Andrew Miller

Andrew Miller was born in Bristol in 1960 and grew up in the West Country. He has lived in Holland, Spain, Japan and Ireland, and now divides his time between Dublin and Paris. *Ingenious Pain*, his first novel, met with exceptional acclaim on its publication in 1997 and went on to be published in a further twenty countries, as well as to be awarded the James Tait Black Memorial Prize for Fiction, the Grinzane Cavour prize in Italy and the International IMPAC Dublin Literary Award. Andrew Miller's second novel, *Casanova*, was published by Sceptre in 1998 and was also widely praised, being described by Hilary Mantel in *The Sunday Times* as 'a source of wonder and delight'.

SCEPTRE

'Miller writes a fine strong prose thickly larded with the sights, sounds and smells of the period, such that one is constantly delighted with strange and vivid imagery, fresh and startling metaphors, flashes of insight, deft twists of plot and resonant variations on dominant themes . . . *Ingenious Pain* reminds one at times of John Fowles's novel *The French Lieutenant's Woman* and the wry historical intelligence manifest in every line of that book; also, a little, in the depth and honesty with which it explores its themes, of Graham Swift's *Waterland*; and, occasionally, in its fidelity to the tones and nuances of the period, of Peter Ackroyd's early flamboyant historical pastiches. But in the end the book is entirely its own creature, a mature novel of ideas soaked in the sensory detail of its turbulent times'
Patrick McGrath in the New York Times Book Review

'A true rarity: a debut novel which is original, memorable, engrossing and subtle . . . As the narrative loops and ducks ingeniously, pain emerges as a creative, restorative force. A fine tale'
Guardian

'In outline, *Ingenious Pain* is partly a fable about love. But it is more impressive than that, thanks to the quality of the writing, the understated wit, the wealth of events, and Miller's atmospheric feel for the 18th century'
The Sunday Times

'A highly accomplished, technically almost flawless first novel'
Sydney Morning Herald

'A positive triumph of a novel, displaying a most inventive and lively imagination and a control very impressive in any novelist, never mind a first timer. It's extraordinary that Andrew Miller can rouse the emotions – can make one feel such sadness and compassion – when he writes so dispassionately. He spices with wit the darkest passages'
Margaret Forster

'It recalls an age when a broken arm could spell death and scientific rationale threatened beliefs which provided the only comfort available to most people. At a philosophical level, *Ingenious Pain* urges us to consider the necessity of anguish for a moral universe, a potent argument for a society increasingly permeated by Prozac, virtual reality and other synthetic modes of experience . . . deeply unshowy, it is concerned with people's need for wonder – from the latest circus freaks to the revolutionary ideas of Newton. It also reminds us that no diversion will enable us to escape from ourselves. The effect is truly wonderful'
Evening Standard

'Miller's writing is richly descriptive, convincing in its evocation of place and era and it has pace, too . . . He is a highly intelligent writer, both exciting and contemplative'
The Times

'The story is never merely a vehicle for illustrating ideas. There are descriptions that are vivid and arresting but he can also tell a story . . . The sense of period is brilliantly handled'
Literary Review

'More than merits comparison with the likes of Angela Carter's *Nights at the Circus* and Partick Süskind's *Perfume* . . . a blistering début'
Time Out

'Miller writes with extreme assurance. He creates a very real world, peopled with outsize characters who entertain at the same time as they offend. He also displays, in the final pages, that most important of all qualities in a writer, compassion. I really enjoyed it'
Sunday Telegraph

'An impressive performance'
Mail on Sunday

'Miller enfolds the reader in the present tense and wields his writing style as coolly and precisely as a scalpel . . . Many of his sentences speak paragraphs, his paragraphs pages'
Independent on Sunday

'The novel's evocation of the period, down to the finest detail, is thoroughly confident; and many of its minor characters are memorably vivid . . . A startling novel . . . *Ingenious Pain* achieves a difficult blend of sadness and loss, joy and laughter'
The Times Literary Supplement

'Stark images, short sentences, metaphors that ambush the jaded reader into fresh awareness of the language . . . A book full of marvels, magic and grotesqueries'
West Australian

'Sometimes you find yourself becoming so captivated by a book that it really matters to you that it be chosen by the Booker Panel as one of the six best novels of the year, if not the best. This year, for me, that book was *Ingenious Pain* . . . a remarkable work of imagination and intelligence . . . an astonishing read'
Antonia Logue in the Sunday Independent

'At one level, this is a rollicking adventure story, written in strong, earthy prose that successfully provides a period flavour and some wonderfully evocative and compressed descriptions . . . In the midst of his gripping tale, Miller takes on no less a question than what makes an individual's life worthwhile. Is it better to be good or to be a genius? Is it better to experience pain than nothing at all?'
Observer

'Fiercely inventive . . . Miller has fleshed out both the period and also the philosophical underpinning of his fable in rich and appropriate language. Minor characters walk around the parlours of one's skull afterwards . . . The true amazement is that this well-nigh immaculate conception is a first novel'
RTE Guide

'A finely wrought and provocative novel'
Daily Telegraph

'Andrew Miller is not only a bold spirit but a talented one'
Australian Financial Review

Ingenious Pain

Andrew Miller

SCEPTRE

RAYMOND CARVER: 'Late Fragment', from
A NEW PATH TO THE WATERFALL.
First published in Great Britain by Collins Harvill 1989.
© Tess Galagher 1989.
Reproduced by permission of The Harvill Press and Grove/Atlantic, Inc.

Copyright © 1997 by Andrew Miller

First published in 1997 by Hodder and Stoughton
A division of Hodder Headline PLC
A Sceptre Paperback

The right of Andrew Miller to be identified as the Author of
the Work has been asserted by him in accordance with the
Copyright, Designs and Patents Act 1988.

20 19 18 17 16 15 14 13 12

All rights reserved. No part of this publication may be
reproduced, stored in a retrieval system or transmitted
in any form or by any means without the prior written
permission of the publisher, nor be otherwise circulated
in any form of binding or cover other than that in which
it is published and without a similar condition being
imposed on the subsequent purchaser.

British Library Cataloguing in Publication Data

Miller, Andrew
Ingenious Pain
1. English fiction – 20th Century
I. Title
823.9'14 [F]

ISBN 0 340 68208 6

Typeset by Palimpsest Book Production Limited,
Polmont, Stirlingshire
Printed and bound in Great Britain by
Clays Ltd, St Ives plc

Hodder and Stoughton
A division of Hodder Headline PLC
338 Euston Road
London NW1 3BH

To my Family

And did you get what
you wanted from this life, even so?
I did.
And what did you want?
To call myself beloved, to feel myself
beloved on the earth.

Raymond Carver

FIRST

1772

1 On a hot, cloud-hemmed afternoon in August, three men cross a stable yard near the village of Cow in Devon. The grouping is oddly formal: the two younger men, like heralds or warders, solemnly precede their host, or, more fancifully, draw him on – his black-coated bulk, his red face – by the reins of an invisible harness. One of the guests carries in his hand a leather bag from which, as he walks to the stable door, there comes a muffled jangling.

It is the older man who, after a pause, opens the door, standing back for the others to enter. They do so, slowly against the darkness. The stable has been swept clean. The smell of horses, of hay, of leather and dung, is mixed with the smell of burnt lavender. Despite the season there is no offensive odour from the corpse. The Reverend wonders if Mary knows the secrets of preserving flesh. In old days the gods kept dead heroes sweet until the funeral games were done, the pyres lit. There are ways, no doubt, still. Ointments, spells, certain prayers. She has been sitting on a milking stool by the table. She stands when they enter, a neat, squat figure, feathered with shadows. 'Well,' says the Reverend, 'I said we should come. These gentlemen' – he indicates the younger men – 'are Dr Ross and Dr Burke. Doctors, Mary.'

She looks past the Reverend, looking not at Burke and Ross but at the bag in Dr Ross's hand.

'Doctors,' he says again, a hushed voice. He wants to call her 'lass', but though, measuring by her looks, she has less years than he has, she seems immeasurably older, and not simply older, but as if she belonged to a different age, a different order; a relative of rocks, venerable trees.

She goes, not just quietly, but with no audible sound at all. Burke looks at Ross, mouths the word 'witch'. They cross themselves discreetly, as if adjusting buttons on their waistcoats. Says Burke: 'We should make a start or we shall be riding back in a storm. Have you a lamp there, Reverend?'

There is a lamp, brought when the body was moved. The Reverend lights it from his tinder box – tac, tac; flint on steel – and passes it to Ross. Ross and Burke come up to the table where James is laid, his length in a woollen nightgown. His hair, almost white when he first came to the rectory, began, in the last year, to darken. Mary has washed it, rubbed it with pomade, brushed it and bound it with a black ribbon. He does not look like he is sleeping.

'A handsome corpse,' Burke says. 'Oh yes, there are features all right.'

Beneath James's crossed hands lies a book in scuffed leather binding. Burke snatches it, views the spine, grins, passes it to the Reverend, who has already recognised it: *Gulliver's Travels*. James borrowed it from the study only a week or two ago. Who placed it here? Sam? Mary? Sam shall have the book if he wants it. The boy should have something.

Ross strips the body, drops the gown on to the floor. From the bag he takes a knife and passes it to Burke who looks along its edge and nods. Burke places a hand on James's chin, and slashes the trunk from the top of the sternum to a point just above the pubic hair. He then cuts across below the ribs to make an inverted cross,

4

bloody-edged, moist. He pauses to take a spectacles case from his waistcoat pocket, fixes the spectacles on to his face, blinking. He mutters something under his breath, takes hold of a flap of skin and fat and peels it away. He uses the knife to free it, to coax it from the matter below. His hands are muscled like a sailor's. Ross holds the lamp aloft. He has a short stick he swooped up on their way over from the house. He uses it to prod at James's guts.

'Would you care for a more intimate view, Reverend? You can see little from there, I think.'

The Reverend shuffles forward. Burke disgusts him.

Dr Ross says: 'The Reverend's interest is in the invisible tenant of the house rather than in the house itself. Heh?'

The Reverend Lestrade says: 'Just so, sir.'

'Now for the heart,' Burke says.

They begin to tear at the chest, working at the ribs with a handsaw, then using the knife to worry through the great vessels. The doctors are visibly excited, bright as eggs. There shall be a paper in this, societies addressed, circles of illuminati: 'Some Thoughts, hm, upon the Case of the Late Jm Dyer. An Enquiry into . . . the Curious and Remarkable . . . who until his twenty-something year was insensible to . . . knew not . . . entirely without all sensation . . . feeling . . . knowledge of . . . pain. With proofs, illustrations, exhibits and so forth.'

The Reverend turns away, looks out at the yard where two birds peck grain from a cake of dung. Beyond, in the wall where he grows sweet-william, a green door leads into the garden. He associates the door with James; James coming through and examining the pears or simply standing in the yard, frowning as if he could not remember what he was about.

Noises, like a boot stepping in mud, disturb him. Ross has got it in his hands, the broken muscle of James Dyer's heart. He looks, thinks the Reverend, as if he might like to eat it, and only some very little shame is keeping him from it. Burke wipes his hands on a rag and takes a folded newspaper from his coat pocket. He opens the paper, spreading it over James's thighs, then takes the heart from Ross and lays it in the paper. 'If you have no objection, Reverend . . .' He wraps the heart, stows it in the bag.

'None, sir.' Dead hearts are not sacred. Let them search it. And he remembers, as he remembers so often, that other searching, Mary standing above James in his chamber in the house on Millionaya, glancing round at the sound of the Reverend's breathing as he stood, motionless in the doorway with the serving girl. Then, knowing he would not, could not interfere, Mary looking back at James, sleeping – drugged? – unbuttoning his shirt, uncovering his breast. The room was dark enough, one small candle by the window. And yet he *did* see something: her hand, seeming to wound James, yet leaving no mark, no more than had she dipped her hand through a skin of milk.

'Reverend?'

'Sir?'

'You are missing some fine things. Here now is the gall bladder.'

'I beg pardon. I was . . . recollecting. A memory of Dr Dyer. We were in Russia together.'

'You have mentioned it, sir. Several times. It is very natural you should think of him, sir, though memory tends a man to sentiment and sentiment, admirable in one of your calling, is a luxury in ours. You must think of these remains not as your former . . . not as a man you once knew, but as the raw material of a legitimate philosophical investigation.'

'A fleshly casket,' chimes Ross, whose breath throws out, astonishing through all the other smells in the place, the unmistakable odour of port and onions, 'containing conundrums.'

The Reverend stares at them. They have shed their coats, rolled their sleeves and are gored up to their elbows, like figures in some absurd Senecan tragedy. Ross takes the knife from Burke and goes round to James's head, cuts swiftly round the back by the hairline and, before the Reverend can guess his purpose, jerks the scalp away from the bones of the skull and lays it over the corpse's face in an obscene, bloody pile. A hot, acidy liquid floods the Reverend's throat. He swallows it and walks quickly out of the stable, across the yard and through the green door into the garden. He shuts the door behind him.

Ahead, the land rises in a smooth sweep to the edge of ancient woods. Sheep are grazing there and a boy is walking by the cool fringe of the wood. In his present mood it appears to the Reverend a delightful lie, but he is grateful for it. It serves him like the little painted screens Italian priests are said to hold before the eyes of condemned men to hide the approaching scaffold. He wonders how it is they gulled him, Burke and Ross, yet they seemed credible, men with reputations, letters. And he too was curious to see if James's body might be made to explain something of the mystery of his life. He had imagined something dry, respectful. Instead he has given his friend into the hands of butchers, lunatics. What if *she* were to see it? She is about the house, doing God knows what, for he has never been sure how she passes her time. The other servants, from fearing her, now take a pride in having her among them. She helps them with their pains. She has, for example, the ability to calm a headache by simply pressing on the sufferer's face.

The door sounds on its hinges. He looks round. Mary is there, standing under the weather-stone, holding out a wooden box. Her coming out just then, as if drawn by the scent of his thinking of her, disturbs him. Worse, he sees there is blood on his fingers and he clasps his hands behind his back, asking: 'Is something the matter? Is there some trouble?'

She unfastens the catch on the box and opens the lid. He says: 'Ah, yes, the device.' He would like it for himself. He, after all, brought it home from Petersburg with the rest of James's dunnage when James disappeared. They thought he was dead.

'It is yours now, Mary.'

She looks at him a while, nods slowly, closes the box and goes back into the house.

There is a faint noise of sawing. When it stops, the Reverend returns to the stable, praying that it will be over, that Burke and Ross can be sent on their road. He will not have them inside. They may take water in a bucket from one of the rain-butts and wash in the yard. James they must patch up as decently as they can – vandals! Killick will coffin him. Tomorrow at noon they will bury him. Clarke is perhaps digging the grave even now, a spot by the wall next to Makin's orchard.

'You have discovered something, gentlemen? Anything?' He tries to infuse his voice with disdain but it emerges weakly. An edge of petulance.

Burke looks up at him. A dozen flies are busy about the mouth of a bucket by the end of the table under James's opened head.

'Nothing,' says Burke, 'I could explain to one not acquainted with the art of anatomy.'

'But the heat, and the vermin . . . He was of your own profession. Surely you have done?'

Says Burke: 'You are exciting yourself, my dear Reverend. Come now. This closeness oppresses you. You are not easy. It were better you retire, yes, and avail yourself of some agreeable eccoprotic. Rhubarb, say.'

'Or pulp of colocynth,' says Ross, openly amused.

'Colocynth is good,' says Burke. 'Or a little of the root bark – *euonymus atropurpureus*. Should you have it by. A man of your physiognomy can never purge himself too frequently. You agree, Dr Ross?'

'A very cleansing measure, Dr Burke. I'm sure poor Dyer would have advised it.'

'We shall inform you of our findings.'

A speck of light on Burke's spectacles wavers in the air like an angry spark. The Reverend hesitates, then says: 'I shall be in my study.' He shuffles out, too fatigued to feel much shame.

2 The yard glimmers: starlight on the backs of the puddles left by the storm. The Reverend closes the stable door, crosses the yard. In the stable, Mary is sitting up with James. Burke and Ross left the body tolerably sealed and the Reverend, with Mr Killick, placed it in the box at dusk, nailing the lid. Killick, a good man, helped sluice and scrub the stable and scatter fresh straw and handfuls of dry herbs. By the time Mary appeared the air was breathable, the horror of the afternoon eradicated but for a few tea-brown stains on the table. They hid these beneath a cloth.

Weary, yet at ease for the first time that day, the Reverend loiters in his garden. It is nothing more than a cottage garden, nothing one might boast of, yet it is one of the things of his life that he loves, solidly and without reserve. Of what else can he say so? His sister Dido perhaps, on most occasions other than when she harasses him to have the panelling changed for something more modern, or lectures him on his dress and habits, which it pleases her to liken to a poor country curate who keeps a drinking-shop.

His patroness, Lady Hallam? She has aged. How vast her bosom has become, what a weight for her! But still the sweetest disposition, the sweetest intelligence. Worth every sonnet he scratched for her, all the hours poring over blotched sheets struggling to make the things scan, to force out a rhyme not utterly devoid of sense. Half a dozen might be good, that out of more than a hundred, two hundred. He must burn them, of course, next year or the year after, and certainly should his health fail. Intolerable they should be read by strangers – the fat vicar at Cow who wished to play bull with Lady H.

He walks to his pond, claps his hands and a dozen ripples break over the surface, threads of light circling out to the banks. Good, clean-fleshed creatures. With Mrs Cole to sauce them one would look in vain for better food on a gold plate in any bishop's palace. He must expect a summons to the palace in Exeter before long. A polite pressing to put Mary out. Her being there while James was alive was part of the Reverend's charity towards the doctor. But such a woman, such a very irregular woman in the house of an unmarried servant of the Church . . .

Leaning down, he dips his fingers in the water, intrigued by the dark bowl of his reflected head. A light moves in the parlour window. He stands and goes closer. The curtains are undrawn. Tabitha is lighting the candles in the sconces. A great, strong, heavy girl, a hoyden, not pretty, her face distinguished only by youth, health. The first month she was in the house she suffered with nightmares, pissed her bed and moped red-eyed about the house, dropping glasses, incapable of following the simplest orders. There was a difficult interview between the Reverend and his housekeeper, Mrs Cole, Mrs Cole threatening to go to her sister in Taunton if Tabitha remained in the house. She had repeated it several times – 'Taunton, Reverend, Taunton' – as if the town lay on the far side of the Bosphorus. But the nightmares passed, the girl became handy, and in the winters Tabitha and Mrs Cole share a bed, the housekeeper curled behind the girl like moss on a warm stone. It has crossed the Reverend's mind he might enjoy that himself.

He takes a last draught of night air, goes into the house, shoots the bolts and turns into the parlour. Tabitha, who has in her hands a tray of his second-best long-stemmed glasses, starts as if he were the devil, come to snack on her. It is a nervous habit that never fails to irritate him. They stare at each other a moment and then he remembers how very naturally she cried at James's death. A generous heart.

He says: 'Are you going to your bed now, Tabitha? Are you tired?'

'Middlin', sir, but if you fancied a posset or what not. Gran'father allus had a posset before bed.'

'Does he thrive still?'

'No, sir.' She smiles happily. 'He fell in the fire one time an' died of it. He were a cheerful make of man, though. Before, like.'

The Reverend sees it: an old man in the fire, a pair of bandy legs, truly bandy, like the metal knacks for taking off the top of an egg. Like something out of Bosch. 'I won't have anything now, my dear. I shall sit up a while. Perhaps I shall read.'

She curtseys; he notes her cleavage, fears again for his glasses. At the door she says: 'An' I can come to the burying tomorrow, mayn't I? Mrs Cole said as I should ask.'

'Surely. I should like to see you there. You were fond of him?'

'Lor', sir, I misses him already. Don' you miss 'im, sir?'

'Very much.'

'I misses him.' She pauses, wets her lips. 'I were gonna ask you summat, only Mrs Cole said I should not.'

'Well, you must ask it now.'

'Whether it were a miracle when Dr James . . . I means, sir, Dr Dyer, when he saved that Negro?'

'I fear, Tabitha, that this is not the age of miracles.'

She gawps at him as if he has said something wildly important, shocking. 'What were it, then, if weren't a miracle?'

'The doctor's skill.'

''E calls 'imself Lazarus now, sir, the black fellow.'

'What did he call himself before?'

'John Amazement.'

'I like that better.'

Alone, he peels off his wig and scratches vigorously at his scalp. A moth, which he vaguely remembers having flown in the previous evening, begins to fly about one of the candles, then settles on the mirror. Its wings are coloured like wood grain and on each there are marks like staring eyes. Nature's cunning.

From a cabinet he takes a decanter and glass, fills the glass with smuggled brandy, drains it with a single gulp. He sets the glass on the mantelpiece, takes up one of the candles there and goes out into the passage, guarding the light with his hand. His study, a small, tightly furnished room looking out from the other side of the house, has scents of ink, sweet tobacco, books. He sets the candle on the edge of his writing desk, his 'escritoire', as Dido has it. The surface is entirely hidden by papers. Letters formal and informal, bills: £1 18s to the wheelwright; a monstrous £10 for silver spoons from London. Of money in, only a note for ten shillings and sixpence from the parish officer for marrying a man in custody to a woman carrying his child. Beside these, some notes for a sermon, three goose-feather quills, a sand tray, a blade, a stoppered bottle of ink.

He holds up the candle and runs its light over the backs of books, pausing at old favourites to tap softly on the spines. His tattered, grammar-school Homer, his father's Collier edition of Marcus Aurelius. *Pilgrim's Progress*, illustrated, bought in Bow Lane on his first trip to London. Ovid, deliciously louche, given him by a friend at the University who hanged himself the following year. Two volumes of Milton in stiff black leather, another gift, these from Lady Hallam on his first being appointed to his living, and valued by him more for the lovely swirls of her dedication than for anything of Milton's. Voltaire's *Candide*, bringing instantly to the Reverend's mind the small, dark, intelligent face of Monsieur About. Fielding, Defoe. A much-unread volume of Allestree's *Whole Duty of Man*. Tillotson's sermons.

Turning from the shelves, he opens a chest beside his desk and pulls from it a canvas sack, lodges the sack beneath his arm and hurries back to the parlour, just as the clock shudders through ten. He sets down the bag, strips off his coat and drops it over a chair. With his back to the empty grate, he finds himself, as usual, face to face with his father, the Reverend John Lestrade of Lune in Lancashire. A very middling sort of portrait, his father's face a shiny, one-dimensional oval against a background of brown varnish, like the reflection of the moon in a muddy pond. They exchange their silent, nightly greeting.

The Reverend endeavours to recall what he knows of James's father. A farmer, of that he is reasonably certain, though whether great or small he does not know. Of the mother he knows, if possible, rather less. Some slim reference to her having died young. What did such reticence conceal? The elusiveness of a self-invented man? Some doubt, some niggle concerning his true progenitor? Ah; what questions he should like to put to that poor, cut-about head in the stable! Mary must know a great bundle of things. He has long considered setting down the Petersburg stuff. The rest might be uncovered, somehow.

He eases himself down a little way, breaks wind into the fireplace. Immediately he experiences the pleasant urge to shit, which, after enjoying the sensation a while, he acts upon, dragging over his close-stool, a noble piece of furniture, solid as a pulpit, and setting it with its back to the candles. With a kind of flourish he debreeches himself, removes the padded seat and settles on the wooden O. The canvas sack is to hand; he leans and draws it up to his feet. The mouth of the sack is closed by a length of cord. He unties it, slips in his hand. The first thing he touches is a smaller bag, this also of oiled canvas, rolled like a small log. He draws it out and sets it on his hairless thighs.

Unrolling it, the implements seem to wake as they catch the light. Knives, scissors, a handsaw, needles and other objects whose name and purpose he can only guess at and which might expressly have been made the better to terrify a patient. He draws out the longest of the knives, double-edged, sharp still as a sack of limes. This surely is the knife James used on the unfortunate postillion, though without it, its very adequate bite, they would have buried the fellow at the monastery. And this curved mirror about the size of a child's palm he first saw the night of their arrival at the monastery when James used it, fixed to a candle, to sew up his own head. None of the implements has been used since then, though when James came to the house, when it seemed he had regained the better part of his senses, the Reverend offered them back. James had not wanted them.

The Reverend rolls the bag neatly and sets it down. He dips again into the sack and withdraws a sheaf of documents, stashed willy-nilly from the last time he examined them. Indeed, he has been through the sack several times, but with James's death the contents have assumed a new and important character. Tomorrow, when the body is in the ground, these will number among the very few proofs of James's existence. The papers he now examines, holding each one up six inches from his face – his spectacles are in his coat pocket and he is loath to disturb the delicate business of making a stool – are mostly certificates, some of which, perhaps all, are forgeries.

The first and prettiest purports to be from the Hôtel Dieu in Paris. Three black seals on it, a half-yard of ribbon and a frantic, indecipherable signature. The Reverend is tolerably sure that James never studied in France. Next, and more credible, is a certificate from St George's hospital in London, stating that James Dyer attended classes in anatomy and *materia medica*. A third is from the Surgeon's Hall, rating James as fit to serve as surgeon's mate on a sixth-rate of His Majesty's Navy. Dated 1756. James would have been barely more than a boy. There is a companion piece to this; the Reverend fishes it out of the sack. A snuff-box, ivory-topped, and inscribed on its base: *A*

MUNRO '*H.M.S. Aquilon*'. He opens it, sniffs. Though empty so many years it yet retains a pungency which, rising through the Reverend's nose to his brain, so stimulates it that Munro momentarily looms, hesitant and ectoplasmic in the shadows beside the window.

He snaps it shut, drops it in the sack, farts tinnily into the enamelled pot. Another sheet; not a certificate but a reference, a most impressive one, for this signature is legible – John Hunter, that Alexander among surgeons, who finds James to be '*most excellent in the treatment of Fractures simple and compound, the management of Contusions and Amputations and the proper use of Bandages*'. It is, thinks the Reverend, as if the Archbishop of York were to write that he finds me particularly devout, an exemplary pastor of my flock.

The last, a fine vellum though much beat up, is in French. A neat, even hand; its carefully flourished Fs and Ys are the work of a secretary at the Russian embassy. It is signed by the ambassador and stamped with the imperial birds. It is James's letter of safe conduct, introducing him as '*Un membre distingué de la fraternité de médecine anglaise*'.

Now there is only the little book. The book that promised so much when he saw it first and which now taunts him more than ever. Surely it is some manner of diary? Yet the entire book is written in a code or shorthand that the Reverend, despite some attempts, cannot make out. Even the diagrams are cryptic; impossible to say if they are maps or visual notes for a surgical procedure, or nothing at all, merely lines without the least significance. The single legible word comes on the very last page – 'Liza'. An old love? Did he have old loves? Liza. That too must remain a mystery. Drowsily, the Reverend wonders if his own life will appear like this, a book in a language no one can understand. He thinks: Who shall sit by the fire for me, puzzling it out?

His evacuation is not progressing well. The matter, though

noisily presaged, will not emerge. The effort of it wearies him and he fears a strain. It would not do to end like unlamented George Secundus. Sleep crowds him; he closes his eyes. The faces of Burke and Ross briefly form like faces in a tobacco cloud. Other faces follow: Mary, Tabitha, Dido; not James. The clock taps out the progress of the night. He wonders: What shall I say tomorrow, what shall I say, what shall I say . . . ?

From his uncurling fist, from the smooth, uncertain surface of his thighs, the papers of James Dyer tumble to the floor. The moth scorches its wings; the Reverend gently snores. From the stable, just loud enough to pierce the open window of Dido's room, where Dido stands, streaming tears, comes a voice, a song, husky and monotonous, utterly foreign, impenetrably sad.

SECOND

1771

Three times a year the Reverend Lestrade and his sister have themselves bled. It is a ritual, like making the strawberry beds in October, or the increasingly tedious visits to Bath in May, which serve to punctuate the year and which, to omit, would occasion a distinct unease. 'Bleeding', so the Reverend's father often declared – and so now, in his turn, the Reverend also declares, more for the pleasure of echoing his father than out of any deep conviction – 'is very good for men and horses. And right good for pragmatic, mithering women.'

Dr Thorne is their usual operator, an able man, but this year, his horse having stumbled in a rabbit hole and thrown him, he cannot come.

'Why not James Dyer, then?' asks Dido, closing her book and holding out her hands to the evening fire.

The Reverend taps his teeth with the stem of his pipe. 'No, sister, I do not think it is well advised.'

'Sure he has seen blood before.'

'Surely,' says the Reverend, 'and enough perhaps.'

'If we cannot have Thorne and you are afraid to ask Dr Dyer – living as he does upon the fat of our hospitality – I shall open a vein myself. Or if I cannot, I may call on Tabitha.'

With an air of studied innocence, the Reverend asks: 'Has Dr Dyer outstayed your welcome, sister?'

'Indeed he has not. No, not so. You mistake me as ever, Julius. It is very vexing. It is because you vex me so that I must be bled.'

'How do I vex you, sister?'

'By crossing me in everything I wish for.'

'Like the spoons?'

'Oh, fiddlededee the spoons. Yes, the spoons. And now this.'

'You might ask him yourself perhaps.'

'I might. And I might walk up to Caxton's place and drink a bottle of his rum.' Dido stands, her dresses rustling like live things.

'Good night to you, brother.'

'Ay, good night to you, sister.'

She goes out of the parlour, very upright. It is, thinks the Reverend, a good twenty years since he bested her in an argument.

The moon, in its last quarter, rises at ten thirty. The Reverend sleeps, dreams of his garden, wakes and dresses, praying on his knees by his window, open-eyed, staring into the golden bowl of a November morning. Bacon and cabbage for breakfast, hot punch, then a pipe of Virginia tobacco in his study, going over Sunday's sermon. He hears the dogs. The sound thrills him, like the sound of bells. He opens the study window, leans out. George Pace, his manservant, is there with the dogs, and Mr Astick over from Totleigh for the morning's sport, sipping from his flask and talking dogs with Pace.

'Morning to you, Astick. Rare morning, eh?'

'Shall there be mornings like this in heaven, Reverend?'

'Assuredly. The dogs are sharp set, George?'

'Larky, but they shall settle.'

The dogs are dancing in their sleek coats, gently biting one another's throats. The Reverend rejoices, feels himself to be twenty.

'I must speak a few words with the Doctor. Then I am yours.'

He finds James in his room, dressing. 'Forgive me breaking in upon you at such an hour.'

James says: 'I heard the dogs. They are merry.'

'They were created for mornings such as this. I am come on an errand and that is to beg a favour of you. You know it is our custom to have Dr Thorne bleed us the day of the tithe supper; well, poor fellow, he has took a fall from his horse and clacked his head and cannot come and the nub of it is will you oblige us? For myself I am content to miss, but my sister . . .'

There is a brief silence while James buttons the legs of his breeches. Below the window the dogs set up a sudden clamour. The Reverend fidgets and steps backwards to the door. 'No matter, no matter at all.'

James says: 'Nay. We must not disappoint your sister.' They grin at each other. 'I wish you joy of your sport.'

'You would not care to join us?'

'I'm a poor sportsman and I've an unaccountable fondness for hares. And this leg' – he pats his right knee – 'would hold you up.'

'As you like, then. I shall see you at dinner.' The Reverend hurries off, takes the steps two at a time. From his room James hears the party move off, the barking of the dogs scraping and scraping at the sky, ever more faintly.

He washes his face in a basin of shocking cold water, smooths his hair and examines his hands. One small scar on the left stands out like a tiny raw nipple, seeps a fluid. Of the other scars, fifteen or twenty on either hand, there is nothing to complain of beside a tiresome itching. Nothing to be unpleased about.

He takes up his razor, holds it out and examines the blade. There is, at first, a quite perceptible movement, a trembling at the tip, but it settles and grows acceptably steady. He shaves in front of his small, cranky mirror. The stubble of his beard is darker than his hair, a more vigorous growth altogether, as if welling from a more wholesome part of himself, some part more atune with his two and thirty years than the weathered mask of his face, the grey hair of his head. He smiles at his reflection. The first true day of spring comes in the heart of winter. Who is to say I shall not grow entirely well again?

He pulls on the supple dog-skin gloves with which he protects his hands, and goes in search of food, walking into the kitchen where Mrs Cole and Tabitha and Mary and a girl by name of Winifred Dade are preparing the tithe supper.

'Lor' but we are boarded!' cries Mrs Cole, seeing James. She leaves off her pie-making to fetch him cold meat out of the meat safe. 'Shall you have some nice eggs, Doctor, what Winny brought from home?'

'A little of the mock goose and a shive of bread will be a feast, I thank you, Mrs Cole. Morning to you, Tabitha, Winny, Mary.' The girls, red-faced from the heat of the fire, look at each other stupidly and bite their lips. James does not see. He is regarding Mary who is sat at the great table, slicing onions.

'The onions do not make you cry?' He makes no dumb show to explain himself, such as the others do. Though he has never heard her speak a word of English, he knows how perfectly she understands him, both when he speaks and when he is silent. Now she answers him by cutting two neat pearly rings from the onion, fetching them up delicately with the knife and depositing them by the meat on his plate. Quietly, he thanks her.

He eats, content among the scuttle of the women. If he sits quietly they will forget him and he can view them in their female world, see them almost as if he were another woman among them.

It moves in him faint, powerful memories of his mother and sisters and the maidservant, a singer of nonsense songs, whose name he has completely mislaid. He revels in their skills. What excellent surgeons these women would make! And might not he make a passable cook? He would like to ask if he might join them, cut vegetables or mix the sweet mess of a pudding, but that would disturb them and the girls would lose their concentration.

When he has done, he slips out of the kitchen, a small pot of warm water in his hand, and enters the garden. He pauses, listening for any sound of the coursing and thinks perhaps he hears it, a faint echo of savage barking. By the side of the parsonage is the Reverend's glasshouse. It is a small construction, too low to stand quite upright in, full of pots, tubs, the reek of geraniums. Here he has appropriated a corner for his experiments, and is pleased to find his cannabis plants, their soil lagged with straw, surviving the cold nights. He checks his sponges on their slatted shelf, brushes away the beginnings of a cobweb and takes one of the smaller sponges, slipping it into his pocket. The sponges are his joy, the ripest success – though heaven knows, a very imperfect one – of his investigations into analgesics. He began it six months back, writing to Jack Cazotte in Dover, whose name he had remembered out of the air, having once had dealings with him during the days of his practice in Bath. Three weeks after writing, the first neat aromatic package arrived, the first of many containing herbs, seeds and compounds, together with Cazotte's advice, and pages copied out in Cazotte's neat hand from learned books such as James had no access to. Thus, from Pliny, James learnt of the properties of the mandragora root, how it might be steeped in wine and how it was often used in former times, mercifully or cynically, to lighten the agony of prisoners under torture. With vinegar and Asian myrrh – and curiously inflamed emotions – he concocted the potion offered to Christ on the cross; offered and refused. The recipe for the sponges came from a manuscript of the Conquerors' time: each sponge soused in a brew of opium, fresh hyoseyamine, unripened blackberries, lettuce seed, juice of hemlock, mandragora and ivy. Permeated with their precious cargo, they are dried in the sun, ready to be rehydrated upon use.

No one, other than Mary, knows the nature of these experiments. She discovered him with her nose, coming into his room one evening, sniffing the air and very slightly raising her eyebrows as if to say, 'Is this all you have learnt?' The Reverend and his sister are devilish curious but ask no questions. He is grateful to them.

From the glasshouse he goes to the barn. The doors of the barn are open. Urbane Davis is sitting on a log eating a fist of cheese. He has been threshing oats and the air is still mazy with the chaff.

'Morning, Davis.'

'Morn'n, Dr Dyer.' Davis raises his cheese in salute.

'I trust you have not been terrifying Sissy with your flail.'

'Nar. I 'ad a squinny at 'er jus' now. Very tranquil she were.'

'I am glad of it. I am on my way to pay her a visit.'

'Sissy? Sissy?' At the end of the gallery, a snug dry spot about the height of a man below the barn roof-beams, there is a movement in the shadows, a fragile mewing, half alarmed, half beseeching. The creature is used to him now, appreciates his footfall, and is anyway too weak to flee him.

She was found in the second week of September; a ginger female cat, panting in a kind of nest she had made for herself in the interior of the Reverend's honeysuckle bush. Sam spied her first and told James, who lay in the grass beside the bush until his arm was numb, talking *sotto voce* while the animal stared at him, steadily, wonderingly. It was a farm cat, a wary old pugilist, not used to petting. With patience and titbits from the kitchen he insinuated himself. After three days, he could lift it out, a surprisingly light parcel, as if it were a smaller cat crawled into the pelt of a greater one. He took it to the barn, laid it in a box of rags and straw and examined it by lantern. The examination had revealed a tumour about the liver. She was old and dying in pain.

What, then, to do? Only three alternatives: leave it die; kill it; treat it. Of these only the latter two struck him as acceptable. He had, after all, already interfered in the creature's existence and having done so had acquired a responsibility beyond merely abandoning the thing. As for killing it, a death swiftly dispensed was the surest relief, and George Pace was a very able killer of things, cosy with the dark gods. Good sharp blows were his stock-in-trade.

Yet should a cat's life be less sweet to it than a man's; sweet even in sickness, even *in extremis*, nay, more sweet then than ever? And if the pain may be abated, sensibly abated, if he possessed the probable means, was it not the best way? Was he not required to do it? Or is the creature only the unwitting subject of his experimentation? He does not like that thought. He shies from it.

Slipping the sponge from his pocket, he tears a piece and dips it into the warm water of the teapot. 'Now then, Sissy, this is what you like.' The animal's suffering has instructed it, and when he places the swollen sponge to its face, it sniffs and chews at it, rubbing the juice on to the sensitive skin of nostrils and gums; pathetic, comical actions. The tumour eats the cat from inside. The dose is increased daily. Each time James comes to the barn now he anticipates finding her dead. It occurs to him that the cat may be willing itself alive principally to consume the drugs. He strokes the dull coat, watches her subside into placid imbecility.

Below, Urbane Davis has taken up his flail, rhythmically striking, humming to himself a hymn. What is it? 'Come O thou traveller unknown.' James takes up his things, descends the ladder, holds a glove across his face not to breathe in the dust.

2 The Reverend, his sister, Mr Astick and James eat dinner at a table in the parlour where tonight the Reverend will entertain the gentlemen farmers. The others will eat in the kitchen, according to custom. The main dining room, unused since Michaelmas, needs a two-day fire in winter to heat it through and is unnecessarily large for the one party, inappropriately fine for the other.

'Another wedge of this good fat mutton, Mr Astick?' The Reverend has thrived on his morning's sport. It has brought him two large hares. James has seen their mauled corpses in the kitchen.

'Nell – that's the silver bitch, Doctor – was like a leopard today. Mad with it she was. Could hardly walk coming home. Trembling and lolling her tongue.'

'Let me charge your glass, Doctor,' says Dido, sitting at James's side.

'Now don't you disguise the doctor in drink, Dido,' says the Reverend, himself somewhat disguised from the punch before dinner. 'We are under his knife this afternoon.'

'I understand, Doctor,' says Mr Astick, 'that surgeons are like to drink as much as their patients before an operation. Equal courage being needed on both sides.'

'I have known it,' says James, pushing a piece of meat about his plate.

'Dr Dyer wasn't one of those,' says the Reverend.

'I meant', says Mr Astick, 'that it must take as much bottom to perform an operation as to undergo one. Is that not so?'

26

James says: 'I have witnessed a very reputable surgeon in a great hospital heave before going into the theatre. I have seen a thousand-pound-a-year man run out in the midst of operating.'

'Pray you, gentlemen,' says Dido, tapping her fork on the table. 'We have not ate our pudding yet.'

'Very true, my dear,' says the Reverend, 'and I have been impatient for one of Mrs Cole's puddings ever since breakfast. Ha ha!'

'You shall dig your grave with your teeth, brother.'

'As you won't eat, sister, I must eat for two. When will you want us, Doctor?'

'When it is convenient to yourselves.'

'Then I shall rob you at Loo first and you shall have it back in blood later,' the Reverend says.

Even Dido laughs at this. A strange excited laugh.

3 He is in the parlour, reading, when Tabitha is sent to fetch him. He has read the same passage out of *Roderick Random* four or five times – Roderick making up to the decrepit Miss Sparkle – but has taken in neither the comedy nor the cruelty of the scene. He has been thinking what excuses he might make, even now, and listening to the rumble of the Reverend's footfall in the room overhead. On the card table by the fire, laid by the cards of his last, losing hand, is a neat tortoiseshell case containing the lancets. It belongs to the Reverend, belonged to his father before him. James does not know what became of his own set. In someone else's pocket now.

Tabitha enters the parlour. 'Miss Lestrade is ready for you to go to 'er now.'

'Miss Lestrade?'

'In 'er room, sir.' She points vaguely upwards.

He asks: 'What have you there?'

She walks over and hands it to him: a tin-glazed, earthenware bowl. 'Reverend said to give it you.'

'Thank you, Tabitha.'

James takes the bowl, the tortoiseshell case, and mounts the stairs, turning left and stopping to knock lightly at the first door on the right.

Dido Lestrade is sat by the table at the window of her room. She has changed her dress since dinner and wears now a gown of pale primrose and a quilted white petticoat. Her face is illumined by the afternoon light, a painter's light. She is, James believes, near the same age as himself. Her eyes are good, very human, but she has plucked her eyebrows to damnation.

He has never been in the room before. He is aware that it is on display for him and that he should admire it. He glances round, notes the Chelsea porcelain, the peacock-feather fans, the petit-point screen, the lacquered commode, the bed-hanging of Indian cotton, decorated with the Tree of Life. Endless frills and knickery-knackery; all in a room older than the church, a chamber better suited to blocks of solid, rustic furniture, the sort of stuff, sepulchral and stinking precisely of time, that stands about the rest of the house. Here is Dido's protest, her discreet rebellion: a Bath boudoir in the belly of North Devon. It moves him, and in some obscure way he would like to comfort her. He is aware that there is a gesture somewhere in the lexicon of such things that would convey his sentiments exactly, but he cannot find it. He says, more gruffly than he meant: 'You have a cloth for your arm?'

She has it ready on the table, a silk scarf, thickly dyed. Her gown is short-sleeved, but James draws it further up before he ties the scarf. He is aware of being physically closer to her than he has ever been. Aware of her scent, the texture of her skin. The blue and white at the crook of her elbow is affecting. 'Not too tight?' he asks.

She is looking away from him, shakes her head. He takes the case from out of his waistcoat pocket, pulls off the lid, chooses one of the little blades, draws it out, drops it, fumbles for it on the Turkey carpet, retrieves it, clears his throat, takes her arm – cool beneath his grip – spies out a vein, positions the bowl, pricks the vein and watches the blood slope off her arm into the bowl. When he has collected, he guesses, six ounces, he presses his thumb over the wound, removes the scarf, breathes. A ball of wool serves as a plug. She folds her arm and holds it across her breast, like flowers or a sickly pet. 'I'm sure Dr Thorne takes twice that,' she says, looking into the bowl.

'It is more use to you in than out.'

'My father thought bleeding the greatest boon for pragmatic women.'

'And was your mother like that?'

'She was thought to be. As, in turn, I am too.'

'I have never thought of you so,' says James, very nearly scrupulous.

'I believe you have not.'

'How do you feel?'

'Pure well, thank you.'

'I shall be with your brother should you need me.'

The Reverend is gazing out of his window; a view over the garden, the rising fields, the woods. He greets James without turning. He is in sombre mood, suddenly sober after the sport, the good cheer of the morning. Out with the dogs, the first hour, he felt he was revisiting his youth, his body a robust, powerful implement, pleasing to use, and even in the thrill of the chase, his mind had retained a delicious coolness, a brightness he strained for uselessly on other occasions . . . Well, he must be grateful for it, for his hour.

James, to whom the Reverend, in a fit of confidence, once confessed that he versified – though not all the port in Christendom could have induced him to say what kind of verse, still less to whom it was addressed – now asks, by way of having something to say, and subtly impressed by the Reverend's aura of melancholy, if he is turning lines in his head. The Reverend, pricked by embarrassment, answers hastily: 'No, indeed. Not that. The Muse deserts me like everything else – hair, teeth, breath. No, I was thinking of . . . of putting some wheat and turnips in the little field. What do you think of it? Did you not say one time that you grew up upon the land? I'm sure you did.'

'I made no study of it. My knowledge of turnips is that I like them roasted if I like them at all.'

The Reverend says: 'I wish I knew a little more. I mean of what is good to do. I should like to set an example. They laugh up their sleeves at me, you know, the farmers. They'll be at it tonight, you wait. Will you sup in the parlour?'

'I thought rather I would play king of the kitchen. We had some fine singing there last year.'

'Whatever you wish.'

It is to be with Mary, of course, but the offer has been made. It is a pity, muses the Reverend, starting to grin, that James does not show more interest in Dido. They would make an interesting pair, but the little foreign woman has him, great, deep cables connecting them. Never seen them touch, though. Are they carnal?

He peers into the bowl in James's hand. 'I see you've done her, then. My sister.'

'I had meant to empty it,' says James, flushing. 'I cannot imagine how I failed to do so. Forgive me.'

'Peace, Doctor. After all, it is the same stuff as animates me – though mine is a less watery soup than hers. Now, sir, I'd be grateful to you if you would open a vessel here.' He taps his right temple. 'Thorne's done it before now and I feel it would relieve me. Greatly.'

James stares at him, looking for a sign to know if he is quite serious. He says: 'The blood circulates about the entire body. To take it from one place is to take it from another.'

'That, I grant you, may be the theory, yet I experience a surfeit, a plethora, quite local to the head.'

'It would be dangerous. Unnecessarily so.'

'Nay, man, not to one of your accomplishments.'

'You confuse me . . . with my former self.'

'Come, come now. I'll sit here still as a wall.' To prove it he takes up position upon a stool, as stiff and unmoving as if he were sitting for his likeness. Thinks James: I shall refuse. Then: why should I not do it? I could have done it before in a blindfold. The devil take us both. I shall do it.

He lays a large handkerchief upon the Reverend's shoulder, selects a lancet and leans close to the side of the Reverend's head, examining the skin beneath the stubbled, grey-blond hair. Free for an instant from all hesitation, he lodges the tip of the lancet, feels the involuntary flinch, absorbs it, digs deeper. He is aware of the noise of rapid breathing; imagines it to be the Reverend's, then realises that it is his own. A trail of blood snails over the Reverend's jowls. The Reverend speaks through his teeth: 'Deeper, Doctor, deeper.'

And something goes wrong; wrong as in a dream where the steady flow of images erupts without warning into something elemental and hideous that sends the sleeper fleeing out of sleep. A spasm – as though his hand had been touched with electricity; a spastic contraction of the muscles, God knows. Instantly, the whole side of the Reverend's face is a sheet of blood. The lancet falls, also the bowl, splashing the Reverend's shirt with blood. The Reverend groans, yaws like a stricken ship, clutches his head. He says, his voice very calm: 'Help me, James.' And James runs out. Out of the Reverend's room and into his own. Seconds pass, minutes perhaps, before he can find the courage to return; minutes of staring furiously at his coat hanging from a nail on the back of the door. Then he snatches up all the linen he can see – a shirt, a nightcap, a square he uses to dry his face – and runs back, like the lover in a farce, to the Reverend's room.

The Reverend is on his bed, a hand pressed to the wound. James drops to his knees at the side of the bed, gently lifts the Reverend's hand. Such is the effusion of blood he cannot at first make out the wound. He wipes, makes a compress with the square and fixes it with the nightcap. He hurries to the top of the stairs, shouts: 'Tabitha!'

Her face, dusted with flour, appears in the stairwell. He sends her for hot water, hot water and claret. His chest is heaving as if he had run full pelt up the lane. Dido comes on to the landing, still holding her folded arm, staring at James in amazement. 'What is it?' she asks. 'Are you hurt?'

He gapes at her, cannot answer, and runs back into the room, leaning over the prostrate Reverend as if sheltering him from rain. Dido follows, issues little cries of alarm, glares angrily at her brother. 'Christ, brother . . . has he shot himself?' There is a noise, ominous at first, a liquid wheezing in the Reverend's throat. 'Is he dying?' asks Dido, all natural colour gone from her face, but for the moment her manner admirably composed.

'Not dying,' says James. He knows that sound better than most. He says: 'I believe he is laughing.'

Out of the curled man on the bed comes a reedy voice, hugely amused: '"Has he shot himself"! . . . oh, very good . . . very good, sister . . .'

A minute later and Tabitha arrives with the tray, the wine, the water. Mrs Cole is behind her, alarmed at Tabitha's description of the doctor waving his arms like a lunatic at the top of the stairs.

What they see is the Reverend sitting on the edge of the bed, pale but grinning, his head swathed in a bloody nightcap, Dido sitting beside him, her mouth shut tight as a mussel, and the doctor, of whom all those stories just might be true, sat on the other side of the Reverend, sobbing like a child.

'How is supper coming, Mrs Cole?' asks the Reverend. What heroics! Yes, sir, the afternoon has been an unexpected success.

4   The two of them go out for wood, a man and a boy, under the November moon. The man, somewhat stooped, limps from an affliction of his right leg, his head bobbing like a swimmer's. The boy, hands tucked under his own shoulders for warmth, walks two steps behind. A frost is building, glittering around the lights of the house.

They come to the wood-pile. James stretches out his arms for the boy to load him. From the logs comes a reek of earth, fungus, rotting bark.

'Take from the back there, Sam. Are they drier there?'

'They all has a little wet on 'em.'

'Fetch out those at the side there – the beechwood.'

It has been a hot summer; a wet, mild autumn; a poor harvest. Wheat is fifty shillings and eight pence per quarter; up three shillings over the previous year.

'We'll take what we have, Sam, and dry them at the fire.'

They move back towards the lights. A young dog, restless at the end of its chain, sets up yapping. From James: 'Hush, sir!' It slinks into its shadow, ears cocked against the movements, the soft calls of the country beyond.

Using his elbow on the latch, James opens the kitchen door. There are sudden, good-humoured complaints about the cold from the men at the table until Sam pushes it shut with his heel. They lay down the logs and brush the earth from their coats. At the table, twelve men, fat and thin, are doing their all to eat back what they have lost by the tithe. To eat and drink it back with a kind of hilarious determination. James knows most of them, most know him – know him, if not exactly what they should make of him.

Tabitha drops a jug, one of the big ones. It explodes impressively at her feet, drenching her stockings in clouds of cider. She cries, more from fatigue than shock or fear of Mrs Cole who is serving in the parlour. The farmers cheer. James goes to her, says: 'Go to bed, Tabitha. Sam and I shall serve them.'

The tithe supper, an event entirely pleasing to no one, is drawing to its end. The table is massed with cups and glasses, greasy plates of dented pewter; with the sucked and shattered skeletons of duck and chicken and hare, the browned, nubbed bones of the beef, sharp mutton bones.

'How then, Sam,' says James, 'will all these beasts find their parts on Judgment Day?'

'Taint just gonna be folk, then?'

'Bless me, no. Chickens, cats, Jonah's whale.' He looks down at Sam: an agile, scrawny, wonderfully ugly boy of eleven years. At fifteen he will be untellable from any red-faced son of the plough in spotted neckerchief and leather breeches, roaring in some market town. By thirty he will be one of these at the table; still lusty, but already half broken by work and worry, drinking to forget.

They sit together on the bench beside the fire. James feels its heat against his face.

Sam says: 'You said as you were gonna tell the story, Dr James.' Dr James: a form of address used openly only by Sam, privately by others.

'What story was that, Sam?' Knowing well what story.

''Bout the race.'

'Oh yes.'

'An' the queen an' that.'

'An empress, Sam. Better than a queen.'

'An' 'bout Mary.'

'Can you hear in all this rumpus?'

Sam nods.

For James this is an experiment; turning his life into anecdotes for a child. A series of small, safe detonations, preventing him, he trusts, from bawling a stream of fearful, undigested revelations to a stranger, or – worse – to one who knows him. And Sam is a good listener, tolerant of revisions, following the story as he follows a plough blade in the fields.

'And where did we arrive to upon the last occasion?'

Says Sam: 'Your friend, Mr Gummer.'

A vision: Gummer's face, that is, the eyes, for the rest is muffled by a scarf against the cold. Could he possibly have described Gummer as a friend?

James drinks from his cup, draws off one glove, wipes his lips with the back of his hand; feels the mottling of the scars.

'You know, then, how I first met Mr Gummer when I was a boy, how he stole upon me while I lay on my belly in the grass on the old hill-fort the day of the wedding and how, after my fall out of the cherry tree . . .'

'An' breakin' your leg.'

'Indeed . . .'

'An' the fella what set it . . .'

'Amos Gate, the smith. Good, then. Now, after my leg was mended – it has unmended since – there was . . . a sickness in the house. A very sharp sickness, so that my mother and brothers and sisters were all carried off . . .'

'All?'

'Ay, all,' confirming his lie. 'Leastways, I was alone, and set out to walk into Bristol to find Mr Gummer, thinking that he, who had shown a kind of interest in me, might take me in. I was younger than you are today, Sam, and yet I walked the whole of that road, mostly through rain as I recall. Have you been in the city, Sam, in any great city?'

Sam shakes his head.

'No more had I. Such a prodigious number of people! Soldiers and sailors and fat merchants; fine ladies holding their gowns out of the muck – for the city is much more filthy than the country. It was the first time that I ever set eyes on a black man or a Chinee. And there were ships from every blue corner of the world, one next to the other like creatures in a pen. And shops, Sam, lit up like Christmas, and a vast to-ing and fro-ing, a vast racket of men and beasts. Now, finding Mr Gummer among this, hmm, entropy, was, you may imagine, a far from simple business, and yet by following my nose I did find him and very surprised and, after a manner, pleased he was to see me, though I must tell you, he was not a kind man. But as I was not a kind boy we were a match of sorts. That was the . . .'

'Hallooo there! There's men dyin' o' thirst here!' Several of the company are waving their mugs as evidence while the others begin drumming on the table with their fists. The beat gains momentum, rings out like the tread of soldiers.

'Come, Sam.' James stands, smiles, apologises to the farmers with a slight bow. He takes the jugs, two in either hand, and goes through the door at the back of the kitchen into a chill, windowless room with a copper and mashing tubs and barrels where the Reverend, at each quarter-year, supervises the brewing of his table beer, and where Mrs Cole creates her country wines, the bottles stacked up against two of the walls. Despite the cold, Mary is sat there, very still on a straw-bottom chair, doing nothing discernible. A candle burns by her feet, which are tucked together, neat as cats. James draws the beer. When he has finished he says: 'Come through. ''Tis cold in here, even for you.'

She observes him, her eyes, two sucked black pebbles.

'They are but small farmers,' he says. 'Sound and fury. It means nothing. Nothing but this.' He raises one of the jugs. 'Come sit with Sam and me by the fire.'

James carries the beer into the kitchen and sets it on the table. He wishes very much he could be sure she is happy; contented at least.

'Aah! Your 'lixir of life, Doctor. You saved us from a dry grave.'

'Long life to you, gentlemen. Health and happiness.'

'You won't bibe wi' us?'

'If it will please the company.'

'Well spoke, man!'

The jug is passed around, beer slopping on to the table at each pour.

'A toast, lads!'

'The King!'

'Farmer George and ol' Snuffy.'

'To the best cunt in Christendom!'

'Nay, boys.' It is Ween Tull speaking. 'To our own Dr Dyer. Not happy in 'is name, I'll grant you . . .' − cheers for this wit − '. . . but as he gives no patents to any man or wife, nor takes up a knife more than to cut his bread, he saves more lives than any in the kingdom!'

The toast is called. Says James: 'Generous of you, gentlemen. Most.'

A voice cries: 'Where's Will Caggershot? Gi' us one of your verses, Will. Gi' us "Sally Salisbury"!'

Caggershot wriggles up from the bench. '"The Epitar of poor Sally Salisbury".'

The company gazes at him like happy schoolboys. Caggershot clears his throat.

'Here flat on her back but inactive at last
Poor Sally lies under grim death;
Through the course of her vices she galloped so fast
No wonder she's now out of breath.

'To the goal of her pleasures she strove very hard
But tripped up ere halfway she ran
An' though everyone fancied her life was a yard . . .'

He stops, gawping over the others' heads towards the door of the brewing-room. The rest now twist in their seats to see. James stands from the hearth bench, his arms open as if hoping physically to bring the company together again. ''Tis only Mary, gentlemen. No need to leave off your songs.'

'We know who 'tis, Doctor.' Caggershot takes his seat. The farmers pool their gaze in the centre of the table. James shrugs and, going to Mary, hands her on to the bench next to Sam. Slowly the talk resumes, like an old pump, temporarily blocked. They drink; the drink is replenished. Mary is forgotten. Caggershot sings his songs, each more lewd than the last. Then Een Tull, brother of Ween, and the undoubted and piteous fool of the company, points his weebling finger at Mary, calling: ''Ow 'bout the woman, Doctor, showin' off 'er teef an' that.'

The request is chorused by others, and so swiftly it is evident that Een has said only what others have been thinking. James has half feared such a turn, yet hoped they would refrain out of respect for him as 'the Doctor', as the Reverend's friend, as Mary's evident protector. It stings him, this apparent betrayal. And it is he who is to blame, he who has exposed her. He stands, loaded with breath.

'NO FREAK SHOWS, GENTLEMEN!'

There is no one in the room, not even Mary, who knew James Dyer as the immaculate young man setting out for Russia in the autumn of 1767. None who have seen him in his finery, his coat of thunder and lightning, shaking the hand of the imperial ambassador as though it were the ambassador who should be honoured by the contact. None even who have imagined such a thing, save Sam perhaps, arranging gorgeous puppets in his mind as a kind of history. For the moment, the farmers are utterly routed.

The stillness is broken by a sound like the onset of rain. Mary moves to the head of the table, her hands neatly gathered at her waist as though about to sing for them. She waits – that sure theatricality of hers – then parts her lips in a snarl, so that the front teeth, neatly filed into points, are bared to the gums. From the table comes a low moan of wonder. How much better this is than a double-headed sheep or a mathematical fish in a stinking booth at a country fair. Their expressions are so ludicrous, some of them unwontedly mimicking Mary's snarl, that James's anger translates itself to laughter, a loud, liberating laughter, which might have earned some angry words had the Reverend not then entered the kitchen, his face, despite the bleeding, dangerously ripe after five hours of food and drink and cards. He peers quizzically at James, then addresses himself to the farmers.

'Gentlemen, I fear I must detain you no longer. I am enough in the farming way myself to know you will be anxious to regain your homes.'

The appearance of a superior, even one so free from glamour as a parson, is unpleasantly sobering. Pipes are tapped out, the last of the beer swilled from the mugs. Their expressions seem already to anticipate the cold sensations the next dawn will bring; the renewed struggle with recalcitrant beasts, the tramping through still, dark fields like the first or last men on earth.

James brings out hats and greatcoats, scarves and gauntlets, sorry now that he has laughed. The yard fills with the manoeuvring, the shuffling and stamping of men and horses. The dog, which launched itself into a frenzy of yelps at their appearance, has received across its snout a sharp slap from the Reverend, and now lies on its belly in an ecstasy of restraint. Hooves on the cobbles ring like showers of flints. The farmers depart, their horses picking their way up the track towards the road, until at length only James and Sam and the Reverend remain, grouped in the emergent quiet, chiaroscuro fashion, around the Reverend's lantern.

The boy shivers. The Reverend looks down at him as if surprised to find him there.

'Had you your wits about you, Sam, you might have had a ride home with one of our guests.'

James says: 'I shall walk him. I've been keeping him up with old stories.'

'Ah, stories . . .' The Reverend nods as though the word signified to him in some special way. 'Well, you've some to tell.'

'And some we share.'

A smile flickers on the Reverend's face. 'We do that.' He sniffs the air. 'Watch your step on the ice, Doctor. Shall you take the lantern?'

'Nay. Sam and I are learning our stars. We shall see them better without a lantern.'

Sam has run back into the house to fetch their coats and James's staff. Waiting in the yard, James eyes the edge of the dressing that pokes from beneath the Reverend's wig. He wants to ask how he goes on with it, but the business of the bleeding continues to trouble him. He is relieved when the Reverend nods towards the open door, through which, visible among the remaining lights, Sam stands beside Mary, taking his leave of her.

'He is fond of her,' the Reverend says.

'Ay. There's something between them.'

'Does she ever speak to him?'

James shrugs. 'He understands how she means towards him.'

Sam brings his coat, the heavy surtout, its pockets deep enough for books and apples and paper for sketching.

'Well, then.'

'God speed.'

'Good night to you.'

'Good night, good night, Sam.'

They are drawing apart. The Reverend turns towards the house, scratches behind the dog's ear and sighs, sighs so heavily it surprises him, as if his body possessed some secret knowledge yet to permeate through to consciousness. His temple throbs; he touches it tenderly with two fingers. Odd that James's nerve should go like that. Odd how a man can change. Finished as a doctor, of course. All that talent! True, he was a hard and unlovable man before. But useful; by God he was. What does the world need most – a good, ordinary man, or one who is outstanding, albeit with a heart of ice, of stone? Hard one that. This dog's too skinny. Needs worming. Time to sleep now. Dream something good.

5   From the house there is nearly a mile of pitted trackway to reach the bridge and the road that runs uphill to the village. It is darker here, under the shadow of trees and tall hedgerows, but the moon still guides them, showing deep ruts sequinned with frost, and the snaking of branches from the invisible to the invisible across bars of diffuse light. Where they find the sky unhindered they stop, Sam following the arc of James's hand as he names the stars, both of them staring up into the depths of heaven until it seems they can feel the earth tumbling under their feet, and they must look down or stagger. Their walking startles

an animal; eyes in a body of umbra, a creature insubstantial as the quick, dry rustle of its escape through the hedge. Sam claims it for a fox, says he shall tell George Pace of it and earn a penny.

By and by James persuades Sam to sing for him. Sam walks a way in silence, pondering his repertoire, then starts in with 'Old John Barleycorn'. His voice is too soft at first, then suddenly he is in his stride, a light treble voice, husky on the higher notes:

> 'There was three men come out of the West
> Their fortunes for to try. And these three men
> Made a solemn vow John Barleycorn should die . . .'

For some three or four minutes, this singing expresses for James more of the natural melancholy of life than anything he has heard in cathedral or concert hall. Or madhouse.

> 'They wheeled 'im roun' an' roun' the field
> Till they came unto a barn
> And there they made a solemn mow
> Of poor John Barleycorn . . .'

They come out at the bridge, a stone hump with low parapets, and turn up the hill to Cow. A single light shows feebly from a house at the brow of the hill – Caxton's place. Passing, they peep in through the half-curtained window, at the backs of men working at their drink. Then they go on into zones of shadow, winding between the shut stone faces of sleeping cottages, the dark gardens, the breathing and shiftings of animals. Far off, yet very clear, comes the call of an owl, and its answer, equally clear, equally distant.

The sexton's house is marked by a glow seeping through the glass of a downstairs window. The light shifts at the noise of their approach and the door is opened before they have knocked. The boy's mother stands in the entrance with her candle.

'I trust he has been no worry to you, Doctor.' And then to the boy: 'What do you mean giving the doctor such trouble, walking all this way in the middle of the night?' There is more relief than anger in her voice.

James says: 'I pray you not be too hard on him. I am to blame. And to walk on such a night is no hardship. Sam has been singing for me. He has a fine voice. I was thinking he should be among the choir. They are not over-endowed with fine singing there . . . Your good husband being a notable exception.'

'You are kind to say so, I'm sure.' She makes the briefest curtsey, only really perceptible in the movement of the candle flame. Despite the doctor's present condition – virtually a hanger-on among the Reverend's household – he carries with him a vague measure of fame, and a certain gentility, which makes him, in her eyes at least, one of the Important People. She is touched also by his friendship for her son. It is a good light for the boy to be in; a good warm light.

'You'll come in and take a smatter of something? For the night air?'

'I cannot impose on you at such an hour, Mrs Clarke . . .' But already he is following her and her light into the house, past the shadow-elongated hat of the sleeping sexton, whose snores just reach them as they gather in the kitchen. Here the bedded embers of the fire give off their steady heat.

The house is but the slightest bit smaller than the one James was a child in, the house at Blind Yeo, and there is much about it, the humble, scrubbed look of things, the complex blend of odours, the play of light on polished surfaces, that is as familiar to him as his own face.

Mrs Clarke brings in her husband's mug, filled with ale, and sets it down in front of her guest. For herself she has a small glass of ginger wine. Sam, standing like a footman at James's shoulder, drinks milk out of a wooden cup.

'Your husband is well?'

'Thank you, sir, he is. But he must have his measure of sleep, mind. He says that working with so many eternal sleepers gives him an appetite for it.'

'An appetite for what, madam?' The sudden warmth after the cold air has made him drowsy. Mrs Clarke blushes.

'For sleep, Doctor. Only for sleep.' She glances at her son, then laughs unexpectedly. 'It is his joke, Doctor.'

James says: 'There is not a profession in the world as does not have its particular humour. I regret that that of medical men is perhaps the grossest of them all. A proximity to the suffering of others produces a drollery more cruel than truly comic. It begins as a defence against horrors but soon becomes merely a way with them.'

'I'm sure it was not so with you,' says Mrs Clarke. There is always, in the doctor's conversation, a gratifying air of imminent indiscretion.

'No, madam, it was not, for the suffering of others did not trouble me in the least. I understood it only in so far as there existed a correlation between the sharpness of the pain and the fee that might be had for its relief.' James, whose gaze as he spoke was directed at the table, now looks up to measure the effect of this confession. There is an instant's confusion in her eyes but it passes quickly. She shows she is determined to be kind to him.

'Sure you knew your business best, Doctor.'

'Depend upon it, madam. I was – and this is no puff – the only surgeon of my acquaintance whose good reputation was not an utter fiction. Most had tongues and fancies that could have turned a tavern brawl into the siege of Troy, but come to the real business of healing and you had might as well be attended by a goose. Gold swords and hearts of the cheapest brass.' He pauses, smiling to take off the edge of anger that has crept into his voice. 'You see how unkind I am to my old profession. There were some good men among them, ay, and good women too. Those who knew how to comfort without touting hope when there was none. In truth, Mrs Clarke, there is little enough we can do, very little. We are born too late and too early – between the secret arts of the old world and the discoveries of the age to come. I had a certain genius, madam, mostly for the knife. But I never had that way of looking . . .' He gestures loosely in the air above his ale. '. . . that quality of attention towards another's suffering which marks out the true healer.'

'Why, I fancy you are too hard on yourself, Doctor.'

James shakes his head. 'No, madam, I am merely just. I was good in the smallest sense of the word. Wonderful dextrous but no man ever came to me for kindness.'

There is a weight in the words and something iron in his tone which makes this last unanswerable. There is a long pause, then Mrs Clarke says: 'You have a sister, I think?'

'I had two.'

'They . . . ?'

'Ay, the pretty one, Sarah. Died as a child along with my brother. I believe the other still lives, my Liza. That is, I do not know of her not doing so. I have not seen her since I was a boy.'

'You told me they all died,' says Sam. 'That you was alone.'

'Hush now,' says his mother, afraid to disturb so fragile a mood.

'Did I say so, Sam? Well, it was near enough the truth.' He falls silent.

Mrs Clarke waits, then offers, 'Mayhap you shall see her again.'

'She would not be glad of it, I think. She has no cause to love me.'

'A sister does not need cause to love her brother, Doctor. 'Tis her duty.'

'There can be no talk of duty. I wronged her.'

'As a boy. And boys often wrong their sisters. Lor', when I think of my own brothers. Yet we are friends enough now.'

James shakes his head. 'I should not be able to look at her.'

'Then she might care to look at you, her own flesh an' blood.'

'Impossible.'

'Forgiveness is a great thing,' she says, 'for those with the heart for it.'

James, his hand on Sam's shoulder, eases himself up from the table. In a quiet voice he says: 'She is blind. Was blind. The smallpox.'

Sam is sent to bed. Mrs Clarke, candle in hand as before, leads James to the door. Stepping out from the house, he says: 'Did I talk strangely?'

'You are always welcome wi' us, Doctor.'

'Thank you. I feel it. My regards to your husband.' Again he marks the awkward curtsey. The door closes, a bolt slides home and the woman's footsteps fade into the body of the house. James makes his way up the path, blinking to clear the imprint of the candle flame from his sight. It feels colder now; the stones grate like glass beneath his shoes. He has reached the road when he is stopped by a softly floated 'tssst!' from the house.

'You'll tell the stories, Dr James?' The voice seeps from a small casement under the eaves. Sam himself is quite invisible.

'I shall.'

'The Empress?'

'Yes, Sam.'

'An' why Mary's got pointy teeth?'

'Go to bed, Sam.' He raises his arm, waves.

The sexton's ale, bright and wholesome as it is, is not quite adequate protection against the frost now fingering its way through the folds of James's coat. Neither, after his conversation with Mrs Clarke, does he feel like trudging directly home – home! – to the Reverend's house and a cold, most likely empty bed. A half-hour of human society, a glass of rum and water, some insubstantial chatter – these shall settle him again. What did he mean, going on to Mrs Clarke like that?

Coming abreast of Caxton's, he bows in through the low door, stands in the choppy light and breathes in the vile air of the place. A small front room with a small fire, benches polished to jet by countless breeches, and four tables upon which single candles give off coarse threads of smut. Caxton himself stands by the fire, arms akimbo, looking over the shoulders of a half-dozen of the Reverend's recent guests who are playing at dominoes, almost imbecilic with fatigue and drink. Seeing James, Caxton works his face into a semblance of welcome and the two men exchange greetings. Not having set foot in the place for months, James had forgotten how much he dislikes Caxton; not for the tavern-keeper's association with local poachers – poachers, by and large, are honourable men – nor yet for the rumours, strongly grounded, of his having sold evidence to the constables which led to the turning-off of a boy on a charge of stealing a gentleman's pocket-watch. His unease concerns the girl, Caxton's daughter, who stands, heavily pregnant and picking at the quicks of her nails, an arm's length from her father. Feeling James's gaze on her, she attempts a smile yet manages to express only a profound embarrassment. Caxton calls: 'What'll it be, then, Doctor? What shall the wench fetch you?'

James orders his rum, turns down an offer to join in the dominoes, and sits by himself at one of the other tables. The girl – for at fourteen or fifteen, despite her condition, it is hard to call her anything else – brings him his glass, wipes the table with a beer-damp cloth, and sets the glass in front of him. He asks her how she goes on, glancing at her great belly which seems on the verge of overwhelming her. Avoiding his eyes, she says: 'Right enough.'

'You shall be brought to bed of it soon, Sally. You are not afraid?'

'I shall be glad to be rid of it, sir.'

'Who shall attend you?'

'Mother Grayley.'

'She has much experience,' says James, silently appalled that a woman known as a hard drinker and with a regiment of dead infants to her credit should be called upon by anyone other than the devil. This must be Caxton's wish.

'Simple is best, Sally. You are young. No need to go dosing yourself with nostrums and the like.'

The girl whispers her thank yous, hurries off. James takes up his glass and drinks. This brief interview with Sally, and the sight of her father, slick and loutish, even of the farmers hunched over their little rectangles, a pile of grubby coins in the centre of the table, all of it depresses him. There is no real happiness here; little even of hope. In the girl's vulnerability and in the hardness of the men there are equal measures of dogged suffering; and though some suffering is earned, some pain doubtless a kind of nemesis, what comfort, what satisfaction is there in that? All pain is real enough to those who have it; all stand equally in need of compassion. God knows he craves it for himself.

The door opens; he looks up. A man of such size it appears he has been made from the material for two men, a man with black skin – or is it brown, or in fact a kind of grey, like night over snow? – enters the little room like an adult entering a house of children. Stooped under the beams, he shuffles in decayed crimson slippers towards Caxton. He holds out a small jug, a cream jug, and whispers in a voice like the soft raking of coals, a single word:

'Gin.'

'Gin?'

The black man nods, points delicately at the jug. Caxton takes the jug and hands it to his daughter, who goes with it into the back room to fill. The black man reaches into the pocket of his short jacket, takes out a purse and shakes a sixpence into his open palm.

Thinks James: You could hide a cricket ball in such a hand. How stiff the fingers are, like an old man's. Still powerful, though.

The Negro receives his jug from Sally, thanks her and waits for his change from Caxton until, seeing he is to get none, he nods wearily and shuffles back to the door. The door swings shut. For two, three seconds, there is nothing but the erratic rhythm of the fire, then the farmers chatter excitedly, each telling the other what he saw, as if each were the sole witness of this marvellous encounter. Caxton is congratulated on cheating the stranger. A farmer warns him he will be eaten in the black man's cooking-pot. Roars of laughter. Another, turning to James, asks if a Negro is made the same as a white man, if perhaps their bones are black like their skin. 'No,' says James, feeling now an overwhelming desire to quit the place, 'they are made as we are.'

'I hear tell their seed is black – beggin' yer pardon, Sally.'

'I cannot say.'

'And what of their hearts,' enquires Caxton. 'Are they black?'

James says: 'No more than yours, sir, or mine.'

To James's irritation the remark is mistaken for humour and he is forced to leave to a chorus of cheery farewells. I fail, he thinks, stepping cautiously on to the icy road, even in conveying my contempt.

He clears his mind with a dozen deep draughts of cold air, thinks of the morrow, trusts it will be another brilliant, fiery day, another with air like champagne. He grins, remembering the Reverend's sudden vigour of the morning. A man must make a quiet store of such mornings, hoard them against more desperate times. If tomorrow is fine perhaps I shall take out my ink and paper, up to Lady Hallam's place, and do that little temple by the water there.

He has begun to sketch it in his head when the sound of iron-shod wheels bouncing over the road behind him makes him step on to the greensward. For some minutes the cart exists only as a collection of noises; the groaning of axles, the crazed timpany of rattling pots and pans; squeaky, inebriated singing. Finally, he discerns the vehicle's form, a covered one-horse wagon, swaying down the hill from Cow. Coming up by James, the voice ceases to sing and calls out: 'Who goes there? Are you a Christian or what are you?'

Says James: 'You have nothing to fear from me.'

He is able now, beneath the soft halo of starlight, to see two figures, one very small, sized as a child, yet clearly, from her tone, and from the clouds of gin that wrap her words, not a child. The other is the Negro from Caxton's place.

'Not decent, creeping 'bout in the 'edgerow this time a night,' says the woman, then, in the space of a breath, her voice fills with honey. 'Ain't you got nowhere to go, then? Poor bleeder. Carn 'e stop wi' us, John? He ain't got nowheres to sleep.'

'Hush,' says the Negro.

James says: 'Your offer is a kind one but I have a roof and a bed a short walk from here.'

'Well, that's all right, then. Get 'er goin', John.'

John clucks his tongue, the horse takes up the strain, and the wagon rolls forward, trailing its thin ribbon of song behind it.

'Wouldyatastethemoontideair . . . toyourfragrantbowerrepair . . . wherewovenwiththepoplarbough . . . themantlingvineshallshelter-you . . .'

James sleeps with Mary, finds her between his sheets when, candleless, he feels his way to his room. He climbs in behind her, his chest to her back. His leg aches like the devil but it does not worry him. He knows he will sleep, inhaling her skin as if it were one of his narcotic sponges. He kisses her shoulder in greeting, also in farewell, for she will have returned to her own small room while he is still sleeping and long before any of the household stirs.

In the next chamber, the Reverend is sitting, in his dreams, naked and perfectly companionable with Lady Hallam over a hand of cards. Dido dreams of a man, tenderly sucking the blood from her elbow. James dreams of a cherry tree large as a house and of looking down through the flaked green flesh of its leaves to where the Negro, dressed in cherry silks and satins, holds up his arms to catch him.

THIRD

1 The winter of 1739 is the worst in living memory: a bitter, petrifying season that grips the country like a biblical revenge, beautiful and murderous. On the Ouse at York, on the frozen Thames, presses are dragged on to the ice to print news of the ice-world, as though from a freshly minted kingdom, suddenly and miraculously overlaying the old. In the cellars, wine and beer choke their barrels; cattle are found rigid in their stalls at dawn; strange lights are seen. The darkness crackles. Crows and other birds fall stiff as ornaments from the open sky.

Driving, bone-infesting cold gathers the poor, the very young, the old, the sickly. Infants are buried beside hooped grandmothers and veterans of Blenheim. The gravedigger's heart-faced shovel rings like an axe on iron, and graves are so shallow there is talk in western villages of grave-robbers, until a pack of dogs tearing at the boards of a pauper's coffin in the yard at Kenn are shot at by the watchman.

In Blind Yeo, a village that has dawdled from the grey walls of a medieval priory, and now, in the thirteenth year of the reign of King George II, straddles the road from Bristol to Coverton like a set of poor teeth clenched on a strap, little is moving save blue smoke uncoiling from thatched or slated roofs, and a few figures out of doors, hugging themselves in long coats, stumbling over ruts, each footfall audible in the glassy air, each breath visible.

Twilight comes hard on second milking, light seeping from the windows of farmhouses and cottages.

Behind the village a hill-fort rises island-like above the moors. From there, an observer, stamping his boots for warmth, might assume the day was all used up, and that the village would slide into the long night like a launch slipping into black water. But by the bank of the river there is a gleam of light, then two more, then a dozen, and with them voices, cries of 'Clear the way!', and the grating, swishing, unmistakable hiss of skates.

The skaters hang their lanterns from the lower branches of the trees. The trees arch, black and shiny, over the frozen river. A party, fifteen or twenty strong, glides over the illuminated ice. Some gracefully, propelling themselves with flicks of the trailing skate, hands clasped behind their backs, bodies leaning forward into the icy tunnels of their own progress. Others are hunched as if preparing to catch an enormous ball, or wave their arms like women folding sheets on a windy morning. Certain heads regularly disappear from view. There are shouts, amiable and neighbourly, shouts of 'Dammeyejohn!' and 'HoldfarstAlice!' – and laughter, high and drunken.

A moon, tight as a fist, is planted in the west above the estuary. Dogs all over the moor, in farmyards where the muck glitters like diamonds, bay at its brilliance. Even the beagles of Coverton Hall press together blindly in their kennels, a velvety mass, and howl. The skaters are touched by it too: midwinter madness; the year's seductive zero.

A bottle smashes on the ice. A figure drags himself to the bank. 'ZatyouJoshua?' The figure leans back against the base of an alder, nods his head and vomits a stream of warm cider between his knees. A young woman with a shawl tight about her shoulders draws up on the ice beside him. She says: 'You're mistaken if you think I shall carry you home. Useless man!'

He ignores her. The voice is scolding, but there is a bubble of hilarity in it, and when a second woman sweeps by and catches her arm, she lets herself be taken.

The air is set ringing from the single high note of a fiddle. A cheer goes up, and the fiddler, an old man, his skull wrapped in a woollen sling, begins a medley of dance tunes, music as familiar to them as the sounds of their own voices – 'Get Her Bo', 'Jumping John', 'Joyful Days Are Coming'. The skaters, sweating in the polar air, dance and fall and clutch at each other with new strength. More come, easing themselves down the bank on to the ice. There is no fear the ice will break. It is hard as bone.

The fiddle stops. The dancers stop, their breath like gauze masks as they look up. Shooting stars! Above Pigs' Green, above Ladyfield; a first, then a second burst. A dozen arms reach up, pointing. The dogs, suspicious of the sudden quiet, fall silent.

Elizabeth Dyer is on her skates by the bank in a block of darkness ten yards beyond the edge of the lantern light. She is twenty-nine, mother of three children, wife of the yeoman, Joshua Dyer. The skates she wears she has had since she was fourteen. Recently she has suffered from indefinable sorrows. Tonight the sky draws a tide of blood through her, so strong she feels in danger of floating up, disappearing over the rooftops of the village.

From behind her comes a soft, granulous footfall; she does not turn to see who it is, and when a hand – not her husband's hand, not any farmer's hand, but a hand long and light and smooth – slips beneath her shawl and presses her breast, she remains looking up, though the stars have flickered out and the sky has resumed its stillness. In his haste, the stranger loses his balance; he slips and drags them both down on to the ice, his weight on top of her, knocking the wind out of her. They writhe in a heap, yet neither tries to stand. Her skirts are up. She knows she has the strength to fight him, to fling him off her. Instead, she gropes towards the bank, scrabbling until she catches hold of a root, cold as brass, and clutches it with both hands, anchoring them, her and the stranger, like some clumsy vessel wallowing off a black coast. He hangs from the bones of her hips, jabs several times before he succeeds in entering her. It is over in seconds: a half-dozen thrusts; the dig of his nails; his breath hissing between his teeth. Then he drifts away from her, her shifts and petticoats and gown falling like curtains.

She remains there long enough, her knuckles numb around the tree-root, to be sure that he has gone. Her body is trembling a little; she has a sharp vision of a man making his escape between hedges of fine lace, across hard, empty fields. She is amazed at her calmness. The risk has been huge and senseless. She cannot explain it. She eases herself up, touches the back of her dress, pulls her shawl tight about her shoulders and skates back towards the lights. The fiddler is playing again, jigging clumsily on the bank. A woman friend takes her arm, skates at her side a moment.

'Don't this air make your skin smart, girl?'

'It does, Martha, it does.'

'You won't have no trouble from your Joshua tonight.'

'No, Martha, I think not,' and Elizabeth skates free, feeling as she goes a lick of the man's seed, already cold, on the inside of her thigh.

 The child is born in September, in a room hot with fire and the breath of women. The women crowd around the bed. Mrs Llewellyn, Mrs Phillips, Mrs Rivers, Mrs

Martha Bell. Mrs Collins from Yatton, Mrs Gwyny Jones from Failand and Joshua's mother, the Widow Dyer, who fills her nostrils with Virginia snuff and looks over the midwife's shoulder. The midwife is sweating out her gin. She has not had a mother die on her for almost a year, but she will not answer for this one. The infant won't emerge. It has been hours now, though she can feel the crown of its head, the wisps of sopping hair, like weeds in the river.

Elizabeth Dyer is growing weaker. Her lips are pale, the skin grey around her eyes. The midwife has seen it often enough, how they pass beyond you, no more screaming, turn their faces to the wall. Another hour or two, then, God willing, mother or infant will be dead; then nothing more will be expected of her. Perhaps the child is dead already.

Liza Dyer, nine years old, stands, caught between the curves of the women's dresses, looking on. She holds the fingers of one hand in the fingers of the other. Her face reveals a normal terror. The others note it, remembering their own initiations at the side of birth-beds and death-beds.

Mrs Gwyny Jones whispers: 'Should Mr Viney not be sent for?'

Widow Dyer says: 'We have no need of a man in here.'

Such exhaustion! Elizabeth cannot think what it is like, cannot imagine words for it. Her belly is frozen. The child, a bung of ice, is killing her. A cold salt sweat burns her eyes, streams off her taut skin, soaking the mattress. How will Joshua survive without her? Who will love the children as she does? Who will make the good butter? Who will rear the lambs of dead ewes or stitch shirts until eyes and fingers ache? She can remember no prayers, not one. Her head is empty. A voice is nagging her, telling her to push, push for all life. How cruel they are to make her suffer so! She screams; a vast sound, jostling the women, rocking them, all save the Widow, the most rooted. Liza is blown on to the floor, felled as though struck between the eyes with a poker. Mrs Collins pulls her up. No one suggests the girl might leave.

The midwife cries: 'It comes!'

'Praise be,' says Gwyny Jones. She strokes her heart; a reflex of joy.

The midwife rakes the infant out, grips its slithery ankles in her fist and holds it up. It is dressed, head to toe, in blood, and hangs limply from the woman's hand.

Says Widow Dyer: 'Is it quick?'

The midwife shakes it; the infant moves its arms and hands, a blind swimmer, an old blind man feeling for the door. It does not cry. It is silent. The women cock their heads. Silent. Liza reaches out. The midwife cuts the cord with enormous rusty scissors.

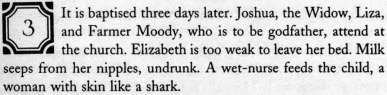

It is baptised three days later. Joshua, the Widow, Liza, and Farmer Moody, who is to be godfather, attend at the church. Elizabeth is too weak to leave her bed. Milk seeps from her nipples, undrunk. A wet-nurse feeds the child, a woman with skin like a shark.

Though it is the middle of the afternoon, the church is so dark they can barely see each other. The child is not expected to live. Widow Dyer has persuaded them so. No healthy child could be so unnatural, not to make a sound in three days. Sleeps, wakes, feeds; does not cry, not once. It has a dozen curls of silk-black hair on its head. Its eyes are baby blue. Widow Dyer says it is best if it dies.

The priest comes late from his lunch, expels, discreetly as he can, the gas from his stomach, takes the child, asks Moody if he abjures the work of Satan, and gives the child its names: James Dyer. One given name quite enough for such a sickly thing, and less work for the mason.

There is no water in the font. The priest spits in his hand and makes the cross on the child's brow, feels it stirring, then passes it to the girl. Joshua Dyer fumbles in his purse, puts the money in the priest's hands, nods solemnly, awkwardly. They trudge home through the scraped fields, Liza hugging the baby tight against her ribs.

4   From inside the house they hear the sound of his horse in the lane. Liza runs to the window. Widow Dyer looks up from her darning, hoists her bulk upright and bustles to the fire. There is a poker dug into the heart of the fire. Elizabeth says: 'Nay, let me, Willa,' but the older woman ignores her, draws the poker out, protecting her hand with a piece of scorched cloth. There is a bowl of punch set ready by the fire. She presses the tip of the poker into the liquid so that it hisses fiercely. The noise wakes the baby. It has been sleeping on a quilt in the kneading-trough. It looks at the fat woman by the fire, looks at her dipping her finger into the punch, then breaking off a piece of sugar loaf and mixing it in. The Widow says: 'He allus liked things sweet. Is his food ready? He'll be leery after the market all day.'

The older children have run to the front of the house to glimpse their father coming down the lane. Now they run back into the kitchen, to the back door where they know he will enter when he has stabled the horse. After a minute they hear his boots and elbow each other to be nearest to the door. There is the sound of the iron latch, then the kitchen door opens and a wave of winter air sweeps across the kitchen.

He lets the children crowd around him for a moment, then closes the door and pushes into the room. Widow Dyer ladles punch into a mug and hands it to him. She says: 'Bide by the fire, son,' and fusses him towards it. She does not ask him about the parcel beneath his arm. He sets it down with exaggerated care on the kitchen table, then drinks the punch as fast as he can bear to. The others watch him in a broken circle. He is a splinter of the outer world. From the deep half-frozen folds of his coat come odours of horse, leather, tobacco. Even the frosty, thrilling smell of the night itself.

Sarah, no longer the youngest now the baby has come, reaches up on tiptoe and places an investigative hand upon the parcel. Liza plucks her away, scolds her. Joshua grins at the older girl. In a teasing voice he asks: 'Now, wouldn't you like a peek inside, wench?'

'You sold the geese then, father,' Liza says.

He laughs and holds out his mug. 'Allus business with you, Liza. Fill this for me, then. Greetings, wife.' Elizabeth nods to him. She has picked up the baby and swaddled it in her arms. Joshua looks away at his mother. 'I got a good price for the birds.'

Elizabeth wonders if Joshua has drunk much at market. She remembers the night, six months past, when he fell on his ride home, covering his side with plum-coloured bruises. She remembers him on the table, groaning, and not a moment's peace until Viney came with compresses and infusions.

This year he seems himself more, but the parcel – a heavy, expensive look to it – worries her. She knows the minds of men like Joshua. Her own father was the same; happy to argue all night to fix the price of a ewe or a bushel of apples, but show him something new, something novel, and he would part with his money as though he were heir to a dukedom. No wonder the quacks and showmen never went without what was good. Fine mounts and fine cloth on their backs.

She says: 'You bought something, then. Something useful.'

Out of the corner of her eye she can see the Widow scowling at her. 'Ay,' she says, seeing her husband colour. He gives her a half-offended, half-angry look, which in the early days of their marriage might have brought an exchange of blows, and then a tumble in their new bed. Her needling sharpened their appetites then, but work, sickness, children, the constant wrestling with the weather, with animals that seemed to know only how to die, all that had worn the life out of them, so that they live only in fits now, in spasms. They hold each other's gaze a moment, then Joshua turns his back on her, pushes his hands close to the flames.

'Food,' he says.

The children step quietly away from him.

He eats. The food dulls his temper. When he has finished, he wipes the grease from his face and lights his pipe from a taper. He reaches along the table and pulls the parcel towards him, so that it sits on the table between himself and Liza. It is wrapped in coarse sacking, exudes a faint distinctive odour of oily wool. He cuts the string with the knife he has been eating with, pushes the parcel closer to the girl. He says: ''Tis for all of you, but as the wench has more sense and age, it's to stay with her to show you as she pleases.' To the boy he says: 'Bring that candle up, Charlie. There. Set it by her.'

Liza, with the gravity of a child queen examining the gift of a foreign court, unfolds the sacking until she has uncovered a polished wooden box about the size of the family Bible. There is a brass catch at the front. She looks over at her father. He says: 'Open it, then, girl. It'll not open of itself.'

She fumbles with the catch, frees it, opens the box, and stares in at its contents, then looks round at the others. All the faces, with the exception of her father's, show the same excited puzzlement as

63

her own. Inside the box is a wooden disc, white, mounted with delicate wires and globes of varying circumferences and colours; red and blue, one black and white, one golden, greater than the others. Around the edge of the white disc are the names of the months and pictures from the zodiac. At the side is a handle like the handle of a little coffee grinder.

She runs her finger over the golden globe. Joshua says: 'Hot, baint it.' His face is fierce with pleasure.

'Baint hot,' she says.

'Hot in summer, cold in winter. All day you see 'im, but at night he's gone.' He has devised the riddle on the ride home and is well pleased with it.

'I see it!' Elizabeth has forgotten for the moment the probable expense. She claps her hands. 'This is the sun, and this is our world . . . and this is the moon?'

Joshua says: 'An' this is Mercury, and this Venus. Venus for love and Mercury for summat else. Turn the handle there, Liza. There, like so.' He places his hand over the girl's. 'See?'

Cogs, the secret workings of the machine, bite and turn. The globes begin to move, each with a motion of its own, slow and stately, like bishops dancing a minuet. The children sit, bewitched, hardly breathing.

''Tis called a horrory,' says Joshua, his voice almost a whisper: 'An' that's Greek for everything.'

Widow Dyer nods sagely; Sarah and Charlie clamour for their turn, and in the liquid of the infant's eyes, the toy universe gently spins – the crab, the lion, the virgin – month after month, year after year.

It is James Dyer's earliest memory.

The kitchen is his first world. The fire jabbing at the irons, light shivering in the backs of copper pans. A cosy abattoir where creatures of the air, the field, the river are shorn and gutted and pampered for the flames. The servant, Jenny Scurl, is an alchemist of the flesh, transforming the corpse of a rabbit or the heaped, snowy carcass of a goose, her fingers thick as bottle-necks; tearing, scraping, cutting, tearing out the roots of guts and stuffing the tender hollows with onions, boiled eggs, sage, parsley, rosemary, chopped apple, chestnuts. To amuse the children she skins eels live.

James lives in the lower regions, crawling on the stone floor beneath the kitchen table where the shadows are haunted by thin, nameless, determined cats who sit beside him, watching feathers drift and flour shiver down, and who fight him in the war of scraps, finding him a hardier opponent than his predecessors. Unnoticed, he spends half his days there following the women's wooden heels and woollen-cased ankles beneath the sea-edge of their petticoats – to and fro, to and fro; never still.

Later, after a score of unprotested falls, he learns to scale the kitchen chairs, sitting, his feet barely reaching to the end of the seat, soundlessly accepting the knocks and caresses, the dabs of bread or sweet pastry that come his way. Increasingly, his muteness draws the attention of the adult world. Some take him for a moon-calf, witless, and bounce him on their knees, talking to him as they would to the dog. The women coddle him for his blue eyes, for the comical gravitas of his stare. When Liza has him to herself she makes his face sticky with her kisses. He sits still upon her lap, remote as a spider or a star.

Elizabeth says: 'He will change in time. Give the child time. Was Sarah not a backward, whispery sort of infant? Yet she speaks well and often enough now.' She watches James as though his first words will be a denunciation. She has put the horns on you, Joshua Dyer! Hearing some commotion in the village, she fears it is the Rough Music, the carnivals of hate that play beneath the windows of adulteresses. God forgive her, she tried a dozen times to lose the child, and it was not as if she had not lost others before their term. The last two had never gone beyond the fourth month. But this one was tenacious, bracing itself in her belly. Now, with his blue eyes, his silence loud as a huntsman's horn, he has come to shame her. The old woman, the Widow, blunt red face and ferret's eyes, her mind wringing intelligence out of the air, does not quite dare openly accuse her. She watches the boy, then settles a look on Elizabeth that needs no explanation.

As the child grows, so the turn of her mind is darker. She senses the presence of darkness; a malevolent look in the eye of a ram, a branch slapping her face, a fly crawling on the white of her wrist. She remembers the stranger's hand, long and light, and the lines of a song she sang as a girl: 'The Devil is a Gen'leman, He dances very neat . . .'

On an afternoon in the child's third year, alone with him, watching him gaze about with that quiet, empty look, as if he understood everything or nothing, she pinches him hard on his upper arm, fixes him with her nails, almost until he bleeds. When he looks at her, merely quizzical, and then looks down, calmly, at the raw, narrow ruby on his arm, she is filled with a horror of him, a nausea. But the panic passes and she is swept by waves of tenderness. How pretty he is! How absurdly sad, bolted into his silence. She hugs him and sucks the mark she has made on his arm, though she cannot shift it and sees it there long afterwards, memento of her shame, terror, love.

Sometimes she is afraid that the Widow will speak to Joshua, yet they both know Joshua will believe only what he wishes to, the thing most comfortable to believe: that his wife is faithful and loves him as he loves her. Once a day he dutifully asks, 'How is it with the boy?', but he does not stay for an answer, nor does he whittle in the evenings wooden dolls and spinning-tops as has done for the others.

Dumb beneath this canopy of adult fears, James's world expands. His mind, a room furnished with fires, cats and painted suns, now fills with the life of the farm. In hand-me-down rabbit-skin breeches he is led into the ooze of the yard, watching the hens squabble and spiders spin their webs about the hinges of wedged and unshuttable doors. He learns the smell of lime in the fields, sees the spoor of hares on the snow, listens to the threshers, their voices ghostly among the dust and shadows in the barn, old hats on their feet to save them breaking the thatching straw.

He meets Tom Purely, the 'strawberry man' on account of a growth of pink skin from his neck. Tom takes the boy to see the pig and they find it in the orchard, a tall white pig with large ears, its breath smelling of apples and cabbage and sour milk from the dairy slops. He watches when it is slaughtered, the men flexing their hands and burning off the creature's bristle with torches of straw.

Jenny Scurl takes him for walks in the orchard. By the hedge at the back she kisses Bob Ketch or Dan Miller or Dick Shutter. Bob Ketch squeezes her bubs and she sighs as if it made her sad. In May she puts flowers in her hair and in the boy's hair too. His hair is lighter, touched with gold in summer. His eyes, which everyone hoped would turn brown like the other children's, stay blue. Mr Viney, stopping by one day, tells Joshua how it is not unheard of, one blue-eyed child among a brood, not unheard of.

As soon as he is old enough he is moved from his parent's room to the chamber next to it. The room is small. Two flock mattresses on either side of the window, and two wooden chests for their things. There is a small fireplace in the corner, and on the wall above the girl's bed is Sarah's picture of a cow, flat and red against a flat blue sky.

Waking in boyhood mornings, coming awake when the world outside is more night than day, this is how it is: the tap and scrape of a horseshoe, the hissed remarks of a ploughboy or horseman to Jenny as she comes from the dairy door to start the milking. Later he hears his parents. His father's boots shaking the house, his mother's whispering. Then the light of a candle inkling beneath the door, the door softly opening and the older children, Charles and Liza, swinging out their legs in rumpled nightshirts, pulling on clothes very fast, and without a word spoken following the candle downstairs.

Later, Liza comes back, her hands scented with cream and fire-smoke and the musky-shitty smell of the animals. She scrubs them – James and Sarah – with a cloth and water she has carried from the well, searching the small folds of their faces with half-tender, half-violent movements. The day is open then. A dozen familiar voices rise out of yards and fields, calling to dogs, herding cattle, greeting neighbours. Saws and hammers and axes begin their work; a flight of doves circles out from the cote at Coverton Hall, and the poor, a dozen widows and orphans and men too sick to work, crawl from beds of straw and trudge towards the overseer's house, or stand, bow-headed, outside a neighbour's door, waiting for a dole of warm milk, a harsh word, a bite of yesterday's bread.

6 In the reign of Queen Anne, Lady Denbeigh presented
to the village of Yeo a modest schoolhouse. The masters
are generally very young or very old, or in some manner
broken down. The present incumbent, Septimus Kite, lives in two
small rooms at the rear of the school. Here, between a small bed
and a small table, he sleeps and eats and doses himself with
laudanum. He has an assistant, a lame spinster out of the village,
Miss Lucket. The money she receives, and money from the sale
of her jams, keeps her, for the time being, off the parish.

All the Dyer children have attended, as and when they
could be spared from the farm. When James goes on his
first day, he walks with Liza, though Liza has long since
finished at the school. They walk the lane, under the hawthorn
hedges where in spring the children chew the tender green. The
schoolhouse, its bricks still raw beside the weathered greys of the
priory walls, stands at the side of the lane. Liza presents the boy
to Mr Kite. Kite stares down, grunts, says: 'This is the one who
does not speak?'

Liza says: 'Not yet, sir, though he understands very well.'

'Sit him there,' orders kite. 'I wish I had more like him.'

James sits on a bench by the window. Liza puts a blood-warm
baked potato into his pocket. She says: 'Do as they tell you, Jem.'
He does not turn to watch her go.

Miss Lucket, one leg three inches shorter than the other, her
walk a grotesque rolling, which the children, following her down
the lane to school, ape behind her back, is a kindly and dedicated
teacher. Young men and women, babes in their arms, will stop

shyly to talk to her, remind her of their names though she has not forgotten them.

From her, James learns to shape his letters, chalk on slate. He is, in his way, an apt and able student, yet there is something about him that renders Miss Lucket uneasy. It is her boast that, within a month of a child coming to her, she has him placed, can see how he will go on with the others, how he will turn out. With James she remains as ignorant of his true character six months after his starting as she was on the morning he arrived. He is not well liked, she knows that, but the children do not tease him. The older boys think twice before making any trouble with him. There is an independence, an arrogance, out of place in a boy of six and which she did not find in his brother or sisters who are moody, impetuous, ordinary children. She has heard the rumours, of course, the pall of gossip that has hung about Elizabeth Dyer since the child's birth.

She wonders if the boy is unhappy, and being herself a kind of expert in unhappiness she tries to draw him out with looks and little gestures of sympathy, none of which he appears to understand. His practical skills are excellent. He sews more neatly than the girls, stitches sized like midges. He draws well, which is to say he is a very neat copier of things; he never draws what is not in front of him. And stories bore him, a thing she has never known before. They seem to baffle him, such that when, during the afternoons that lie like vast blue or grey lakes over the moor, she reads from *Gulliver's Travels* or tells the tale of the Moonrakers or Tom Thumb, his is the one inattentive face; blank, almost moronic.

There is one boy at the school – Peter Poundsett – a year older than James, whom every child delights in tormenting. There is nothing obviously different about him. He is neither fat nor thin; his features are regular. He is strong enough for his age, can throw a ball or jump a ditch as well as any. His father is a carpenter, his mother a baker of excellent cakes, and their house is far from being the meanest in the village. But the children, as if they saw on him markings such as bees see on certain flowers, markings invisible to adult eyes, twist his name into nonsense, into childish obscenities. His lunch is stolen and flung in the river. His back pelted with dung. He is accused of fornicating with farm animals, of stealing marbles and pennies from other children, of uttering curses that make them sick. Those who hound him most mercilessly are the same as accuse him most virulently. It is the most notorious thieves who accuse him of stealing, the kickers of kicking them; and those who trap him and strip him of his breeches – a thing that occurs at least twice each winter – are the ones most likely to accuse him of precisely this offence against them. They wheedle at Miss Lucket's knee, or more daringly at Mr Kite's, in the hope of getting their victim thrashed. Often they succeed, and Peter Poundsett is stretched over a chair at the front of the class while Mr Kite works with the strap, the half-yard of seasoned leather that hangs from a nail beside Lady Denbeigh's portrait.

James takes no part in these games, though he watches them from a distance, a small questioning frown on his face; and this Miss Lucket takes as evidence of a gentler heart. So too does Peter Poundsett who, desperate for an ally, makes eyes at James and does for love what he has never done from greed or fear; stealing titbits of food, and pennies from the box beneath his parents' bed, gifts that James accepts or refuses strictly according to whether or not he wants the thing itself. Peter Poundsett trembles with hope. His tormentors draw back.

A month passes. The children watch. A second month, and still they hesitate. It is as if James has drawn a circle around the boy, and though the children press their toes against its edge, none of them dares step in.

Until at last they do. It is a Friday, morning break, a week before the school is closed for the hay harvest. Kitty Gate, the blacksmith's girl, broad and ten, flings a stone at Peter Poundsett's leg as he crouches beside James, playing marbles by the priory wall. James hears the noise, hears Peter's gasp, looks at him, looks at Kitty. Keeping her eyes on James, she reaches slowly down to clutch a second stone. James looks away. It is his turn to roll. Peter whispers: 'Jem?' Then louder: 'Jem!' There is no answer. Kitty understands, enough if not all. She lets out a whoop, then throws, hard and true, striking her victim in the face and tearing his lower lip which instantly blooms into a rose of blood, velvety petals tumbling and splashing on to his shirt.

Miss Lucket has witnessed the entire scene from the classroom window. Now she swings like a lame fury from the schoolhouse door, the strap trailing from her hand. She is afraid that they will scatter before she can reach them, but Kitty is transfixed by the sight of Peter Poundsett's face, and the first she knows of Miss Lucket's approach is the sear of the strap across her back, the shock of it knocking the girl off her feet. But Kitty is not Miss Lucket's true target. She hurries on, opening and shutting on the hinge of her good leg towards the wall where Peter Poundsett stands, and where his betrayer calmly watches her come. More than anything she wants to bring the strap down across his face, a thing she has never done nor even contemplated before. She draws up breathless before him, raises the strap, but as their eyes meet the rage goes out of her. Blue as the cornflower in the fields beyond them, his eyes contain no malice. It was not goodness she saw in him before; neither is this its reverse. They stare at each other for several seconds. Then she turns away from him, takes Peter Poundsett by the collar, and marches him into the schoolhouse, the boy, like something incompetently butchered, bleeding and howling beside her.

7   Harvest. The village prepares itself like an army on the eve of campaign. Joshua Dyer takes on what help he can afford; ninepence a day plus vitals for a man, a penny for boys and women. Most years, local cottagers supply his needs, once they have brought in their share of what remains of the common meadow. Now and then the road delivers strangers: soldiers, sailors even, deserting, lame, or paid off after Dettingham, Fontenoy, Culloden.

It is during the harvest of 1749 that Widow Dyer, carrying bread and cider out to the workers, suffers a paralytic seizure, and it is James, sent to find what has become of the refreshments, who discovers her, stretched out on the track like a mound of laundry. The sight is intriguing. He walks around her twice, observing her fat calves, her hair, tumbled out from beneath her linen cap, and the great congested moon of her face. A blue-bottle parades on her cheekbone.

He waits to see if she will do anything, if, for example, she will die. Her mouth is working, mouthing silent pleas. He drinks from one of the dropped flagons, spilling some of the liquor over his chin. Then he goes to find his mother.

It takes eight men, half winded and shuffling in their boots, to carry the widow back to the farmhouse. They set her on the trundle bed in the parlour then send for the parson, who sends for the curate, who comes sweating from the fields to read the prayer for the dying. The family stand around the bed awaiting the moment of her departure. Her breath is like a sack of coals dragged over a stone floor, but by the evening she lies more easily. Charlie is sent to Madderditch to bring Mr Viney.

Viney arrives, his grey mare glowing like milk in the dark. He examines the Widow, Joshua holding a candle beside his mother's face. Viney bleeds her, then says: 'Let her bide where she is. If she lives out the night, send for me again. Prayer is the best physic for her now.' He drinks a glass of cider with Joshua, then mounts his horse and rides up the darkness of the lane.

Joshua and Elizabeth sit up in the parlour. Elizabeth works with her needle. The house settles, groans; the widow wheezes and snores. Dawn reveals her living still. Charles is needed in the fields. James is sent to bring the apothecary.

It is an hour's easy walking to Madderditch. Viney's house, dressed in ivy, stands on the outskirts of the village. The front door is answered by Viney's aunt, a gossip of the Widow's who reads the note – penned by Liza – explaining the boy's errand and leads him inside. She sends a servant to fetch the apothecary then stands eyeing the child with some interest. So this is Elizabeth Dyer's bastard, her shame. They say the child is dumb. She does not like his looks at all. A bastard should be the humblest creature on God's earth. This one contemplates her as if she were the cook. She says: 'Do you not know what you are? Do you not know what your mother is? Shall I tell you, child? Shall I?'

Viney comes in; his face – shrewd, worried, kindly – is bright with heat. His aunt passes him the note and leaves the room. He reads it through a pair of folding spectacles, nods his head. He says: 'I think, then, we have some hope of saving her. Shall we make her well again, child, eh?'

He gestures to the boy to follow him. They come to a passageway, then to a door. The room inside is warm from the sun that cuts in through the half-open shutters. A spacious room but almost sunk beneath the clutter of the apothecary's trade. James sniffs the air. Here are scents unlike anything he has experienced before. Bitter and metallic, but also sweet, as if the apothecary had mixed together flowers and anvils, gunpowder and rotten eggs, to create a unique, stinking perfume.

In the centre of the room is the work-bench, crowded with mortars, gallipots, smoke-blackened knives. There is a rolling-board for making pills, a small pile of crabs' claws, a human skull, and several books with crinkled yellow pages, as if they had once been under water. From the ceiling hang bundles of dried plants.

Says Viney: 'Now, child, we shall find something to make the Widow mend. An infusion of borage perhaps.' He reaches up and takes a fist of blue, star-shaped flowers. 'And something to purge her. When evil is at work in a body we must expel it.' He takes senna leaves and ginger. 'My art – do not touch that! – is to mediate between man and nature. This art was given to our forefathers by God – Ay, pass me the pot – thus all healing is divine – set it upon the stove – It is the arrogance of modern doctors that is their undoing. We can neither heal – that is the lung of a fox – nor be healed without humility. There now, the water will draw the goodness from the plants. You are an able assistant, James. I shall mention as much to your father.'

When they ride back to Blind Yeo, James sits in front of the apothecary, his fingers tangled in the mare's coarse mane. The country people say: 'Gad speed 'ee, Mr Viney', 'Good morrow to 'ee, sir!', 'Be that the Dyer boy ridin' up so mighty wiv 'ee?'

The to-ing and fro-ing to Madderditch for medicine is James's particular duty. He spends longer and longer in the apothecary's den, watching and then helping in the preparation of mixtures and ointments and gargles. He learns to roll pills, to make an emulsion from the yolk of eggs, to prepare oils from lavender and cloves and ginger. Viney himself is more engrossed with his metals, his crucible and furnace, his pyramids of numbers. More than once they are forced to flee from clouds of noxious smoke, running out into the garden to gulp lungfuls of air while the aunt shakes her fan at them in exasperation.

But the Widow rallies, though now she is as mute as the boy, her voice lost for ever above the summer fields. At Christmas she leaves her bed, her back pocked with sores, her face sunk on to the bones of her skull. There are no more visits to Madderditch. More than ever the boy keeps his own company, comes and softly goes. His silence, his dumb indifference, is taken for revolt, for insolence. Joshua beats him, flies out in real anger. Even Elizabeth treats him coldly, enraged that he should draw such attention to himself, and thus to her and to history. She watches him one morning, climbing up the side of the hill-fort like some grim diminutive tribesman, and thinks: Would that he does not stop. Would that he goes on, climbing and climbing. Would that this were farewell.

Yet it cuts her heart to think it.

8 It is the summer of 1750. The year of the London earthquakes. The hottest summer of the boy's life, hotter even than '48, when the locusts came. He is lying on his belly on the side of the hill, watching the wedding preparations in the orchard below. Small figures, just recognisable, are fetching and carrying from the house. He does not hear the stranger approach over the muffling grass until a hand catches him about the scruff of his neck and hoists him to his feet.

The stranger eyes him; eases his grip, says: 'Now here's a pretty bird for the bag. Hiding, child, or spying? Are you a native of this place?'

James wriggles free, rubs his neck, nods.

'Then, Robin Goodfellow, you are hired. Which is the Dyer farm?'

James points down the hill. The stranger squints, fans himself with his hat, spits at a bee. For a time he seems to consider it, the wisdom of descending. At length he says: 'Lead on, boy,' and they go, crabwise, towards a knot of sheep in the shade of an elm tree by the gate that leads to the road. As they walk, James steals glances at the man: the holy blue of his eyes, the pock-marked skin, the goat-hair wig dusting the shoulders of his coat with its powder. The stranger wears ribbons on his coat, yet it is difficult to imagine him as an acquaintance of Joshua's, still less of Jenny Scurl or Bob Ketch. Certainly he is no farmer; nor does he seem a pedlar, for he has no pedlar's pack. Nor a gentleman. More than anything he reminds James of the actors who played at Moody's farm two summers past and who he watched through a knot-hole as they changed and danced and bellowed to each other among the rat-gloom of Moody's barn.

Coming to the road, the stranger begins to talk more loudly, as if he distrusted his surroundings, yet did not wish to appear on his guard.

'. . . A wedding, boy, why, 'tis one of the finest things imaginable, most prodigiously, of course, when one is not related to any of the parties involved. You have attended one before? Your parents' perhaps?'

James shakes his head.

'A funeral, however, is to be preferred. A fellow with a respectable suit of clothes may live comfortably on little else but the vanity of the dead for years together. I attended one one time at Bath. The burial of a notorious gambler who . . .'

The stranger stops in the road by the lane to the farm. He leans down. Peers at the boy.

'You do not appear, child, to be made of mud and straw like

the other inhabitants of this place. Indeed you put me in mind of someone. You have never been in Newgate? The Fleet? Bridewell? No . . . well, 'tis only my humour. Tell me, do you have money in your pocket? A penny perhaps?'

James shakes his head. The stranger shrugs.

'Then nothing is something, for we have it in common. You are schooled here?'

A nod.

'You can read?'

A nod

'God's teeth, child, I could have a better conversation with my hat. Do you never speak? . . . Ah, the creature shakes its head. And is the creature happy to be dumb? . . . It does not know. And where does the creature live? . . . Behold! It points . . . Here? Here! Is Dyer your father?'

Before James can move his head to answer, the stranger takes the boy's face between his hands, studies it like a portrait. His hands smell of tobacco juice. He laughs, more like a bark than laughter, then whispers, 'I'll be . . . I'll be . . .'

From along the road comes a burst of voices. It is the wedding cart, freshly daubed with yellow paint, turning out of Church Lane with Jenny Scurl and Bob Ketch and a half-dozen of the wedding party on board, singing and shouting and passing the bottle.

The stranger looks a moment longer at the boy, then hurries off towards the orchard, the sole of one of his shoes flapping as he goes.

James runs into the house. The women are sweating in the kitchen. He goes upstairs unnoticed. Sarah, Liza and Charles have long since changed. Their common clothes lie sprawled upon the beds. Now that they are older the room is divided by a curtain. James fingers the wool of his sisters' dresses, and the wooden combs where strands of Sarah's red-gold hair catch the light. She is the beautiful one. Half the village are enamoured of her, her name carved into the bark of a dozen trees, and though Joshua talks loudly of his blunderbuss, its cargo of rusty nails, they still come, men and boys, misty with lust.

Liza also has admirers, but treats them so fiercely most go off in search of easier conquests and softer hearts. In truth, her affections are already spoken for, split like a divining-rod between her father and her youngest brother.

James undresses, pulls on a pair of leather breeches and a linen shirt. He studies himself in the mirror. He is tall for his age, fineboned, his skin slightly burnished by the sun. Such an enigmatic look; such a silent, knowing face. There are moments when he thinks the face will speak to him and tell him secrets, remarkable secrets. He looks until he is dizzy.

On the stairs he hears the patter and stamp of wooden soles, then Jenny Scurl and his mother, laughing and chiding each other. He goes on to the narrow landing. Jenny Scurl's face is round and pale as a sliced apple. She has already drunk a good deal, and the sight of the boy seems to mulch something in her heart. She bends down and kisses him fatly on the cheek. Elizabeth says: 'Go out now, Jem.'

In the orchard, the noises of the wedding party are already unnaturally loud. The guests sit at a long, white-clothed table, feeding themselves upon Joshua Dyer's food and drink. Joshua, squeezed in the coat he wore at his own wedding, sits beside the Widow Scurl, a threadlike, nervous woman in a large, unsuccessful hat, the brim of which strikes the parson's nose each time she turns to talk with him. The parson barely notices. He is sweating and telling a story no one can be bothered to listen to. An empty bottle of port glints in the grass behind him. Next to the parson sits Widow Dyer, a dense and disapproving cloud. Beside her is Bob Ketch, and his sister Amelda, the girl looking at something the stranger is showing her in the palm of his hand, and nodding her hot, pretty head as he talks. Beneath the table is a dog, black, thick-necked, scavenging from foot to foot.

The harvest looks like being fair again. Joshua, revelling in his part as stand-in for Jenny's sea-deceased father, has seen to it that the table is well spread with dishes. Seeing James, he calls him over and in an awkward movement drags him on to his lap. The bride totters to her seat, a large grin adrift in her face. Widow Scurl flashes her gums, tears a piece of white meat from the chicken and pushes it between the boy's lips. He keeps it there, on his tongue, until Joshua picks up the knife to carve. Then he slides from the farmer's lap, sidles beyond the nearest trees and spits the meat into the grass.

He weaves between the avenues of fruit trees, comes by and by to an old cherry tree, the tallest tree in the orchard, and taking off his coat he circles the trunk until he finds a knot in the bark to serve as a foothold. He climbs, smudging his shirt-front with lichen as he stretches up for the lowest branch, then swinging his legs, rotating his body until he is topside of the branch like a drowsy cat. He sits up, finds another branch within easy reach and sees how he may go from one to another as if ascending a spiral staircase. Birds, thieving the cherries, go off like small explosions as he climbs towards them. Now and then he pauses in the hot shade to eat the fruit, letting the stones fall from his mouth to bounce off the branches below. Watching them fall, he sees a black shape moving at the base of the tree. The animal catches sight of him in the same moment, raises its snout and gazes up at him longingly. James resumes his climb, more carefully now as he feels the branches bow beneath him. The foliage thins, and then, among a tangle of delicate wood, as though he has hatched from a jade egg, his head is in the sky and he is breathing the tangy breeze and narrowing his eyes against the sun.

He eases himself round, takes his bearings. The hill-fort,

Moody's farm, the church tower, the moor. Round and round until he comes to the white flash of the table where most of the guests are still eating, though a small group has gathered about Amelda Ketch, who has her neckerchief unpinned and is being fanned by Elizabeth. Joshua and the parson knock their mugs together, shout Tory toasts. Sarah and Charles are teasing the dog, running in and out of the trees with the dog loping determinedly after them. A voice calls for dancing, and the old man, the same who played by the river in the great freeze, crooked as a root, pulls a long quavering note from his fiddle. The groom, the bride raucous in his arms, leads out the dancers. Soon, the others join; circling, ducking, hopping, spinning. Even the Widow Scurl, who moves over the grass like a small, mysteriously propelled sofa.

The music ends and the dancers, breathless, are applauding themselves and preparing for the next dance, when Liza, shading her eyes, points and calls to Elizabeth who calls to Joshua who, after struggling to see, sees and shouts out: 'Down from there, James. Where's your sense, boy!'

James, figuring himself to be immensely high, immensely distant, finds it hard to believe they are pointing at him, waving too, sharp downward movements of their hands as though droving the air. He steps higher, to the V of two fragile branches. Their waving is more insistent. Joshua shouts like a distant cannon. James leans from the tree. The shouting stops. Even their hands freeze in front of them. He feels as if, stepping out, he will have no difficulty in flying. He stretches out his arms, gazes into the far ends of the afternoon. His weight passes a line, fine as a human hair, and then he is flying, amazingly fast into the green sky, and then nothing, nothing but the memory of flight, faint and fading, and the iron taste of blood in his mouth.

9 'How be 'ee, Jem?'

The entire party has crowded into the little room by the hall where Widow Dyer lay through her sickness. The room still smells of her and the medicines James carried over from Madderditch. Amos Gate, big as a cloud, leans over the injured boy, frowns at his leg. The foot hangs slack like a loose stocking; one could pull it off with bare hands. Amos turns, addresses the company: 'All you bodies wi'out business here best shog. Baint a dog fight.'

They go, glancing back, the faintly shocked expressions of people who have sobered too quickly.

Joshua, Elizabeth, Amos and the stranger remain. 'Marley Gummer,' says the stranger, 'at your service, ma'am. I have some experience of chirurgical procedures.'

Amos puts a hand on Joshua's shoulder. 'You take off now wi' yer lady. I'll work fasser and cleaner wi' just Mr Gumly here.'

'Gummer, sir. Marley Gummer.'

Joshua looks to his wife. She is sitting on the edge of the bed. She gazes for several seconds into the boy's face, then kisses his brow. 'Why, he's brave,' she says. 'See how brave he is?'

With Joshua and Elizabeth gone, the two men strip off their coats, Amos to his last good shirt, Gummer to a fine though faded waistcoat, in sea colours. Across the bed they hold a hurried consultation. Several times the blacksmith urges the boy to rest easy. Gummer observes that he does, remarkably so.

Amos, with blunt fingers, examines the break. He has set

perhaps twenty bones in his time. He has never seen a break so complete as this. The longer he delays, the less hope there is of saving it. It may already be too late.

'Daft business climbing trees, eh, Jem?'

'Surely', says Gummer, 'the folly is in falling rather than climbing.'

'Then as don't climb . . . Damn, but I'd feel easier if 'e'd squeal a bit. Baint natural jus' lying there.'

'He never speaks?'

'Never.'

'And yet he seems to understand. James Dyer, are you sensible of having broken your leg?'

James glances down, looks at his leg, then at Gummer. He nods. Gummer holds the boy's gaze then looks over at the blacksmith. Gate says: 'We'd best be doing it.'

Gummer holds up a hand. 'A minute more, sir. I begin to be intrigued. James, do you feel something here? A kind of fire?' Gummer sharply taps the swollen foot. The boy's expression is thoughtful, as though he were listening for a stone to sound in the bottom of a well. He shakes his head.

The men exchange stares. Gummer jumps up from the bed, searches rapidly around the room and takes from the table next to the window a candle and tinder box. He lights the candle and brings it to the bedside.

'Close your eyes, boy, and give me your hand.' There is something avuncular in his tone which for the first time makes the child wary. After a moment's hesitation James closes his eyes. He feels Gummer take his hand, a firm grip; then a sensation as if Gummer were brushing the tips of his fingers with a feather. He smells something, burnt meat. The blacksmith says: 'Thars enough now, Gumly.'

When James opens his eyes there is a red, smoky weal across the fingertips. Gummer blows out the candle.

'Most suggestive, Mr Gate, is it not?'

Amos rasps his fingers in the stubble at his neck. 'You think as the fall has smashed his senses?'

'The odd thing here, sir, is not so much that he feels no pain, *as that he does not expect to*. What do you make of that, sir?'

''Tis past believing.'

'Not quite, please God, not quite. What is truly past believing is worthless, and I doubt not but this could sell better than the rabbit woman of Godalming – dealt with correctly, of course. There would have to be the right man in charge . . .'

'Charge of what?'

'My dear Mr Gate, come now, you appear perplexed. Do you not see it? If my surmise is correct we have with us here an oddity of the most subtle kind. Eh, boy? An aberration of nature. A true *rara avis*. A . . .' – lowering his voice – '. . . a commodity.' He laughs, throws his head back with a curious jerking movement. 'My, but today has had its surprises. Life, Mr Gate. Do you not find it voluptuous?'

The blacksmith's face is solemn; it is the face he assumes when straightening horseshoes. 'Josh Dyer's son is not for sale, nor ever shall be. I can tell 'ee that much, mister. And we have a bone to set. So let's to it. Hold him fast now.'

Standing by the end of the bed, Amos takes hold of the boy's foot. Gummer shrugs, pulls off his wig to reveal a head of unevenly cropped hair. 'As you wish, Mr Gate. Though I hardly think we need trouble to restrain him.'

He binds the child in his arms. 'Haul away! Ha!'

For two weeks James lies on the trundle bed watching the light ebb and flow on the whitewashed walls. Bees, flies, butterflies nose in through the open window. His leg is splinted with two boards left over from the building of the cow-stall. At some point the chickens have excreted on the boards as they excrete on everything. James picks at the hard black-and-white matter, flicking it at targets on the opposite wall. For three days there is fever, then the fever abates. The fall, in memory, in dreams, in waking fantasy, is the axis round which he slowly spins. Twice, on evenings when he is left alone with the candle, he repeats Marley Gummer's experiment. He does it once when Liza is there. She snatches his hand away, horrified. Thus he gathers the evidence.

His leg mends with a speed amazing to all, all but himself. Viney calls, stays half an hour examining the boy, says he has never seen the like. Miss Lucket comes with a basket of strawberries from her garden. Elizabeth brings him his food, watches him eat, studies him as if she seeks to catch him out. One morning the Widow lumbers in, dips her finger into the water of his chamber pot, sniffs it, scowls at him. Gummer does not come. He wishes Gummer would come.

Liza is his most frequent visitor. She brings paragraphs she has copied from the local papers. She reads them to James, sitting on the end of the bed and doing her best to bring out the gossipy or sensational tone, to breathe life into the comings and goings of ships and lords. Rinderpest has broken out again; a Quaker has been robbed at gunpoint on St Phillips Green; an old woman who left a candle by the curtains has been burnt to death. Their Graces the Duke and Duchess of St Albans are arrived at the Hot Well in Bristol. The death of the Irishman John Falls is announced, his life remarkable for his having once drunk two quarts of whiskey at a sitting and afterwards being able to walk home.

She can feel him listening, peeping at the outer world through these chinks of information. When she has no more to read to him she chatters, telling him who she has seen during the day, who said what to whom. She asks him questions and answers them herself. It is a mode developed over the years; it is how one talks to James. She finds it restful, and all the family have long since ceased to expect him to talk. So when, one evening – she is sat at the end of the bed massaging his leg – he answers her, she looks round at the door to see who has come in. He has only said 'Yes' or 'no', neither can afterwards recall his first word, but it is enough. His silence, like an immense pane of glass, is shattered. Inside of a minute everyone is gathered about the bed. Liza says: 'Ask him a question!'

No one can think of what to ask.

Elizabeth says: 'How is your leg today, son?'

For a long stretch he does not answer. Then he says: 'I wish to sleep now.'

Joshua takes off his hat, shakes his head in wonder. It is like the lifting of a curse. He smiles broadly at his wife. 'Whatever next?' he says. 'Whatever next, eh?'

A breeze curls into the room. Liza goes to the window, sniffs the air. 'Like rain,' she says, tears in her voice. She pulls the casement closed, draws the curtain.

10   On an evening four days after the wedding, Amelda Ketch discovers a rash of red pimples on her forehead which, by the following morning, covers most of her body. Mr Viney is called, makes a cautious diagnosis of measles. Six hours later he is called back, Silas Ketch banging frantically on the front door. When he examines the girl a second time and sees how the pimples have formed into thickly grouped clusters, he warns them to prepare for the worst. On his way home he stops at a high place on the road and looks over the quiet country where death is stealing across the fields. He prays in the saddle, rides home, and knowing he will be at

one bedside or another for weeks to come, goes straight to bed and sleeps.

The following day he sees the papules are already changing into watery sacks that will shortly distort her face to the point where it is no longer recognisably her own. He does what he can to comfort her, both for the physical pain and the mortal terror that has gripped her, but there is little he can do and he knows she has sensed as much. He orders the family to keep the fire banked, and to give her what water she wants together with a little wine to fortify her. More importantly, she is to be attended only by those servants and family who have themselves already suffered the smallpox. No children are to visit her. Any mirrors should be removed from her room. Yes, he has seen worse cases come through. There can be no excuse for losing hope.

That evening the pustules form; by midnight she is delirious, and to the petrified relief of those who watch over her, the girl dies two days later, an hour before sunrise.

Viney is not there when she dies. He already has five new cases, three of them children. They are the kindling; he can only guess how the fire will rage, how it will spread. He rides from one stricken home to another, eating his meals on horseback or standing in the kitchen while some sobbing woman cuts a slice from the spit. Were he a heartless man it might have amused him, how his powerlessness spurs them on to greater faith in him, as though his very shape atop the grey mare were enough to ward off disaster. He is lonelier than he has ever been in his life.

The first death. The news is everywhere within hours. Elizabeth hears it from Dan Miller's wife, Ruth, who has heard it from Biddy Bidewell who has heard it from another. The Dyer children are sat about the table in the kitchen, all but James, still laid up in the little parlour. She does not say anything to them but her face betrays her. Liza gives her a worried, questioning look. 'Who was that at the door, Mother?'

'Just Ruth Miller with a pot o' gossip.' She knows they will find out soon enough. Of the family, only Joshua and the Widow have been with the smallpox.

Elizabeth takes a basket into the dairy, fills it with cheese and butter and cream to go over to the Ketch family the next morning, then goes upstairs to her room. When Joshua comes, the two of them sit on the edge of the old casement bed, hand in hand, wordless and pale, hardly a sound in the world beyond the rise and fall of their own breath.

Hearing of Amelda's death, Sarah and Liza cry for an hour; then there are chores in the dairy, the hens to feed, a shirt to be darned. They do not feel especially threatened; they are full of strength and youth, and though they have seen the marks of smallpox on the faces of their elders, they have never seen the sickness at work. Life goes on. A half-dozen cases are reported in Coverton. One of Lady Denbeigh's kitchen servants is said to be in the balance. Elizabeth holds to what comfort she can and tells herself that the disease is not spreading as fast as they had feared, that there has not been much dying. Perhaps the disease is of a mild type and it was Amelda's constitution more than the sickness which carried her off. Then too, no near neighbours have been affected. The worst of it seems to be Kenn way and towards the sea. For a day, two days, she relaxes her vigilance. Then, as if the sickness had been waiting for a moment's inattention, it comes.

Sarah complains of a persistent headache. Her limbs ache. She feels feverish. When the marks come Elizabeth resigns herself to saving what she can. Sarah is followed by Liza. Then Charles. She nurses them without tears or sighs. She sets her face against the power of the disease, attempts to resist the onslaught through the unremitting exercise of her love. James remains free from infection. She keeps him away both from herself and from the other children. The house divides into camps. Elizabeth, Sarah,

Liza and Charles. Joshua, the Widow and James. From one camp come strange, pathetic cries, the air of fever. From the other, a tense and impotent silence.

Elizabeth carries her bedding into the children's room and lives there with them, spooning honey-water, changing sweat-soaked clothes, mumbling prayers as she goes from one to the other. She feels oddly calm, as she did that night on the frozen river, but now the ice is thin and cracking and the voices of her children, seeping through the swollen membranes of their mouths, are the sound of the dark, cold-flowing river beneath.

Joshua, on the understanding that he will not afterwards go to James, visits the sick-room, hanging above his children like an ineffectual planet, touching them with a despairing tenderness. Sarah, whose beauty has given him such great and quiet pride, affects him the most cruelly. The disease has turned her face into a mask of livid blisters, so that when she dies he is almost glad, though in the hour of her death he feels himself wrapped in a cloak of madness. Viney comes and helps lay the girl out and wrap her in her shroud. He sees in Elizabeth her will, hard and tempered. He knows that she will last at least as long as the storm. Joshua he persuades to keep to his work, tells him of other families, also grieving. Joshua hardly hears him.

On his way out, Viney speaks to his old assistant through the door of the parlour. 'Your sister Sarah is with God, Jem, but your mother is a fine nurse. I have great hope of the others being well again.'

The boy's voice comes muffled through the wood: 'Shall I die too?' The question is cool, undistressed.

'We must all die one day, Jem.'

'But shall I die now? Like Sarah?'

'I think not, child.'

'Nor I,' says the voice.

A tumbril, the wheels muffled with sacking, comes next morning. Joshua goes with them to see his daughter into the ground. Elizabeth remains with Liza and Charlie. Delirious, their voices loop and shudder in the air. Charlie dies the day after his sister is buried. The last thing he does is to reach up, as if to pick an apple. Liza lies, one hand with her mother, one hand with death. In the hall the clock has not been wound. The hands stand at half past three. There is no fire in the kitchen. Even the cats have gone.

James becomes a reader of sounds, recognising the muttered voices of Pegg the undertaker, and Viney and the parson. Sometimes there is a neighbour, kindness overcoming caution. Often he hears Joshua, the wheezing in his chest, the sudden, thunderous oaths. Widow Dyer brings James his food, a bare cold diet, yet he eats it with great appetite, licks the plate clean.

He waits for Liza to come down like the others but the pustules on her face dry and scab over. Elizabeth holds down the girl's hands to stop her tearing at the scabs. On the morning of the twelfth day Liza sits up in bed and calls in a weary voice for her mother. Elizabeth, folding and refolding Sarah's clothes, sees the girl's blind gaze, the glutinous eyes, and goes to her, embraces her, presses the last of her strength into the girl's ribs. One has been saved, an immeasurable victory, and she notices, with something like indifference, the red marks that have risen on her own hands.

 Kitty Gate is the last to catch it; a boy called Slight is the last to die. The villagers bury their dead and the burial yard is raw with turned earth. The stonecutter has a new apprentice. Some find solace in the church, some in the bottle. Viney stables his horse, sleeps in the day and sits up at night, drinking brandy and muttering to those who ran past him into eternity; ran past him like children in a game, fleet of foot, easily ducking his clumsy hands.

There are many, mainly young, whose faces show the marks of the sickness. Passing each other in the village, they nod warily and look about themselves as though in search of their former lives. But the old rhythms re-emerge. The first laughter, the first forgetful children spinning their tops on a flagstone; the first lovers walking the paths their mothers and grandmothers walked. The fruit is ripe and must be harvested. This season there are fewer arms, fewer quick hands. The shortage leaves the others numbed, too tired to think, too weary to grieve. Apples are 7s 6d a bushel; winter will not wait on their grief. Thus time, the sheer weight of days, turns them like water on a mill-wheel paddle.

Farmer Dyer, his blind daughter and lame son, are pitied. In the aristocracy of suffering, Farmer Dyer is a lord. Not a great lord, but grand enough to be avoided, to be spoken of in a solemn voice. He appears to be losing his wits, growing wild. Goodwife Kelly, meeting Goodwife Coles on the Madderditch road, remarks that Dyer will be on the parish before Easter. The other replies with a shake of her head. Josh Dyer will be cold in the ground before then and it's a poor look-out for the children and the old mother. Who would take them in now, even as servants? A word hangs between their heads unspoken. Workhouse.

The yard, once the bright unblinking eye of the farm, becomes cluttered, overgrown, useless. The pig is sold, as are the sheep, and the grass grows high in the orchard. Christian Vogue, estate manager for the Denbeighs, rides down, speaks to Joshua from the saddle. When Liza asks what Vogue wanted Joshua will not answer, stares at her, too ashamed to speak. James he has ceased to notice.

When drunk, the farmer calls for Liza to sing to him; lullabies. On nights when he finds no consolation in her voice he staggers into the yard to rant at the sky until exhaustion drives him in again.

In the New Year Joshua comes into the parlour where James has slept ever since his fall. He wakes the boy, shaking him and pulling him from the bed. He says: 'I've seen her! In the barn! She be an angel now, Charlie.'

Liza, a cloak around her shoulders, is standing by the back door. She reaches for her brother's arm. The three of them cross the frosted yard, a lantern swinging from Joshua's hand. They enter the barn. Tools and aromatic sacking hang from the walls; grain-seed crunches under their feet. Joshua holds up the lantern.

'There!'

Liza says: 'What is it, Jem?' She tugs at his arm.

James peers forward to where the light laps faintly against the blackness at the far end of the barn. Something is moving there, white and faintly luminous. It is several seconds before he can distinguish it, the soft S of the neck, the slender head where the eye is set like a diamond.

James says: ''Tis a swan.'

'A swan? Father, Jem says 'tis a swan.'

'Glory be,' says the farmer. 'She has come back.'

The bird stays several nights and then, disturbed by Joshua's frequent visits, it leaves as suddenly as it came. Joshua does not appear troubled by its going. The change in him, the extraordinary reverse of his decline occasioned by the bird's arrival, continues. He does not drink, he shaves his face and wears his church-going clothes. Much of his time he is alone in his room, in prayer or meditation. The farm he has no interest in. His thoughts are on higher things, and when Liza gently chides him, he smiles at her and strokes her face saying: 'Soon, wench. Soon enough.'

James knows that soon means never. He is curious, a little impatient, to see how things will end. He suspects that Joshua will one day disappear, leaving without warning, without any indication of where he has gone.

It is the spring thaw when the day finally arrives. There are violets growing on the banks at the side of the road and the first brimstone butterflies are flying over the hedgerows. Joshua has not been seen since the previous evening. As darkness comes, Liza, hoarse from calling, sends James to fetch Tom Purely. Tom comes back with James. The Widow is already red-eyed, silently keening. Tom takes a lantern and sets off to go around the farm. James goes with him but Tom is less friendly than in the old days. He is not alone in thinking the boy is somehow at the root of the family's disasters.

They do not have a long search. Joshua is in the barn, at the back where there are still feathers from the swan. At first they do not see him, but the light catches the nail-heads in his boots. He is lying face down in his dark suit, his knife gripped tight in his right hand. There is blood, a black pool that frames his head. Tom inches closer; the light trembles in his hand. He reaches down, takes a hold of Joshua's shoulder and slowly turns him until he lies upon his back. Above the slashed throat the mouth seems to smile still and the open eyes gaze upward as if, in his last agony, Joshua Dyer had seen something wonderful moving in the air above him. Tom runs out of the barn, hollering. James stays in the dark a moment, nudges the corpse with his foot as if to be sure the farmer is gone, then turns, feels his way into the yard, pauses, looks one last time at the star-illumined litter of the place, then fetches from his room dead Charlie's winter coat.

Dawn finds him walking steadily on the Bristol road, a parcel tucked beneath his arm. In Blind Yeo, in a dead house, a girl cries and cries his name. No one comes.

FOURTH

1 'Pain, friends, is from the devil. It is his touch, his caress. His venemous embrace! Who here has not heard a man in agony cry out and curse his God . . . Or a woman in childbed, blast the unborn infant's ears with groans and shrieks . . . The loving parent is transformed into an ogre. The child by pain is parted from his prayers, the good man from his goodness. It is a hell on earth! It casts us into the flame while yet we live . . . And doctors! We know how much they may do! We know how their ministrations can double our suffering . . . And then they rob us when we are too weak, too much out of our wits to boot them down the steps of our house. Death is sweet release. Think now, I ask you, think now of your greatest suffering, of a day, a night, when some raging pain in your tooth or bowels, in your skull, in your leg . . . a burn from the fire, a fall from your horse, or one of the thousand noxious diseases that rend us from within. Remember, how each and every one of you, in your torment, would have exchanged your skin with the most wretched in the kingdom, just but you might have a minute, nay, a half-minute's relief.

'Yea, I tell you this: it shall come to you again, and worse than you have known before, worse tenfold. You are the candle; your suffering is the flame. It feeds on you! What would a man not then give to have at hand some inexpensive remedy he might himself administer? Think of that, friends. Think what you would not give for such a boon . . .' Gummer pauses to let the words do their work. He is in good voice today and there is a good crowd to hear him, as many perhaps as fifty, crammed into the stale, grassy, boozy air. There is the sound of money, very faint, but quite audible to Gummer.

James, who has heard the speech a score of times, twists about to take a better view of the people he will shortly be performing for. Farmers in hot broadcloth steaming like cattle; apprentices in fustian, hungry for any diversion, something to hoard in memory and nibble at through the tedium of the week. Market women in linen caps and gowns, some with their chapped hands clutched by local beaux in leather waistcoats. At least two faces he recognises from other fairs; professional showmen. One walks a high-wire, the other sells charms to protect against gunshot wounds, or the clap, or toothache. They will recognise him, of course, but there will be no trouble. An unofficial guild exists between the showmen. A good new act is more an asset than a threat. More punters, more excitement. Purse strings loosen.

The woman beside James delivers a surreptitious dig to his ribs. It means: 'Keep still. Draw no attention to yourself.' The woman's name is Grace Boylan, former prostitute, though still available to those who favour a larger, motherly sort of whore. Gummer says she has a good face, that is, a face that betrays almost nothing of her character. Nor does she play her part too strongly like the strumpet they used in Devizes who waved her arms and wailed like a village Thisbe. The crowd laughed at her and things went dangerously wrong. Grace behaves herself; she is credible. Best of all, she is oddly unmemorable.

Gummer draws a handkerchief from his sleeve and wipes his brow. He is dressed in a good black coat, part parson, part physician. The sweat is real enough; so too are the heat and the breath and the gawping hundred-eyed creature gazing up at him.

The deceit is very physical; the hard but stylish end of the market. It is something to be proud of, and Gummer is proud. His sole ambition, from his brathood in some unspeakable neighbourhood of an English city, has been to become Marley Gummer; and by virtue of his unstinting effort, his unerring eye for another's weakness, he has achieved it. Mentally, he walks through fields of cloth of gold. Only now and then, liverish on dark, inclement days, does he look over his shoulder at the young wolves coming up behind him; looks and shudders.

'Friends! I am a Christian gentleman. As such I come among you today. I do not seek personal profit' – he waits for the jeers; a half-dozen come; he closes his eyes in the manner of one long used to such injustice – 'I do not seek personal profit more than that which will enable me to continue my crusade. For if pain comes from the devil, then to fight pain is to fight with angels!'

Behind Gummer is a box, iron-bound. He opens it and lifts out a bottle of dark brown fluid. For the rest of his pitch he holds the bottle over his heart with both hands.

'I was, in my youth, betrothed to a girl of infinite sweetness. A girl of such loveliness and virtue . . .'

A voice calls: 'One or other. Never the twain t'gether!'

'. . . of such Christian virtue I shall never look upon her like again. Not in this world. She was my bride but one brief year, then took sick of a complaint that baffled the most eminent minds. The sight of her suffering' – he gulps; there are moans of sympathy from some of the women – 'brought me to the very precipice of madness. I prayed that I might take her place, that I might die and she live. 'Twas not to be.' His eyes fill; a plump tear winds down his cheek. For a moment he seems incapable of continuing. He groans.

'Why, I asked, was I spared? For what? There was no happiness in the world without my bride. And then it came to me in a dream, that I, Marley Gummer, had been chosen as the instrument through which the burden of man's suffering might be eased.

Heavy task! I searched for years among the wisdom of the ancient world. I devoured libraries. I studied Galen. I corresponded with the great Boerhaave. All to no avail. I was, I confess it, on the point of abandoning my search when, in the great library of Alexandria, a scholar of that place, a man of antique manner, brought to me a volume crusted with the dust of centuries and said . . .'

'With what tongue did he converse?'

The heckler possesses an alarmingly cultured voice. Gummer's face betrays a flicker of discomfort, an instant's loss of poise. He cannot see who called out. He lobs his reply in the general direction.

'He spoke, sir, with his own tongue, and I with mine. We had but one apiece. "This," intoned the relic, "is what ye seekest." I opened the tome and began to read, ay, and was reading still when the cock crowed and the sun climbed into the sky. This book, friends, was writ by the very doctor who cured the archer Philoctetes of the serpent's bite . . .'

'Does it cure warts?'

'How much is it?'

'Patience, patience . . . In those pages I discovered the recipe which, with some alterations to render it palatable to a Christian people, I present to you this afternoon.' Gummer holds the bottle aloft like a communion chalice. 'Yet I would not have you take my word on it. Indeed, I forbid you to purchase even one bottle until its efficacy is proved beyond doubt.'

'How you gonna do that, then?'

Grace leans again into James's ribs. This time it means: Get ready.

'I intend, before your very eyes, here upon this dais' – a dozen tea chests covered by a sheet of muddy canvas – 'to demonstrate in the clearest manner imaginable the miraculous force of this draught. I carry no testimonies, though I could pave the road from here to Scotland with them if I chose. I prefer the witness of your own eyes. Thomas, after all, was no less a saint for wishing to place his fingers into our Saviour's wounds.'

'You blaspheme, sir!' Again, that voice.

Gummer says: "Tis in the gospels, friend, should you care to read them.' He sets the bottle on a small table on which there is also a candle stub, and something that catches the light: an implement.

'In pursuit of *verus*' – his voice booms – 'it will of course be necessary to inflict pain before I may relieve it. The suffering will not be lengthy but the sharper the fangs the sweeter the relief which follows. Who among you will come up? Who will sacrifice a little blood for his fellow men. The risk, I assure you, is very nearly negligible.'

He takes up the implement. It is a steel pin turned to a very obvious sharpness. 'Come now, somebody . . .' He hits upon the least likely among the crowd, gathers their refusals, their hurried 'Not I, by God'. His eyes settle on James, then on Grace.

'Madam, are you the mother of that fine boy?'

'Ay, sir. His sole parent since his father died in the French wars.' Murmurs of approval and interest.

Says Gummer: 'Gave his life for his country. Noble. And might the boy, madam, give a drop of his father's martial blood for something greater than nations? I mean, madam, for the Truth!'

'My Billy! Never! Why, 'is skin's like silk. He has but to graze his knee and he turns white as eggmeat.'

'A sensitive child?'

'Oh, very, sir, begging your pardon.'

'Then do you not see how he is precisely the subject I require? Madam, if you will but let me have him' – some cries of 'Let 'im!' – 'it shall, I promise you, be your proudest boast that your Billy brought the light of understanding, the beacon of hope, the balm of ease to these' – a grand sweep of his arm – 'goodly folk.

Come, madam, the suffering will be but a moment. A blink of the eye. For his father's memory.'

James says: 'Let me go, Mother. Let me be brave like my father.'

It is Gummer's experience that one can never be too obvious in these matters. He reaches out over the heads of the crowd, exalted as a Methodist. 'Pass the boy up! Pass him to me.'

James is handed forward. A local butcher, dried blood black beneath his nails, lifts the boy on to the stage. 'There,' says Gummer, 'there now. This is a great day for you, Billy. A great day.'

James faces the crowd. He has never felt a moment's stage fright. Gummer's hand is on his shoulder. James looks down at the foolish open faces. Near the back of the booth, by the opening, he catches sight of a large wig, half a face, an intelligent eye, a collar and shoulder of good cloth. For a moment the eye holds him, probes him, then Gummer turns him and the act begins.

Gummer invites the butcher on to the stage to hold the boy steady. The butcher grins, pleased, self-conscious. Gummer flourishes the steel pin for the crowd to admire. He asks the butcher to touch its point. The butcher dabs the point with his finger. It draws a pearl of blood. The butcher frowns at his finger, then grins again and holds it up for the crowd. Gummer takes hold of James's fingers and turns the boy's hand palm up. For several seconds, as if wrestling with a tender conscience, he holds the needle poised above the taut skin of the boy's palm. Then he pricks it, the point of the needle making a tiny shallow wound. James screams and faints in the butcher's arms. The crowd bursts into excited chatter. Gummer waves his arms to silence them. He puts the pin on the table and lights the candle. Salts are waved under the boy's nose. He revives. The butcher pats his shoulder like a worried uncle then, at Gummer's request, seizes the boy in his arms. Taking hold this time of the boy's wrist,

Gummer quickly runs the flame over the delicate skin. James writhes in the butcher's grasp; he screams, howls, begs; he laughs. He faints again; he is revived. The candle is returned to the table.

Now the bottle containing the remedy is uncorked and held to the boy's lips. James takes in as little as he can. He knows the taste well enough; vinegar, laudanum, honey. The bottle is stoppered. The crowd scrutinises every movement. After only a few seconds the child's strength seems to return. He stands up strongly. It is amazing how little fear he shows. Gummer takes up the pin once more. The butcher makes ready to grab the boy but Gummer shakes his head. Again the point of the needle is held above the skin of the boy's palm and slowly, slowly, Gummer drives it through the flesh until a half-inch of steel appears through the back of James's hand. The butcher's jaw drops. It is a moment Gummer adores. There is not a mind in the place he does not now command. He withdraws the pin, wipes it on a white cloth and holds up the cloth like a bride's wedding-sheet. He fetches the candle and burns the boy's skin. The child does not so much as sigh.

Even before Gummer has extinguished the flame, the first voices are clamouring for the potion. James jumps down to rejoin Grace Boylan. Some of the crowd touch him, as if for good luck. Gummer gets down to business, dealing with several customers at a time – money from this one, change to another, orders from a third, smiling encouragement to a fourth. It lasts an hour. People who have not seen the show but see a steady stream of people emerge from the booth with bottles in their hands go in to buy for themselves. Something this popular must be good. With the last twenty bottles Gummer doubles the price. It is a gamble, but no one complains. The last bottle is bought by a gentleman with green eyes.

James and Grace have left the fair. They are sitting under a tree eating bread and cold bacon. It does not do to be seen too much.

As night falls they make their way back to the booth. The flaps of the entrance have been roped together except for an opening at the bottom through which, on hands and knees, James and the woman crawl into the silence of the booth. A servant, Adam Later, is sleeping under a sack. Gummer is sitting on the boxes. To his right the candle burns, throwing watery shadows over the canvas. Next to the candle is an ornate, long-barrelled pistol, cocked.

'Aha!' He beams at them, already a little drunk. 'The changeling and the tart! Come hither, boy. Claim your reward.'

James approaches. The blow knocks him backwards on to the trampled earth.

Says Gummer: 'Let that remind you to keep your amusement to yourself. Laughter, by God! We had trouble enough teaching you to scream.'

James stands, brushes the grass from his jacket. Gummer shakes his head. 'Alas, 'tis almost pointless to strike him. What a prodigy! What a very dangerous child. Come, I shall not hit you again.' He rests a hand on James's shoulder. For some seconds they gaze into each other's eyes. 'Sleep,' says Gummer. 'Mistress Boylan and I shall finish the bottle.' He draws a watch from his pocket. 'The pair of you leave two hours before sunrise. We meet at Lavington.'

Says Grace: 'We shall settle accounts first, mind.'

Gummer nods. 'You shall have gold, dear Grace. Gold and silver.'

'And shall I?' James is standing just beyond the candle's first ring of light.

'The boy gives me the creeps,' says Grace, helping herself to the bottle. Gummer shrugs. 'You do not need to love him. He, after all, could no more love you than this could.' He taps the barrel of the gun.

'Ay,' says Grace. 'God forbid he should ever grow to manhood.'

2   James lies awake beneath his coat for an hour, listening to the hum of their voices. Figures pass by the booth, some singing snatches of song in drunken voices, some quarrelling; a dog sets up barking. How familiar these sounds of the human forest have become to him. At first they kept him from sleep, listening, weighing up each cry. He was wary, and though never fearful he kept himself in readiness for flight. It did not occur to him that Gummer might protect him.

He had found Gummer in Bristol, in a house in Denmark Street, hard by the hustle of the docks. He was not hard to find; it was merely a case of enquiring from those who in looks most approximated Gummer himself. Thus, by a trail of card-sharps, showmen, impersonators and pimps, he was brought to the door of the house. A middle-aged woman admitted him and passed him on to a younger woman who led him to a chamber, a bare room with clothes strewn on the cot and floor, a table with the remains of a meal, a glass broken at the stem. Gummer was kneeling by a wall, apparently in prayer. He turned at the sound of the door opening. He did not seem surprised to see the boy. He looked at him, then back at the wall, then waved the boy over. There was a small knot-hole in the wall. Gummer moved aside. James placed his eye to the hole, felt the coolness of air against his eye. The room he was looking into was larger than Gummer's and there were pictures on the wall and a four-poster bed with a cat and a chamber pot beneath it. On the boards an old man, naked, on hands and knees, was being ridden by a woman, who struck his flabby arse with a riding-crop and made him carry her about the room, though his breath wheezed and the sweat dripped down his shanks. When she struck him the man's face flinched with delight. The woman looked towards the hole in the wall, stuck out her tongue, grinned.

'The delineations', whispered Gummer, 'of human pleasure.'

For the first weeks of their new alliance, James accompanied him around the city: a rat-run of taverns, bagnios, gaming-rooms, cockpits. Men eyed the boy shrewdly, weighing him up as they might another man's horse, another man's luck. The women, tempted by the prettiness of his face, approached him with a cautious, weary kindness.

At the end of June, sitting in the room in Denmark Street, sunlight in an orange flag unfurled over the black floorboards, a fly indolently tapping the diamond-patterned glass, Gummer hinted at the means by which he – no, they – should make their fortunes. He had already, on several occasions, satisfied himself that what he had witnessed in the parlour in Blind Yeo was no accident. Pins, candles and slaps had met with no more response than if he had tortured the table. To be quite sure, he borrowed a tool from a builder and extracted one of James's teeth. The result was so convincing, so overwhelming, he had stooped and hugged the boy, his shirt smeared with the child's blood. The boy was incapable of suffering! The boy had never suffered in his life! More than this, any wound he received healed at such a rate one could almost sit and watch the flesh draw together, knit, blanch, resolve. The site of a burn would be quite invisible three days after it was given, and though the child's hands had been pierced a dozen times the skin was smooth, untroubled.

The plan was simple. If they carried it out boldly they would make more in one summer than Gummer had made in ten years of laborious swindling and sharking. Naturally it was not without some attendant risks. People did not take kindly to deception, to being made fools of. The greatest danger lay in James being recognised. To avoid this they would do fairs that lay at some distance from each other, move swiftly from one part of the country to another. It was vital, however, that the child should be convincing. He must learn to imitate suffering, he must study it, its effects. He should study it like a foreign language and for this he must have a teacher.

Gummer had a man in mind, ran him to ground in a drinking-shop by Christmas Steps where, among the sloped backs, the insensible roar, the close stink of the place, Cato Leigh, decayed thespian, legs swollen with the dropsy, his face a dozen faces, each slapped redly upon the other, underwent the familiar inferno of his nights.

He was declaiming, for the price of a drink, lines from Faustus, when he saw, out of the side of one large eye, through the prism of a tear, the lank figure of Marley Gummer, a hound on its hind legs, with whom, in the year seventeen something, he had passed himself off as a Spanish grandee in an elaborate scheme to defraud a cartel of sherry merchants. And next to Gummer, a boy with eyes like blue stars.

'This fellow, James,' said Gummer when they had lured Leigh back to Denmark Street with the promise of strong drink, 'will be your tutor.'

Leigh looked down at the boy. He was uncomfortable with children. He found it hard to believe he had ever been one. He said: 'And what, pray, Mr Gummer, am I to teach the boy?'

'You are to teach him how to suffer.'

'Life, sir' – Leigh's arm flourished through the air – 'will teach him soon enough.'

'But you shall teach him sooner, Mr Leigh. Start tonight. He must know how to scream, how to writhe, all the usual horrors. He must be good. He must convince. You have a week.'

'What manner of child have you discovered, Mr Gummer?'

'One I conjured up in the country, Mr Leigh. A most delightful, cold-blooded monster of a boy. Now then, where shall you begin?'

At first James did not understand what was required of him. The man's antics were utterly mysterious, but Leigh persisted and the boy caught on. Soon, the bawd who ran the house complained that it was driving away her business. A constable beat at the door with his iron-tipped pole and had to be shown from room to room before he would believe there was no murder, no witchcraft.

From quotidian miseries they progressed to the mimicking of more spectacular disasters; the contortions induced by poisons, and all possible woundings from daggers, pistols, toledoes. At the end of the week Gummer tested the boy, having him fall down on the street and clutch his knee, or howl in dismay upon receiving a slap, or run about hopping and bellowing from a scald. The first experiments were too fulsome or too feeble. Onlookers were confused, suspicious. But James was no sluggard. What he did not learn from Cato Leigh he took from others, following a man being whipped through the streets, squatting down to observe the torment of a street crier, her leg shattered by a cartwheel. One bright afternoon he sat on Gummer's shoulders to observe, over the heads of the crowd, the hanging of a felon outside the gates of Bristol gaol. It was everywhere, this thing called suffering. And such an infinite variety! People skulked in horror of it, prayed to their god to be spared it, and yet it seemed that nobody was; no one, that is, apart from himself. Even Gummer was not immune, living like the others at the mercy of a rotten tooth, a loose slate, a tainted oyster.

They set out in July through the green gut of a country road. The city ended suddenly; there was a house, a brick stack, smoke, ugly children. Then only fields and the scrolled canopies of the trees, and farmhouses where old dogs, eyes ajar, stunned themselves in the sun, and a woman in iron pattens paused outside an open door, shading her eyes with her hand to watch them pass. Marley Gummer, Adam Later, James Dyer and Molly Wright – first of the 'mothers' – jolting, shoulder to shoulder in a high-sided wagon, piled high with boxes and poles and rolls of canvas.

The first fair was a market town in Gloucester. The show was an unqualified success, almost too smooth, so that Gummer fretted that they would be unable to repeat such a marvel. Three days later, in Somerset, they did so, and again, a week later, across the border in Wales. They rode east then, through the harvest to Oxford, then east again through a flat land, travelling from spire to spire, to Norwich, the great roll of its cathedral bells heard on the breeze while the city was still invisible.

'Mothers' came and went. The potion itself was rarely the same, the ingredients bought from local apothecaries who were well paid to keep their curiosity in bounds. Only the crowd was always the same, the crowd and the act, though on occasion Gummer would extemporise, convolute his tale of secret recipes, bearded magi, magical ingredients.

By his own lights Gummer treated the boy well; new clothes and shoes, sugar plums, a neckerchief as green and dark as the sea they had walked by at Cromer. He taught James secrets of the underworld: how to cut out a purse, how to cheat at cards, how to conceal a blade so that it drops neatly into the hand when needed. And stray, unprovoked advice on women, what they care for and how. In the country outside Lincoln, after a lunch of rabbit cooked on the spit, Gummer showed James a length of lamb's gut he called a London Overcoat. Protection, he said, from Signor Gonorrhoea, and he winked and wiggled the thing in the air, laughing. Only once did he feel it necessary to chastise the boy. It was nothing he had done, nothing he had said. It was a look, a quite shocking look, such as Gummer had seen once before, in the eyes of a hanging judge at the end of a long quarter session at Dorchester. For this insubordination he strapped James tight to the wheel of the cart and left him there all night. Grace Boylan, now James's 'mother', swore that she could find a way to hurt him, her with her background, her talents, and for a minute or two Gummer let her try. Then he pushed her away, freed the boy and tenderly walked the life back into his legs. 'James,' he sighed, 'where would we be without each other, eh?' And as they walked back to the cart through the shadows of the trees he sang:

> 'In summer when the shaws be sheen
> And leaves be large and long,
> Full merry it is in fair forest
> To hear the fowles song . . .'

3 Grace wakes him with the toe of her boot. It is time to go. James moves easily into wakefulness, shrugs off his dreams, inhales the pre-dawn air. He takes up his bundle, pulls on the coat he has been sleeping under and waits by the flap. Grace comes, shivering, rubbing at her face with the heels of her hands. She is at her worst at this time, full of speechless fury at the darkness, the chill air, the long walk ahead of them. Also at fate, the too-many years on her back, and this strange untouchable boy walking the road beside her. An old soul he has, or no soul at all. You'd think he might whistle or ask how far it will be or when they will eat. Not this one.

Black; black and gold. Night disperses. Light hangs in rags from the trees. Clouds the size of villages drift westwards. For five minutes the tips of the corn-stalks catch the sun and scintillate. Already there are gleaners at work, women gathering the left-behind, the second crop. They gather a clutch, bind it and pass it to one of the children who run to the gate where a boy stands guard.

Grace and James breakfast in the corner of a meadow. When they have eaten, Grace lies back in the grass, belches, sinks the lids of her eyes. The breath whistles in her nose; a horse-fly settles on her belly. James opens his bundle. The orrery is wrapped in an old coat. He sets the box on top of the coat, slips the catch. The planets reflect the morning light. He turns the handle. There is some rust on the cogs, just a little, but it means he must use more force to turn them. The wires shudder, the planets vibrate. When Grace sits up he is still with it, Liza's old toy. Grace has not seen it before. She comes close, kneels heavily in the grass and watches. A smile unfurls across her face; she touches the brass sun. James lets go of the handle, closes the box, wraps it in the coat. They go. It is a long empty road.

 4 'Pain, friends, is from the devil. It is his touch, his caress . . .'
Salisbury, 10 October 1752.

The sides of the booth are buffeted by winds; enormous soft fists beating at the canvas. Gummer must raise his voice above the noise of it. The wind makes the crowd restless. It distracts them. They think of roofs, lost washing, journeys home. Only when Gummer begins his exchange with Grace Boylan do they hush and lean slightly towards the woman and the pale handsome boy in his blue coat beside her.

'Let me go, Mama. Let me be brave like Father.'

'Well spoke, boy! Pass him up! Pass him up!'

On stage again. This time it is a young man, forearms thick as hams, a cast in his left eye, who will help with the torture. The pin, the flame, the potion, the pin once more. There are some marks, red freckles where the pin has been before, but nothing to arouse suspicion. His flesh seems to have no memory.

As Gummer brings the candle, James sees again, at the back of the booth, the same green eyes he has seen now in four of the shows. He has not told Gummer. He is waiting to see what the man will do. The flame laps at his hand. The green eye studies him. The crowd gasps, a voice calls, 'I'll take two!' A commotion, a swirl of figures, the wind beats twice, thrice upon the canvas, and the green-eyed man is gone. Gummer rubs his hands, gets down to business.

Outside, the wind flings birds around the chimney-stacks. A man chases his wig towards the river. A newspaper torn from the hand of a lawyer suddenly wraps the head of a beggar. Grace and James head for the cathedral. Inside, the wind has a solemn echo. Grace slumps on a pew, wriggles a bottle from beneath her skirts, empties it and slides the bottle under the seat.

'Better, by Christ.'

She looks round for the boy, does not see him. She closes her eyes. There is a tiredness in her, a black water in her bones that no sleep can ever ease now. A dozen voices in the choir sing the first lines of the *Te Deum*. High above her bowed head bats swim through the arches, disappear into the shadows.

James walks towards the altar, looks at the boys in the choir. They are much of an age with him, faces candle-pale, their eyes following the hands of the music master. There is one boy with a face like Charlie's. James thinks of his dead brother, then of his mother; he remembers her lifting him – how clearly! And he remembers the smell of her. Flesh, milk, the warm appley breath. The blood thuds in his ears. He raises a hand to his chest, then to his face, touches his own hot face. There is something on his hand – water. He licks it. Salt water. The boys are singing; their voices rise like a fountain, fall like rain. He goes towards one of the side doors. A man is standing by the door, hat in hand. He nods to James, pulls aside the curtain in front of the door. James stops, looks around, looks for Grace Boylan. In a distant pew he sees a shape that may be hers, a figure bowed in sleep or prayer. When he looks back the man has gone. From different points in the cathedral voices, hushed and unintelligible, are murmuring. James steps forward. Behind the curtain someone is waiting for him. From across the body of the church there comes a blink of light; Gummer strides in, tiny among the pillars, the great tombs, the cliffs of grey stone. He sees James, waves at him. James moves towards the side door, goes through it. He does not see the man but feels the grip on his arm. A voice says: 'Hurry!', and pushes him forward through yards of disordered air. A carriage and four is waiting. James and the man are running now, down an alley, over a bridge. The river flashes, an empty boat scuds crazily on its surface. As they reach the carriage another man leans out, hauls James up, snaps the door shut. The coach lurches backwards, then forwards. Gummer's face shows suddenly at the window, an arm snakes about his neck, drags him off. James stares back and sees at the side of the road two men knock Gummer down. One has a stick. They start to beat him. There is no noise other than the wind. The man with green eyes gently pushes James back into his seat and draws down the window blind, hooks it. From out of darkness he says: 'You are safe now, child.' A hand reaches out, pats the boy's knee. 'Quite safe.'

5 A land smooth as bottle glass. Trim gold woods, the green and steel snake of a stream. A lake of manageable size with the spire of a submerged church just breaking the surface. A driveway stippled with the shadows of young trees; Italian gardens; avenues; prospects; miles of red-brick wall, iron spikes.

James opens his eyes. He does not know what has woken him. A bird is staring at him, cocking its head from side to side on the top of a bush. James looks at the shadows to see how long he has been asleep. Two hours at least. The sunlight surprises him. He has been dreaming of snow, a world of snow, and a voice, calling him, closing on him.

He clambers to his feet. He sleeps so much now, so deeply, as though his body were preparing for another life. He claps his hands; the bird flies off, takes the dream with it.

In the evening air the house is splendid. The pale stone soaks up the pink and honey of the light; each window bears its own unique sun. Generous Palladian arms stretch out on either side of the main house. As he approaches, his feet crunch on the raked gravel. He walks up a flight of shallow steps to a double door. He does not need to knock. Invisible eyes have always seen him. Hands, tightly gloved, admit him. Servants in yellow coats.

This is the door through which he entered when he first arrived, the green-eyed man beside him, his hand sometimes brushing the boy's shoulder as though to reassure him. The gentleman had passed James into the care of a servant and James had followed the man beside a swirl of banisters, through corridors broad as roads with doors leading off as far as the eye could pierce. There were voices in the air, a language he had not heard before, a leisurely, expressive chatter, and looking up he saw men on scaffolds, dark-haired with elegant faces, long brushes in their hands. They were working on a frieze above one of the great windows. They paused in their work, looking down at James, grinning, shaking their heads. '*Ah, povero ragazzo!*'

He was shown into a room with a curtained bed and a fire burning quietly in the grate. The servant had looked at the boy then, his expression no longer deferential, like an actor stepping suddenly out of his part.

'When you wants to eat you pulls that wire there.'

And James had asked: 'Will the man come? The man I came here with?'

'Mr Canning?' The servant shook his head. 'He'll send for you when he wants you. He's a busy man. You're not the only one, you know.' The door was already closed before James thought to ask: '"Only one" of what?'

No one comes to see him other than servants, though not the same as the one who led him up on that first day; not as familiar or sly or informative. They order the room and bring trays of food. After the greens and bacon and penny loaves of his life with Grace and Gummer, the diet is gamey and sweet. A rich diet that makes him restless. He cannot decide if he is a prisoner or a guest. Certainly no key is ever turned in the door, and no one stands on the corridors playing gaoler. He begins to explore, candle in hand, going out when the house is quiet, his own footfall swallowed in the plush of the carpet and nothing but a stream of cream-coloured light to betray him.

The first time he meets nobody; the house is ostentatiously empty. After an hour, he becomes lost, deceived by symmetries, and only recovers his room towards dawn, his candle long since gutted, his door suddenly appearing before him when still he thinks himself on the wrong floor, the wrong corridor.

The next night he goes further. Two servants, the light of their candles draped over their yellow coats, cross ahead of him through some large stately space, linger an instant to look towards the finger of James's flame, then disappear. What secret lives these people lead, secret as eels. When James tries to follow them there is no sign of where they have gone, no betraying glow.

It is the third or fourth night before he encounters anyone with whom he can speak, a night so sharply lit by the moon its light penetrates even into the windowless corridors, lying like sheets of new paper under the doors. He has been walking the greater part of an hour when midnight chimes from clocks in a hundred rooms and he hears a voice, soft yet querulous, and traces it to a great door that stands just wide enough to admit him. He enters and sees by moonlight a man, the silvery shape of a man, standing in a kind of pulpit at the side of a shelf of books. The man, reaching up to replace a book, turns and peers at the boy.

'What are you, eh? And what do you want in here? This is a library. Boys, I find, do not care for libraries. Perhaps you were looking for the kitchens.'

With a grunt of effort he slots the book in its place and clambers down. He seemed quite tall. Now it is evident he is no taller than James.

'Come, then, now you are here. Let me show you about. I am Collins, Mr Canning's librarian. I was with him in Spain and Italy. Oh, indeed, we were in Italy for many years. He speaks the language like a native. Can recite Dante by the hour. These shelves are history. Herodotus, Pliny, Tacitus. Homer. Here is philosophy. Aristotle, Bacon, Newton, Erasmus . . . Hobbes, Locke . . . In this place, for which only Mr Canning and myself have the key, are certain rare and . . . particular volumes. How old are you, boy?'

'Thirteen.'

'You have amorous thoughts?'

'Amorous?'

'Ay. Hot thoughts. Lewd. Are you a peeper through keyholes? Are you inflamed by the heave of a bosom?'

James considers a moment the bosoms he has seen. Liza's once, white puppy-heads as she lifted her shift one night in summer. The actresses at Farmer Moody's place. Grace Boylan's when she gave them to be squeezed by Gummer. He shakes his head. The librarian shrugs.

'You won't be pestering me for the key, then. Where had we reached to? Philosophy? These shelves here are poetry, a particular favourite of Mr Canning's.'

He stops. Holds up his hand. He is listening, and looking over James's shoulder towards the door. He says: 'Did you hear them?'

James counts the fingers on the librarian's hand. One, two, three, four, five, six.

'It is the twins,' says Collins, and for a moment the oddest smile lives on his face. James turns. Two heads have appeared round the door. Four eyes examine him, then the heads withdraw and he hears the hiss of their slippers, running.

'After them!' The librarian prods James between the shoulder-blades. 'Make haste, or you shall lose them!'

James sets off in pursuit, stopping now and then to listen, then running on. He glimpses them on the stairs, then at the far end of a gallery, slipping through a doorway into the dusk of another passageway. For half a minute he loses the trail completely; then comes a muffled crash, a cry of 'Damn! Damn!' He follows, finds the shards of porcelain, but no sign of the girls, no noise of their slippers.

They are in a room that he learns later to call the 'Hall of Statues'. The moon is wedged between two cypress trees outside the window, and the statues throw long sharp shadows on to the marble floor. Men with coiled hair, their naked bodies slackly muscular, lean on spears or gesture wearily with absent arms. Women, goddesses, hands draped across breasts, heads without noses, eyes blank, staring inwards.

The girls are on a bench near the window, sleeping. He goes close to look at them. They are huddled together; their heads with high white brows lean one against the other. The eyes beneath their bloodless lids seem unusually large. Their mouths are small; the lips bunched, babyish.

One of the girls opens her eyes, very suddenly, as if her sleep has been a ruse. She smiles. 'I was dreaming of you,' she says. 'And now you are here.'

'How do you know me?'

'Mr Canning said you were to come here. And then I saw you from my window. Mr Canning said you look like any other boy but that you are not so, not at all. He would not have brought you if you were.'

'I have not seen Mr Canning. Not since I arrived.'

'Oh, you must not expect to see him. At least, not often. He will send when he needs you. My name is Ann. This is my sister Anna. We were in the circus before Mr Canning found us. We did not like it. You were in a circus too.'

James shakes his head. 'I was in a show. It was to sell medicine.'

'Was it a good medicine?'

'It was nothing. Nothing good.'

'Mr Canning gives us good medicine. He prepares it himself.'

'What is wrong with you?'

'Hardly anything, except that our heads sometimes ache and we are so tired we fall asleep in the middle of our sentences.'

'You are always with your sister?'

She laughs, a snort, as if he has said something amusing

though in questionable taste. 'Of course; and she is often such poor company. But soon we shall be apart and then I shall not see her for a whole week, or even a month, so when we meet we may have a conversation, like ordinary people do.'

And then he understands. It is something in the way they are nestled together on the bench like the two halves of an ink blot. He asks: 'When are you to separate?'

'When we are sixteen. Mr Canning has promised us.'

'How old are you now?'

She is asleep. The other sister is looking at him. 'You tire us out with so much talk. Why are you not in bed?'

'Why are you not in bed, since you are so tired?'

'We like it here. We like to look at the statues. We like that one especially.' She points to the corner of the room. A squat figure with a great tumescent cock thrust to the sky. 'Mr Canning says he is the god of gardens. Priapus. We call him . . .' She whispers a name James cannot hear, then giggles, a sharp hysterical sound. The other sister does not wake. Her big head lolls on her chest.

James asks: 'How long have you been here?'

She shrugs one shoulder. 'Since Mr Canning found us . . . We are having our likeness done. Mr Molina does it. Perhaps he will paint you too if you come.'

'Where does he paint you?'

She points upward, a gesture as wearily elegant as any of the statues. Then she too is asleep.

For a long time he stands, observing their sleep, waiting to see if one of them will wake. He feels towards them a kind of kinship; not a warm emotion, not friendship. Mr Canning, then, is a collector, and he, James Dyer, like the twins, like Mr Collins, has been collected. Or in his case, stolen. He is quite untroubled by it. Canning will serve as Gummer has served. And there are things in this house, things that he wishes to know more of. A six-fingered librarian; two girls as one. What did Gummer call him once? *Rara avis*. How many of them are there here, in Mr Canning's gilded cage?

6 It is many days before he speaks to them again, though several times he sees them walking in the park beneath twin white parasols, Ann and Anna, waiting for their sixteenth birthday. Twice he has seen them accompany one of the servants to the little house that stands on a rise near the lake. The servant always carries a bucket; full when he goes, empty – to judge by the way it swings upon its handle – on his return. As for Mr Molina's studio, he cannot discover it. He has begun to wonder if the painter exists only in the twins' mind.

Whenever he is bored or wishes for some company, he goes to the library. Mr Collins – as Viney before him, both men quickly aware of the boy's capacity to absorb knowledge – persuades him to slide the leather volumes from their shelves and read. Not poetry, of course, or stories – the boy is blind to them – but books of anatomy, books of maps, books of experiments; books with complex seductive diagrams, books of astronomy, geometry . . . With Mr Collins at his shoulder, December rain on the windows, candles flickering against the long afternoon twilight, James stumbles through some pages of Latin in Harvey's *De Motu Cordis*. But it is the pictures which snare him: the world beneath the skin; the skein of guts, the globes and bulbs of the great organs; the sheets of muscle strapped around the trellis of the bones; the intricate house of the heart, veins and arteries radiating, curling, branching into tiny tributaries.

Through the slough of the year, Mr Collins feeds the boy Borelli

and Malphigi ('*I have sacrificed almost the whole race of frogs* . . .');
Fabricius of Padua; and from its high shelf, the librarian on tip-
toe in his mobile pulpit, Vesalius's anatomy, *De Humanis Corporis
Fabrica*, the title page showing the great man, knuckle deep in the
abdomen of a female cadaver at the theatre of public anatomy in
Padua. James even learns a dozen words of Greek.

Molina's studio, discovered by James as he discovers everything in
this house – the chance turning of a handle, a door untried – is
high among the warren of servants' quarters, above the crowns of
the trees, level almost with the circling of the rooks. It is cluttered
with the painter's domestic junk: paint-streaked shirts, cups and
kettles, empty wine bottles, a large broken clock, brushes in jars
of fluid. A grey cat squats by a plate of fish-heads, undisturbed
by the boy's presence. Molina has his back to him, does not
turn from his canvas but reaches back with one hand to wave
the boy to a seat, some exploded oriental couch near where the
girls are sitting. The twins seem stunned by the fixity of their
pose, their dress sparkling, their faces feverish in the light from
a dozen candelabras.

Says Molina: '*Ya está* . . . rest now.'

He steps around the canvas, drops the brush into a champagne
flute, stretches mightily.

He says: 'So this is the boy they have told me about.' They hold
each other's gaze, the painter nodding his head: a tall, gaunt man
with thick eyebrows, and a head of thick brown hair tied in a black
ribbon. 'And have you come to be painted, my friend?'

The twins say: 'You must finish us first!'

'Have no fear,' replies Molina. 'Your immortality is almost
complete.'

The twins jump up from their couch, stand before the canvas,
clap their hands delightedly.

'Will you paint us *afterwards*? Will you? James, you shall never guess what has happened! Mr Canning says he shall present us at court! Imagine!'

Molina laughs. 'Perhaps James can go too and dance with you at a ball. One after the other. You must ask them now, James. They will be in great demand. My dears, you must sit again, a little while more . . .'

'We're bored! We want to talk to James.'

'James will sit here with us and listen to your chatter. Now, like before, yes . . . Your hand, Anna, more so . . . perfect. Now I paint.'

Molina works. When the twins have fallen silent, have entered again the trance of their pose, he says to James: 'The measure of an artist is the quality of his attention. You understand? The way he is looking at his subject. Perhaps that is also the measure of a man, no? Tell me, James, you like your new home?'

'Well enough.'

'So, so. I understand you have a very special, hmm, ability. No feeling, no . . . sensation. Truly I cannot imagine such a thing.'

Says James: 'What is your "ability"?'

'This, my friend. Only this poor business with the paint. Look, they are asleep. It is their condition. They must share the same blood. It is not enough. You think they are pretty? I show you something. When they sleep like this you can fire a pistol and they do not wake.'

Molina walks up to the girls, reaches down and takes hold of the hem of their dress. 'Come, James.'

He ravels up the material. Four plump legs in red stockings tied with ribbon above the knees. Four white thighs, very nude, and two neat beards of tight coppery curls. The join is at the hip. Molina takes James's hand, places it just where the flesh is fused; the confluence of bone and blood. There are tears in his eyes.

'It is so soft, no? So . . . *No sé cómo se dice* . . . It feels as if, a little push, and your hand would be inside. I saw this, James, one time in my home, in Granada . . . A man, a Moor, a healer . . . he reach into a boy's flesh and take out a part that is bad. No knife, no blood. I saw this myself. The boy had some pain, but little. His mother held him. The Moor reached in . . . like he pulled a fish from a pool. I would like to paint them without their clothes but they are timid. I think if I give them a little wine. Then perhaps they will do it.'

James gently palpates the flesh. He is wondering how the major organs are shared between the twins: bowel and colon, spleen, kidneys, pancreas . . . what if there were not enough, if, for example, they shared a single liver? Was there some way of knowing beforehand, or only once they were on the table? Did Mr Canning know?

Molina lifts the boy's hand away, covers the girls with their dress.

'Have you ever painted, James?'

'At school I used to draw things. I found it easy.'

'I think so. These are painter's hands you have. Artist hands.' He looks at the boy, smiles. It is a kindly, a pitying smile. 'You really feel nothing, my friend?'

James shakes his head. He does not care to be pitied.

'No pain?'

'Never.'

'And pleasure? You feel pleasure?'

No one has asked him this before. He looks at the cat gnawing daintily at the last of the fish-heads.

'Pleasure?'

Certainly there are things he likes: the knowledge in Mr Collins's books, certain foods, the orrery, Canning's wealth. Are these things pleasure? Or did Molina mean something different, physical, a sensation? In some remote and virgin world within, he knows the answer. Pain, pleasure. He has glimpsed their coast, their high cliffs; smelt in dreams the loaded offshore breezes. But still he is

123

surrounded by a calm insensate sea; his ship high-sided, inviolable, its great grey pennants streaming. How could it be otherwise? It is a thought he does not entertain.

Molina is by the canvas again, working white into blue on the old dinner plate that serves him for a palette.

James asks: 'What is in the house by the lake? I have seen a servant go there. The twins go too.'

Molina nods, still intent upon his mixing. 'That is one of Mr Canning's most wonderful . . . things. Of course, he does not tell the world. Only his friends; the learned gentlemen.'

'You have not said what it is.'

'That is because I wish you to see it with . . .' Molina searches in the air for the word. '. . . a clean mind.'

'You will take me?'

'I will take you.'

'When?'

'Tonight.'

'What else does Mr Canning have?'

'Many things. Many. There is the boy from the moon.'

'That I do not believe.'

'There are people, James, who would not believe in a boy who feels no pain.'

'What does he look like, this boy?'

'Very strange, and then, not so strange at all. Not very big or small. No horns. You shall see him too. One day.'

James studies the side of Molina's head but there is nothing to learn there. The painter is utterly absorbed. He is painting the blue of the girls' eyes and finding blue elsewhere.

The cat has finished its meal. It licks its paws, very thoughtfully.

Dusk brings an hour of light; the world flares up. There is colour, birdsong: the grass capped with silver. An hour, then clouds, night-bearing, sweeping in over the hills, the village, the lake. The light recedes into a slender golden tower. In the house, servants hurry from room to room lighting candles. The fires are stoked, shutters barred.

James meets Molina on the back stairs. The painter winks, swings a key from his hand.

'Ready?'

They exit through a low door at the side of the house. Molina has taken a lantern from one of the servants, a feeble light but sufficient to see the next two, three footsteps. They do not talk, not until they reach the house by the lake. The house is small, a mock temple. A statue of Neptune stands beside it, pot-bellied, dyspeptic, frowning towards the lake. Molina scratches the key against the lock.

'What you are going to see, James, Mr Canning found near the island of Capri. It is said the Emperor Tiberius also possessed such a one. That he used it for his pleasure.'

The lock gives. Molina opens the door, cautiously, as if whatever is upon the other side may take fright. James follows. The stench of fish is physical in the air. The light of the lantern marbles the surface of a pool. Molina crouches by the edge of it.

'Come, my friend. It will not harm you.'

But James is not afraid, he is suspicious. He is thinking of Gummer, holding up his bottle of trash above the wide-eyed crowd. Is Molina duping him?

There is a movement, the writhe of a shadow in the bottom of the pool. James kneels beside the painter, stares down into the water.

Molina says: 'Did you see?'

James says: 'I saw nothing.'

The water is not clean. Where the light pierces it he can see particles of scum, brilliant green. Molina dips his hand into the water.

He croons like a lover: '*Venga, carina, venga.*' The water breaks, the light zig-zags crazily over the surface. A form is thickening, rising towards them, parting the slack muscle of the water. A shape – a head? – skims just below the skin of the pool. There is a flash of bronze, a cry, gull-like, forlorn, awful. For an instant James sees it, outlined in the boil of its own movement; an eye, unmistakably human, unmistakably alien; a powerful blonde shoulder, a long arched back, a tail trailing black weeds and crusted with shells; the broad ragged comb of its fin. It cries out again, turns up its belly, the white and rose of its breasts, and dives, pulsing its tail, passing beyond the shallow net of their light. The water slaps against the stone edge of the pool; slowly, slowly settles.

Molina eases himself up. He gestures to the boy to go ahead of him, out of the room, then he pulls the door shut, locks it, pockets the key. It has started to rain. The rain shows in the surface of the lake like a field of tiny white flowers. They run to the house, and as they run, Canning's dowdy marvel swims deeper into the lairs of the boy's brain, and circles there, stirring dreams, currents of unease.

7   January freezes. February brings a sudden thaw. The rivers lap their banks, the roads turn to mush. On the feast of St Valentine's James receives a locket of hair bound with a length of thread. Also a riddle, the spelling wildly idiosyncratic. When next he meets the twins he looks to see which of them is missing a scissor-bite of hair, but among the rings and curls, the sheer abundance, it is impossible to tell. It is from them both perhaps. If they suffered the same thoughts, why not the

same emotions? For a week he uses the lock as a bookmark, then loses it, leaving it perhaps inside a copy of *De Revolutionibus*, or among the pages of Mr Canning's first edition of Newton's *Opticks*. The girls' great day is coming. They sometimes faint at the very thought of it.

Visitors. A dozen coaches, wheels gummed with mud. Servants at the door like bees around the entrance of a hive, Mr Canning in a coat of thick green velvet, the serene host. The gentlemen bow, clasp hands, utter their pleasantries, yet their mood seems sombre, abstracted, as though in their heads they carried delicate pyramids of thought that must, in every moment, be attended to. They grip their canes, hurry into the marble hall. The last arrives, horses spattered to the bit with mud; a fat gentleman is carried wincing over the puddles to the stone steps.

'My dear Bentley.'

'Greetings, Canning. Filthy weather.'

James spies on them through the banisters above the hall. Canning glances up, sees him and nods, nothing more, yet an intelligence has passed between them: Canning will see him later, James will come to him. Everything is perfectly understood.

The men talk below, their heads in clusters, then follow Canning towards the west wing. The house swallows them. A servant scrubs away their footprints.

James waits in Molina's studio. The painting of the twins is finished, propped unceremoniously against the painter's bed.

Molina says: 'I was afraid for the twins to see it. Painting is not a kind art. Art is not kind, not polite. They came and looked at it, looked a long time. They are very happy. So happy they are crying. Then I am crying also because I know that the painting is true. I have thought of you, my friend, of painting you. I think it will be very hard but I would like to try. Shall we try, eh?'

They try. James stands with his back to a tatty brown drape. On a table beside him Molina places an open book, smuggled from the library while Mr Collins attended to a call of nature. It is a rare edition of Bartolomeo Eustachio – *Tabulae Anatomicae Clarissimi Viri* – the open page shows a male figure, feet planted into the lower corners of the page, hands pressing against the sky. The head is turned to one side and has the appearance of an angry moon. All the outer skin has been removed to show the blood vessels. In the drawing these appear like a complicated system of roots. For an anatomical illustration it is weirdly expressive. The man seems all too sensible of his condition, pained and disgusted by it as though he were the victim of some outrageous and inexplicable surgical procedure. His exposed heart is a parcel, clumsily wrapped. Even the tiny vessels of his cock have been exposed. It hangs, a small dark spike between the flayed musculature of his thighs. Above all, he has the air of one waiting, flexed in horror, for the return of his tormentor. Molina finds it fitting for the portrait. He does not say why. James assumes it is to reflect his interest in such things.

Molina draws, first by the light of day, then with the help of the candles. The first sketches he throws aside; the later ones he nods at cautiously. James glances at the broken clock, says: 'I must go now.'

Molina nods. 'The gentlemen will be expecting you.'

A servant is waiting for him in his room. Clothes he has not seen before are laid out on the bed: a suit of red satin, silk stockings, shoes with silver buckles. He has never worn clothes of such quality. He looks in the mirror. The servant waits, careful not .to impose his own reflection. When James turns to him, he leads the way to where the gentlemen are gathered, a room on the ground floor smelling of pipe smoke and chemicals. A single strong light stands on the table. Next to it, the complicated focus of the room, is a device, slender at the base, and at its top a shining glass bowl. Inside the bowl is a dove, sometimes still, sometimes beating its wings against the glass. The base of the glass is splashed with the bird's excreta. The gentlemen are gathered around the table. Several wear spectacles; one of them scribbles notes on a sheet of parchment. Mr Canning stands by the machine holding a handle attached to a pair of leather-cased pistons at the base of the machine. By means of these pistons the air will be removed from the glass. Mr Canning calls the glass bowl 'the receiver'. Beyond the light's frayed edge the room is very dark. There may or may not be others in the darkness. James steps forward. Faces turn to see who has entered, their glances linger a moment, then return to the experiment. They have seen it before a dozen times but Canning's machine, built with his own hands, is a peculiarly luxurious specimen.

'Now, gentlemen,' says Canning. He begins to turn the handle. Immediately the bird reacts to the change in its atmosphere. A last wild attempt at flight, to burst the glass. A furious knotted energy. Then an invisible hand settles on its back, pressing it to the bottom of the receiver. Some of the gentlemen nod their heads. The one who was writing looks up through spectacles, mutters: 'Ah, yes, yes.' Another gazes away into the darkness. Mr Canning turns the handle; the bird is convulsed, its wings half spread, flattened against the glass. The body distorts. Spasms are increasingly marked. Then they weaken to a kind of feeble trembling. The only sound is the steady clicking of the ratchets at the top of the pistons. The bird is still. Mr Canning lets go of the handle. There is silence, then the noise of sobbing. Someone outside the light. Mr Canning smiles. He has the face of a wise angel. He reaches up and adjusts a mechanism at the top of the receiver. There is a hiss of air, the bird is instantly revived, though its movements are drunken. Mr Canning reaches in, carefully removes the bird from the glass, cups it tenderly in his hands. The twins, dabbing at their tears but reassured now, drift from the shadows. Mr Canning hands the bird to Ann. It appears quite docile, as if it has already forgotten its suffering. The gentlemen applaud, more lights are brought, and behind the lights, servants bearing crystal decanters of port and claret and brandy. The visitors drink toasts:

'The future!'

'Knowledge!'

'Newton!'

Mr Canning walks around the table to James. 'You look very well in your new clothes, dear boy.' He straightens the edge of James's coat; a maternal touch.

'Gentlemen! If I may command your attention for a moment ... I should like to make known to you this young man – Master James Dyer – who has been living in my house for some while now. I hope in the spring to bring him to London with me that I might introduce him more formally at one of our regular meetings.'

The men inspect the boy; some make a shallow, good-humoured bow. The twins come and stand beside him. Canning is behind them, one hand on James's shoulder, one on Ann's.

He says: 'They are my family. Dear to me as children of my own. Come, I think they are of an age when they might take a glass of claret.'

The twins are much admired. The claret colours their cheeks, their eyes catch all the candle points, their noses quiver. The gentlemen, drinking freely, are increasingly gallant. They seem to savour the twins' particular appeal. The girls smile their favour on James. His manner makes him seem much older, self-contained. But for the richness of his coat he might have been a Quaker child. Some of the gentlemen take an interest in him, discreetly quiz him, but soon grow tired of the closeness of his answers. They turn away to the decanters or the twins or to each other. The fat man, Bentley, remains, his head toad-like upon the wattles of his neck. He makes desultory enquiries about the boy's diet, sleeping habits, general health. All the while his nails are fixed in the flesh of the boy's wrist, digging until the skin is broken and drops of blood discolour the lace of James's new shirt.

Bentley says: 'How very clever of Canning to discover you. We shall have some times together, you and I.'

He pulls a large handkerchief from his pocket and dabs the boy's blood from his fingers.

8

There is no warning.

He is woken early one morning, told to dress warmly, given chocolate to drink, a plate of eggs for breakfast. Mr Canning is waiting in the hall, a servant smoothing the shoulders of his travelling coat.

Canning says: 'You have not been in London before, I believe. Some say it is the greatest city since imperial Rome. Others that it is the devil's drawing room. Both descriptions are true. Have you been to see the twins?'

'No, sir.'

Since the night of the air pump the twins have been laid up in bed with fevers: dreams of smoke, dreams of fire.

'Never mind,' says Canning. 'We shall bring them something back from London. A fan, a comb. Something *à la mode*. I do so like to surprise them.'

They step out, cross a corridor of late March sunlight and mount into the cool leathery interior of the coach. There is a cry of 'Hey! Get up there!' and the wheels crackle over gravel, draw them through the tender shadows of the trees, along the drive, out through iron gates. Canning pulls a copy of *Philosophical Treatise* from his pocket and begins to read, now and then nodding or shaking his head at some choice or controversial item. James leans up against the window. It is the same from which he last saw Gummer, sprawled on the cobbles at Salisbury while the men beat him. He would like to see Gummer again, see what has become of him. They were a good match in their way, and it was amusing to fool so many people. Perhaps Canning's men murdered him, or else he is swinging at some junction, body in chains, pulled at by crows. Who exactly would mourn such a useless, cunning man?

By dusk they are passing Kensington Gardens. Despite the chill, Canning pulls down the window so that the boy can see better, see and hear, for the city with its elegant lamp-lit squares, its soldiers on horseback, its barrows and carts and hawkers, makes a most satisfying racket.

At several points there is a crush of coaches and sedan chairs. Then the coachmen and the chairmen roar at each other, vicious and comic, their chained obscenities oddly formal. Children, huge eyes and fragile limbs, weave between the traffic. Beggars hold up their hands to the window, flinch at the coachman's whip. A whiff of burning, a whiff of drains, even a thread of scent as the coach of a fashionable woman passes close beside their own.

Up Piccadilly, past St James's, then Horse Guards Parade, the Strand, Fleet Street . . . The coach halts, the footman opens the door, James and Canning dismount. They turn into a narrow court on the left. At the end of the court is a house with a lamp outside. As they approach, an elderly man with a gown and staff comes out to meet them.

'Welcome, Mr Canning, sir. Most of the other gentlemen are gathered.'

'Very well, Lute.' Canning presses a coin into the man's hand. 'Lead on.'

They enter the building, ascending the stairs past portraits of the society's presidents and alumni.

'Do you know who this is, James?' Canning has stopped in front of the most imposing of the portraits. A thin-faced, humourless man, apparently much irritated.

'Sir Isaac Newton, James. I had the honour of knowing him when I was young.'

Lute brings them to a door at the back of the house. Above the door, in a gold scroll: 'Nullius in Verba'. When Lute opens the door there is a sea-sound of voices, hushed as they notice the arrival of Canning. Several of the faces – including Bentley – James recognises from their visit to the house. Lute bangs the heel of his staff on the floor, announces them. Canning takes James's arm and steps with him on to a raised platform. There is a table there with a glass and a bottle.

Canning says: 'Did you find those things for me, Lute?'

'I have 'em here, sir.'

He passes Canning a small leather bag. It looks very new. Canning quickly opens it, looks inside, nods. The clock strikes eight. Outside the hour rings across the city. James stands next to Canning, looking over the men's heads to the gardens. It has started to rain.

'Gentlemen! Fellow members . . . I am here tonight – as I promised I should be – to discover to you the latest of my prodigies. It is a boy I found performing – quite innocently – in the booth of an itinerant quack. The rascal used the boy to demonstrate the powers of an analgetic. The demonstration was remarkably convincing, but when I investigated the nostrum I found it to be entirely bogus. Yet I had seen with my own eyes this boy here apparently unaffected by the application of pain. If this was not – as it plainly was not – an action of the drug, then how might it be explained? I attended a number of these 'demonstrations' and had my agents at others. Naturally I suspected some imposture, a sleight of hand such as card-sharps and conjurers are adept in. Only when I had satisfied myself that this was not the case did I rescue the child from his unhappy situation and bring him to the protection of my own home. I should like now, with the indulgence of the company, to perform a small experiment which will I am sure convince the most sceptical that here is an extraordinary subject worthy of the society's attention.'

From the bag Canning takes a seven-inch needle. It has a more medical look to it than the one Gummer favoured, but is in all important respects the same. Canning pricks his own thumb to demonstrate the needle's sharpness. He turns to James. James holds out his hand, palm up. Canning takes hold of the fingers, poises the tip of the needle and drives it through the boys hand. James screams. Canning stares at him. The room is silent; someone chuckles.

In a low voice Canning says, 'This is not the booth, child. We are not selling anything.' His eyes are not friendly now, nothing parental. He addresses the company. Behind his back James stares at the fat man, who grins fatly back.

'I should explain, gentlemen, that the boy was required to mimic pain in the first instance in order to convince the crowd that he was a normally sentient being, was indeed one of them. If I might crave your further indulgence I shall repeat the experiment.'

He repeats it. This time the boy does not flinch. A growl of astonishment from the company. A sound the boy knows well.

Canning delves in the sack, pulls out a pair of pliers, holds them up amiably before the company, then uses them to tear off the boy's left thumbnail. It requires considerable force and sets up a sweat on Canning's lip. He holds up the pliers, the nail between their steel teeth. There is applause. Some of the gentlemen are standing. Canning binds the thumb, pats James's head.

'I wish, gentlemen, I could say I have discovered how it is that a boy, otherwise quite like any boy of his years, should feel no pain. Alas, I have not. It is – as you have witnessed – as if the faculty of suffering were frozen, and indeed we know that the application of cold to a hurt will often give relief. It may be in this instance the expression "cold-blooded" is more than merely figurative. And should this prove to be the case – that the senses are in some way frozen – it is a nice question to consider how this ice may be thawed, and what the effect would be should the child experience pain for the first time . . .'

The next speaker is the Reverend Joseph Seeper. He has a curious vole from his garden in Stroud. Neither seem at ease. The company drifts out.

It is past midnight when the carriage rolls up Charles Street into Grosvenor Square where Mr Canning rents a small but luxurious dwelling. They have been kept up by their admirers, the gentlemen of the society, who have wined and dined them in the upstairs room of the Mitre in Fleet Street. Several were anxious for Mr Canning to repeat his experiments but he would not, claiming that it would compromise the dignity of the society to do so. James meanwhile worked his way through a bottle of wine, largely unobserved. He was curious to see what effect it would have, if it would make him as loud as the others, but there was nothing beyond a distant sensation of warmth, a slight quickening in his thoughts. Poor stuff to place such value on.

As they mount the stairs into the house, Canning is in good spirits. He sings softly in Italian, greets all the servants by name, allowing them to kiss his hand as though he were the bishop. In a room full of crystal globes he binds the boy's thumb. The needle wound already shows signs of healing.

James is taken by a servant to a room on the first floor. When the servant leaves, the boy sits by the window looking out over the gardens in the square. Despite the hour there are still people about, still a to-ing and fro-ing of carriages. The watch comes – 'Past one of the clock. All well!' A fellow in a ragged coat scuttles across the square like a cockroach. James uses the chamber pot, then climbs into bed.

It is still dark out when he wakes, no sign of morning. His mouth and throat are dry as cloth. He does not know how long he has been asleep. He climbs out of the bed. There is a candle by his bed but nothing to light it with. He feels his way out of the room. The corridor is black except for a single arc of light from a half-open door. He pads towards it, hears from within a muttered singing. He peeps in; he has an excellent view. Mr Canning is sitting naked by the fire in his bedroom reading the *St James Chronicle*. The paper rustles, Canning turns the page and then, as if suddenly tiring of it, folds it briskly in two and drops it on the floor beside him. At first it seems a trick of the light. Canning, in spite of the cock curled between his thighs, has breasts. Not large or full, not beautiful, but undeniably breasts. Some movement of the boy betrays his presence, Canning looks out, eyes darting in a face of stone, then seeing who it is he smiles, as if to say, 'Had you not guessed? Surely you had guessed.'

9   In the middle of July there is a storm of hailstones, stones big as pigeon eggs, large enough to stun sheep, to kill them. For a week it is spoken of as an omen, then forgotten in the work of harvests. Mr Collins in his summer coat throws open the windows of the library; blue-bottles stumble in, zag the bookish air. James reads or dozes. He has made two more trips to London with Mr Canning and lost two more nails. Nothing is required of him now. The twins continue sickly: vomits in May, spotted fever in June. When, in August, they take the air

for the first time in weeks, leaning on Molina's arm, they appear from the library windows like two ancients out for a turn with their favourite nephew.

The season recovers them; they achieve a fragile vivacity. Soon, James's company is required on expeditions to collect wild flowers. When Molina comes he sketches them together and some of these he works up with oils: two girls and a boy, sat beneath trees, hazy in the smashed sunshine. Of all the pictures of James Dyer – the freak boy, the fashionable physician – these of Molina, little more than sketches in paint, the paint handled very freely, little by way of detail, these are to be preferred. The girls are shown with their tragedy intact; the boy sits up straight against a tree, his expression as unflinching as one of Mr Canning's statues. It is the face of a child assassin, an idiot king. Even a casual viewer is unsettled. They are in the presence of an enigma.

What prompts James to go, finally? Why one day rather than another? He is caught in something, the moist cogs of a vast machine. He does not know how to call it. There is light and hay-dust in his glands. His dreams are littered with dogs. The previous week he gazed for an hour at the dissected genitalia of a woman in a volume of anatomy, studying it like the map of a country he would shortly be travelling in. This morning he wakes, shrugs on his dressing-gown and goes straight to the girls' room, as though he has received a message from them, an invitation threaded secretly through the air from their room to his.

He finds them still in bed, sitting up, peeling boiled eggs. It is a week before their birthday, a fortnight before his own. Round their necks each wears a string of pearls, an early present from Mr Canning. They smile, and where he stands their smiles intersect. The girls put down their eggs, half peeled. Ann pulls back the covers. James climbs in, lies back, gazes at the canopy.

Later, he remembers how much giggling there was, how much

the girls seemed to know. And years later, riding in an open carriage in Bath, two young wives huddled on the seat opposite, he realises that the twins' knowledge could only have been the fruit of experience. With whom? Canning? Molina? Were they Molina's mistresses?

Between the giggles, odd concentrated silences. Whole minutes of hard physical work. Being joined, each of the twins feels the other's pleasure. Stroke one breast; both sisters sigh. How long does it last? Long enough to bore him. The girls pant like invalids, coo and chide him, grow momentarily fierce. He goes along, wishing the experience to be tidy, to have a proper end. After half an hour the string of Anna's pearls snap; the warm pearls run like quicksilver between their bodies, into the creases of the sheets. The girls squeal, kneel up, start to pick them, placing the pearls in their mouths as they find them. James watches them a while, scrabbling in the sheets, their mouths full of pearls. Then he puts on his gown, goes back to his room.

Another day. It is still dark. The fat man is sitting at James's bedside. He has a candle in his hand. He smells of rain and brandy.

'How is my marvellous boy?'

He reaches out a cold hand, touches the boy's cheek.

Says James: 'Is it today? For the twins?'

'Ay, today.'

'And I may watch it?'

'Why, of course you shall.'

'Will they die?'

'And what would you care if they do? But you are the one I'd like to cut. I'll wager there are secrets in you. What d'you say, boy – shall it be you? I could count on you to keep still. Keep your trap shut.'

The door opens, Mr Canning leans in. 'Bentley?'

'Ay, Canning. I'm with you.'

They leave.

The boy lies awake.

He enters Mr Canning's private operating theatre by a door high at the back of the room leading directly to the benches on the balcony above the operating table. Molina is with him, his drawing things beneath his arm. Canning has asked him to make a record. Molina looks unwell; his breath is tainted. When he takes the charcoal his hand is shaking.

Canning wears a satin coat, white and embroidered with silver roses, as if this were his wedding day. Beside Canning, several gentlemen from the society are already in their seats. They chatter excitedly, somewhat loud. Daylight slides in evenly from the skylight, and around the table, a bare wooden table such as kitchens have, with wooden blocks for the girls' heads, there are three tall candelabra and a servant with a trimmer to trim their wicks. Boxes of sawdust are tucked neatly beside the table.

The lower doors open. A quartet of musicians enter. They sit, fumble with their music and examine their instruments as though they have only recently discovered them. They play a few tentative notes then fall silent. Next comes Mr Bentley with his assistant, Mr Hampton, and Mr Hampton's assistant, the doorman Lute, who carries a large tray covered with a cloth. The gentlemen on the benches applaud. The operators bow, neatly and in time. Then Mr Bentley detaches himself, goes to the door, opens it and escorts the twins into the theatre. More applause. The twins are wearing a kind of shift, cut down the middle and tied with ribbons. The applause is louder. Mr Canning stands; the others follow. Molina starts to sketch at speed, charcoal hissing on the paper. The sketch looks like an attempt to hide something.

The twins look up at the balcony, the benches, the men leaning over with their chivalrous smiles, wigs newly dusted, fresh shirts, fine coats, barely one who has not had Canning's barber run over his face with a razor. The twins are dazed, squinting. Drugged, perhaps drunk. When their eyes reach James they hardly seem to recognise him. Bentley's hand is at Anna's elbow. Lute waits between the girls and the door as if to bar their way should they try to run. The gentlemen resume their seats. Canning makes a sign with his hand. Bentley nods, leads the girls to the table, helps them up, settles their heads on the wooden blocks. Lute draws two handkerchiefs from his fist like a conjurer and places one over each girl's face. The handkerchiefs rise and fall rapidly over the girls' mouths. The tray is uncovered; below the covering it is bright with knives. Bentley and Hampton pick them over as though they were thinking of buying one. Lute murmurs in a musician's ear. The violinist taps his foot and the theatre fills with a dainty overture from something popular in town. The operators take up their implements, the ribbons of the twins' shift are pulled undone. Bentley gropes at the girls' hips, finds his place and drives in his knife. The girls' bodies jerk up from the table. Lute and Hampton press down. The room is suddenly very warm. The girls do not scream, not until the fourth cut. Molina leans back with a groan; James leans forward. The screaming lasts about a minute, then there is a sudden access of blood, a red wash of it, tiding off the table. Lute kicks one of the boxes to catch it but kicks too hard so that the blood splashes off its side. Hampton is trying to collect the vessels Bentley has cut. He sees one, clamps it, starts to tie it but the blood is unrelenting. The musicians have lost each other; each plays what is left in his own head. Bentley's knife slips from his hand, clatters on to the floor. He swears and seizes another from the tray. His apron is sodden. James turns away to see Molina, slumped, ashen, vomit over his shoes.

The cloths over the girls' faces barely move now. Hampton is working furiously; his wig has slipped down by his right eye and when he pushes it back he leaves on it a scarlet handprint. Bentley steps away from the table, waves to the servant to bring him a glass. The servant pours the brandy carefully yet still spills it. He brings it on a little tray. Bentley downs it; goes back to his work. The twins are attached now only by some matter at the shoulder. Bentley leans with his big shoulders and sunders them. Hampton cannot keep up. He shouts, something utterly garbled, at Lute. Another wash of blood, this time caught in the box. Bentley to Hampton, pointing at the offending vessel: 'Pick it up, man! Pick it up.'

The oboist has left the room. The violinist and flautist play on, dreamily, quite separate now. The handkerchiefs no longer rise and fall. Bentley puts down his knife, looks around for a cloth to wipe his hands and, not discovering one, takes the handkerchief from Ann's face. The girl's face is turned towards her sister, mouth open, eyes ajar. There is not the slightest sign of life. Molina has gone. James takes the paper and charcoal, begins to draw. Hampton is crying, still fiddling with something, some artery. He says, as though speaking to the girls: 'Poo past! Poo bloody fast!' Canning stands, says quietly: 'Thank you, Bentley. I am sure that you did your best.' He walks out like a French king, his courtiers behind him. Bentley waves a hand dismissively. When next he looks up at the benches only James is there, finishing his sketch.

That night, stripped to the waist, washing, James finds on his skin minute fragments of eggshell. They are surprisingly hard to remove.

The musicians, altered men, stay on to play a dirge in the chapel at the twins' funeral. Mr Canning weeps copiously for ten minutes, looks stricken in the pew, then recovers, and is quite his old self at the party after, walking the length of the gallery arm in arm with Mr Bentley.

The girls are buried in separate coffins, a private graveyard of the estate. James is there, looking over the lip of the grave to see the coffins stacked. He wonders briefly which is which, if it is Ann or Anna on top. There is no way of knowing. It is cold for September; the mourners do not stay past the throwing of the first clod.

He does not see Molina until the following week when he comes upon him urinating into one of Mr Canning's amphora. The painter is drunk but not very.

'Well, my friend. All things must end. You, me, Canning. Even this fine house will be dust one day. For me, I prefer to leave my bones in a civilised country. English cruelty is like English games. I do not understand. I am going home. Goodbye, James. Get away from this place.'

James says: 'You said once you would show me the moon boy.'

Molina looks around, frowns incomprehension, then laughs as he remembers. 'You want to see?'

The boy nods.

'*Bueno, vamos . . .*'

Through the great salons, past the gilded mirrors, the tapestries, the looted idols; past enormous paintings, past elegant furniture . . . Now up the stairs, corridors, sudden windows, the disappearing back of a servant, the distant shutting of a door.

'In here,' says Molina. 'In this room.'

James looks back along the corridor, momentarily lost. He thought they had come to his own door. Now he realises that they have. Molina opens the door.

'Come, James. Do not be shy.'

He takes the boy's hand, not too gently, and pulls him into the room, over to the mirror.

'You have met before?'

Molina backs to the door. '*Adiós*, my friend. This is a dangerous place. *Peligroso*. Even for you.'

James stares. The moon boy stares back. Outside, a fine blue rain is falling. A servant with a bucket is tramping to the house by the lake.

11

A boy, twelve-months taller, steps out of the woods carrying in his arms the luminous globe of a puffball as though it were the head of an ogre he has slain. Behind him lollops a dog, a grey, three-legged mongrel. They are companions of sorts; the dog indiscriminately fond, the boy content to let it be with him, his awkward shadow. Now and then he throws a stick for it, amusing himself with its comical gallop, its enthusiasm. It serves him in other ways too. The previous spring it came to the house, left ear hanging on, hanging off, by a strand of purple flesh. With needle and thread and Mr Collins to hold it down, James sewed the ear back on, neatly if not quite straight. It was his first patient, and when the dog failed to pick up more wounds, James administered them himself, with knife or stick, such that the dog that runs past him now towards the topiary in the Italian gardens bears a dozen scars, some livid, some pale, but each more cunningly tailored than the last.

He follows it towards the garden, loses sight of it among the clipped green walls, hears its nervous bark build to a crescendo, then abruptly cease. He calls to it; it does not come. He enters the garden, sees the gardener's barrow half full of prunings, but no gardener and no dog, though the animal's three-pronged track is visible in the grass. The hedges glisten. A family of birds is flung suddenly upward, wheeling off towards the woods. A voice is singing, faintly, huskily, a servant perhaps, illicitly to his sweetheart. Then the voice speaks to him, addresses him by name, out of the heart of an evergreen globe.

'James! Over here.'

By burrowing near its southern pole, the globe may be entered. James crawls in. Gummer is sitting, pleased as punch beside the body of the dog.

For the moment James says nothing. He is looking at Gummer as though he has come across him floating in a jar of preserving fluid. And he *is* preserved, though there are grey hairs in his nose, and his teeth are another shade of brown and the skin looser at his neck. James feels as if he has dreamt this meeting in the green dripping gloom of the garden, even its details, such as the wide-bore short-barrelled pistol Gummer casually aims at his belly.

'When do we go?'

'Well spoken, boy! Soon as ever you like. May I trust you to fetch your accoutrements from the house? I think I may. And should you happen to pack some of Mr Canning's silver, why, 'tis only recompense, a paying back without the trouble of forcing the rogue to law; for you were my property, boy, and the bastard stole you. Some cheese while you're at it, and meat, and a bottle of good wine. I shall take up my station over the way such that I may see you come and go. Any surprises and you shall join poor Cerebus here.' He pats the carcass kindly. 'Comprendy vous? Damn, but I'm glad to see you, boy.'

James goes into the house, toys momentarily with the idea of alarming the servants to Gummer's presence, then swiftly packs the better part of his wardrobe. He goes to the library and helps himself to those of his favourites he can quickly lay hands on. From one of the galleries he takes four silver snuff-boxes, and from the kitchen where the cook snores in her seat toasting her feet by the fire, he helps himself to a pair of cold roast pigeons and a half-bottle of the cook's gin.

It is not hard to leave. He rides behind Gummer on Gummer's horse, rides south, his bag slung between them. Wherever possible they keep off the roads and out of villages. Now and then some rustic with a mattock over his shoulder, or a girl out berrying, gives them an enquiring look but mostly they are alone, observed only by the cattle, by sheep and by those creatures drawn to the light of their fire at night.

On their third day they ascend a winding lane between hedge-rows blue with fruit. Sea-birds balance overhead, then a hundred yards beyond the crest of the hill, the world ends and a salt wind throws off Gummer's hat and flicks it idly down in swoops to the sea.

They cross Southampton Water by the ferry and come in sight of Portsmouth in the last hour of daylight, the first of night. The water stays light longer than the land. Not even at Bristol has James seen such a congregation of ships, ships in the Pool, and a great mass of them, more than could be quickly counted, out by Spithead. Between the great ships all manner of smaller vessels – wherry boats, jolly boats, gigs – rowing to and fro, the voices of the sailors carrying clear as the cries of sea-birds. They ride down into the city. Everywhere the rolling walk of sailors, libertymen in bum-freezer jackets, all conversation at the bellow, and on their arms scruffy whores, loud as their men. James and Gummer ride under the lights of a recruiting inn. From its upper windows hangs a white flag with a red cross, big as a sail. Men in uniform, dark faces, bright assessing eyes, watch them pass. One calls: 'Ho there, lads . . .' and Gummer presses his heels into the horse's flanks, urges her on with a soft click of his tongue.

The house is in the back streets. The horse must pick its way through trash. Figures swish past them in the darkness.

'Here's home, boy – for now. Come meet your step-mama.'

Home, from the vague shadowing of its form, appears like the outhouse of a farm and may once have been so before the city swallowed it. Inside, however, there is a sense of rudimentary housekeeping. A fire growls in the hearth, there are pictures on the wall, china in the dresser, even two geraniums at the curtained window and, above them, a large, vicious-looking parrot, rocking edgily on its perch.

Grace Boylan stands at the door with a candle, a shawl over her hair. She glances at the boy, then searches over his shoulder for Gummer, reaching out to take his arm and lead him into the warm. She sits him on a chair, knocks up a glass of curdled milk and ale, and as he drinks it she strokes his cheek, coos and settles her bulk upon his knee.

Gummer drains his glass with a sigh, beams and says: 'I said I should fetch him. See how tall he has become. My, they must have been feeding him well.' He pushes the woman off his knees, winces and stands. 'First things first.'

He covers the space with remarkable agility, fetches the boy a clout on the side of his head. While James reels Grace fetches him another, then a third, sweetly weighted, sweetly timed. James goes down. They begin to kick him.

'Not the head!' cries Gummer. 'Not the head!'

They keep at it for five minutes, then flop in seats, wheezing. Boylan looks done up, bad as if they have been kicking her, yet peaceful, as if it has done her some good, brought her some peace.

James sprawls on the floor. He is not uncomfortable; it is only that he cannot find his breath. The ceiling pulses like a skin. The room is growing darker. He sees Gummer take off his shoes and warm his feet above the coals. 'Tomorrow, Gracie, we shall celebrate. Drink the town dry. What do you say to that?'

The parrot, like a decayed angel, swoops from its perch and settles on the back of Gummer's chair. 'Not the head!' it cries. 'Not the head! Not the head!'

When James wakes he is in bed, fully dressed. Opposite the bed is a small window. The day's grey beginnings ooze over the roof of the house across the way. He sits up, strips off his shirt and looks at the welts on his chest. Impressive. He slides from the bed, goes to the window. No parkland, no maze, no purple woods. In the street below, the cobbled gutter, a girl-child, one arm round the neck of a dog, squats and watches the golden rope of her water wind through the crevices between the stones. A man leans out of a window, rubs his face, looks up at the weather.

At the foot of the bed is a parcel. James sits on the bed and lifts it on to his lap. Old clothes, most quite useless now, too small, too ragged. He drops them on to the floor. Underneath is the box, its sides scratched, splintered in places. He opens it. Venus rolls about like a marble. The sun is dented. The moon leans drunkenly away from the Earth.

Patiently, he sets to work, restoring his universe.

In town, to the casual observer, the three of them are like a family. Gummer remarks on it; even Grace seems taken with her part, and when, in the tap-room of the Anchor, Israel England, pimp, points out the likenesses – father's hands, mother's nose – she turns to James and detonates in the region of his cheek a kiss of oysters and porter.

From the Anchor to the Sailor's Return, then to the Black Horse, the Queen Anne, the Star, the White Horse, the Grapes; back to the Black Horse; then roaring and skittish into the Lobster Pot, Gummer cracking his forehead on the lintel, but for the moment as insensitive to pain as the boy, the youth, the young man behind him.

Grace dabs with her handkerchief, orders gin and hot water. They drink as if they have not drunk in days. Only James sees what is happening, sees the hands held like playing cards hiding the men's mouths, hears the faint susurration of their plotting, knows without quite understanding it, the presence of danger. If he speaks now, will he save them? Does he care to? He looks over at Gummer. He was not sorry to see him in the bush, the sly grin, the quick, amused eyes. But Gummer has changed, or he himself has changed. What was it he liked about him? That Gummer recognised him when the others did not, or at least pretended they did not. For that there was a store of goodwill, a meagre store, all used up now. 'Down the hatch, Gracie!' says Gummer. A fellow in white ducks, hands tattooed with blue webs, goes out, looks along his shoulder at the boy as he passes. To meet those eyes is to become a confederate. James meets them; he says nothing.

The others finish their drinks and stagger out. It is dark now. Gummer dances, very freely, then, propped on the boy's shoulder, shouts: 'This is what you'll never know,' waving his arm to introduce the night. 'I pity you. Pity you. Christ!' He crashes on to his knees. Grace hauls him up, works him on to her back, clasps his arms about her neck, his head drooped on her shoulder, toecaps dragging on the ground behind. James looks around for the sailor, thinks he sees him in the shadow of a boarded chandler's shop; he and another.

Homeward now, James at the tail. Gummer sleeps serenely on the woman's back. The moon peeps out, gives the streets a black shine. Somewhere to the rear of them, the men are following. At the door of the house James glances back but the street is empty. Grace says: 'Help me with him.'

James takes the feet. The stairs are very narrow, very dark. Grace lights a candle at the fifth attempt. Gummer is on the bed, mouth slack, a peep of white between his lids. Grace pinches his cheek. He wakes, sits up and sings: 'Bring forth in Sabine jar the wine four winters old, O Tally-arkus . . .' Then falls back, smiling, deeply asleep. To James, Grace says: 'Bolt the door.'

James goes down. There is still a little of the fire left. He finds a stub of candle on the shelf, lights it from the embers. He opens the front door, two inches, and goes upstairs to pack his bag. The orrery he wraps in his velvet coat, buries it deep in the bag, then carries the bag down to wait by the fire. It is a short enough wait. There is a noise, soft, like the nosing of a dog in garbage. He goes to the door. The man is standing there grinning, a cosh in his hand. He puts a finger to his lips. James points upward.

To one behind him, a huge Chinese, the sailor says: 'Stay here, Ling-ling. Look after our new shipmate. Warren, Kinnear. With me.'

As they go on the stairs James sees that their feet are bare. The Chinaman puts things in his pocket. It does not look like stealing. James, who gave only three of Canning's snuff-boxes to Gummer, gives the fourth to Ling-ling. The Chinaman takes it, strokes the top with his finger. He says: 'They call me Ling-ling, like bell. My name Easter Smith. My old name Li Chian Wu.'

From the ceiling, a mighty thud, as if someone has picked up the bed and flung it down. One of the seamen, Warren or Kinnear, staggers down the stairs, spitting teeth. From above, Grace Boylan screams: 'Murder! Murder!' Ling-ling goes up. Thuds, oaths, the sound of something large and empty smashing. A sudden hush, then Ling-ling with Gummer in his arms and behind Ling-ling the other sailors and then Grace Boylan, descending on hands and knees.

'Oh mercy,' she cries, gulping a great sob out of her heart. 'He's sick, can't you see? Sick. Some awful catching sickness. Green shit. You'll all be dead by Monday.'

Says the sailor with tattoos: 'I know his sickness, Mother. Good sea air will set him up. Cast off, lads!'

She rears; he whacks her with the jack, once, and once for luck.

Then they stream out into the night. Passers-by shrink back from them; an old woman shakes her fist. Left, left again; Gummer, still in Ling-ling's arms, limps as a doll, murmurs but does not struggle. They emerge on to the docks. Beside a bollard, a man in a blue coat, a hanger at his side, watches them come. He calls: 'Anything likely, Hubbard?'

'Couple o' landsmen, sir. The young 'un come willing.'

The officer peers into James's face. 'You volunteer?'

'Yes.'

The officer takes a coin from his pocket and gives it to James. 'Welcome to King George's Navy. Ship them aboard the tender. Tell Mr Tedder to enter this one in the books as volunteer. Sharply now!'

They set out over the water. The oars creak in the rowlocks; the men talk lingo. They are hailed from other ships:

'What are you there!'

'Aquilons!'

How tall the wooden walls of ships are! Some of the men-of-war have their guns run out and from the gun-ports comes light, music, a hubbub of voices. Gummer, curled tight, shivers in the bottom of the boat. James rests his feet on him, hugs his bag to his chest, tastes the salt breeze. A lantern shows from a ship dead ahead, a voice rings out – 'Ahoy there!' – and Ling-ling, Easter Smith, Li Chian Wu, pulling at his oar, whispers: 'This home now.'

Kingswear, 10 January 1773
Rev Dvd Fisher to Rev Jls Lestrade
Sir,

*Mr Buller at the Admiralty informs me that you are desirous
of knowing something of the sea career of James Dyer whom I
understand to have been your particular friend. Knowing that I
sailed upon the* Aquilon *as Chaplain throughout much of the '50s
Mr Buller suggests I might furnish you with some recollections
which – craving your indulgence for the distortions of memory
occasioned by the passing of some twenty years – I shall now
endeavour to do. It may also be in my power to provide you with
the names of other former 'Aquilons', in particular Mr Munro,
for whom I believe I have an old address in Bath which may yet
find him.*

*In order that I may situate myself in this narrative, let me
say only that I came aboard the* Aquilon *in the spring of '53
having finished at the University – I was a New College man
– the previous year. I had had hopes of a living at Mere but this
falling to another I did not care to take some poor curacy and
so petitioned an Uncle, then Captain of the* Furious, *to obtain
a posting for me.*

*I knew then as little of the sea and of life upon a Man of War
as any Englishman may, and had I known of the hardships, the
tedium and discomfort of such a life I doubt I should ever have
set foot up the gangplank, and thus have missed those youthful
adventures which I fear I have grown too fond of relating, much
to the exasperation of my poor wife – Mrs Nancy Fisher née*

Arbott of the Exeter Arbotts – you may know of the family –
But as a man gets older he likes to look back upon those times in
his life when he was among the doing part of the world and did
not take his knowledge of it entire out of a newspaper.

To come to the point, I sailed with Captain Reynolds – of
whose character I shall say more anon – first to Gibraltar and
thence to Port Mahon, and from there to Saint Lucia in the
West Indies where I suffered with the black vomit, and but for
Mr Munro's ministrations would I believe have ended my days
off that unwholesome coast, as indeed did some score of the ship's
company.

We returned to Portsmouth in the summer of '54 where I left
the ship to try my fortune upon terra firma, *but finding myself*
no better off than before, I engaged again with Captain Reynolds
and was but newly reinstated when I first set eyes upon James
Dyer, which is to say I must have clapped eyes upon him then,
for that is when the new people came aboard. I cannot, however,
remember noticing him then, or indeed any of them in particular,
apart from a fellow called Dabb who ran mad and leapt over
the taffrail and was seen no more. As you know, Sir, it is the
sad and iniquitous business of the Navy to provide for itself
largely out of pressed men and you never did see such naked
misery as upon the faces of those wretches when first they
are brought aboard and surrounded by a world as strange to
them as might be the moon. If, Reverend, you have not had
the honour to walk the deck of one of His Majesty's ships I
fear it is very hard for you to comprehend the world your
friend had come to. The seamen themselves – in their looks,
their language and their character – are quite unlike their
earthbound cousins. One's ears are constantly assailed by talk
of futtock shrouds and gantlines, halliards, topgallants, spars,
capstans and I know not what. And, Sir, it is such a very nice
world, so very particular and jealous of its customs – who may

walk the Quarter Deck and who may not – who is accounted a gentleman and who is not – that nothing is more easy than unwittingly to give offence.

I of course was an 'idler', like the schoolmaster – there were always several young children aboard – and such as the purser, the carpenter, the surgeon and his mates; that is, all those who did not stand watch. There were a number of advantages in this, not the least of which was that we might enjoy, under most circumstances, an uninterrupted night of sleep, while no seaman ever slept for more than four hours at a stretch, and even this meagre portion was at the mercy of the weather. Such would have been the fate of your friend – crammed into fetid quarters between decks, hammock slung side by side with his greasy shipmates, everything too hot or too cold, everything regulated by whistles and oaths and the rope's end – for the Boatswain and his mates rarely gave an order but it was accompanied by a lash – and this on a ship accounted very moderate in the severity of its discipline.

Now, Sir, I fear you will be growing impatient to know when I did first notice James Dyer. I have been asking myself the same question while here at my desk, and have but two minutes since been rewarded with a true memory, quite as if it had been preserved in amber.

We were in the Bay of Biscay and I was taking my regular morning turn with Mr Shatt the schoolmaster when he pointed Dyer out and said that Mr Drake – a very amiable officer, somewhat aged for a midshipman – had remarked on the boy's coolness and how he had seen him walking upright along the yards as if he had been at it twenty years. When I looked I saw a young person aged about fourteen or fifteen, dressed in canvas frock and baggy breeches, well formed, handsome, though with a rather grave expression, indeed, if I may say without offending your memory of him, a somewhat supercilious expression, and this, I doubt not, helped give rise to the rumour that he was well-born. *Other evidences seemed to bear this out. For example, he had with him when he came aboard a bag of clothes containing some fine coats and waistcoats etc. and also a boxed orrery, which Mr Munro prevailed upon the boy to show to him. Besides these proofs – suggestive rather than conclusive – there was a persistent whisper that one of the pressed men, an older fellow, name of Gunner, who had come aboard at the same time, was, or had been, Dyer's manservant. How such stories start I cannot say. I used to think they were like Herodotus's bees, self-propagating, and of course, once they exist, they very shortly swarm over the whole ship. Gunner, as far as I know, denied any such connection.*

At first I imagined how these intimations of gentility would do James Dyer no service at all among the common seamen, and yet, whether out of a natural deference to one born better than themselves, or whether on account of his great coolness, he became quite a favourite with them – which is to say they respected him, though I do not think any loved him.

Now, Sir, Mr Dnl Tusker, my Rhetoric master at Grammar school, begged me never make a general statement without then furnishing some particular instance by which its truth may be demonstrated. Let me do so then in the matter of this coolness – or bottom or bottle or neck or whatever we shall choose to call it. I dare say you saw several examples of it yourself. I have mentioned his walking out on the yard-arms – this in all weathers. Then there was the fact that he was utterly uncowed by Mr Cladingbowl the Boatswain, who was a very considerable bully and a great supporter of 'starting', a noxious custom of unofficial beating towards which the senior officers turned a blind eye. Dyer, for sundry offences real or imagined, was beaten very fiercely by Cladingbowl and also by his mates Dominic and Muddit, such that on one occasion Mr Munro was summoned to attend and found the boy greatly marked upon the back and haunches for which Dominic and Muddit spent a week in Irons, though

Cladingbowl scaped his just deserts until Minorca, where he took a canister of grape full-on and all but evaporated.

What amazed Mr Munro upon this occasion was that the boy, though stunned, shewed no evidence of the suffering that must be consequent upon such a thrashing; and what amazed him further, what amazed us all, was the speed with which the welts on his back disappeared, for he was not, I think, in the sick-bay above a single day before he declared himself fit for his duties.

Another particular that I should like to give I fear I may not in good conscience, for I was not a witness to any part of it and heard it second-hand only from Lt Williams of the Marines. It concerns an attack on the settlement of Baracoa in the island of Cuba in which your friend played a notable part. I cannot ask Lt Williams to recount it for you as the fellow was so unhappy as to succumb to the bloody flux, but Mr Drake who lives in Brixham may be prevailed upon.

It was shortly after the raid on Baracoa that James Dyer was taken on, at Mr Munro's request, as his Loblolly boy, that is, as a kind of assistant to himself and his mate, Mr O'Brien. This freed the boy from the rigours of the Watch and enabled him to remove his mess to the cockpit, which, despite the gloom there – it is in the very bowels of the ship – and the stink from the purser's office hard by, must have been a veritable palace by comparison to his old quarters. It also had the happy effect of placing him beyond the tyranny of Cladingbowl and this no doubt had been part of Munro's purpose in requesting him, for Mr Munro, in spite of some weaknesses common enough at sea, was a very considerate gentleman.

It transpired soon enough that the surgeon would have no reason to regret his decision, at least as far as the question of the young man's competence was concerned. He very shortly shewed himself the equal of his work, and what he did not already seem to know he learnt without effort and became so proficient as to excite the resentment of Mr O'Brien. So much were Mr Munro and your friend in each other's company that I am sorry to record they became the butt of an ugly and infamous story, put about in the first instance by Mr O'Brien but then gaining general currency. I should not mention this, Sir, and risk offending you with ancient tattle, were there not certain repercussions that make the relation of even so unsavoury an episode pertinent.

To my dismay, Munro did little to protect either his own name or that of your friend, and indeed, gave every evidence of being besotted with the boy. I cannot well explain his reluctance to act, other than to suggest that his sense of outrage had been dulled by his consumption of Laudanum which he confessed to me he took at one thousand drops a day, quite sufficient to destroy one less habituated to the drug. Rum he also took in considerable measures, partly on account of the condition of his teeth, which were very rotten and only rendered bearable by regular swilling with the spirit. Poor man, he was never quite happy, and the presence of his young assistant was such an evident boon to him it seemed quite callous to prise them apart. Notwithstanding this I determined to speak with young Dyer and stress the necessity of confronting these calumnies. I spoke with a certain frankness and proposed that he should be less in the surgeon's company. He did not at first appear to understand what I was saying and when I made myself more plain he only smiled and rebuked my impertinence in the strongest language and indeed, Sir, quite made me fear for my safety, though I am not a small nor a cowardly man.

As for Mr O'Brien, he did at length succeed in provoking the boy, and did not, I am sure, understand what a dangerous enemy he had made. I believe I may trust to your knowledge of your friend's temperament to bear this out and think you will not be surprised to hear that O'Brien shortly came to grief. He was beaten, severely beaten, while on shore leave at Colombo. No one witnessed the encounter and O'Brien never said more than that

156

he had been attacked while cutting back to the quay through some narrow streets. However, it was generally accepted as being the work, directly or indirectly, of James Dyer. As for O'Brien, he was out of his wits for a week, so that when we next touched at Portsmouth he discharged himself and was not heard of again. There were no reprisals of an official nature. It is as Captain Reynolds has it – 'The navy is no profession for milksops.'

Being now without a mate, Mr Munro petitioned Surgeon's Hall to examine James Dyer to be O'Brien's replacement, and by virtue of Munro's influence with some members of the Board your friend had an early opportunity to shew his talents, travelling from Portsmouth to London in the company of his mentor and going before the Board the following day. I do not remember the precise result of the examination and yet it was sufficient for him to obtain a Warrant and I hazard he was one of the youngest ever to have obtained such a post, though let it be said that in the Navy a man – or boy – whose star is bright may rise more quickly than in almost any other profession you may think of, some having been made Captains before they are twenty, Admirals before they are thirty.

Now, Sir, I must come to that event which will I think be of most interest to you. It is an event that shall remain at an instant's recall to my dying day. Indeed it figures largely still in the collective memory of the nation. Yet there is one matter, a curious business, I should like to relate beforehand and which I should have mentioned earlier except that other relations forced it from my mind. It concerns James Dyer's putative servant – Gunner – and occurred some two months after they came aboard at Portsmouth. The body of a woman was discovered in the bread-room, sewn into a hammock, a large woman, somewhat gone and very necessary to be buried before she rendered the bread unfit for consumption. An investigation revealed her to be Gunner's 'wife' – it was not so uncommon for men secretly to carry their women to sea – though her own name at such a distance I cannot remember. I was called upon to read the burial service, and the body, with a 32 lb shot at her feet, was consigned to the deep by Gunner himself and two other men while we were some degrees south of the Azores. Gunner was very struck by it, calling the deceased his 'Lamb', which was remarkable when you consider we could but barely pass the woman's corpse through the gun-port and that her form, wrapped in the canvas, plunged beneath the surface of the sea like a White Shark I saw by Botany Bay. There is truly no accounting for the way in which men place their affections. I dare say not every man finds Mrs Fisher quite the form of female perfection I do.

You will not need reminding, Sir, of those events in the spring of 1756 when the French, under the Marquis de la Galissonière and the Duc de Richelieu, landed at Minorca and drove our garrison back into Fort St Phillip, blockading the island and laying siege to the fort. Aquilon was one of the ships dispatched with Sir John Byng to the Mediterranean, arriving off Minorca on the nineteenth day of May. We were subsequently ordered forward to attempt a communication with the fort, but were frustrated by the appearance of the main French fleet to the south-east of us. Though I had been at sea some years and had been present at numerous chases and small engagements, I had never seen so many enemy ships together and the sight of them set up a clamour in my heart such as I have never experienced either before or since. Our own fleet of thirteen doughty Men of War formed up on a line to intercept the enemy, but the wind dropped off and darkness came before we could engage, and we were forced to spend a sleepless night full of the most tense anticipation. Some of the people asked me to write letters to their loved ones, fare-ye-wells, which I did, sat in the waist, writing by starlight from the sailors' dictation, and several of these fond missives it was my melancholy duty to send home from Gibraltar after the battle. About four of the clock I went down to my quarters to eat a little salt pork from my private store and was distressed to see Mr Munro slumped against the door of his dispensary with a bottle of liquor in his lap. I attempted to rouse him, failed, and called James Dyer to help me shift the surgeon to his cot. Your friend was in his hammock and not at all pleased to be roused — I do honestly believe he was the only man on the ship to be sleeping then — and told me very plainly to go to the D——. In the end I moved the surgeon with the help of Mr Hodges the purser, and then went back on deck, for I could not abide to be below at such a time.

The morning found us wrapped in mist and I could but very faintly discern the masts of Intrepid ahead of us, but the sun ate up the mist, and the French fleet were spied twelve miles to the south and east of us. The signal gun sounded, and our ships, which had become somewhat scattered during the night, came back into the line and we tacked towards the enemy in two divisions, one led by Admiral Byng and the other, which included Aquilon, under the command of Rear Admiral West.

I was ordered below more than once but could not for an hour tear myself away from the spectacle of the enemy, now very clear to us, almost abreast on a port tack, their cannon run out, and small figures quite visible upon the decks.

At length I was prevailed upon by Mr Drake, and travelled down through the decks where the gun-crews crouched by their pieces. I recall Lt Whitney bowling into me and knocking me quite off my feet and then using the most shocking language before he realised who I was, after which he begged my pardon and had me escorted by a vast Chinee sailor down on to the orlop deck.

You may imagine my dismay when Mr Hodges informed me that the surgeon was still in his cot. I went there directly and saw at once that the case was hopeless. Though I was angered by this display of negligence, I was also afraid for him, for had it reached the ears of Captain Reynolds it might very well have come to a court-martial. I said – 'What is to be done, Mr Hodges?' – James Dyer answered – 'It is already done' – words to that effect. He was wearing Mr Munro's operating apron and stood beside an operating table of sea-chests spread over with a sheet of sailcloth. He had his instruments – Munro's instruments – all about him, and had the air of a man about to sit down to a good dinner. I said – 'Sure you do not mean to manage alone, James?' – To which he replied that he did not, and was pressing me into service as his assistant. I did not like this idea at all but Mr Hodges seemed to think it a good one and offered his own services as a dresser so gamely that I felt it impractical to decline.

I put on an old jacket out of the slops and then joined the others at cards, though how I played I do not know for I longed to go above and see how we stood with the French. Shortly before three in the afternoon we felt the ship go about. Mr Hodges, who had been at sea some twenty years, nodded his head saying we would shortly be at it and would I say a prayer for our success and protection. I said something, I could not repeat it now to save my life, a rather rambling prayer to be sure, but the others in the cockpit – two women, two young children, Mr Shatt, and Stoker, a syphylitic case two poorly to fight – bowed their heads. All, I am sorry to say, except Dyer. My 'Amen' was lost in the sound of gunfire, not ours but the enemy's, and I felt the poor old Aquilon shudder in the water as she took its force.

This, as I was able to establish after, was the first of the broadsides to rake Admiral West's squadron as we bore down on to the French line. Two more followed at intervals of four or five minutes before we felt the ship once again alter course. 'Now' – cried Mr Hodges, jumping up in the midst of dressing a man's hand and suddenly very martial – 'Now we shall bloody their noses!' – He was a true oracle, for the words were barely out of his mouth when our guns fired. Lord, Sir, and how they kept it up! The lanterns dimmed and brightened as the concussion from the decks above sucked the air from the orlop deck, and after each broadside there was a mighty roaring of the gun-carriages and a general thunder of feet racing to the magazines and the shot-lockers.

I lost all sense of the passage of time. I remember my mouth was very dry. I shall not pretend I was not afraid. I could not understand how the ship could endure such punishment, how there could possibly be anyone alive upon the upper decks. Indeed, many were not and there was a steady flow of wounded men brought down into the cockpit, some screaming, some in a swoon, some bearing their lacerations with the most exemplary fortitude. Pretty soon it became difficult to walk there for the numbers of poor wretches who lay about on the boards. Always a cry of 'Surgeon!' and very many, even among the elder men, called for their mothers.

In the midst of this was James Dyer. Never for an instant did his concentration waver, never did he pause to rest or wipe his brow or drink. We brought the worst cases to him – dangling arms, crushed legs, gaping bellies – and he cut and sewed and pushed men's innards back into their natural cavities. I swear to you, Sir, he took pleasure in it, this demonstration of his genius, and I cannot believe any man ever cut human flesh with a cooler head or a steadier hand, certainly not while the world itself was shaking so.

At some moment I became aware of a commotion behind me and saw Mr Drake was there shouting that the Captain was hurt and demanding that the surgeon go up to attend to him. Mr Munro of course was in no case to attend to himself, still less the Captain, so it fell to your friend. I intended to go on with the men in the cockpit but Mr Drake said that my services might also *be needed and thus I found myself going up through the ship at Dyer's heels.*

The gun-decks were all billows of grey smoke. Each gun, the enemy's and our own, firing quick as they could be brought to bear, the pieces growing so hot they were skittish as colts, leaping high and recoiling with truly frightful force.

In several places we were forced to step over the bodies of dead men, ay, and dead boys – for I recall very well seeing the face of poor William Oaks, whose tenth birthday had fallen on the day prior to the battle. I could not see how he had been killed for there was no mark on him more than a small bruise above his eye.

On the upper deck the carnage was even greater, and as we made our way to the Quarter Deck the blood splashed on to our stockings. There was such a whistling of ordnance I firmly believed I should never get below again, that my hour was come, for it did not seem possible that a human being could survive in such murderous air. Indeed, I had the unreasoning conviction that the entire French Navy had set their honour upon destroying me, though I have since discovered that this is a by no means unusual conviction for men in battle. It is certainly an unpleasant one, for somehow, while waiting for the bullet's impact, one must endeavour to comport oneself like a gentleman, that is, you cannot hide or crawl on your belly, most particularly when you are in the company of a fellow who walks through the Valley of the Shadow as though it were Ranelagh Gardens.

Poor Captain Reynolds lay in Mr Drake's arms beside a huddle of dead marines. His left leg was entirely off and Mr Drake said he thought it must have gone over the side for he could not find it anywhere. The Captain asked where Mr Munro was. I said he was engaged below. The Captain then smiled and said he was happy to see Mr Dyer for he was sure he knew what he was about. He said – 'Shall I live?' – Dyer answered that he would as the limb had come off neatly and there was not much stuff in the wound. The Captain thanked him, and we were on the point of getting him below when an enemy ball struck the mizzen mast, spraying the Quarter Deck with splinters, one of which struck me in the eye.

Beyond that point I can tell you very little. I thought at first I was killed and yet somehow I got below, as did Captain Reynolds who, as Dyer prophesied, survived the battle and retired as a Yellow Flag Admiral. For the battle itself, well, Sir, you know how that fell out, and the consequences for poor Admiral Byng. The Enemy broke off the action and fell away to leeward, that they might reform their line out of range of our guns. They were faster than us and there was no signal from the Admiral to chase. In truth, our ships were badly mauled, and though, with an Anson or a Hawke, we should no doubt have pressed on, at the time we were glad enough of a respite. Certainly no one may accuse the English sailors of wanting the stomach for a fight. They are endlessly brave. I do not believe they ever think of being killed. They live only in the instant. The future is nothing to them.

I left the ship at Gibraltar, together with the Captain and those of the crew too poorly to face the rigours of the homeward passage. The last occasion on which I saw your friend was when I was carried past the dispensary and happened to look in with my one good eye and see him there apparently dissecting a human hand. But as I was somewhat feverish, I may have been mistaken. Yet, now I think of it, that was not quite the last time, for I saw him once in London, near Temple Bar, almost two years later, walking with an older gentleman, somewhat gross, whom Mrs Fisher assured me was one of the famous Hunter brothers.

Well, Sir, I trust I have been able to satisfy your curiosity. Your friend was a very remarkable person and I was not at all surprised to read of him going to Russia to inoculate the Empress. I should be interested to know how he fared for I do not think I heard of him after. If you are ever in this part of the county pray be so good as to call on us. We live very quietly but there is good sport on the river. I am, Sir, Your Most Humble Servant,

David Fisher

Solomon Drake to Reverend Lestrade
April 1774 at Brixham

Sir,

Rev Fisher asks that I rite you conserning James Dyur of the Aquilon *and that you have an interest in that genlemans time at sea, particully the rade at Cuba. I understand Rev Fisher has told you the rest of it.*

The place we rayded was called Baracoo and the short of it is we went to keep our people sharp and see what might be had of any use or value to us. We rowed in in four boats with Leftenant Whitney commanding and strict orders to keep are tongs still in are heads that the enemy might not be alurted. I commanded the third boat − Benson MacNamara Johnson Dyur Gummer Parks Austin O Conner Lower and the chinee Arthur Easter − all with cutlasses axes pistols or clubs acording to there fancy.

An ower before first light we came into a small baye and could see the town very faintly at the end. The place was quite as the grave cepting a dog that got wind of us and set up barking. We landed at the darkest part of the key by some steps an under the lee of a tobackoo wherehouse.

Leftenant Whitney led the first party out to look for the Mayors house and my party followed incase there was a garryson. For five minutes we had the place to ourselfs then a bell rung out from one of the churches and mery Hell broke loose. Had they nown we were a party of no more than thurty-five souls we might have had are work cut out but they thort we were a thousand come to murther them in there beds. The town was empty in side of an ower. Then are people began to go into the houses and leftenant Whitney dare not say ort nowing there temper an how they wood sooner put a bullet threw him than stop there fun.

In an out of the houses they went like bees at there hives. Anything of value they took but best they liked the fine close particulally the laydes close and when they could not carry more they pulled them on and ran about like women out of Bedlam. Sir I ashore you it was the strangest site in the world.

Now the cubans came back in to fight, some on whorses, others on foot. I saw them kill Able Seaman Parks, but are men, encumburred as they were by there booty, gave the enemy good service. We were in the plaza mayor which is the mane sqare of the town. I had taken down some fine felow from off his whorse an thinking such a fine whorse would be a grand presant for my late wife could I but get it home when I saw James Dyur standing in the sqare loading a pistol quite an careful as if he had been in a room alown. One of there soldery, a lad about the same age as Dyur, was stood twenty feet away loading his musket like fury an when he has it done he snatches it to his sholder an fires an misses. Well he was not a cowardly cur this cuban like most of them are for he has a wicked bayonto long as his arm an he ran at Dyur yelling at the top of his voyce. Blow me if Dyur dont then rase his pistol an hold his aim until the cuban lad is all most upon him. I think that cuban thort he had done it for his bayoneto was a hands bredth from Dyurs westcot. Well if so that thort was his last for Dyur put a ball threw the fellows brayn-pan and so made an end of him. It was the most complete thing of its kind I have ever seen. Yet what was stranger still an made me wander what manner of young man this Dyur was was that he did not look at the lad he had killed. In my experiance a man always looks at the man he has killed but James Dyur walked away as if the memory had erazed like chalk off a slayte.

We fort are way back to the boats and cast off. The cubans turned some guns on us but then Aquilon came up and made it hot for them. We went on bord with only Parks dead and some wounded inclewding Leftenant Whitney who had lost a finger and a thumb. You wood have shaken your head Sir to have seen the men go up the side in their mantua an lace all bloody an unshaven. I still think of it sometimes an shake my own head. That was the rade at Baracoo.

I do not know what else I may tell you except I sometimes thort James Dyur encouraged Mr Munros love of hard licker. Mr Munro left the ship in 56 and Dyur was surgen an in fareness a very safe one thow kept himself to himself. He left the ship in 58. I askt him where he was headed and he answered to finer things what you could dream of Mister Drake an made the money sine. He went very quite in the jolly boat one night. I think his old servant Gummer went with him for we never saw him more.

I hope this letter is what you expeckted and I hope you will forgive my ruff stile. I went to sea at nine years of age and a Man of War was my universaty. I am Your Obediant Servent

Sol. Drake

14 *Mrs Robert Munro to Reverend Lestrade*

Bath, June 1774

Sir – No name is more repugnant to me than that of James Dyer. If you say he is deceased then I rejoice for he killed my husband sure as if he had murthered him with his own hands. My husband was a good man whose only folly was to be too fond and trusting of one who deserved neither. And though my husband took his own life I am sure he is in Heaven and I am sure James Dyer is in Hell. Pray never write to me of him again for I could never entertain a correspondence with one who called him friend. I am respectfully,

Agnes Munro. Widow.

15 The outside passengers slither down from the top of the machine, their coats sodden with the rain that has pummelled them since they came through the village of Box. They stand in the yard while servants from the inn haul their trunks from the basket at the back of the coach. The coachman opens the door.

'Bath!'

The inside passengers descend, six in all, pulling on their hats, frowning at the sky. Most have been drowsing and have the pale, crumpled faces of recent sleepers. Only one looks indifferent to the rain, unmolested by the long haul from London. He steps lightly over a puddle and speaks with an older man, one of the outside passengers. The man nods as if he has received his instructions.

The landlord, tenting a cloak over his head, bids the travellers enter, and they squelch behind him into the inn. There is a smell of roasting meat, of damp clothes and damp dogs. James orders a room. One, two nights, not longer. A girl shows him up, holds open the door, holds herself against the door as he enters. He looks round at her. She raises her eyebrows; silently offers.

'How much?'

She says: 'Five shillings. In advance. Nothing fancy or unchristian.'

He looks at her. The neck of her dress is absurdly low. On her right breast the half-moon of a cicatrix peeps from her tucker.

He touches it. 'What was this?'

'A hard bit, sir, that the surgeon cut out before Christmas.'

He presses her breast around the wound. The girl pulls his hand away. She looks rattled, as if his touch has disturbed an old nightmare.

'In advance, I said.'

He has found two more lumps. She pushes him away and steps back into the passageway. In the grey rainlight of the passage she is already half ghost, and in a ghost's voice she says: 'Five shillings.'

James shakes his head: 'I would not give sixpence for you. Have a fire made up. When a man called Gummer comes in, send him to me.'

It is long after dark when Gummer, peevish and half cut, returns.

James says: 'You found him?'

Gummer walks to the fire. 'I have always loathed this place,' he says. 'Founded by a swineherd, they say. I believe it.'

168

'I asked if you had found Munro. Be so civil as to answer.'

Gummer spins round from the fire. His look is very straight, cool, murderous. He says: 'You'll go too far with this.'

'There are no children here for you to terrify, Mr Gummer.'

'I mean it,' says Gummer. 'You and your airs! You forget, mister, that I know exactly where you come from.'

'You are more drunk than I thought. I suggest you get into the bed. What is it you are mumbling now?'

'I was saying – you pup – that there will come a day. By God, Grace was right about you.'

'When you bark like this, sir,' says James, 'you put me in mind of an old dog that has long since lost its teeth and sits all day in its own stink waiting for someone to do it the kindness of clubbing its brains out. Old men should not threaten. Did you see Munro?'

'I found his house.' There is no more fight in Gummer's voice. He is staring at the flames.

'And you delivered the note?'

'Yes.'

'Then we shall call on our old shipmate tomorrow morning.'

The fire is out. Gummer snores in the bed. James sits at the table, pulls open a purse, pours the coins into his hand, sorts the gold and silver into neat piles. A little under twenty-five pounds. A man might easily live two or three months together on such a sum, were he content to live quietly, to eat in chop-houses, stay away from the cards and have a fire only in the evenings. James has no such intentions. That life is behind him in London – his student lodgings in Duke Street at three and six a week (landlady: Mrs Milk, a widow and clergyman's daughter); tramping to St George's hospital in the hope of seeing John Hunter operate, or over the new bridge at Westminster to St Thomas' to trail behind Dr Fothergill on his rounds. Sitting in Batson's coffee house in winter for the sake of a good fire and always having to watch every shilling he spent. Enough of that.

He slides the money back into the purse, drops the purse into his pocket, strips off his coat and waistcoat and shoes and lies down on the bed. Gummer snorts, gasps something unintelligible. James blows out the candle. The rain has started again.

 'Oh, dear boy! Dearest James! Well met indeed! You cannot know how often I have thought of you since our sea days. Our salad days! Come now, come and meet Mrs Munro. She has been all agog to meet the famous James Dyer.'

'Hardly famous yet, sir.'

'Time will see to that, James. We both know it. And this fellow I think I know. The name escapes me now.'

'Mr Marley Gummer, sir. Yours to command.'

'Gummer, eh? It comes back to me now, somewhat. Well, I am sure you are welcome also. Mind the pooch there, Mr Gummer. One of Mrs Munro's. Say hello to my old comrades, Chowder.'

The dog darts at Gummer's leg, humps his stocking.

'Affectionate little devil . . . Here they are, my dear. Pipe them aboard. Ha ha. Damn.' Munro trips over the end of the settle, staggers, clutches at a sideboard and pulls it over, sending glasses and bottles of Bristol blue-glass cascading to the floor. Everything smashes. The four of them look down at the debris, then James looks up at Mrs Munro. There is a red flush on her cheeks. She is young, mid-twenties, a face that verges upon handsome. Her eyes say: See what I am wed to? See what I must suffer? She looks over at her husband.

'Why, Robert, I declare you are more of an ox every day. He has been in a lather to see you Mr Dyer. I swear I have never seen him so pleased to see anyone.'

'No more than I am to see your husband, madam. He was a most considerate teacher when we were at sea. I am greatly pleased at the prospect of working with him once more.'

She darts a look at her husband. 'You are taking on a partner, Robert?'

Munro looks back at his wife, then at James. 'A partner?'

'Why, Robert, that is what I have often said you should do.'

James bows, says: 'I am sure that you count half the town among your patients, sir.'

'Half the town! Ha! No, my boy, we go on very quietly but we live. Don't we live, Agnes?'

'We have meat on the table, indeed, though I sometimes think you are too easily satisfied.'

'Wives, sir! One has to be a duke to afford to marry these days. You cannot satisfy them with less than a thousand per annum. It is a cold morning. Let us have a pint or so of mulled wine, some biscuits, and then I must be off to Mr Leavis. Took a tumble last night coming home from a ball at Simpson's rooms. Fractured femur.'

'You must take Mr Dyer with you, my dear. To keep you in good heart. Is there not a great deal of pulling in these cases? I am sure he may assist you in that.'

'He may, he may. Where are you lodged, James? You must send Gummer round for your trunk. No, no, I shall hear no dissent. Mrs Munro will be grateful for the company of a being more her own age. Now then, where is that blasted wine?'

Agnes Munro hints at it; James sees it with his own eyes: the slow foundering of the practice which, upon Munro's arrival in Bath, full of the energy of a man newly married and determined to reform his character, had seemed so promising, and had indeed, during that first season, succeeded beyond all expectation. And when he is sober he is still competent, even the occasional gleam of something more, but those who call for him now do so more out of loyalty, out of a liking for the man, than from any great faith in his abilities. He is courteous, old-world, sitting at the bedside of some tediously dying single lady, stilling the fluttering of her hands, knowing all the while that she cannot pay her bills. He will bleed old men and their wives then drink with them half the afternoon, discussing politics and chiding in the gentlest vein the follies of the young people, though now he will turn to his new assistant, nod and say: 'Present company excepted,' and the old people crinkle their eyes and beam beneficence at Mr Munro's good fortune.

In the unremitting cold of March – the blackthorn winter – Munro is too drunk to leave the house. Messengers who call for him are sent home to ask if Mr Dyer can be of assistance. Most agree that he can. After the first visit it is him they want, not the old fellow.

In ballrooms and salons, the lame, the ailing and the bored, their breath sour with nostrums, discuss the New Man, only twenty if you can credit it. Very able. Very able indeed. Not as genial as old Munro, of course. Robert Munro, decent a man as you could meet in a day's walk, but . . .

Mrs Nigella Pratt's ingrowing toenail, botched by Mr Crisp of Beaufort Square, is remedied by James Dyer. She says: 'It is almost indecent the speed he works at. Why, I don't imagine he was in the house five minutes before it was done. God's truth – one moment he was walking through the door handing his hat to the girl and the next he was stood in the hall having his guinea off Charles. I don't believe he said more than five words the whole time he was here.'

Tobias Bone, Justice of the Peace in the County of Middlesex, a great mole removed from the end of his nose. Recounting in a coffee house by the Pump Rooms he raps the table for emphasis, makes the china jump: 'James Dyer is the only competent surgeon in Bath, apart that is from old Munro himself. Reminds me of a man I had before me once accused of poisoning both his parents.'

'Munro?'

'No, sir, Dyer. Damn good hands, mind. Hands of a lady, eyes of an eagle, heart of a something or other – how does it go?'

Salvatore Grimaldi, musician and intimate friend of Lord B, is cut for the stone. He has left it late. There is a total suppression of urine, and he is carried into the house, faint, sallow, shot through with spasms. Despite his agony, he comports himself with great patience; only once, when the chairmen knock him against the table as they lift him up, does he shout, a brief and furious burst of Neapolitan blasphemy. He begs pardon immediately and asks if Mr Munro will be with him soon.

Munro, wrapped in blankets, a sealskin cap on his head, is sat in his bedroom breakfasting on Madeira and hot water. He has heard the commotion and when his wife comes in he asks her who it is.

'Some foreigner with a pain. James can deal with it.'

He nods. 'Where should we be without him?'

She knocks at James's door. It is opened by Gummer who carries in one hand an open razor. Behind Gummer, James sits coatless at the dressing table.

She says: 'Mr Grimaldi is below. A foreign gentleman of some influence. He suffers with the stone and Mr Munro begs that you would be so kind . . .'

'As soon as we are finished here we shall come down.'

She pauses. 'I pray you not to be too long for the gentleman does suffer so.'

James looks at her in the mirror. 'That depends on Mr Gummer. You would not have me operate in a beard, I take it?'

'No indeed. I am sure that would not be proper.'

It is half an hour before he appears in the chill back room used by Munro as his theatre. His face shines from the razor, and a sweet expensive scent creeps through the air where it mingles with other, less agreeable stinks; the sweat of suffering, old blood. James examines the patient. The patient's eyes flicker; he looks at the young man across a dim and widening gulf. He mutters something about a priest. James ignores him, orders the chairmen to strip off Grimaldi's breeches and then changes his own coat for one of the blood-stiff jackets that hang from a wooden peg behind the door. From the third button of Grimaldi's waistcoat a thick gold chain leads to a watch pocket. James draws out the watch, a gold repoussé pair-case, enamel dial, London-made. He frees it from the waistcoat button and hands it to Agnes Munro, who has retired into a corner of the room. He says: 'You time from the first cut and stop as soon as the stone is out.'

He goes to Grimaldi, leans by his ear. 'Mr Grimaldi, the fee for this operation is your watch. Is that agreeable to you, sir?'

Grimaldi's lips twitch into a smile. There is a perceptible nod.

'Draw up his legs.' James takes a knife, forceps and staff from the drawer, then looks over at Mrs Munro. 'From the first cut, madam. And you' – he addresses the chairmen – 'will be witnesses. So . . . now!'

One minute and twenty seconds.

James holds up the stone. It is about the size of a small pickled walnut.

Munro comes in, blinks at the party gathered around the table. He steps over and admires the wound.

'Lateral cut, eh?'

'As recommended by Mr Cheselden. But I am twenty seconds or more outside his best time.'

'Cheselden! We must celebrate this, James. How is the gentleman? Is that not Mr Grimaldi? How do you go on, sir?'

Grimaldi whispers: 'I have lost my watch.'

Says Munro: 'Lost your watch but kept your life. I tell you, Mr Grimaldi, I have seen these operations last above an hour.'

Grimaldi swivels his eyes to James. '*Caro dottore*. He is . . . an instrument of God.' He sketches a cross over his heart; the chairmen ease him back into his breeches, back into the chair, carry him off. Grimaldi waves feebly through the glass. Munro fetches a bottle of Frontiniac, the last of his prize-share from a French privateer overhauled by *Aquilon* off Brest and saved for just such an occasion. In the theatre James changes his coat, stretches luxuriously.

'You have my fee I think, madam.'

He holds out his hand for the watch. Agnes Munro snaps shut the lid, gives it to him, then, as he turns to the door, she draws a handkerchief from her sleeve, reaches up on tiptoe and wipes a spot of blood from his cheek.

'You are the strangest man I ever knew, James.'

James considers his reply. Something gallant, something out of a novel, a play. But he reads no novels and the few plays he has seen, at Drury Lane or Covent Garden, have made precious little sense to him. The game is too tiresome and his mind is still enamoured of his work with Grimaldi's bladder; the neat way he was able to dilate the neck, his skilful avoidance of the artery. A gold watch was little enough for such work, for an instrument of God.

He bids her good day, goes out. She stays a minute, watching the blood darken the floorboards. She smiles, then shivers. The abbey bells tumble out their music.

Grimaldi recovers. Lord B sends James a diamond ring, then sends his friends, his circle. By midsummer the practice boasts three baronets, a general, an admiral, a bishop, a celebrated painter and two Members of Parliament among its patients. The competition is not pleased. Mr Crisp in particular has been busy spreading rumours, calling them barbers and quacks and saying old Munro could not rise in the morning without a bottle of port wine, could not rise at night either. Perhaps his young protégé could? He places two fingers above his head, waggles them, grins, gets his laugh.

But Crisp loses the wealthy Mrs Davy to them, and then the Robinson family, a populous tribe whom James inoculates against the smallpox. Three guineas a head, an outrageous sum, yet Mr Robinson is convinced that the lives of his loved ones are safer in this man's hands, young as he is, than in those of any other operator in Bath. Munro is there, of course, to keep an eye on things, to soften the young man's presence and nod senatorially at his work.

They advertise in the papers:

> *MUNRO AND DYER, SURGEONS in the ORANGE GROVE BATH beg leave to announce they are willing to receive a SMALL number of NEW PATIENTS due to the RECOVERY and COMPLETE RESTORATION of those formerly under their care. INOCULATIONS, CUTTING for STONE, REMOVAL of TUMOURS WARTS FIBROUS GROWTHS, the SETTING of LIMBS, the HEALING of GUNSHOT wounds a speciality. Favoured by the QUALITY and all who DEMAND the BEST service. LADIES treated with the utmost DISCRETION.*

Gummer takes care of such matters; advertisements, puffs. His figure, tall and weathered, is a common sight among the gardens and Palladian walkways, arm slipped through the arm of some influential gentleman who nods and smiles, half amused and half flattered to be in the company of such a worldly rogue. Gummer also handles the billing; he knows people who know how to see that a bill is never left unpaid. Masters of the nudge, the honeyed threat, and when other means fail there is never a shortage of brawlers in tight coats who, for a shilling, will loaf outside the debtor's door. So the money comes in: gold, silver; large, beautiful banknotes. Also hogsheads, bolts of cloth, heirlooms.

Munro's old sign comes down. A new one – *Jms Dyer & Rbt Munro, Surgeons* – swings from the iron scroll above the door, and beneath its shadow come the citizens of the republic of pain: the chronic sufferers, and those struck down suddenly by some bloody disaster, and hustled in, faint, in the arms of friends. And most come out again, if not precisely healed, at least somewhat easier than when they entered, and all dazzled by the young man's skill, soothed by the elder's kindness. Some even die grateful.

On James's twenty-first birthday, Munro gives a party, crowding the first-floor dining room with friends and feasting them on beef and oysters, summer pudding, syllabubs and champagne. Grimaldi sings for them, a sweet tenor voice that carries across the half-lit Grove to where a band of homegoers stops to listen.

At the end of the port decanter's second round, Munro throws down his napkin, attains his feet and makes a speech. There are tears in his eyes, a web in his throat as he speaks. 'My boy,' he says, 'my boy,' gesturing to James at the opposite end of the table, and there are those among the guests who wonder if Munro means it, if James might be the progeny of some youthful adventure of Munro's. They look from one to the other, trying to discern some likeness. That mouth? The chin? And then their eyes turn to Agnes Munro, and even the dullest are struck by the transformation in that face.

She could not say exactly when it started. Perhaps that first day when he strolled into the drawing room svelte beside her bumbling husband; or when he spoke to her through the mirror when she came to fetch him to attend to Grimaldi; or on any one of those occasions, frequent as she can contrive them, when she has watched him work, his face like clear water.

She is careful, wary of the force of her feelings, but her life is already slung between one encounter and the next, the anxious suspense of not seeing him and the anxious joy of his presence. With Munro she is polite, more so than at any time since their wedding. Yet the harder she plays her part – good wife, loyal wife, wife not enamoured of the beautiful young wolf they have brought under their roof – the more intent he seems on throwing her in James's way. The shopping expeditions, the visits to balls, the evenings at the theatre, the Sunday promenades, all at Munro's suggestion, while he himself takes off to the house of a crony – Kent or Thomas or Osbourne – coming home crapulous in a hackney or a chair and sitting out the night in his study, dozing, browsing in old books, mumbling to the dog. It is as if he were grateful to James for taking up the burden of his marriage. Is he making a gift of her? She knows well enough what kind of wife she has been to him, keeping him out of her bed, upbraiding him in company, particularly in company. Yet she does not doubt his affection. It is as large and clumsy as the man himself. In the lacquered box in her bedroom she has a sheaf of his poetry to her, passionate lines, full of allusions she cannot understand. She waits for a sign, a word, a scene. How can he not suspect? How can he not know? And yet he does nothing.

As for James, no man could seem less ardent, but his composure inflames her, draws her deeper into the indignity of her passion. She cannot help herself. Soon she does not care who sees, who knows, who gossips. She has never felt so free, so hugely embarrassed. She discovers in herself a cunning, a salaciousness, a daring she would never have suspected. She is a stranger to herself. Everywhere there is the marvellous whiff of imminent disaster.

The town is amused. Nothing diverts it more than a domestic farce, and the more stolid, the more respectable the players, the better it is liked. What did Munro expect, a man of his years marrying a green, headstrong woman like Agnes Munro? And then to invite that creature Dyer into his house. Half the women of Bath would lie down for him, particularly the married women. Does Dyer return her passion? No one can say, for when they search it appears he has not a single confidant, not a single friend, other than his henchman Marley Gummer. And Munro himself, of course.

New Year 1762. The festivities bring on a recurrence of Munro's gout. He is put to bed on a diet of steel and angostura bark. James and Agnes spend their evenings by the fire in the drawing room, drinking tea and playing backgammon. She asks him about his life; he tells her nothing, or nothing she actually believes. She invents a life for them both. A life of glamour, of riches, of curly-haired children called George or Caroline or Hester; of a house in Grosvenor Square, of neighbours' envy. Lord, what if her husband were to die? What then?

James gammons her, sips his tea, looks up at her. He understands what is required of him. She is there to be taken, part of the world's munificence. When the pot is empty, the last game finished, and the candles, good wax candles with their clean smell, are down to the last inch of their lives, he crosses over to her, lands a kiss on the hot of her mouth and fingers her into a sweat. She jerks her head back, shudders, kicks, sends the card table, the board, the counters tumbling over the blacks and sumptuous reds of the new carpet.

She sobs, cannot stop herself from asking if he loves her, truly, as she loves him, utterly, for ever, ever and ever.

James is setting up the board again, laying out the counters on their leather spikes. Agnes is on her knees beside him. He does not know what she is saying. Is she happy, afraid? Frankly she seems drunk. He helps her to her feet, answers all her questions with yes, yes, yes, of course. He is thinking of the twins, of pearls and boiled eggs. The memory of them is like a finger pressing his chest. He stares at the miniature of Munro above the mantelpiece, tries to clear his mind. Molina's studio, the light there, the light in the girls' hair as they slept. The finger presses harder. It is like the tip of a cane, but hot. He does not like this feeling. Shakes his head to clear it. Agnes asks: 'Are you well, my love?' He says something to her, he does not know what, and makes for the door. The stairs are immensely long. He hauls himself up by the banisters. His heart is beating violently. He is afraid he will not reach his room. Munro is snoring. Is that Canning's voice? Canning?

'What did you expect, James?'

'Not this!'

'No one is safe, James. Not even you. Especially not you.'

He is lying on the bed. There is a small fire in the room. His hand hurts, his fist is clenched. He opens it. He is holding the dice from the backgammon. He lets them roll on to the floor. He lies a long time, uncertain if he is awake or dreaming. Some perceptions – the rattling of the window, the creak of the fire – remain with him; but there are visions that rise like smoke from the other world. He says: 'I have a fever, I am sick.' He feels himself seeping out of his body; the room glows, very bright, and looking down he sees himself lying across the bed, and sees Agnes knocking at her husband's door and Munro's blind, drugged face climbing out of sleep. For one awful moment he seems to experience Munro's emotions, the vast resources of the man's unhappiness. He fights it, flounders in the air, escapes to new horrors. A line of men and women shuffling through the mist, heads bent to their chests as if they carried a great burden on their backs. Ahead of them is an evil-scented, vaporous pit, like the common grave in a city racked by plague. Those at the head of the line stumble into it, some screaming, some with a profound groan like a death groan. Others go in silence. One looks round, wildly, sees James, points, then waves him towards the line. The line halts, others look, two step apart to make a space; a voice cries: 'This is your place, James Dyer!'

There is no repetition of the incident. In the following months his strength, the fine powers of his concentration, are greater than ever, as if the episode had purged him. Despite Munro's insistence that he should take more rest, he works harder. Plans are laid for a building in Grand Parade to be purchased and used as a private infirmary. Six months later they open with Chinese lanterns and concert parties. The upper floors are for inoculations and on the ground floor there is an operating theatre, fine as any in a London hospital, with seating for thirty guests who, for a modest fee, may watch James Dyer cut, slice, and saw his way to eminence.

Munro can also be seen, free of charge, but more often he is to be encountered by the river, sipping from a flask, feeding cake to the swans, or drowsing in nooks of sunshine, wig askew, his hat over his eyes. Occasionally his wife will be with him, sitting at a distance, leafing impatiently through a novel or frowning at the hills, but the denouement – the scandal, the duel, the flight – fails to materialise. Mrs Vaughan, whose opinion is always to be trusted in these matters, declares that the Munros and James Dyer have reached an arrangement, a very improper thing in people of their class, like a farmer's daughter learning the harpsichord. Munro has evidently resigned himself to the inevitable. As for Mrs Munro, she has shown herself to be a very brazen piece, for which the women of Bath have a duty to despise her. James Dyer – well, he could hardly be said to be human at all. A machine for cutting. An automaton. Dangerous.

'Dangerous?' ask the women, pausing with their needles.

Mrs Vaughan inclines her head. 'He appears to have been born without a soul. What, then, has he to lose?'

17   Patients come from Bristol, Exeter, London. In Grand Parade, James and Munro purchase a second house. James refines his techniques, designs new instruments: probes and forceps and cunning scissors. In the upstairs rooms of the new house he treats victims of the pox with mercury. They lie in the little wards in suits of flannel, gums swollen from the mercury, dribbling their saliva into pots, two to three pints of it in a day, until they are cured or can stand the treatment no more.

These salivations, and the inoculations in the other building, bring James four hundred and fifty pounds in 1764. Add to this the lithotomies, the amputations, the bleedings, the settings, and his income is close on seven hundred pounds.

In the winter of '64 he has a new and potentially even more lucrative service to offer the people of Bath. He becomes a man-midwife, an *accoucheur*, after he is called on one night to save the life of a mother in childbed. The woman, a Mrs Porter, had been in labour for three days with Dr Bax and Mr Crisp in attendance. Bax, on the evening of the third day, rubbing his chin with the gold boss of his cane, decides she cannot be helped. Nor will it garnish his reputation to be at the bedside of a dead mother. He gives her over. Mr Crisp stays on, glad of a clear field. He leads Mr Porter on to the landing and in a whisper that fills the house he counsels the extermination of the infant, its corpse to remain inside the mother, two, three days, such that it might soften sufficiently for them to extract it. There is a steel hook he has, so long, which he has used before with considerable success. Thus the mother will be spared; that is, perhaps she will be spared, he can give no assurances; hands of God, the lady's constitution, etc.; these cases, sir, very unfortunate, very uncertain. Mr Porter is aghast, takes hold of Crisp's coat, shakes him violently.

'Damn your hooks! Damn your incompetence!' He runs to the top of the stairs, shouts to one of the servants below: 'Fetch Dyer!'

'Dyer?' cries Mr Crisp. 'That mountebank!'

Exit Mr Crisp, face in a cramp of anger, shouting from the window of his coach: 'On your own head, sir! I wash my hands of it! Folly, sir! Lunatic folly!'

When James arrives it is three o'clock in the morning. The weather, bad all night, has deteriorated into a full storm. Before morning a dozen chimney stacks will be down, and already roof tiles scythe through the darkness. There is no moon, no stars. All the houses are shuttered, all save one.

Mr Porter is waiting in the dining room, holding a lamp up to the window. He has drunk a half-bottle of brandy but has never felt more sober, more appallingly conscious, in his life. He catches a glimmer of his servant's lantern, and then the horses, heads down, looming.

The moment James enters the panelled hallway and the door is shouldered shut against the wind, his physical presence, the unconsidered precision of his movements, quieten the house. He walks up the stairs carrying his green baize bag. He refuses to be hurried.

Mr Porter has only seen him from a distance, and once only, from the far side of the abbey courtyard. It was raining, and Dyer was sheltering under the west door of the abbey with his friend – his servant? – Marley Gummer. Waiting for someone, for something. Mrs Porter pointed him out. 'That man', she called him. She was only just with child then.

James opens the door. The lying-in room. The sick-room. The death-room perhaps. The hearth is chock with fire. The air is thick, over-hot. Three women sit around the bed. The eldest of them James recognises as Mrs Allen, a woman said to have powers, connections with unseen forces. Her presence speaks clearly of Porter's desperation. She is chanting over the bed, over the figure in the bed. She stops when she hears James. Turns on him.

'Come to finish her off, have you?'

To Mr Porter James says: 'If this witch is to stay she is to keep her mouth shut.'

He leans over Mrs Porter. Their eyes briefly connect, hers looking up from the well of suffering, his responsive as moons. He gets his hands on to her belly. She flinches at the coldness of his fingers. It is her first child. She whispers: 'Do not kill it, sir.' James throws back the blankets, prods, squeezes, reaches his decision. He goes to Mr Porter, says: 'Her pelvis is narrow and the child has not turned. There is a way to save her and to save the child. But I must cut her.'

'Cut her?'

'As Caesar's mother was cut. An incision of the abdomen.'

'Cut?'

'Ay, sir, cut. We cut her belly to let the child out. It must be now. If not I shall have to leave you to Mrs Allen's spells. There is a calling-out fee, of course.'

'And if you cut her, you can save her, and the child?'

James shrugs. He wants the operation, believes he can pull it off, though he has never done one before, nor seen one performed other than on Mr Smellie's leather woman during an obstetrics lecture in London six years since. He also knows that his profession universally condemns it as being little better than an assassination of the mother. He has heard of no instances where it has been performed successfully.

'I have your permission?'

Porter's eyes film with tears. 'There is nothing else?'

James looks at Mrs Allen, looks back, raises his eyebrows. Porter gives his permission.

'Get these women out,' says James. 'No, leave this one.' He points to one of the younger women. She has a strong, calm look to her. Not a flincher.

'And bring me some water, warm water, and wine and fresh linen.'

James strips off his coat, opens his bag, selects a knife, examines briefly the rosy skin, then cuts, fast, a vertical incision from belly button to pubic hair. Mrs Porter roars, swings a small white fist with considerable power against his left ear. He laughs, does not look up. He says: 'A good sign, I think. Now hold her still. I have some delicate work here. Jog my knife, Mrs Porter, and you shall bleed to death.'

He cuts through the muscles of the abdominal wall, opens the abdominal cavity, then makes a transverse incision, right to left across the lower part of the uterus. Behind him there is a crash as Mr Porter succumbs to the sight of a stranger's hands lodged in the slashed belly of his wife. The infant seems determined to resist, to fight off this terrible invasion. Feebly it kicks at James, plucks at his hands with its daisy-stalk fingers, clings to the bloody gubbins of the womb. It comes at last in a drench of its mother's fluids. James passes it to his assistant, ties the cord, cuts it, delivers the placenta and drops it on to the boards, where a dog, hiding under the bed, stretches out and takes it tentatively in its teeth. James seals up the mother; those stitches Miss Lucket so commended. Rather surprisingly, Mrs Porter is still alive.

The young woman is binding the child in a shawl. She asks: 'What shall I do with it? Give it a posset?'

He says: 'Do whatsoever you like.' He looks around the room. The father groaning on the floor, the mother in a swoon in the bed, the infant mewing in the young woman's uncertain grip. He wraps his knives.

'Tell him I expect my bills paid promptly.'

She starts to say something, but he has gone.

18 Robert Munro is a man coming slowly from a long sleep. Or, as he sometimes thinks of it, a man on the trail of himself in the midst of a sunless forest. He does not hurry. He is afraid of what must come; afraid that he will not have the strength.

Towards his wife he has never felt a greater tenderness. Certainly he does not condemn her. She has conceived a passion. Her slender sense of duty could have been no match for it. He himself is to blame. Who but he brought them together? Brimstone and tinder. There is a justice to it, a considerable justice. And if he believed James Dyer loved his wife, that it was truly love, then they may indeed have reached an arrangement. But Dyer does not love her; he wears her like a coat, puts her on or off at will. And that is monstrous, worse than the betrayal of friendship – for in fairness there was no friendship on Dyer's part – worse even than the visions that haunt him of their couplings, the sounds of which sometimes wake him, an awful noise, not at all suggestive of pleasure, more like the muffled distress of a child.

What must be done, then? Kill James? Kill them both? He would swing for it but hanging does not signify. He is more afraid that he will fail in this supreme test of his life. Fail himself. Fail Agnes. Fail everyone. Voices whisper – 'Take up your sword, Munro!' – but his limbs are heavy and the blood ticks so slowly in his veins. How good just to go on sleeping in his favourite chair in his study, shutters drawn, a single candle for company. Distant bells, distant footsteps. Just to sleep, past morning, past all mornings. Endless sleep.

The door slams; he rouses himself, goes to the window and sees their backs departing. What is it tonight? Another ball, a charity concert, a trip on the river? He goes up to his room, stands there vacantly a while, then carefully selects a suit of clothes, changes, and goes back to his study. His watch says half past eight. Chowder is squatting on the floor, staring up at him, black, beseeching eyes. 'Good dog,' he says, then pours himself one last drink, hearing in his head, again and again, until they are like nonsense, the words he will have to speak.

James and Agnes are at the theatre in Orchard Street. It is a short walk from the Orange Grove. There is no need for the new carriage. The theatre is crowded, rowdy. Tattered plush, yellow mushrooms of light from the chandeliers. Figures call to their acquaintances; the men offer each other snuff; the women gaze out from their white faces, stroke their hired diamonds, tap their fans. There is an air of stupendous boredom, as if nothing in the world remains beyond fashion, beyond manners, beyond the predictable mechanics of intrigue. There is not even a war on.

James and Agnes settle in their box. She feeds him sweetmeats with her fingers, and all throughout the play asks him why such and such a character does this, and if that is not Mrs Lewis below them, and if he does not think that the actress in the red is egregious ugly. Would he care for another sugar plum?

James takes no interest in the play. He is dimly aware of characters larking among the painted trees, of certain voices, words, the laughter or hush of the audience. There is a fight, a reconciliation. A song. A joke about the City Corporation. A joke about Wilkes. Another song. The lovers die, then come to life again. Someone is recognised. Someone is lowered from the flies on a cloud and throws paper flowers at the audience. Everyone claps like mad, and stamps their feet until the building shakes. It is all so pointless. Childish. He does not care for it at all.

They eat supper near the theatre – fried fish, boiled mutton in a caper sauce – and walk back through the clammy air to the Orange Grove. James is tired. He has a woman's foot to take off in the morning, a half-dozen inoculations after that and then a ride to Marshfield to examine a farmer whose gun went off in his face. Agnes is chattering about a garden, a hat, a friend, a day last week when something occurred that quite amazed her, or didn't, or saddened her or made her laugh. A servant with a candle lets them in. Dinah. She is looking at them oddly.

The door of Munro's study opens. Munro is there, filling the doorway. He is dressed as though expecting a visitor of consequence. He does not look like a buffoon, a cuckold.

'A moment with you, James.'

'I am sure it may wait until morning.'

'No, sir, it may not.'

James has his foot upon the first stair. Ignoring Munro has never been difficult. Until now. He turns. Between himself and Munro is the servant, clutching her candle.

Agnes is standing very still in the dark place by the front door. She whispers: 'Robert?'

Munro says: 'Good night to you, Agnes.'

James says: 'Be brief if you will, sir.'

Munro steps back for him. James passes, Munro closes the door. Agnes stares at the door, then at Dinah. Dinah starts to cry.

It is a long time since James has been in Munro's study. For several months Munro has forbidden the servants to come in, afraid they will disturb the delicate disarrangement of his papers. By the various chairs in the room are stacks of books, and beneath the chairs the light picks out forgotten glasses, empty bottles. On the desk, sheets of paper, heavily blotted. Beside the sand tray is a pair of spectacles with one of the lenses missing.

'I would ask you to sit, James, but I fear this is a conversation best conducted upon our feet.'

'To the point, sir.'

Munro inhales deeply. 'The point, then. It is this. You have offended me. You have abused me. Done so in my own house. Done so for years. I know the blame is not entirely yours. I have a measure of it, as does my wife. You were strong; we were weak, deplorably so. I have earned your contempt. Well, sir, I know you do not care for speeches. You are a man of action. A remarkable man in your way, ay, and a very considerable surgeon . . .'

'The point, sir!'

Munro is sweating heavily; it shows through his coat, dark continents spreading from beneath his shoulders. He says: 'Your frolic here is at an end, James. You will give me the satisfaction of meeting me at the earliest possible instance. In the meantime you will shift yourself from under my roof. I shall arrange for someone to call upon you tomorrow. I doubt it is the first time you have been engaged in an affair of this kind so you will know the form. That is all.'

James bows. 'You will make a generous target, Mr Munro. I bid you good night.'

It is dusk when, the following day, James returns from Marshfield. The farmer was dead. Turning into Grand Parade he spies Mr Osbourne standing alone by the balustrade. He rides up to him. Osbourne greets him dryly, says: 'I cannot dissaude him from this course. However, it is still possible that an apology and an undertaking never to see Mrs Munro will be sufficient.'

James says: 'I have been challenged, sir. Whether or not I see Mrs Munro is neither here nor there.'

'If you kill him, Dyer, you will be taken up. Have sense, man. It's over. You are young. You might go anywhere and prosper. It is not so with Munro. You have left him nothing to lose.'

'You are to act as his second?'

'I cannot with honour refuse him.'

'And this is an affair of honour, is it not?'

'It is.'

'Then you have come to tell me a time and place where honour may be satisfied.'

'Lansdown. Follow the road to the top of the hill. I shall be waiting. Tomorrow morning at six. If one of you is fatally hurt the other will have a day's ride to get clear.'

'And how are we to kill each other?'

'I shall bring a brace of pistols.'

'To be loaded in my presence.'

'Naturally.'

'Then we have no more to say to each other.'

He rises at five, takes a light breakfast, and leaves written instructions for Mr Timmins, factotum and dresser, informing him that he shall not be receiving any new patients that day.

The city is mostly empty as he rides through. A pair of dazed young men returning from a night of gaming and drinking. In Queen Square, a herdsman leads his flock of goats. A milkmaid sits on her upturned pail and plaits her hair. An ordinary morning, a hint of autumn in the air.

James has been out twice before, both times in London, both times with fellow students over quarrels he has forgotten. On the first occasion the pistols were faulty, tampered with perhaps by one of the seconds. The next occasion, James's ball lodged in his opponent's shoulder. There were a dozen other students with them in the garden and no shortage of volunteers to cut the ball out. Afterwards there was a brief hullaballoo, then the matter was dropped. Two young men of no importance quarrelling in the garden of a tavern was of little concern to anyone.

On Lansdown Hill he has a sudden glimpse back over the city, the houses huddled around the abbey, their chimneys drifting smoke, the river tranquilly signalling with its light. For the briefest moment it occurs to him that he might lose it all, that he will kill Munro and have to run – to France perhaps, or Holland. He mentally shrugs. He is not interested in shooting Munro, bears him no animosity. Certainly he is not fighting for Agnes. Munro is welcome to her. When he kills Munro it will be for Munro's folly, his audacity in issuing a challenge. What did he think he was doing? That absurd scene in his study! James should have given him a sound kicking then and there and had done with it. So much tedious form in these affairs.

Osbourne steps into the road ahead, raises his cane. When James comes up, Osbourne says: 'You are alone?'

'I am as you see me, sir. Where is the party?'

'This way.'

He leads James through a break in the trees and through an old stone gateway, a broken crest on one of the pillars.

James says: 'What is this place?'

Osbourne says: 'It was a garden once.'

Munro and another man are waiting at the far end beside a tulip tree. Osbourne walks down to them, then returns with Munro. James dismounts. Munro says: 'Good morning, James.'

He has the same steady manner, the same despairing calm.

Osbourne says: 'I beseech you both to give up this most unchristian business. Even at this late hour you may reach some . . . accommodation. How do you say?'

'If Mr Munro will withdraw his challenge,' says James, 'I am content not to shoot him.'

Munro says: 'I cannot withdraw, sir. The offence is too strong.'

James shrugs. 'I hope for your sake, sir, your hand is steadier with a pistol than it is with a knife.'

Osbourne signals to the other man who comes forward with a box. Osbourne opens the box and loads the pistols. He holds them both out to James. James takes the one from his left hand; a good-quality flintlock: blued octagonal barrel, gold touch-hole, checkered grip. A sliding safety catch on the lockplate. In the off position.

Munro takes the other gun; they turn, walk a dozen paces. Munro calls: 'One moment.'

He hands his pistol to Osbourne and then strips off his coat and waistcoat. James says: 'You need not worry about cloth in the wound, sir. I shall be aiming at your head.'

No reply. Munro takes the pistol. Osbourne walks away. The morning is very quiet.

Osbourne says: 'Are you prepared? . . . Fire at will.'

Munro's shot follows almost immediately. A flash, a puff of smoke, a report that must have echoed for miles.

James raises his pistol. He feels extraordinarily good this morning. Braced. Capable of anything. He does not think 'I shall kill Munro', or 'I shall not kill him'. He raises his pistol to the target and discharges. Munro spins round on his toes and plunges into the grass. Osbourne runs over to him. James calls: 'Is he dead?'

Osbourne says: 'I do not think so.'

James goes towards them, curious to see what manner of wound he has made. He looks down. Osbourne is cradling Munro's head on his knees and wiping the blood from his face with a handkerchief that is already crimson. Munro has his eyes closed but is visibly breathing. The middle of his face is a mess. Bone and torn flesh.

James says: 'We shall need to procure him a new nose. Take him to the house. I shall attend to him there.'

'Attend to him?'

'Ay, sir. You have not forgot my profession?'

He drops the pistol on to the grass beside Mr Osbourne, bids them good morning, and leads his horse out from the garden.

When Agnes Munro sees them carry her husband into the house, she asks: 'Is James hurt?'

Osbourne shakes his head, and as they manoeuvre the stricken man up the stairs, mutters: 'It's you they should have shot.'

The wound prospers. James dresses it daily, peering into the cavity of Munro's head and making a number of sketches he later has engraved. Neither man speaks. Munro speaks to no one for fourteen days, and when he does, his voice is as mangled as his face. Curiously, the only person who is able to understand him is James Dyer. Munro's friends look on, perplexed, frustrated. There is no remorse in James's manner, no resentment in Munro's. Between them is an odd complicity, peculiar perhaps to lovers, or to those who have offered each other death. Agnes is excluded. She wanders the house in a raggedy dress, complaining to herself and living on cup after cup of expensively sugared chocolate.

The nose is fashioned by a watchmaker in Pierrepont Street, working from James's designs. It is light, made of polished ivory and attached to a pair of Munro's spectacles. There are several fittings before James is satisfied. Munro sits up in bed and examines himself in the looking-glass. When he hands the glass back there are tears in his eyes.

James says: 'It will outlast you, sir, by some considerable margin. You shall be outlived by your nose.'

Munro replies: 'Show much ish shertain. A vegy ig-genious construction. I ham grateful to you, sher.'

There is no irony. He reaches out and shakes James's hand.

19 For three months, while Munro's friends look on, the two surgeons act like an old married couple. It is not that anyone suspects James of making up to Munro. James Dyer continues to be precisely himself: hard, headstrong, ambitious; hugely efficient. And there is not the least evidence of any tenderness towards Munro, any remorse. Yet they are often seen walking together, sometimes in conversation, more often in silence. They walk at dusk, aimlessly about the city.

For a time, the sight of them hoving into view is enough to make people step out of a shop or coffee house to gawp at them. Munro's nose is discreetly pointed out to children and visitors. There is a great deal of speculation as to whether he wears it at home, or in bed, or ever mislays it, or if it ever falls off his face while he is adjusting the buckle on his shoe. Does it pain him? What if he takes a cold? Munro himself seems remarkably at ease with it, now and then reaching up to stroke it.

Agnes grows portly and faintly mad, hauling Chowder about, staring malevolently at strangers she suspects of uttering slights. The sight of her evokes some pity and some satisfaction. More than one preacher adumbrates her case from the pulpit. Leaning out, they slap the air with their Bibles. God's justice! God's wrath!

The hands of the congregation curl round stones of air.

And then the preachers have their feast. Candlemas, 1767. The streets perfumed with coal smoke and frost, the night sky richly hammered with stars. James has been at Grand Parade, trepanning a young man kicked in the head by a horse. The young man survives the drill and is handed back to his friends, feeble, bewildered, but very much alive. A woman, immensely pretty, kisses James's hand, despite the spats of blood still on his fingers. James carries their money to his strong-box in the basement, dons his coat and sets off for the Orange Grove.

In the drawing room he finds Gummer by the fire, peeling a bun from the prongs of a toasting fork. They look at each other, say nothing. He rings for the servant. She is engaged now to a journeyman baker in Trim Street. James orders supper, eats it off a tray in the drawing room. Overhead he can hear Agnes mumbling, interrogating the emptiness of her room. Gummer goes out on some louche or venal assignation. Chowder curls before the fire, shivering and farting.

Towards midnight, James retires, goes up to his room, pulls on his nightgown and nightcap and lies between the sheets, waiting for sleep. But sleep does not come. He waits, impatient, unused to those phases of sleeplessness familiar to insomniacs; the sly hallucinations, the endless settling of the bones, the beating of his heart vibrating through the whole bed. He loses any sense of time, hears the watchman's voice but not the hour. Two o'clock, three?

He hears a noise. It is not loud. Somewhere on the ground floor. Something falling. Gummer perhaps, tripping over a table leg in the dark, or Dinah, full of noisy caution, sneaking in on her return from Trim Street. Yet some instinct warns him that the sound is less innocent, that it comes as the small report of calamity. He swings out of the bed, stands in the dark, listening.

He feels for the tinder box he keeps beside the bed, lights a candle, takes a cane for protection, and goes on to the landing. If there is some unlucky whoreson below filling his sack then he has picked the wrong house and the wrong night. But even as he descends the stairs, cane at the ready, he does not believe in it and is unsurprised to find the downstairs rooms cold, unmolested, empty. All except Munro's study, where a dim light ripples from beneath the door. And there is a smell here, as if Munro – or someone – were burning cloth.

When James opens the door he sees two things: a fire, not yet serious, where a candle has been knocked on to the carpet; and Munro, stood in the air in a corner of the room, a chair on its side beneath his feet. Munro's coat is folded on the armchair by his desk. James throws it over the flames, stamps them out, opens the window. When the smoke has cleared he examines Munro and satisfies himself that the man is dead. Those stories of men reviving on the surgeon's slab after being hanged, how interesting that would be! Munro, however, will not be reviving this side of the Last Trump.

He considers cutting him down, but the man's girth is intimidating and the rope at his neck is taut as a ship's hawser. Munro is in no hurry. Morning will do. James takes up his candle and notices upon the desk, next to a half-dozen envelopes sealed with black wax, Munro's spectacles and ivory nose.

James does not attend the funeral. He is seeing a patient, a woman with puerperal fever. In James's world, people would be dropped into lime-pits or, like Grace Boylan, bundled through a gun-port with a shot at their feet. One moment here, the next invisible; nothing but sea. None of this dressing up, this lugubrious to-do.

Officially Munro has died of heart failure, but the truth leaches out and within a fortnight, from Taunton to Gloucester, the word is that Robert Munro has hanged himself, or some say shot himself or swallowed poison, and that it was his wife and that rogue Dyer who drove him to it. Everyone, it seems, had seen it coming.

Three days after the funeral Agnes is hissed at as she walks through the abbey courtyard with Dinah. She does not go outside again for a month.

A week later, James arrives at Grand Parade to find all the windows on the ground floor smashed. Mr Timmins meets him at the door, explains that he cannot continue under such circumstances and must therefore, respectfully, regretfully ... James thrusts him out of doors, sweeps up the glass, has the glazier at work inside of an hour.

He is shunned. His practice slumps. Soon only those past caring what the world thinks, whose minds can travel no further than the relief of their pain and who hold like a precious secret the reputation of James Dyer, not as a man but as a surgeon, continue to come.

Those whose condition is less insistent, who still have one foot in the stream of the world, go to Mr Crisp, who is able, or Mr Farbank or Mr Boas, or any of the dozen other men who can flourish a certificate and wield a knife, and who have drunk damnation to James Dyer. They have their wish now. He shall feel the pinch soon enough. Then they shall see.

March. A shower of stones is flung at James's back as he walks to the Orange Grove after dark. The same night the new windows at Grand Parade are smashed.

April. Four new patients in the whole month. Dinah and the cook give their notice. Replacements are hard to find. Agnes takes to her bed, lies among the sour linen clutching a silhouette of her late husband. James does not visit her. They live in the house as strangers.

The hissers, the stone-throwers, grow more audacious. James, dozing in the saddle on his return from seeing a patient in St Catherine's valley, opens his eyes to find the road barred by four men carrying staves, their faces masked with scarves. One runs forward to strike. James kicks the man in the head, sends him tumbling. The others come up; one seizes the reins; they wrestle James on to the road. The fight is short, almost silent. James has no compunction as a fighter, no fear. He lashes out at eyes and throats, but four is too many. They overwhelm, pound him with their staves. Vaguely, he is aware of their leaning, their whispers, their hard breathing. Then he hears them running. Then nothing.

When he comes to it is light. A yellow dawn. A fine rain. A crow watches him from the edge of the road. When it sees him move it hops into the air, flaps heavily away over the glistening valley. The horse is sheltering under an oak tree, the horse as still as the tree. Very slowly, James pulls himself into the saddle. There are not many to see him on his way home, yet enough for the news to spread: the bastard's black and blue! A modicum of justice for old Munro.

When Gummer finds James at Grand Parade next morning he shakes his head, laughs, then later on brings food and wine. The welts, the gouges, the imprints of boots on James's back, legs, arms, blossom, then melt back into his skin. He tends his own wounds; compresses, needle and thread. Within two days he is able to hobble about with his cane. In four he is quite recovered, sees the few patients who remain in the inoculation chambers and the pox ward, operates on a child's putrid tonsils. There is no search for his assailants. He does not think of them. None of this matters. He is James Dyer. Even his enemies call him remarkable, brilliant. He does not suffer. But for the first time in three, four years, he opens the old orrery and comforts himself with the sight of it, and the memory of himself at Blind Yeo, a boy convinced of his greatness.

The planets do not fail him. On the fifteenth day of May 1767 he receives a letter from Dr Fothergill in London.

My dear James,

Though you choose to forget your old tutor, he does not forget you. I take an old man's pleasure in following the progress of my more promising students, and I am reliably informed that you have put your talents to good use in the West Country. I understand you have made inoculation against the smallpox, that most vital of measures, something of a speciality.

Mr Pouschin, the Russian Ambassador in London, has made it known that the Empress Catherine is desirous of having herself inoculated as an example to her people, that the scourge of the disease in her kingdoms may be abated. To this end she has required her ambassador to discover an English operator, our people being renowned throughout the world for their skill and knowledge in this matter. Several names have been put forward and I have taken the liberty of placing yours among them. I trust you will not take it amiss.

Who it is who shall, at the last, perform this piece of business depends on who shall arrive in the city of St Petersburg first, for it is decided that, all those on the list being equally fit for the task, all should have a fair opportunity. A day shall be set when those who are willing to undergo the journey will be assembled in London, that they might set off together for the Continent and thence, as speedily as they may, to Russia. Though I cannot entirely approve, it is thought this will afford some sport and amusement, both here and in Russia.

Should you wish me to confirm your name, I ask that you call here as soon as you are at liberty to do so, as it is anticipated that the matter shall come off before the end of this year.

Were I a younger man I should be tempted to go myself. The risks are not inconsiderable, but the rewards are likely to be very handsome indeed.

> *I am your Humble Servant etc*
> *Fothergill*

James is in London the following week, with Fothergill in Fothergill's garden. There is not a mark left on him from his recent beating. He wears a suit of excellent cloth, has clipped his hair and wears a wig, a new one, expensive and faintly scented.

Though it is possible that Fothergill has heard of the Munro affair, may even, in some way, have been prompted to write by his knowledge of it, there is no dark hinting, no gesturing at his candidate's questionable moral credentials. James expounds his method of using a charged lancet for the inoculations. Fothergill nods, approves. They drink wine on a bench under a flowering cherry tree. They drink a toast to the Empress. Fothergill says: 'What an adventure, Mr Dyer.'

They have supper with the family, plain fare, the sun setting through the window. Fothergill's daughter blushes at the way James observes her, this beautiful man, as though she were laid on his slab.

After supper Fothergill leads James to a room in the upstairs of the house. It is full of stuffed birds startling from the walls, of bones and fossils, and dead butterflies with wings like cut silk.

'Come,' he says. There is a barrel next to the table. When Fothergill takes off its lid, a waft of tobacco, bitter-sweet, fills the room.

Says Fothergill: 'My agent in North America, Mr Samms, packs his prizes in tobacco dust. This arrived yesterday on a slaver out of Charleston. Pray, hold back my sleeves.'

Fothergill reaches into the dust, draws the creature into the twilight of the room.

James asks: 'What is it, sir?'

'*Mephitis mephitis*,' says Fothergill, holding it up like a darling. 'The Wood-pussy. The common skunk.'

 The houses at Grand Parade are sold. An actor buys one, a retired captain of the East India Company the other. It is July. James's last week in Bath. A crowd is gathered by the river where a rope slants steeply over the bowling green and the Orange Grove to the east tower of the abbey. He walks over and stands at the back of the crowd. Everyone is gazing up at the tower. A small figure is manoeuvring on to the rope, lying down with his chest on some manner of breastplate that balances precariously on the rope. Someone shouts: 'He's coming! He's coming!', and the figure is suddenly in flight, hurtling down the rope, a stream of smoke trailing behind from the friction of the board. A pistol shot, the bray of a trumpet ringing over the hills. The figure plunges like a shooting star, a falling angel. Insane! Astounding!

The crowd cheers. James is pressed forward, until he finds himself looking over the shoulders of those nearest the point where the lower end of the rope is fixed to a scaffold. He sees a man, small and gristly, dressed in a patched coat, and beside him, the trumpet still in her hand, the wind tears still in her eyes, is a girl, fourteen or fifteen, conceivably his daughter. A woman next to James in the crowd says: 'It was her what done it. A short life, eh? Short and merry.'

He is studying the girl. She is laughing, as though her life at that moment could not be more lovely to her. She looks at the crowd, returns for a second James's stare. Such a face she has. Such fierce joy in her eyes.

James shoulders his way out of the crowd, gets free of it and walks, heavy as a corpse, towards the Orange Grove. He cannot think what has disturbed him so. It was a circus act, part of this rage for flying that has swept the country. A thrill for the rabble. He enters the quiet house, goes up to his room. It was always bare, green and bare. Now it is barer. He goes to the mirror, wipes it. Such a face. Is he alive? What is it to be alive? What does the girl feel that he does not?

He adjusts his cravat. Chill, dexterous fingers. He thinks of Russia, Russia, Russia . . .

FIFTH

Rev Jls Lestrade to Lady Hallam

Paris, 22 October 1767

Dear Lady Hallam,

Forgive me for not having written sooner. The truth is that I have been very loath to to do anything at all and find the smallest task wearying beyond description. This, I fear, makes me very poor company to your friend Monsieur About, who begs that I send his warmest regards and says with what fondness he recalls his stay at the Hall.

I do not believe you have ever been in his house which is on the Quai de Bourbon and but a minute's walk from the cathedral of Nôtre Dame. Do you admire the Gothic style? I was in there the other day and the air was so charged with incense it made my head spin. The windows are very fine things.

Alas! The city has too many palaces, too many churches, too many monuments. It would, I suppose, be the same for a foreigner coming to London, but I have no enthusiasm and I am glad to say Monsieur About does not bully me. As you know he is a man of business, though I am not certain what business, only that he seems to work for some Jews in the Faubourg Saint-Germain. Often, I have been left in the care of his friend Mme Duperon, a very elegant and witty lady with whom I may practise my poor

French. Her English is eccentric to say the least, and her accent renders the most innocuous statements curiously improper.

This, however, is by the by. I have been stung into this tardy correspondence not only by the recollection of my promise to write to you, but by a very odd turn of events, such that it now seems we are to abandon Paris and set off – lest a night's sleep puts paid to the notion – for Russia! I do not myself quite understand how we came to this. I am not at all sure it is wise, but About is all for it, says he has been three or four times to St Petersburg and that he would rather be there than Venice or Rome or any of the great cities of the South. We were all at supper when he made the suggestion and doubtless somewhat inflamed by his hospitality, which is never less than generous.

I say 'we' and should, as a matter of good manners, introduce the company. About, of course, and myself and Mme Duperon. In addition, an English couple by name of Featherstone whom we met last week in the Tuileries when About was able to assist Mr Featherstone, the latter having suffered the indignity of having his purse stolen. The matter was so happily resolved we agreed to visit Versailles, ensemble, that same afternoon. We did not see the King but saw some strange things in the menagerie, viz: a small black stag of China, a young elephant, and a rhinoceros with its horn broken. The Featherstones have been our companions ever since.

Mr Featherstone is a man of middle years, robust, wealthy I think, and very recently wed. His new consort is half his age, pertly pretty and I believe a very good match for him. They are honeymooning in Paris. He has been here before on business. She has never been outside of Hereford and is wonderfully unimpressed by Gallic sophistication. At least once an hour she tells About, or Mme Duperon – who does not understand at all – that the place is full of vile odours and execrable manners. Even, it seems, in matters of fashion, the women of Hereford have it over their Parisian sisters. I must confess I find them somewhat

*wearing, though in my present state I find almost all company so,
which indeed makes ME very tedious. Also perhaps a somewhat
muddled correspondent. Was I not writing of Russia? Permit me
to explain.*

*The whole matter was precipitated by this extraordinary race
between the doctors. I feel sure your Ladyship will have read of
it or heard talk of it. A – what is the collective noun for doctors?
– say, a 'funeral' of physicians, has set out from London. They are
to pass through Paris and afterwards Berlin on their road to St
Petersburg where one of their number shall gain immortality by
inoculating the Empress against the smallpox. The rules – Mr F
is my informant – are these: the first into Paris will be the first to
leave again the following day, his departure being as many hours
ahead of the other competitors as was his arrival. The same shall
apply in Berlin after which they go pell-mell to St P's. There are
receptions arranged both here and in Prussia with the British
ambassadors, and when the first of the doctors came in today at
the Place Royale there was a little crowd to receive him, though
at least half of the locals appeared to be expecting one of the King's
mistresses.*

*It was more or less by chance we were there. Mr F wished to
see the fortress of the Bastille which is no great way from Place
Royale. Ten minutes after we entered the square a very dusty chaise
bowled in with a most comically flamboyant postillion in a bright
yellow coat, yodelling to the horses and cussing the crowd. The
doors opened, we all craned our necks and down hopped Dr Dyer
and his attendant, the doctor dapper as you like, the other with the
expression of one who will never again be amused by anything in
the world, which put me rather in sympathy with him!*

*The next in – though we did not see him come – was
Dr Dimsdale, three hours after Dyer, and apparently already
accusing the others of foul play. What sorry creatures we are! My
companions, however, were very struck by the whole adventure,*

still full of it when we gathered here at chez About for dinner. We were on the meat when M. About, in his most droll manner, tapped his glass with his ring and proposed our jaunt. He threw it off so lightly none of us I think took him at his word, but then he fixed us with such a questioning eye it began to dawn on me, and then on Mr F, that our host was quite in earnest.

It was Mrs F who took up the gauntlet, turning to her husband and seconding About's proposal. Mr F, no more than any new husband, cares to be seen as lacking in manly resolve, and thus met his wife's zeal with a greater one of his own. Then only your correspondent remained to be seduced. About addressed me in French, that we might have the privacy afforded by the Fs' ignorance of the language, and put it to me that a man in my condition could only benefit from the effect of such a journey, one to stimulate the body and rouse the mind with so many delightful impressions I should be quite freed of my present melancholy. He spoke so sympathetically, and as it seemed at the time, so wisely, I was, with the help of his cellar, won over.

Mr F then enquired when it was proposed we should set out. To our amazement About replied that it must be tomorrow morning, that he would take care of the arrangements and that all we needed to do was prepare our bags. We should buy all we needed on the way. No special preparation was necessary. We would follow the same route as the racing doctors, even perhaps contrive to arrive in St Petersburg before them!

I can only say that in the light of his candles the scheme appeared delightful and we admired ourselves greatly for having the bottom to undertake it with such a show of nonchalance. It is now, by my watch, a quarter before three in the morning. The city of Paris is quiet though I can see a boat gliding on the river and can hear what sounds to be the sobbing of a woman in the street below. I have become quite an expert on these little-visited hours of the night. Sailors, I believe, call them the 'graveyard watch', and it is odd to think of them, even as I write, steering by wind and star over the great desolate oceans of the world.

It is also, perhaps, the hour of fanciful thoughts. I beg your Ladyship's indulgence. I do not believe I have properly thanked you for your goodness to me over this matter. The somewhat public decay of my faith must have been an embarrassment to you if not indeed an affront to your own strong belief and Christian righteousness. To be treated so graciously places me for ever in your debt. It is my profound wish that one day I may find the means to repay it.

I shall now lie down, close my eyes and at least play-act the part of a sleeper. Morpheus may then take pity and come to me. I shall write again in the next days and give you news of the Great St Petersburg Expedition, though I fear – hope? – it will be quite forgotten by the time we drink our morning chocolate.

I remain, Madam, your most humble, grateful, wayward servant,

Julius Lestrade

Rev Jls Lestrade to Miss Dido Lestrade

Paris, 22 October 1767

My dear Dido,

A word from your errant brother. I hope you are not still in a pet with me. I know my actions have caused you much uneasiness. I can but ask for your tolerance and patience and assure you of a brother's love. Paris is pretty enough. My French holds up though is not as elegant or correct as your own. How are things at Cow? Is Mrs Cole taking care of you? What of your headaches? Does Dr Thorne's medicine give you some relief?

Listen, my dear, there is some talk here that we may go to St Petersburg in Russia. Do not be alarmed! Monsieur About, whom you would like mightily, has persuaded me to it though I cannot say if it will come off. Not very likely, I think, yet it may be better than kicking my heels here. I have written to Lady Hallam. Do you ever see her? How does she seem? I do not know why I ask you all these questions; Lord knows where you could send a reply.

Do not be angry with me, Diddy. You and I should always endeavour to be well together. See that George Pace fixes that hole in the roof before the weather is really bad, and do, I beg you, give some attention to the garden.

I am your affectionate, foolish brother,

Julius

Rev Jls Lestrade to Lady Hallam

Berlin, 31 October

My dear Lady Hallam,

I am writing to you from the Hotel Phönix in Berlin where I have a very dainty room and a better desk than in my study at Cow from which to write to you.

I cannot quite believe that I am here. About is a magician, a benign Faustus. His energy is prodigious. We left Paris a week ago, the servants rousing us before first light on the morning of our departure, and all of us gathering, with vague remembrance of our undertaking of the previous night, at the breakfast table for hot chocolate and buns. About was there already, tucking in and looking as if he had slept twelve hours.

Mr and Mrs F and myself, carefully avoiding one another's eyes, were forced to display a zeal we in no way felt. Yet which of us cared to stand revealed in the character of a mere talker? A blabbermouth! Within a minute About had us toasting St Petersburg, the Empress, the travelling life. Thus a man's concern with how he looks to the world will allow him to be dragged halfway across its surface. It was, I assure you, a very comical scene. I dare say it would come off to good effect in the theatre.

After breakfast, our trunks were hastily assembled, and we

mounted into our chariot. It is a rather old machine, very brown inside and out, apart from the spokes of the wheels which have some old yellow paint on them. The stuffing in the seats has bunched in places, one of the windows will not completely close, and there is a continuous eerie lament from the rear axle, but we have become quite attached to it, for it is a very sturdy machine with a good, dry smell and plenty of space for us all, even Mrs F's hoops.

By the time we made our first stop, a pretty inn outside the town of Compiegne, we were all remarkably resigned, the more so when the innkeeper regaled us with an exquisite stew of duck and bacon, and About persuaded him to part with a half-dozen bottles of his best red wine from his 'cave'. The weather, which had been grey in Paris, ripened into a glorious autumn afternoon. Our coach, which glories in the name of 'Mami Sylvie', after one of About's elderly female relatives, quite consumed the distances, racing between the hedgerows and bouncing us through settlements which, despite their evident poverty, were picturesque to us. That night I had my first good sleep in many weeks, at least seven hours of blissful slumber. I wonder now how much of our suffering, our mental anguish, is occasioned by the lack of it. It may be that the cure for many of our ills is no more than the administration of a potent sleeping draught.

You may consider, madam, that we are an oddly assorted band of voyagers, but I must report that we agree with each other very well. Mr and Mrs F are honest folk, easily ruffled, I fear, and Mr F never far from bluster, but essentially well-meaning, and one cannot ask for more. They are delightfully and consistently contemptuous of all things un-English. All that we see – cows, trees, buildings, the very men and women we pass upon the road – have to the Featherstonian mind a more lovely counterpart in Albion. This, far from exasperating About, makes him roar with laughter, and where a smirk might offend, such open amusement is taken in good part. Mrs F is cuter than her husband. I catch her sometimes with a very shrewd expression on her face. Before this honeymoon is over she shall have Mr F well tamed.

As for our Captain, Monsieur About, you already know something of his character and abilities. Did you not find something – how shall I say? – something mysterious about him? I have not fathomed him at all and yet I have a perfect confidence in him. If any man may bring all safely and expeditiously to the Imperial court it is he.

At Brussels we had a look at Dr Dimsdale and another of the competitors, a Mr Selkirk, and in Hanover we saw Ozias Hampshire. We could not tell which of them was leading but upon our arrival in Berlin we discovered that Dyer was still the front-runner and that the accusations against him, and against his man, grow ever more furious. There is even some talk of his having hired brigands to waylay Dr Lettsom's chaise and certainly Dr Lettsom would seem to be out of the race.

I have passed the day in sightseeing – the Opera House, the old Royal Palace, the new Protestant cathedral in the Lustgarten which they call 'old Fritz's tea-cup' on account of its dome. 'Old Fritz' himself is in the city and About has gone to the Palace in hopes of an audience. He did not wish to be accompanied, claiming that the matter was one of business and would be too dull. He took with him, carried by a servant from the hotel, one of the stout boxes he loaded in Paris. I do not know what is inside of them, and when this morning I gave it a hard look, About winked at me in a very curious manner. I cannot believe it is anything improper. Does Frederick have any foibles your Ladyship knows of? Great men sometimes do. I believe that Monsieur About delights in teasing us.

Mr and Mrs Featherstone have been with me doing the sights.
They are rather pleased with Berlin and as the Prussians were
our allies in the late wars they have a greater claim on Mr
F's affections than the French can ever hope for. Tonight
we dine at the Bristol and retire early to make the most
of our good Prussian beds, for About advises us that the
further east we travel the less salubrious will be our quarters.
So be it.

I trust this shall find your Ladyship both healthy and happy.
Shall you be going up to Town this winter? Now Monsieur About
is at the door. I am your humble and obedient servant,

Julius Lestrade

Jls Lestrade to Miss Dido Lestrade

Berlin, 1 November

Dear Dido,
Your brother is in Berlin! Yes, I know, he has no business being
there but . . . there he is and there's an end on it. Are you well?
I have sometimes wondered whether Thorne knows what he is
doing. Most doctors are incompetent. Quite a number of them
are mad. All are greedy. The trip from Paris might have been
worse though my back is sore from the confounded coach and I
have been seized with the worst attack of piles I can remember
having suffered. I often wish I was back in Cow, but as I am
still unfit to serve as the people's spiritual guardian I should only
have to go away again and cause more distress to those I hold
dear. Perhaps God is in the East. Perhaps I shall become a
Mohammedan. Would you let me back in the house, Dido, if I
became a Mohammedan?

Besides Monsieur About I am travelling with some people
called Featherstone. Mr Featherstone, who has shares in a
couple of Bristol slave boats, is a great red-faced child.
Mrs F is a flirt and has married him for his slave gold.

Incredible as it may seem, she has been making eyes at me! They say travelling induces a slackening in a man's moral character; what effect might it have upon a woman? We shall see.

Tomorrow morning we are on the road again. Things I fancy will be considerably less convenient from here on. Of course, there is nothing to stop me returning to Paris, or for that matter returning to England, but I intend to see the journey through. I shall then at least have some stories to tell, even if I have no grandchildren to tell them to.

I had a dream last night and you were in it, wearing one of Mama's old dresses, the grey one. Do you recall it? When I woke I had for a time a strong emotion. I wonder if Father was happy at my age. Are you happy, dear sister?

My next from the chilly land of the Poles. Give my best to old Askew. Remember me in your prayers.

Julius

Rev Jls Lestrade to Mr Askew, Esq

Bydgoszcz, 8 November

My dear Askew,

I doubt not but Dido has kept you informed of my peregrinations. She was not at all pleased with me when I left, swore she could not understand my mind at all. Accused me of pleasing myself at the expense of others. I am afraid there is some justice in this, though I hope that you, old friend, are not so hard on me. How could I discharge my office as a conscious hypocrite? A lawyer may perhaps practise his profession without much faith in the law or a soldier attend to his duties without believing his war to be a just one, but a man of the cloth cannot decently continue without his faith. I know, my friend, you are wagging your head and saying if such were the case half of the divines in England would have to relinquish their positions. I sometimes think that what I fear most is that I could live quite contentedly WITHOUT religion. Is this the spirit of our times? An overweening age.

How are the dogs? That lovely bitch of yours will be a terror for the hares this year. I trust Miss Askew thrives. An odd business the other day – I had a stand-off with a mob of the local soldiery. I quite feared for my life, though I do not think I showed it. They came upon me while I was pissing on a wall behind the inn where we had passed the night. Ugly devils. Paid them off and they let me be. The country here is very poor. The peasants wear the bark of trees upon their feet for shoes. Danzig on the Baltic is our next stop and we hope to have some news of the flying doctors there. I shall have to buy myself a decent cloak for the weather is turning. Keep an eye on my sister, she is not used to being alone.

I am, Sir, your most obliged and humble servant,

Julius Lestrade

Jls Lestrade to Miss Dido Lestrade

Kashubia, 12 November

Dear Dido,

We are nearing the Baltic coast and the city of Danzig, which About tells me is a thriving merchant city much populated by Scots. The land here, though fertile, is poor, worse than France, but the people seem less oppressed. It is also damn cold, a wind that blows in our teeth for it comes out of Russia. Yesterday eve my back seized up completely while I was lying in bed trying to read Candide by the candlelight. For several minutes I could not move at all and even fancied I should die there, a godless clergyman in a hovel in Poland. Punishment no doubt for my reading Voltaire. It is About's book. He has made me a present of it. He met Voltaire in Geneva.

It is a mistake to travel in the hope of solving one's problems. One merely transports them and is thus forced to endure them among strangers. How is that for a pensée? *It will be a great relief for us to reach a civilised town. Even About's equanimity has been somewhat ruffled by these last two days of slog. I will not say he quite snapped at Mr F; it was more the soft growl of a very big dog, rather impressive and comical when you consider one could make three Abouts from the flesh and bones of one Featherstone. It is dangerous for Mrs F to see her husband constantly in the company of a superior man. I am sure Mr Featherstone shines like a star among his fellow slavers but he sputters like a damp brimstone next to About.*

I believe I can smell the sea. A cold green sea.

I am, affectionately, your brother,

Julius Lestrade

2   Konigsberg, first city of ducal Prussia, basks fatly under blue skies. Mami Sylvie clatters in through the slushed streets, a bell rackets in the cold air. Mrs Featherstone desires to make some purchases. They link arms and set out from their inn. The Reverend buys senna and tobacco. About buys a fine fur hat. In the same furrier's the Featherstones purchase pelisses, 'This for the lady, this for the gentleman – *sehr schön, nicht wahr*? And this other gentleman, he will also be wanting?'

The Reverend considers his diminishing hoard, and settles for a pair of gloves. Outside they admire themselves in the shop window. 'Now,' says About, 'we are fit to meet an empress!'

With fresh horses they set out the following morning, travel hard, deep into the night, chasing the Pole Star towards Riga. The snow, half thawed, freckles the landscape, but on the afternoon of the second day, clouds roll in from the east: blue, grey, white. Throughout the night, snow, shifting stealthily around the shuttered windows of their inn, falls steadily, pausing just long enough next morning to persuade them to continue on their way, then falling again, relentlessly, a soft crushing weight of snow. It is exhilarating at first, its weird dances, weird beauty. Then, quite suddenly, as though a mental spark has flown between the travellers, they are alarmed by it. What if the coach should become bogged? Where would they seek help? Have they not been rash to travel so late in the year? About raises his hands. Peace! In Riga they shall have Mami Sylvie fitted with runners, a very usual way to travel in this part of the world and wonderfully pleasant. They shall skate into St Petersburg! He has done it a thousand times. For his own part he is very glad to see such weather. They will go twice as fast on the runners. All for the best in the best of all possible worlds! He winks at the Reverend, and yet to the Reverend's eyes even About appears unsettled, glancing furtively at the impossible curtains of snow, the failing light. How slow the horses go, up to their knees in the drifts! It is agreed, in the very next village they come to, they shall seek shelter. No point tempting fate. They do not have a race to win!

They stare out anxiously, searching for the silhouette of a house, the flicker of a light.

'There!'

'Well espied, Mrs Featherstone!'

It is little more than a hovel. About jumps out, beats at the door. The others peer through the window at him, wiping their breath from the glass. The door opens, About enters. Five minutes later he returns, the snow melting from his boots as he settles back in his seat.

'We are saved!' He chuckles. 'The delightful fellow informs me there is a monastery no more than a half-hour's ride from here.'

The half-hour passes. An hour. There is no sign of any monastery. No sign of anything. Mrs Featherstone enquires testily if Monsieur About understood the directions. Monsieur About fixes on her a hard and intimate look. The Reverend is quietly calculating their chances if they are forced to remain out in the storm. They have some biscuits and there is the last half-bottle of the French brandy. Might a fire not be possible? He has a tinder box and there must be a great deal of wood about.

The word 'wolf' leaps into his mind like the beast itself. Childhood wolf stories. Childhood dreams of animals with spiky fur and ice-coloured eyes, slouching, watchful, scenting the dreamer in the forests of sleep. No Mama here to vanquish the horror with a lullaby. This, thinks the Reverend, looking round at his companions, might be a good moment to recover the comforts of prayer, and he has formed a single, silent 'Our Father', the words cumbersome, large as eggs in his mouth, when all prayer, all thought, is instantly suspended.

Says Mr Featherstone: 'Was that . . . ?'

The second shot is more distinct than the first. The coach halts; no one speaks. A cry? They hold their breath. They hear only the beat of their own hearts, the sweep of the wind.

The Reverend says: 'Hunters?'

'In this?' scoffs Mrs Featherstone.

'Perchance it was a signal?' says the Reverend. 'A traveller in distress. Should we not investigate, monsieur?'

Mr Featherstone asks: 'Are there bandits in these parts, monsieur?'

About shrugs. Shrugs again. 'I regret, some things are unknown even to About.'

Mrs Featherstone says: 'Why does one of you not look into it? Why do you all just sit?'

'Surely, dear,' says Mr Featherstone, 'my first duty is to protect you.'

About says: 'Bravo, monsieur. For myself, I have been out once and did not care for it. My stockings are still quite wet.'

They look towards the Reverend. He holds their eyes a moment then buttons the neck of his coat, forces open the door at his side, and drops, lightly as he can, into the roaring world.

 The coachman grips a blunderbuss across his lap. Only his eyes remain unmuffled, humanly alive. His coat is crusted with snow and the snow sits thickly in the gutters of his hat.

The Reverend says: 'Let us go forward together!' He speaks in German, seeking, as the snow thrusts at his face, the appropriate grammar. Imperative or conditional? The driver shakes his head; a small gesture of unshakable resolve.

The Reverend turns away, pats the nearest horse, a sorrel. He feels the warmth through his new gloves. Poor beasts. How unhappy they look. His hands sheltering his face, he gazes forward, up the road towards Riga, then walks, leaning into the storm, twenty yards before he remembers he has no weapon. He stoops, picks up a branch, wipes the snow from it, holds it like a musket. Through this weather it might be mistaken. No more shots now. No sign of life at all.

How far is he supposed to go? He must not lose sight of the coach. It would not take long to become lost then; to wander off the road, lose all sense of direction, steadily colder, weaker. Lying down he would be covered in minutes. Buried till the thaw, some peasant with his dog coming across the frozen corpse in spring. A lonely place this. The whole land giving off a continuous low moan of absence.

He looks back. Mami Sylvie, though much obscured, is still visible. Ten more paces, then back. He counts them out, reaches seven, and stops. Something is moving in the storm ahead. A man? Two men. One standing, one lying in the snow. At the side of the road there is a vehicle, a chaise, wheels deep in the snow. One horse.

Grasping his branch, the Reverend approaches. Whoever they are they do not look like cutthroats. More like the victims than the perpetrators of an outrage.

'HALLOOOOO!'

The man has a pistol, briefly points it at the Reverend's face, then lets his arm drop to his side. The Reverend moves closer. He lets go of the branch.

'Dr Dyer?'

They are standing together now in the road. Dyer's cropped head is gashed, gory.

'Dear sir, what calamity is this? Are you robbed?'

'You know me, sir?'

'I saw you in Paris. Place Royal.'

'I did not see you.'

'The Reverend Julius Lestrade, sir. Is this your companion? Is he badly hurt?'

'That is the postillion. My "companion" shot him while he made his escape.'

'Shot him?'

'Having first struck me and filled his pockets with my gold.'

The Reverend kneels in the snow beside the post-boy. No boy this, but a man in his fifties, shocked, frightened. The ball has struck his wrist and exited by his elbow. When the Reverend looks up, Dyer is leaning into the coach, pulling out a bag, a travelling bag and another, smaller, of green baize, which faintly jangles as he lifts it.

'I assume, Lestrade, you did not walk here from Paris.'

'Indeed not. The coach is yonder.'

'Then I should be grateful if you would assist me to the nearest town. If you know of me then you know where I am bound.'

'I fear we shall none of us get far in this. Aha! Here they come!'

Mami Sylvie creeps silently towards them. Mr Featherstone is sat up beside the coachman. Featherstone has the blunderbuss at his shoulder. Thinks the Reverend: It will be a miracle if I am not shot in this adventure.

'HO!'

'HO THERE!'

The wounded postillion is carried inside the coach; Dyer follows, the blood making a crazy web over his face. The remaining horse from the chaise is tethered to the basket at the back of the coach. Mr Featherstone elects to stay up with the driver. Inside the coach the Reverend fusses ineffectually with the groaning postillion. Mrs Featherstone offers a handkerchief to Dyer to wipe his face. He wipes, hands back the cloth. Mrs Featherstone receives it, drops it discreetly by her feet.

Says the Reverend: 'The rogue shall not get far in this.'

'The devil looks after his own,' says Dyer. 'I swear that when they come to hang him the rope will snap. Where are you headed?'

'Wherever at all we may reach. We are told there is a monastery . . .'

There is an excited cry from Mr Featherstone. About pulls down the window.

'La,' says Mrs Featherstone. 'Can that be it? That ruin?'

The building looks like the hulk of an ancient ship. Two central towers, two low wings, one of which is clearly derelict, the snow visibly falling behind its gaping windows. The other wing is more hopeful, though there is no light to be seen, no welcoming plume of smoke.

They draw up. Monsieur About and Mr Featherstone beat at the wooden door between the towers. Looking out, the Reverend does not believe the door will open. Yet open it does, though by whose agency he cannot see for the moment until Mr Featherstone comes trotting back to the coach. Even then it is hard, among the piling shadows, the last of the daylight, to see more than that it is a man, aged, and carrying a tiny light which somehow contrives to endure the plucking of the wind.

Mr Featherstone and the Reverend carry the postillion between them. Behind, like mourners, come the others: Dyer bare-headed; Mrs Featherstone shivering inside her fur; Monsieur About, humming under his breath, now and then declaring: 'Everything shall be charming. Just wait and see!'

Silent corridors. Unlit empty rooms. Everywhere the reek of damp and cats.

'I believe', whispers the Reverend to Mr Featherstone, 'that this fellow is on his own here.'

Featherstone concurs, says: 'So long as he has a fire and something in the pot. Are they not under obligation to share what they have?'

There is a fire, though it is almost lost in the great stone hearth. Also a pot, which the old monk peers into, stirs, and hangs from a tripod over the flames. They lie the postillion on the table, a noble piece of furniture that may, fancies the Reverend, have served once as the abbot's desk.

'Is he dead?' asks Mrs Featherstone.

The Reverend says: 'He lives, and yet his signs are very faint.'

There is a laugh from Dyer, sharp and humourless. The Reverend says: 'Perhaps, sir, you would examine him. If, that is, you feel able.'

Dyer comes over to the table, looks quickly at the wounded man, goes to his green bag, pulls out a roll of bandages and tosses them to the Reverend.

'You seem to like the part.'

The Reverend, very conscious of his audience, binds the postillion's arm. He is tying the knot when the man lets out a piercing scream, half sits up, then faints away, his head banging heavily on the table. The Reverend steps back like a stage murderer. Everyone except Dyer peers at the man on the table.

'Is he dead now?' asks Mrs Featherstone.

Later, with the postillion on a couch of old straw in the corner of the room, they eat from the monk's smoke-black pot. Some manner of gruel flavoured with pork fat. They drink goat's milk from a communal bowl. The old monk, in the patched and faded habit of a Benedictine, heavy wooden crucifix around his neck, observes them with his small, incessant smile. With him is a boy, fat, fourteen or fifteen years old, the wide open face of an idiot.

About, the polyglot, attempts to draw them into conversation. When language fails, he mimes and sketches maps on the palm of his hand. The monk nods amiably, mutters a dozen words of some incomprehensible dialect, then points to the boy, grins, and says: 'Ponko.'

'Ponko?'

'Ponko.'

The boy slavers, churns his tongue, points at himself. 'Ponko. Ponko.'

Mr Featherstone belches. His wife says: 'Ain't there no beds to be had?'

About leans his head on his hands: a child's mime of sleep. The old monk speaks to Ponko. Ponko goes out. The travellers look gloomily at the cones on the fire. Now and then snowflakes come down the chimney and sizzle in the embers. James Dyer touches his head, says: 'Madam, you possess a looking-glass?'

Mrs Featherstone does not. Monsieur About does. A travelling mirror in a snakeskin case. Dyer, from the green bag, takes a candle-holder to which is attached a curved plate, silver, highly polished. There is a stub of candle in the holder which he lights from the monk's lamps. Further rummaging produces a needle and thread. He arms the needle. He says: 'Monsieur, I should be obliged if you would hold the candle, so, that the light may reflect from the shield. And the mirror, so, that I may see what I am about.'

Mrs Featherstone says: 'What are you about, sir?'

Dyer looks at her. 'That, madam, I should have thought self-evident.'

He begins to sew up his head, drawing together the ragged lips of the gash, and with such swiftness, such unconcern, it is – as the Reverend later writes to Lady Hallam – as if he were sewing only the head in the glass. Everyone, with the exception of the old monk, who looks on as if this were a conjuring trick he has long since fathomed, is vastly impressed.

'Bravo!' says Monsieur About.

The Reverend says: 'Remarkable.'

'I do not', says Mr Featherstone, 'think I could have stood it so well.'

Dyer ignores them. Ponko comes back. The monk rises from his stool, grasps with cramped fingers one of the lights, and leads the party to their rooms, cells of the former brothers. The Reverend remains, sitting up with Ponko and the postillion. The monk returns, shuffles to his stool, sits. Stiff as old wood. The Reverend smiles at him. They nod to each other. Then the Reverend folds his arms on the table, lays down his head and sleeps. His last conscious image is James Dyer, plying a curved needle through his own flesh. His own flesh!

Remarkable.

When they gather next morning, somewhat tatty from a night on cold pallets, they discuss their predicament. James Dyer insists they push on. To hell with the snow. Are they afraid of snow?

The Reverend says: 'Have you seen the snow, sir?'

Dyer says: 'You intend to stay the next week here? The next month?'

'Better here', says Mr Featherstone, 'than what would happen to us out there.'

About says: 'I must agree with Mr Featherstone. It would be folly to make an attempt at travel in such conditions.'

'I do not travel idly, sir,' says Dyer. 'I am not here for my health.'

Mrs Featherstone says: 'For my part I shall not set a foot out of doors. We may not be quite comfortable here but we shall not be destroyed. Sure this weather cannot last.'

Dyer stands. 'If you, Mr About, would be good enough to obtain some provisions from the monk, I shall be on my way.'

The Reverend says: 'You truly intend to go, sir?'

'I do.' He goes out. The others look at each other, big-eyed.

Mr Featherstone says: 'He's mad. Stark mad.'

The Reverend concurs. 'His accident has perhaps hurt him more than we had thought. I have seen men concussed before, not quite in their right senses for a while. I shall attempt to reason with him.'

About says: 'Be so good as to see he takes no more than is his. Whatever he takes is sure to be lost.'

The Reverend fights his way along the edge of the building to the stables. Outside, Mami Sylvie is heaped about with snow. Inside, the stable is surprisingly snug. Two lamps taken from the coach are burning. There is a smell of horse skin, horse dung and last summer's hay; the monastery's meagre tithe, evidence perhaps that the old monk has more visitors than they have imagined. James Dyer is examining his horse's shoes. The coachman, puffing on a short pipe, is tending to the other horses. Ponko is also there, chewing on a piece of straw.

The Reverend stands behind Dyer, talks to him in a low, soothing voice. Dyer is angry when he finds the Reverend has not brought out food for him. He goes back into the monastery. The Reverend waits in the stable, grins at Ponko. The coachman points to the roof. The Reverend cannot understand what the man is saying to him. The coachman speaks to him like a child. The Reverend hears 'red' and 'schnee', then sees what it is the coachman is pointing to. Lengths of wood, curved at the end. About's famous runners, surely. When Dyer returns, the Reverend tells him of the runners. They could not do anything today, of course, but tomorrow, the next day. Dyer says: 'You were of some use to me yesterday. I thank you for it.'

'Thank me, sir, by remaining here another twenty-four hours. You are not fit to travel. And what of the postillion? You alone have the skill that might save him.'

Dyer leads the horse out of the stable.

The Reverend, hands sheltering his eyes, watches him go, the horse picking its way, the rider urging it on. 'I should have stopped him,' says the Reverend to himself. 'There goes a man to certain death.'

It is late in the afternoon before Dyer returns. The company are sat by the fire, the backgammon board spread between the Reverend and Monsieur About. Ponko watches their moves with fascinated incomprehension. There is a distant booming at the door. The old monk wakes from his meditation, is gone a quarter of an hour, and returns with Dyer, the surgeon buttoned in his surtout, a bag in each blue fist. He cannot speak; the wind has frozen his face.

They sit him as close to the mound of glowing cones as they can. His clothes drip, then smoke. Mr Featherstone offers his flask. Dyer swallows, the blood comes into his face. In a voice like the voice of ice itself, he says: 'The horse failed me.'

He does not speak again that night.

For breakfast there is only a mouthful of cheese and black bread, the bread so solid it must be thawed at the fire before they can eat it.

About says: 'How is the wounded man this morning?'

The Reverend replies: 'You may see for yourself, monsieur. The arm is mortifying.'

'It will not be easy to bury him,' says About. 'The ground will be like iron.'

Dyer comes in and sits at the table. He says: 'The snow has stopped.'

About says: 'It has, sir, but I hope you are not thinking of repeating your adventures of yesterday. If you leave today you must do so on foot.'

Smiling, he takes the force of Dyer's stare. The Reverend says: 'Since we must remain a little longer, will you not attend to the postillion, Doctor?'

'He is not my patient, Reverend. He is not of any consequence to me at all.'

The Reverend persists. 'Your oaths as a physician should make him of consequence to you. And if not that, your common humanity.'

'Do not presume, sir, to tell me what I should or should not do.'

'Sir, it seems that someone must.'

'You are impertinent, sir. Idle and impertinent.'

'It is impertinent to wish that we might save a man's life? Is that idle?'

'My business, sir, is with the Empress. I have not come this way to dance attendance upon every post-boy, footman, or lady's maid that falls sick or has themselves shot. I should never have got past Dover.'

Lack of sleep, lack of hot food. The Reverend hears the anger in his own voice. 'This man was in your employ. He was shot by your companion.'

'Mr Gummer was no companion, sir.' Dyer points to his head. 'This was not a kiss he left me with.'

'He was in your company. Zounds! A dog has more compassion.'

'Are you calling me a dog, sir?'

'No, sir, for a dog would have more heart than to leave a man to die, and for no better reason than that he is too eager to keep an appointment.'

'How should you like, sir, to feel my boot on your arse?'

Dyer stands, walks round to the Reverend. The Reverend stands. It has been many years since he felt like this. Black bile. He clenches his fists. He says: 'Nothing would give me greater satisfaction than to bloody your face, sir. I am amazed a man such as you should have lived so long.'

About says: 'What is your price, Doctor, to attend to this' – he gestures – 'unfortunate creature?'

'You refer, monsieur, to my fee?'

'Indeed. The word eluded me.'

Dyer sits down. He is quite calm. It is as if nothing of the last three minutes has actually occurred. The Reverend sits, dizzy with anger, shocked to find that he is disappointed. He stares hard at his nails. His fingers are trembling.

Dyer says: 'It will cost you a horse.'

About shakes his head. 'No, sir. Already you have lost one horse. It was yours to lose. You shall not now lose one of ours. Consider your position. With us you will, not today, but shortly, have passage, either to the nearest town where you may hire a conveyance, or even to St Petersburg, for we also are headed there and would consider it a privilege to deliver you to the Empress. Without us, however . . .' He shrugs expansively. 'You see, sir, it is us who have the whip in hand. Does it not seem so to you, Reverend?'

'Both seems and is, monsieur.'

Dyer picks up a piece of the black bread, examines it, puts it down. He says: 'What I require, sir, is your word of honour you shall fetch me to St Petersburg with all possible dispatch. That there will not be an hour's unnecessary delay. It is agreed?'

About looks to the Reverend. The Reverend nods. About holds out his hand. 'It is agreed.'

Reverend Julius Lestrade to Lady Hallam

Plunge? 18 November

Dear Lady Hallam,

I do not know when I shall be at leisure to post this letter. I am at present in a monastery between Konigsberg and Riga, and apart from a little village – of which more later – we are quite in the wilderness and up to our noses in snow, having been overtaken upon the road by a very considerable blizzard.

Our party, all of whom are well, though somewhat in need of good beds, has been joined by none other than one of the doctors we were following to St Petersburg! It is Dr Dyer, who had the misfortune to be robbed and assaulted by the man he was travelling with. A very mysterious business with nearly fatal consequences for the postillion, who was shot in the arm and is dangerously ill, poor man, and lying no more than two yards from where I now write to you. Dyer, who was struck a terrific blow to the head, has recovered remarkably and is indeed an unusual man in every way. Cold-blooded and apparently indestructible. We hope he will operate on the postillion tonight or tomorrow morning, for it is evident that the man's arm must come off if his life is to be spared. His tongue has a covering of brown fur and is very red at the edges.

How long we shall be detained here it is hard to say. The weather improves, which is to say there is no new fall of snow, but there is a great deal of it upon the ground and the road may remain impassable for weeks! Our salvation may lie in the discovery of some wooden runners in the stable here which are commonly used in these parts to turn a coach into a kind of sledge. Unfortunately this metamorphosis will not be easy to enact, adjustment being necessary both to the runners and to the axles of our machine.

Today at noon we had an expedition over the snow to the village to obtain provisions – myself, Monsieur About, Mr Featherstone, and a boy who is named Ponko, who was our guide. We were at first deterred by the thought of how we should travel over such deep snow. Yet to all things there is an answer. An old monk, who, apart from the boy, is the only inhabitant of the monastery, led us to a great cupboard, which, from the prodigious quantity of dust and old spider's webs, might have dated from the time of the Ark. Here he showed us the ingenious footwear of his former brothers; shoes like racquets made from strips of hide bound to a wooden rim, each about the size of a large frying-pan. Many had decayed, but we did at length find four pairs to suit us, and in this manner set off over a white, sparkling sea.

Monsieur About had sensibly provided himself with a pair of painted spectacles against the glare of the reflected sun, the brilliance of which incommoded Mr Featherstone and myself a good deal at first. More troublesome, however – until we had to some degree mastered their use — were the snow shoes. I do not care to remember how often I up-ended myself, and once down, your Ladyship has no idea how difficult it is to regain one's feet, not to mention one's dignity! Mr Featherstone was at a similar pass and even Monsieur About had his Gallic nose in the ice upon two or three occasions. Yet we learnt from our mistakes and from Ponko's example, and were soon progressing like water beetles over the surface of a pond.

Our first intimation of the village was a haze of grey smoke; one of the houses at the edge of the village — which are all of wood — had burnt down. From the way in which the snow was trampled around the smouldering beams it seems that the villagers had all come to their neighbour's aid, though, to be sure, to little purpose, as the house was destroyed. Ponko was quite excited by it and no doubt told us the whole story, for he babbled and drooled, poor boy, and pulled the most extraordinary faces.

In the village proper there was not a soul abroad, the only sign of life being a large mastiff that snarled very menacingly at our approach but retreated as soon as Ponko fired off a few snowballs. There was no church in the village, nor any place of Christian worship. When I mentioned this to About he said the denizens of these parts were not necessarily Christian at all, and that they preferred the gods of their ancestors, that many still worshipped Nature, and that the priesthood was forced even now to cut down certain trees sacred to the people. Did I not wonder where all the brothers from the monastery had gone? I said I thought there were villages in parts of England where Christianity had yet to take root, but About said the superstition was very profound here, and while we were in the village I saw a number of carvings that make me believe he is right. I was glad then we had Ponko with us, for I do not know how we should have been received without him.

There was little to be had in the way of food. No doubt the people were hoarding against the long winter, yet we did obtain some sausages, butter, a capon, some hard yellow cheese and a leather sack of their local 'wine'. For these we exchanged a good knife, some gloves I bought in Konigsberg, and Monsieur About's dark glasses. I was sorry for the gloves but one cannot eat them. The capon escaped from us on the return journey and we had to chase it. Mr Featherstone, who has a fine appetite and was thus well motivated in the pursuit, overtook the animal just as it reached the treeline and thrust it into his coat where it remained, very quiet, until its neck was wrung. About is in charge of the cooking; our friend the monk has provided some potatoes and we have even discovered some antique herbs left hanging to dry from a roof beam. The juice will make a very nourishing soup for the postillion. I trust it may give him the strength to survive his coming ordeal.

For myself I believe my health is improved. The air is very brisk and clear. I hope and believe I may return to Cow not only somewhat wiser as to the manners of the world, but able to serve you in all conscience in the office to which you were gracious enough to appoint me. Truly, the Almighty moves in mysterious ways.

Monsieur About commands me to send your Ladyship his best compliments and begs that I be excused any further writing until I have taken my turn in stirring the pot. I am therefore your most obliged, faithful and humble servant,

Julius Lestrade

 The food has stunned them. For an hour after eating they sit around the table pouring the wine from the skin, their thoughts drifting, circling, settling. The Reverend

fills his pipe, offers his tobacco. A cat jumps softly on to the table and begins to gnaw at one of the chicken bones.

About asks if he might offer the company some entertainment. It is agreed that he might. What does he propose – cards, backgammon, a guessing game?

About shakes his head, stands up from the table, excuses himself. When he is out of the room, Mr Featherstone says: 'He has quite altered Mrs Featherstone's opinion of the French.'

The Reverend says: 'For the better I trust?'

Mr Featherstone says: 'Quite altered.'

About comes in carrying three boxes; two of them about the size of an infant's coffin, the other one smaller, of highly polished boxwood. He says: 'I was afraid the cold night have hurt them, but I find it is not so. First the table must be cleared.'

They stack their odd assortment of knives and dishes on the floor. The surface of the table is wiped. The cat jumps down then up on to the monk's lap. About has the boxes at his feet. The Reverend hears him open them and then a sound like the winding of clocks. About says: 'Allow me to present to you two most elegant members of society.'

He lifts on to the table the figures of a man and woman, exquisitely dressed in Paris fashions, each somewhat less than two feet in height. He touches a switch on their backs and they begin to walk, the man swinging his tasselled cane, the woman turning her head and raising her lace handkerchief as though to sniff its perfume. The cat stands on the monk's lap, arches its back. The figures stop opposite James Dyer at the head of the table. They bow, turn on invisible wheels, and continue their parade, back towards Monsieur About, reaching him just as their springs are exhausted. About returns them to their boxes. The Reverend says: 'These are your business, monsieur? You trade in automata?'

About says: 'In France, a gentlemen will never admit to be in business, but among the English I may confess to it without exciting prejudice. These are my trade, Reverend. My customers are dukes, princes, kings, and I hope also an empress. The dolls are the finest in Europe, also the most expensive. For this I am a little discreet when I travel. My apologies. Will you see . . . *autre chose?*'

He places the smaller box on the table, opens it and lifts out the most elegant duelling pistols the Reverend has ever laid eyes on. He cocks them both and looks round at the faces of his audience. 'Dr Dyer, would you oblige me, sir? Mr Featherstone, please to be so kind as to pass this to the doctor. Gently, sir, the mechanism is very delicate.'

Featherstone takes the pistol. He says: 'Not loaded, I trust!'

When About turns to him there is no smile on his face; no trace of the amiable host, the gay, resourceful travelling companion. Featherstone is visibly disconcerted. So too is the Reverend. He thinks: If this is acting, it is very good acting.

About says: 'They are of course loaded. One does not trifle with a man like Dr Dyer. I assume that you are a doctor, sir, and not merely a barber.'

Dyer takes the pistol from Featherstone. He says: 'Doctor enough for you, monsieur.'

About stands. Dyer stands. Mrs Featherstone coughs. The monk strokes the cat.

The Reverend says: 'I should like to see those dolls of yours again, monsieur.'

About ignores him. 'Mrs Featherstone. Will you please give the command to fire. Whensoever you wish.'

The Reverend looks at About in amazement. What a face! Eyes narrowed to points of darkness, mouth shut tight, jaw set firm. His arm is outstretched, the pistol aimed directly at Dyer's chest, at his heart. Dyer slowly raises his pistol. The Reverend thinks: How excellent all his movements are to watch. Makes the cat look clumsy. About is up to something. Does Dyer know that? About is a stranger to him. What should he think, a pistol pointed at his heart? He does not seem to care. Nothing more dangerous than a man who does not care. Or does he think himself immortal? Is that it?

'Fire!'

Impossible to say whose finger is first to pull the trigger. The Reverend, sitting equidistant from both men, hears the snap of the pistol actions almost as one, though if he were forced, he should say that Dyer was a fraction quicker. There is no flash, no report. Yet something, some bright object – what? Birds! – small jewelled birds are emerging slowly from the end of both men's pistols, flapping their golden wings and singing a mechanical song, half a dozen notes, which, in the profound silence of the room, are the most delicate and pretty sound imaginable.

From behind them comes a scream, ecstatic, terrified: '*Jesu! Bin ich tot?*'

The postillion is sitting up, staring madly at them from his bed of straw. In Dyer's hand, in About's hand, the little birds fold their wings and glide back into the barrels of the guns.

 'Time?'

Mrs Featherstone, Grimaldi's old watch in her hand, says: 'Three minutes. Somewhat less I think.'

Dyer says: 'How did you like that, Reverend?'

It takes a moment for the Reverend to find his voice. He says: 'I congratulate you, Doctor. It was . . .'

Dyer washes his hands in a bucket, releasing from his fingers clouds of blood. He takes his coat from Mrs Featherstone, his watch, then leaves the room. The others step forward and look down at the unconscious man on the table. Mrs Featherstone says: 'What shall we do with him now?'

Her husband says: 'Not much work for a one-armed post-boy.'

Dusk. The Reverend Lestrade moves clumsily towards the woods in his snow shoes. He has left the other men in the stable working on the runners for Mami Sylvie. They have all been at it most of the day, have dug out the coach, removed the rear wheels and fitted two of the runners, though only after much shaving and hammering. Much cussing too, in which he, to his shame, was not the most backward.

He has come now for solitude and for the beauty of the evening: a white sun settling over the forest, snow the colour of slate, the air pierced with light, the sky an immense glass bell in which the world's few sounds swell the silence, the plaintiveness. It is a world, an hour, created for solitude. The Reverend relishes it, feels with each hissing step the expansive inner presence of his soul. Hymn-writing weather!

The black fringe of the forest is half a mile from the monastery, possibly less, yet it approaches with the slowness of a coastline watched from the deck of a ship, and in the same way it is suddenly there, leaping into focus, each tree its separate self, no longer black but green and purple. At the treeline he stops and looks back. Someone stands by the monastery wall. He cannot tell who it is. He waves but the figure does not wave back. Very likely, under the shadow of the forest, he is invisible. He turns and steps past the first trees. He does not intend to go far; no more than a few yards. Yet how seductive it is; a forest for a fairy tale! He goes deeper, threading his way towards the ogre's lair, the dragon, the fair princess.

In time to come, when he is growing stiff and old and there are no more adventures but the last, he thinks how things might have been if, on reaching the forest, he had turned back. Was that what the figure by the monastery wished him to do? Or were they all unwitting agents of a power that had long since decreed he would not stop but walk deeper and deeper until he saw the lights and the dogs and the silent woman fleeing for her life . . .

She runs soundlessly on top of the snow, so silent he might easily have taken her for a spirit, a ghost. It is the grey stream of her breath which tells him she is real. She stops a dozen feet from where the Reverend crouches, looks directly at him. The lights of the men move through the twilight towards them. Adulteress? Witch? He holds out his hand to her. It is an instinctive action, and for a moment it seems she might come to him, but she dives away, light and fleet as a deer, running between the trees while the torches of the men fan out into a glittering net. The Reverend thinks: They will catch her, kill her here. And if they catch me? What law will protect me in a place like this? All sense tells him that he must escape, that this is not for him to meddle with. But he waits, even creeps forward a way. There is a great confusion of barking and voices. The lights are congregating. Have they found her? His knees are trembling. He edges closer, sliding over the snow, hardly daring to breathe. He sees below the lights the dance of shadows; the woman's persecutors. Have they found her? He waits for a scream, for the sound of men killing. But the lights disperse and move away through the forest, the voices of the men and the dogs fading swiftly.

This is where they were; here where the snow is turned over. He can smell them, the fat from their torches. He looks about, sees on the ground the body of the woman. He goes towards it, expects to see some horror, the snow discoloured, a gaping throat. But when he kneels, touches the dress, it is empty. Dress, shoes, stockings, scarf. Everything she was wearing. It disturbs him almost more than if he had found her body. Truly, then, perhaps she was a witch, and has taken off, naked into the air. Or have they stripped her, taken her with them to murder at their leisure? He gathers the clothes. There is still some vestige of human warmth in the fabric, and it is then, as he bundles the clothes under his arm, that he has the strongest sense that she is with him, somewhere close by. He whispers, his voice odd and strained, strange to him. He says: 'I am a friend, a friend. I am a friend.'

He takes her scarf, ties it to a low branch, then runs with long, powerful strides through the surf of snow, out of the forest and across the luminious plain to the monastery. The company is sat in a half-circle by the fire. They look round, amazed to see the Reverend with such a look on his face and clutching what appears to be a ball of women's clothes.

For the moment he does not explain, says only that they must come with him, and such is his air of urgency, of certainty, that Monsieur About immediately buttons his coat. Featherstone also stands, but his wife plucks at his elbow. Most strange is Dyer, though in the moment it does not seem so. He goes out with About, ties on snow shoes at the door and follows the Reverend, who is already stretching out ahead of them.

They do not talk until they are close by the forest's edge. The Reverend says: 'There is someone we must help. A woman. The people are hunting her . . .'

About asks: 'You know where she is?'

'I know where we must look for her.'

Dyer says nothing, caught in some confusion of his own, harassed onward perhaps by the same compulsion that has the Reverend in its grasp.

They pass, breathing heavily, under the first trees. Moonlight lies like bones under the broken cover of the leaves. The Reverend wonders if he will find the place again, yet even while wondering, knows that he shall and is not surprised to see the scarf hanging darkly from the tree.

He begins to search, prodding with a stick among the dense architecture of the fir and snow and shadows. The others, after watching him a moment, do likewise. Half an hour they keep at it, circling out then back, coming together again. The Reverend feels himself cooling. Has he led them on a wild goose chase? Why should the woman be here? There is no sense to it at all. Yet he was so sure she would be here, hiding, waiting for his return. He catches the gleam of Dyer's eye and is forming his apology when Dyer says: 'Those were her clothes you had?'

'They were.'

About says: 'She will not live long in this cold.'

Dyer says: 'She did not want the dogs to scent her.'

He is looking over the Reverend's shoulder. Now he brushes past him towards a hump of snow by the roots of a great tree. Something darker is showing from the snow. Dyer crouches beside it. There is a moment of hesitation before he touches it. It is a hand.

They dig, hunched over the mound like grave-robbers, scooping the snow, throwing it behind them. They work along the line of the arm to the just-warm crevice of her armpit. They uncover her shoulder, a breast, her neck. Then working up around her face. Chin, mouth, eyes.

'Does she live? Does she breathe?'

Dyer feels at her neck for a pulse, lowers his face by hers, his cheek by her mouth.

'Does she live, Doctor?'

'Faintly.'

'She does not appear to have any wounds, praise God.'

Dyer says: 'The cunning creature buried herself.'

The Reverend removes his greatcoat. He says: 'We must lift her out. Get her to the monastery.'

They lift her. About says: 'How small she is.' They wrap her in the Reverend's coat. The Reverend rubs her hands, feels them come to life between his own. She opens her eyes; The whites throw back the moonlight. He says: 'Madam, we are here to help you. Do not be afraid. Tell her, monsieur, not to be afraid.'

Dyer says: 'She is not afraid.'

'We must carry her,' says About. 'We must leave this place. Now. You are the youngest, Mr Dyer. The strongest, I think. You carry her first. We take turns. *Allez!*'

Dyer gathers the woman in his arms. Her head leans easily against his shoulder. They walk in a line out of the forest. Now and then, from far off, comes the howl of a dog, even perhaps of a wolf. The Reverend shivers, feels the want of his coat; he is suddenly very tired. The moon sails on, low across the surface of the sky. He does not know exactly what has happened, only that it has happened. He does not understand how things have changed, only that they have. He is glad James Dyer needs no help to bring her in.

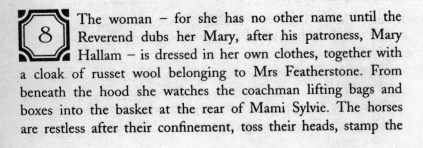

The woman – for she has no other name until the Reverend dubs her Mary, after his patroness, Mary Hallam – is dressed in her own clothes, together with a cloak of russet wool belonging to Mrs Featherstone. From beneath the hood she watches the coachman lifting bags and boxes into the basket at the rear of Mami Sylvie. The horses are restless after their confinement, toss their heads, stamp the snow. The coachman carries out a last inspection of the runners, makes a face, shakes his head. Reverend Lestrade, coming out of the door of the monastery, asks the ladies how they do; how shall they like skating to St Petersburg? Mrs Featherstone declares she will be happy to leave in any way at all, would go on the back of an ass so long as it would take her to some more civilised part of the world.

The Reverend rubs his hands, briefly wonders who is now wearing his gloves, then helps the ladies into the coach. Featherstone comes out in his pelisse.

'Well, Featherstone. Do you think she will run?'

'God help us, sir, if she does not. You still think it quite wise to take the woman?'

'I think it is our duty.'

'I mean only that they, her pursuers, may have had their reasons for . . . They may not take kindly.'

'It is my hope, sir, they shall not know of it.'

'We shall be very cramped, what with the doctor coming with us too.'

'Would you leave them behind, Mr Featherstone, for the sake of a little comfort?'

James Dyer comes out, brown coat and breeches, a long grey coat. He looks at the sky, looks at the coach. The Reverend says: 'You are satisfied, sir, with the condition of the postillion? Myself I thought he looked almost easy this morning.'

Dyer nods. 'He shall live.' He is looking past the Reverend, through the open door of the coach. Featherstone has climbed in and is leaning forward to talk to his wife. Between them is the woman.

The Reverend, following Dyer's gaze, says: 'She seems none the worse for being frozen. We must consider what is best to do with her. We cannot take her to St Petersburg.'

Dyer asks: 'What is your intention, Reverend? Place her in a convent?' He laughs, or something near to a laugh: the sharp expulsion of air from his nose. 'How would you explain those teeth? The tattoos?'

The Reverend says: 'I had forgot the tattoos.'

Monsieur About emerges, inhales mightily. '*Tout est prêt?*'

'There is only ourselves to go in now.'

The old monk raises his hand; a blessing.

The coach rocks, then slides forward, wonderfully smooth.

About says: 'All we need are bells. Ting ting ting!'

Ponko runs beside them, running and falling until Mami Sylvie outpaces him, and he is left behind, kneeling in the snow and waving, as though the coach contained his last and only friends on earth.

Mrs Featherstone sits by the right-hand window, looking back along the smoothly curving track left by the runners. Next to her is her husband, and beside him is Mary. Monsieur About is opposite Mrs Featherstone (his view: the uncut plain, a glimpse of one of the horses, the spray from the leading runner). Beside him is the Reverend Lestrade, book in hand, occasionally taking the view from either window, now and then arching his back to relieve the tension there. To the Reverend's right, James Dyer, looking at his feet, looking out of his window; very often looking closely, unguardedly, at the woman opposite him.

After two days' sledging they are in Riga. They stay at an inn under the shadow of the castle. The Featherstones, About and the Reverend share two rooms. Dyer and Mary have rooms of their own, paid for by Monsieur About. They feast on wild boar. Dyer finds an English merchant, asks if he has heard of any English doctors *en route* to St Petersburg. The merchant says he has not heard of any. His Latvian wife shakes her head. So many people pass through Riga now. More than Berlin. More than London!

Early the following day, with fresh horses, the company board into the chill interior of their coach, clutching rolls and spicy sausages and boiled eggs. Mary is with them still. No one protests. Even Featherstone smiles at her and gallantly peels her an egg. They ride north towards Valga. The Reverend makes notes and sketches on the end-pages of *Candide*.

Nov 22. *Rds poor but it is easier on snow. Lght fall today. Feathers. Sky the colour of wood ash. Pm – Mrs F vomits, face quite green. We stop. M presses her about her eyes. Mrs F easier. Bad smell in coach but too cold to have the wndw down. Not much talk today.*

Nov 23. *Jms Dyer – at times he seems hardly to know what he is about. NOT the same man as sewed his own head, cut Pstllns arm. Always looking at M. Cannot believe he has flln for her yet she has some power over him. About says it also. He is amused. About told us risqué stry of the Empress and her horse. Mrs F laughing too much. My bck easier than at any time since Paris. M nvr speaks a word, least not in my hearing. Thght I saw a bear today at twlght.*

Passed a trp of cavalry on the road. The officer looked in and saluted us. Fine figure. Elgnt scar on his cheek.

Nov 24. *Lst nght in Pskov. Fortress and churches. Drank my first glass of Kvas, made from malt water. Very quenchy. We are not to go to Novgorod. I had hoped to see it. We will pass along the shre of Lake Peipus twrds Narva. We shll then be on the Gulf of Finland and very nr our destination. All in gd spirits excpt D who lies under some uneasiness. M has her own wrld. Her eyes – gives one odd feeling to look at them. No blck cat though and nthng malignant in her face. This below: a sktch of Lake Peipus.*

Nov 25. We have wlkd on white sand beside the Gulf. Hurrah! Helsinki is acrss the water. Askd D if he was confident of winning race. I mght have been speaking in Dutch, for he did not answr. I wndr what opinion M must have of him. He it was found her, carried her. Cannot for life imgne her as a wife! Icy. Saw a ship, English, heading out of the Gulf. Last before the Sprng I thnk. Returning to coach I noticed D was limping. When I askd what was the matter he said he did not knw, then said he had fallen, which was odd as the place was entirely flat.

Nov 26. Lst evning we drnk a grt deal and are very subdued in the coach tdy. At our party D was almost human. Strtd telling stry about his sister and how he had wronged her. Seeing him in this mood A pressed him: Who are yr parents, Sir? D shks his head. Was Gummer yr frnd? D answrs that he had been once. That G had been hard on him but that he in turn had been hard on G and that he was sometimes sorry for it. He seemd affected by the memory of smthng. I had a very lewd dream by virtue of all the fruit of Bacchus I had drnk. I shall not write whm it concerned. I am ashamed of it and yt it was v sweet. When I came down in the mrning for breakfast I saw M on a bench with a grt fierce hound that had alarmed us the evning before. It was slmbring lke a puppy at her feet. My head very thumpy tdy. Am temptd to ask M to rub it. It would not look right hwvr. Below is a picture of a sleeping Mr F who is sat oppste me wheezing lke a bllws.

Nov 27. Tnght we arrive at our destination − if the hrses and the rnrs and rds hold good. Thnks be to God, and to his servant M. About. I have not spoken with him but suspect he is a deist or an agnostic or some such. No matter. He is my friend. Wthout this jrny I might have languished mnths or yrs. When man is at his wit's end he must hve some actvty. I have been foolish and yt I embrace myself and take comfort from knowing I shall be a better shphrd for this falling off. I long to see Diddy. Cow too and Lady H and my grdn which evn in Wntr is a comfort. The Fs I shall alwys remember with fondness thgh we shll not meet in England, I am sure of it. D likewise I shall not see again after St Ps. M likewise not. I trst she shall be left in peace. She is a type that will alwys arouse the prejudice of the ignrnt. This is a picture of her teeth. I passed a vast stool this mrning of gd colour which gave me satisfaction. I have almost begun to think that D may be a lttle mad. I pray it is not so. It may only be the bgnning of some physcl disease — evn of love! There is nthng to be feared like madness. How mny have felt the shdw of its sable wngs. Sure, to be mad is to be damned this side of the grve.

9 They enter the city by night. Braziers burn in the streets and the *drovsky* drivers beat their arms for warmth, watching with eyes ignited by the flames as Monsieur About enquires after the residence of the British Envoy. Fingers point; the drivers speak a language like the grating of pebbles. Mami Sylvie trundles through the city; lights show on the Neva, on its back of ice, and in the tall double windows of several of the finer houses they see the shadows of dancers. Everywhere, it seems, there are palaces, pavilions, golden-spired churches; and between them, behind them, the wooden slums, the wastelands. The air smells of the marshes, the river, winter.

At the envoy's residence a party is in progress; parties are in progress all over the city. The Reverend, descending stiffly from the coach, says: 'One could stand in the street and hear nothing but the popping of champagne corks!'

Servants admit them into the hall and they stand beneath a portrait of King George III, breathing on to their finger tips, dabbing at the water from their noses. The envoy appears at the top of the stairs. He is chewing something. His napkin is tucked in at his neck.

'How may I assist you?'

They wait for Dyer to answer, to introduce himself. When he says nothing, the Reverend points him out. 'This is Dr Dyer, sir. Come from England.'

'Dyer? A physician?'

About says: 'He has come to inoculate the Empress.'

'Has he so? Yes. Of course. Damn. We had better go, then. Allow me to change my coat. I have some Burgundy on this one.'

He disappears, returns ten minutes later, steps lightly down the stairs shouting for a servant. 'How was your journey? No unpleasantness, I hope. You have eaten? What is new in England? I believe I would stand the amputation of a limb to feel English rain again. I have Nikita Panin's mistress upstairs together with a pair of Cossack generals. One is required to drink them under the table, you know. I only pray they do not rape her while we are at the palace.'

Says Mrs Featherstone, flustered: 'Should we not change our clothes?'

'Lord, no. It's all quite informal these days. Not Peter the Great any more. Anyway, she likes foreigners. French is best but English is quite acceptable. Do you speak French, Doctor?'

Dyer shakes his head.

The envoy says: 'No matter. I shall translate for you. You don't hear Russian spoke at court at all. Not unless you're in the servants' quarters. French language, French manners, French fashion. We call it the monkey on the bear's back. What do you think of that? There's our sledge. Crowd aboard. These furs are wolfskins. What was your name again?'

'James Dyer.'

'I believe they have a place for you on Millionaya. Everyone's being looked after handsomely. We shall pass by on our way to the palace.'

The air brings tears to their eyes. The driver shouts, cracks his whip above the ponies. The envoy is asleep. The Reverend thinks: Why did Dyer not ask if he is the first? Was he afraid to know the truth? Surely the envoy should have said. Said something.

They turn, the horses kick up snow. On their right is the freezing artery of the river; to the left it is Amsterdam, Venice, Athens. Amazing, thinks the Reverend, snug beneath his wolfskin and grinning with the strangeness of it all, amazing that the place does not sink. Yet, for all its weight, it seems the mere outline of a city, an enormous stage for some improbable piece of theatre. No business being here at all.

'Is that the palace?' cries Mrs Featherstone, pointing ahead.

'Lord!' says Featherstone. 'Candles enough in there to light the whole of Bristol.'

About laughs. 'At last we have impressed you! But how far you made us come.'

The palace swallows them. The envoy says: 'Stay close! I lost the youngest son of an earl here once and have not seen him since.'

Two men with diamonds in their shoes are wrestling at the foot of the stairs. The travellers ascend, glimpsing themselves in the abundant mirrors, their faces flushed. About says: 'One could grow oranges in this heat!' Squatting at the base of a marble pillar, a dozen Kalmuck women watch the strangers pass. One points at Mary; the others lower their eyes, mumble. A Mongol officer, black-eyed, skin tight as an apple, nods his head to the envoy. The envoy waves his gloves, hops over a pair of sleeping wolfhounds and runs up the next flight of stairs. A gob of wax drops on to the Reverend's sleeve. Dyer is next to him. How pale he looks. That leg is troubling him again.

'Take my arm, Doctor. Or we shall be lost like that other fellow!'

Servants scurry past with trays, the bottles steaming and glistening with the snow they have been pulled from. One servant carries a fish, big as a piglet, slips, lets go of the tray and launches the fish into a dive through depths of yellow air. The envoy asks directions from a child who stands eating candied rose-petals beside a door through which a hundred, two hundred ladies and gentlemen are sat at cards. '*Tout droit*,' says the girl. The envoy kisses her and dives among the card tables, waving the others on without looking back. On the walls, expensive and ignored, slung in cumbersome gold-leaved frames, are paintings from another world. Ruby limbs, bloody heroes, profligate gods; princes with their attendant angels, all unsmiling; and through a background window, a glimpse of hot brown hills, the red tiles of Tuscany.

From some of the tables, between rounds of Ombre or Boston, a powdered face looks up at the newcomers, smirks, whispers, loses interest, goes back to cards.

In this room, tables are laid out with delicacies for the players' refreshment. Sterlet from the Volga, veal from Archangel, beef from the Ukraine, pheasants from Bohemia. Icy jugs of gluckwa, orgeat, almond-flavoured ratafia. 'These melons', says the envoy, coming to the end of the table, 'are from Bukovina.' He dips a finger into a bowl of caviare, licks off the glittering eggs, summons a flunky who disappears and returns.

The envoy says: 'We may go in now. Try to be interesting.'

To the Reverend it seems they have entered the rehearsal room of an opera company, yet the gold is not painted, nor are the diamonds glass. Like all the rooms they have passed through, it is too bright, too exquisite, too crowded with the purchases of Russian agents who scour Europe with their deep purses. So many fine things, any one of which, alone, would have been remarkable. Together they are like the piled booty of a Khan; toys of power.

In the centre of the room a woman is leaning over the billiard table. There is the sound of struck ivory as she makes her shot, then she looks up at the strangers, her blue eyes, her blue gaze, travelling from face to face

Amid the chatter, the polite and boorish laughter, floats a voice, distinctly, exotically English.

'. . . every third night at bedtime eight grains of Calomel, yes indeed, and eight grains powder of crab's claws . . .'

The woman at the table speaks French with a German accent. She says: 'Who have you brought me tonight?'

The envoy bows heroically. 'Your Imperial Majesty, I have brought you Dr Dyer from England. Dr Dyer, and his companions.'

Dyer steps forward, bows. The Empress, in an English sentence clearly learnt by rote, says: 'You honour us by coming so far. We are pleased to welcome you to our city.'

Somewhere among the hunchbacks, the bored dwarves, the maids of honour, the gentlemen of the bedchamber, the Englishman is still talking.

'. . . then I recommend an eighth of a grain of tartar emetic and, upon waking, a dose of Glauber's salts . . .'

The Empress turns, the crowd parts. The Reverend has already guessed who they will see; he has heard the voice once before, in Brussels. Dr Dimsdale, sleek and plump, glides to the Empress's side, already a favourite. The room watches, grows hushed. The gentlemen, the sombre-suited foreigners, regard each other; a long, intelligent exchange. In Dimsdale's eyes, a cool relish of his victory; in James Dyer's eyes, a look of incomprehension, as if the guiding genius of his life had suddenly, inexplicably betrayed him.

Someone giggles. In schoolroom French, Dimsdale says: 'And what is your opinion of Glauber's salts, Mr Dyer?'

The Empress claps; the whole room claps. It is as if the court has never heard such wit, such flare.

10

'What is that? It is an orrery, is it not?'

'It is.'

'It must be a particular favourite of yours, Doctor, for you to have brought it all this way.'

'I have had it years together.'

'A charming piece. I suppose that is the Sun, and these the planets?'

The room is feebly lit. James Dyer is by the window, the orrery on the table beside him. The window is not shuttered. A light snow is falling. In the street below, sleds and carriages are bringing home the last of the card players, the revellers, from the Winter Palace.

'I believe, Doctor, that the girl has lit the stove in your room.'

There is no answer. The Reverend thinks: I will merely rile him if I stay. He must digest his disappointment alone.

He goes to the door, then, unable to suppress the instinct to console, he says: 'The envoy assured me there was much to be done here by a man with real ability. Much to be had. I trust you will not think your trip entirely wasted.'

There is a movement at the far end of the room. Mary. He cannot tell if she is looking at him; the light is too poor, his eyes are too tired. He understands, however, understands perfectly, that he must go.

'Good night to you, then. You both.'

He goes to his room, obscurely troubled. Why does this prickly man, who surely cares nothing for him, provoke his pity so?

He undresses, is briefly naked in the wood-warmed air, then

draws on his nightgown, his pointed nightcap, a pair of thick woollen stockings. When he lies down he prays, the habit resumed after what now seems an unimportant interval of silence. He prays for Dyer, for himself, for his loved ones: a childhood prayer. He snuffs the candle. Strange how the darkness comes all at once. Where is it when the light is there?

11   The Featherstones, Monsieur About, the Reverend Lestrade, in two hackney sledges, go to see a bear belonging to the Empress baited by dogs. Two dogs are killed. The dogs look sorry for themselves only at the very end. A man comes in to hoick their bodies out. The bear is led away to lick its wounds. Fifteen degrees of frost. The drivers' breath freezes in their beards.

A supper at Princess D's. Cold soup, caviare and postilla. The ladies are carried up the stairs by servants. For a wager Monsieur About drinks off a bottle of champagne at a single draught. The Princess says to the Reverend: 'Did you not come with one of the English doctors?'

'Ma'am, we did, but he is indisposed.'

Parting, the Reverend kisses the Princess's hand. She says: 'You must come here every day.'

A man called Bootle takes them to the Newski market. The meat is deep-frozen, hard as stone. Bootle asks after Dyer. The Reverend says: 'He would not come out today.'

'He is unwell?'

'He is weary after his journey.'

'What of the woman?'

When they are alone, About says that Bootle is a spy. St Petersburg, he says, is full of spies.

Bootle takes them to the bath-house. One rouble for a private room, five copecks for the public. 'Let us not be parted!' says Monsieur About. James Dyer is with them. When they are stripped the Reverend sees a dozen red weals upon Dyer's back, like the marks of a lash, and a mottling of bruises on his chest and legs. There are also marks on his hands, as if he has reached for something through a briar. About is unsettled, offended. He says, loud enough for the Reverend to hear: 'That is too much. Too far.' The day is spoiled.

The adventure is coming to an end. This adventure. About has sold his toys to an agent of the Empress. She is known to be delighted. To have paid handsomely. About says they will amuse the court for a week, then be dropped in their boxes and forgotten. It does not matter. It will happen to them all in time. To the Empress herself! Forgotten, forgotten. He fills their glasses. It is evening at the apartment. The Reverend and About are alone there. James Dyer and Mary are at one place, the Featherstones at another. The stoves are hissing: good Russian stoves, nothing like them in England. The Reverend thinks: I could be home by the New Year. A fresh start. Home.

About comes up, smiles, takes his arm, says: 'I am to go to Warsaw, the first of next week. Then as fast as I can to Paris. Come with me. I should not like to travel without you now.'

The Reverend asks: 'Might we take the doctor? And the woman if he will not part from her?'

About says: 'Why not?'

The next day they call at the palace again, but the Empress is away. There are only visitors like themselves, walking the empty corridors, talking in hushed voices. There are no players at the card tables, no servants running with champagne. The servants sit about on the stairs, drink and eat what they have stolen from the kitchens. Only a few of the lights are lit. It is cold, echoing. A spectacular barracks.

At Millionaya they have an evening of backgammon and Loo, coffee and wine. The Reverend retires at midnight, goes to his room, then, taking his quill and ink-horn, sharpening the tip of the quill with his pocket knife, dipping it in the ink, wiping it, dipping it, he begins another letter to his sister.

Rev Jls Lestrade to Miss Dido Lestrade

St Petersburg, 9 December 1767

Dear Dido,

I write now to say I shall be returning to England and may even arrive before you receive this. I shall go to Warsaw with M. About and thence back to Paris and so home. You cannot think how I long to be among you again. Not that I regret my coming here. It is something to be able to say one has met the Empress of Russia. I do wonder how that poor postillion has fared and if we might not have some intelligence of him on the way back. Our little party, soon to disperse, is all well, with the exception of Dr Dyer who has taken his being beat by Dr Dimsdale very hard.

The cold here is shocking but they know how to be warm, and I have been no more uncomfortable than I should have been at home.

Let me tell you of all we have done since my last . . .

He lays down his pen. The letter can wait until morning. He rubs the stubble of his face. Who was that fellow he knew shaved three times a day? Collins? Johnstone? Someone at the University? Paston?

He thinks of his little opium pipe and finds the box at the bottom of his bag. He took the drug first as a boy to quieten a persistent cough; took it later as a student for the dreams it brought, and on those occasions when his allowance was all used up it was cheaper and more pleasant to take opium than to eat. He is the mildest of addicts; Dido takes more. He smokes in the armchair, hugging the smoke at the base of his lungs. His mouth becomes dryer. He smiles. He knows he shall pay for this tomorrow: languor, constipation, headaches perhaps. His smile broadens. Tomorrow can take care of itself. Who is to say any of them shall live so long?

When he has done he lays the pipe down carefully on the box and goes out to get a mouthful of wine to smooth his throat. He takes a candle with him; his shadow moves over the wall like a grey, ponderous sail. The decanter is still on the table in the drawing room. He takes one of the dirty glasses, sniffs it, and pours out a small measure of wine, swills his mouth and swallows.

Going out again he sees there is another light, flickering in the corridor outside James Dyer's room. Who is standing there? He squints, and makes out Zaira, the servant girl. He goes towards her, thinking how he has not properly noticed before the loveliness of her hair, very black against the white of her skin. He expects her to turn at his approach; he does not wish to startle her, but she is staring fixedly into Dyer's room. When he sees the expression on her face he wants to be back in his own room. He wants nothing to do with this. He whispers her name; she clutches his arm, transmits to him her terror. Dyer is in bed, lying on his back, eyes closed. Mary is beside the bed. The Reverend opens his mouth to speak but Mary looks up at him, silences him. For a moment he wonders if Dyer is dead, but then sees the slow swelling of his chest, the slight palp of the skin over his heart. Zaira whimpers. There is the noise of her water running off her leg on to the floor. The Reverend starts forward, a single step, then stops. The room is sealed. There are forces here he knows nothing of, a magic more powerful than his own. He cannot prevent her. One of Mary's hands is in, now the other works in beside it. There is no blood; the flesh parts like water, like sand. Her arms are trembling, her face racked with the effort of her secret business. Dyer does not move, only sometimes sighs like a sleeper in a dream. When it is finished she sits heavily in a chair, her head falls forward, her shoulders slump. The room is suddenly calm; ordinary. A man sleeping in a bed, and a woman next to him, sleeping in a chair. The Reverend goes in, sets down his candle on the bedside cabinet, buttons Dyer's nightshirt, then pulls up the covers. Zaira is watching him. Is she afraid of him too? He takes her hand and leads her away, quickly, along the corridor.

SIXTH

1   The instant before he wakes he experiences an ecstasy, a moment of luminous terror, such as a man who stumbles from the edge of a cliff must feel, somersaulting over the distant rocks. Or a felon, launched to eternity by the hangman's shove, flying through the crowd's hush. Everything is seen, everything is understood, in clear light, in calm air. Then the wind breaking in waves over his head. The light shrieking.

James Dyer dies. Wakes in hell.

At first he knows only that he must escape from the fire in the bed. Then from the fire on the floor. Then from the fire in the air. Not until he reels towards the door does he realise: he is the fire; the fire is himself. And only by escaping from himself shall he escape the flames. There are knives in his bag, and he is not yet afraid of knives. He could die like Joshua, slaking the intolerable thirst with a razor. He gropes for the bag, cannot find it, cannot see anything, his bag, his hands. There is nothing but a slab of paler dark where one of the shutters is open. He opens the others, fumbles with the catch on the window. He hears himself sobbing. The catch gives, the window opens. Snow dances in upon his face. He drags himself on to the sill, coils as if he means to spring on to the frozen river. Then he is gripped from behind, pulled down to the floor, lies there, writhing like an insect. He wants to fight her,

259

but cannot find the strength. She is full of purpose. She is making him dress. She does not understand that he cannot go on, that he is enduring the unendurable.

Outside they take the darkest streets. The wooden houses are asleep, clinging to the ground, heavier than palaces. A dog whines, an infant bawls, a lamp flickers in a house. Someone is sick there perhaps, the family kneeling by the bed. The doctor will not come on a night like this, nor the priest.

Mary does not wait for him; neither will she let him go. He labours behind her, on two legs, on four. He knows that she is his only hope, the beginning and the end of the nightmare. What else is there to hold to? He is one hour old, trapped inside of himself, a blind man inside a burning house. He is like the others now.

2   When he opens his eyes it is light. There is no sign of the city. He tries to sit up but when he moves the fire courses through his body. He tries to speak but his throat is too dry. He licks at the snow. Slowly, as though crossing a river of the thinnest ice, he moves. His hands curl, uncurl. He turns his head. A bird is watching him, blue-black feathers shivering in the wind. It studies him. The eye has no depth. A black light trembles on its surface. The bird hops closer. Fear of the bird is greater than his fear of the fire. He sits up, screaming, flinging from his hands fistfuls of snow. The bird unfolds itself, flies low over the ground, wingtips almost touching the snow. Then it climbs, caws, circles over him and disappears over the trees. He falls back, face to the sky. Now perhaps, in the light, someone will come to help him, take him to a warm place, heal him. The sky turns red; he hears

footsteps; he raises his eyes. The woman is there. She crouches by his head and places a hand over his eyes. She smells of smoke and feathers. He sleeps.

A small flame weaves near his face. Over the back of the flame he sees the woman, stirring a pot. She looks round at him. He speaks to her but does not understand what he has said. They are in a room, a small wooden room. There are no windows. He is lying under a pelt. Under the pelt he is naked. He is too weak to move, too afraid to start the burning again. The woman feeds him from a horn. The liquid tastes of earth. He swallows. Later she takes his hand and leads him from the room. The burning is all around him, a cloud in which he moves, but it does not make him suffer as before. When they are outside she points. There is a man, spreadeagled, face down in the snow. James goes closer, naked over the snow. He does not feel the cold. He kneels beside the man, turns the body over, touches him, the cold-pleated face, the stubble like splinters in the skin, the dark lips showing dark teeth. In Gummer's eyes golden lights are moving. The lights are flames carried in the dark. James bends closer. He sees the face of his mother, tiny, young. Above her the stars are raining over the moor, the village, the hill-fort. He sees a mass of strangers, and a boy lying calmly on a bed. And there is Joshua Dyer in his best coat, frowning, red from sun and drink; and Jenny Scurl, petals in her hair; and Amos Gate, rubbing his chin. Charlie stands at the door and Sarah peeps past his arm. Liza is there, sat on the bed beside him. She is crying for him.

James lays his head against the dead man's chest, curls against the cold body, holds it in his arms. Howls.

Ice mirrors tell him of what he has become. They show him the blur of a man, beard matted with drool, the dark band of his eyes like a blindfold. Often she makes him drink from the horn, the liquor that tastes of must and earth, that tastes of cellars. Then he is a ghost and sees ghostly sights, talks with the dead, or the wandering spirits of those who are yet living. At night he sometimes hears devils; they are like men whispering at the far end of an enormous room.

And he finds a word for the burning. A word that springs from the lips as it is spoken; that is spoken as if it were a seed to be spat from between the lips: pain. It throws out wind enough to stagger the flame of a candle but not to extinguish it, not at first, not unless the flame is feeble, the candle all but gone.

His flesh remembers; every break, every beating, every stab of the needles, every burn from the candle. In pain he discovers his history, and the air grows truculent with voices. The night is not long enough to answer their accusations, nor to shed the tears they demand of him. He had thought his hours were like bonfires that consumed themselves, leaving only the palest ash. Now he learns that time trails men like a killer, thorough, even-handed, collecting the evidence of the years. Nothing is lost. That was all arrogance and ignorance. Nothing is lost and the silence was not silence but merely his own deafness.

'Who are you?'

'Answer!'

'Why does he not answer?'

'He has not spoke to us at all, sir.'

'Where is he from? What papers does he have?'

'Mr Callow read the papers, sir. He is called Dyer, an English-man run mad in Russia.'

'Mad from what cause?'

'The cause was not set out. Only the name and that he is come from Russia.'

'I wonder they could not keep him there. Who was it sent him?'

'Mr Swallow, the ambassador.'

'And was there money sent, for his maintenance?'

'There is money. Mr Callow has it.'

'Tell Callow to charge him at seven shillings a week. I knew a Dyer once. Dyer!'

'Answer!'

'Do you know where you are, sir? This is the Royal Bethlehem hospital in Moorfields. We shall make you well, sir, or one of us shall perish in the attempt. Why does he wear a restraining jacket?'

'Sir, he kicked at one of the keepers when he was stripped.'

'Who was that?'

'Mr O'Connor.'

'Did O'Connor vex him?'

'No, sir.'

'Very well. Tomorrow I shall begin the treatment. We shall loosen your tongue, Dyer. It is naughty to be to be so stubborn. Who is that screaming?'

'I think it is Smart, sir.'

'Why is he screaming?'

'I cannot say.'

'Well, we shall go to him.'

'And this one, sir, shall he wear irons?'

'Upon his legs. Until we know him better. Then we shall see.'

'Dyer!'

'Answer!'

'Nay, do not kick him. He is still a Christian. How do you like your new home, sirrah? Does he speak yet?'

'Some words, sir.'

'Portending?'

'Sir?'

'What does he say?'

'It was mad talk, sir. It was nothing.'

'When you hear him speak you must make some note of it, or if you cannot, remember the words in your head.'

'I shall.'

'How does he like his irons?'

'He does not complain.'

'He is to go to the water today.'

'Ay, sir.'

'He is to vomit.'

'Ay, sir. And shall we bleed him?'

'Keeper!'

'Sir?'

'Sit him up upon his pallet. Does he take his food?'

'We put it in his mouth, sir. He will not always swallow it.'

'If you are casual with your food, Dyer, I shall have Wagner here force it down your gullet with a stick. Ay, like a French goose. How did he like the water?'

'He cried out.'

'From the cold, you suppose?'

'Ay, sir.'

'Was it a cry only? Was there some word?'

'A name, sir.'

'What name?'

'I fancy it was Maria or Mary.'

'Very good. Tell us, Dyer. Who is Maria? Wife? Sister? Whore?'

'Perhaps he is a papist. I might make him talk, sir, if you wished it.'

'No, Mr Wagner. Nothing of that. This is an enlightened age. Nature and philosophy are our guides.'

'OOOWWWWWWWW! OWW OOOOWWWWWW-WWWWWW!'

'Gag him!'

'My name is Adam. I have brought you some drink. Do not spill it. It is milk. Fresh milk. If you have money you may buy what you will here. If you are easy they will let off your chains and you may go out into the galleries. I have been in this place three hundred and nineteen nights. Three hundred and twenty days. I shall go free when the world grows sane. They are madder than us, friend, but do not tell them so. Tell them only what they wish to hear. They are fragile men. Now drink, for one must be strong to be mad.'

'Dyer!'

'Answer!'

'Shall you speak to us today?'

'Yes no yes no yes no yes no yes . . .'

'What does he say?'

'He says he shall speak.'

'You will not howl today?'

'No.'

'Howling, sir, is for dogs. How came you those marks upon your hands?'

'I do not remember.'

'Note, Wagner. The lunatic is a very cunning creature. I wager he made those marks himself. Who is the woman you call Mary?'

'I do not know.'

'He is a great fluent liar. You know your own family, I suppose?'

'They are all dead.'

'What of your friends? Even a madman may have friends.'

'I have none.'

'Dyer! You wish to be free? To walk in the galleries?'

'Sir, I do.'

'What would you give to be free?'

'I have nothing.'

'And if you had, what would you give?'

'Everything.'

'Everything is too much, sir. It is a mad answer. Ha! We have him there, Wagner. Is the patient civil? Is he compliant?'

'There are others worse than him.'

'Well, we shall see. Another month. If he is a good fellow he shall have the irons off. See that he has fresh straw for his bed. I have never known such stinking. My dog would not step in here.'

'Adam. I think I must die here.'

'Many think so at first.'

'And then?'

'Those who do not die, live.'

'How do you live?'

'By being no man's enemy.'

'That is enough?'

'I go away inside my head. There I may travel where I like, speak with whom I like.'

'I heard a woman. Singing. Last evening or yesterday. I do not know when.'

'The keepers bring them in at night. They are for the keepers' comfort.'

'And are there mad women here?'

'They are locked up separately. You may sometimes see them or hear them.'

'Adam? How long have you been here?'

'Three hundred and sixty days; three hundred and fifty-nine nights.'

'Dyer!'

'Sir?'

'I wish to blister your head.'

'I beg you do not.'

'Why do you beg?'

'When you blister my head the pain is very fierce.'

'Come now, there is no remedy without a little discomfort.'

'I beg you do not.'

'I think you do not wish to recover.'

'I do.'

'I think you do not.'

'Sir, I do.'

'Then I shall blister your head. I always get my way. Ain't that right, Wagner?'

'Ay, sir, it is very true.'

4 All Hallows 1768. James Dyer is freed from his chains. Though now at liberty to walk in the galleries he stays in his cell until Adam leads him out and introduces him to the society there. Cromwell, Pericles; half a dozen Old Testament prophets haggling with the beer-seller, the boy with his bucket of shellfish, the girl with her basket of oranges. O'Connor is the keeper; he remembers James and prods him in the chest with the end of his stick, up-ends him, then loses interest.

From the stairs an addled Methodist, preaching in dumb, wards off swarms of diabolic bees. Other inmates sit or lie or stand: in rags, in motley, in blankets. They pick at sores, rock on their heels, moan, slobber, weep. At the feet of the Methodist a bald tailor sews nothing to nothing. The noises echo, like a bestiary in a cathedral.

James points through the bars that separate the men from the women. 'What is that?'

Adam says: 'They call it the Coffin. It is to punish those who are violent.'

They walk to the bars. On the other side is a narrow box, five to six feet in height and set on two small iron wheels. Near the top of the box is a hole six inches across. Through it, James sees the pale dial of a woman's face.

Adam says: 'It is Dot Flyer.' He calls to her: 'Good day to you, Dot.'

Says James: 'How she must suffer.'

'She is used to it. She is wild. The keepers fear her.'

'Sure she is not always in the device?'

'She has her calm seasons.'

A voice speaks out of the Coffin, distant and solemn as an oracle. 'What is thy name?'

'It is Adam, sister.'

'And the other?'

'He is called James. Lately sprung from his irons.'

She starts to sing. Adam says: 'Her father was a musician. He drowned himself in a well.'

Her voice swells, the song booms inside the box. A woman keeper, Passmore, raps on the wood. Dot Flyer rends the air with her song, chases out what silence is left in the place. In Bedlam. Another keeper comes. They wheel the Coffin away. The song dwindles.

He sees her the following day; the shadow and glaze of her face. He goes to the bars, leans against them, presses his cheek against them. Sometimes her face seems to disappear, and then the device is like an empty clock case, standing on its trundle wheels amid the slotted light and dark of the gallery. The light comes through the windows of the open cells. On the wind he hears the sounds of the world without, its small music. The calling of cattle on Moorfields, the drumming of coaches and the swooping calls of the hawkers on London Wall . . .

Then she blinks or turns her head and he is aware of her again. He does not speak to her. He wonders if she is watching him, or if, in her suffering, she watches no one other than herself. He whispers his greeting, waits, then shuffles back to his cell.

She is not there the next day, nor the next. He does not see her for a week, and when he does there is no Coffin but he knows her by the quality of her stare. She is stood amid a court of madwomen and keepers, her copper hair shaved on to her skull, one eye bloated in a green bruise, a cold-sore flourishing on her lower lip. When he goes up to the bars she whispers to one of her gossips. All turn, laugh, Dot Flyer loudest of all. James is ashamed; of his rags, his old man's face, the way his movements are all graceless and cringing. Ashamed that he should want her to like him.

Seeing him discomforted, the women laugh louder. One turns her back, hoists her skirts and moons him; a vast crumpled arse. Dot Flyer is not laughing now. She is looking at James, and there is something of Mary in her expression, so direct is it, so penetrating. Then, as if she has conclusively seen the presence or absence of what she was looking for, she walks away from him into the women's wing, her court processing behind her; a robust and miserable sisterhood, a sorority of the damned.

In the darkest and most troubled reaches of the night, the graveyard watch, he seeks to know what it is he has become. What is he? A madman in a madhouse. A stranger to himself. At night incontinent in thought, sometimes in body. There are coarse grey curls in his beard. His hands shake like the palsy. Some mornings when he wakes his leg so pains him that were there a weapon to hand he would destroy himself in an instant. He lives in terror of the Physician, of Wagner, of O'Connor, of all the keepers, even those who treat him kindly, for nothing disturbs him more than kindness. His heart is raw, and this woman, this daughter of a drowned father, moves him. Her name seeps into his sleep like water into a cellar. He thinks of her continuously. He avoids her. It is her name now he mouths when they force him naked into a corner and fling iced water over him; when they burn him for blisters; when they cup him; when they physic him on to his knees, the vomit burning in his nose, afraid he shall bring up his own stomach. Dot, Dot, Dot. What a beautiful name!

To his amazement he acquires a despairing vanity. He begs the barber to shave him more closely, though the razor jags his face and makes the skin burn as though his sweat were the juice of an onion. He binds his hair with a ribbon of straw, digs out the filth beneath his nails.

On the water in his pot one morning, as the bell rings for slopping out, he sees the reflection of another man. Not what he was, nor what he has become. It is the mirage of a possible self, unborn as yet, perhaps never to be born. A man poised on the edge of a lit and crowded room. He is smiling, and the eyes, though haunted, are calm. The memory of it dogs him for weeks. What impossible efforts must he make to become such a man? He must lose the carapace of madness; adopt the common valour of a common man. For that he is not ready. Not yet. In his prayers, his urgent mutterings to whatever god waits on lunatics, he begs deferment of this grace; the long postponement of salvation.

 'Mr Rose,' says the Physician, 'this man was brought to us from Russia. Precisely such a case of vitiated judgment as I describe at length in my *Treatise on Madness*. Mayhap you have read it?'

Says Rose: 'I have heard it spoke of. How is he now?'

'He is not outrageous. I think we may make him right by and by. Should you care to feel his skull, sir?'

'I thank you, no. What was the cause of his insanity?'

'That is not established. There are many ways to madness, sir. One may take it from a parent, from a fever, from a blow to the head. Some are mad from love or grief. From liquor. From religious enthusiasm. From sunstroke. From too much reading, or tainted meat, or dog bites.'

'He has been educated?'

'I believe he has. You have your letters, Dyer? You may read and write?'

'Yes, sir.'

Rose examines him. He does not stand too close. He says: 'Is he free of disease?'

The Physician says: 'Quite free. And should he serve your turn we shall scrape him. Make him somewhat respectable.'

'Then I believe he may serve. Though I should like to hear more of his voice. It is the voice that counts.'

The Physician says: 'Speak up, Dyer. Come now. None of your tricks.'

James says: 'I do not know what to say, sir. I do not know what this gentleman would have me say. I have no conversation, sir.'

Rose says: 'He is originally from a western county. Somerset or Gloucestershire. Undoubtedly he is educated and has at some time kept good company. If not precisely a gentleman he was one of those who might wait upon a gentleman. A steward, a scrivener. A genteel barber.'

The Physician says: 'Why, that is a marvellous facility, sir, to tell a man so nearly from his voice. Were you ever on your uppers, sir, you might live by it.'

Rose steps closer to James. He says: 'I hope that shall not be necessary.' He takes hold of James's left hand, holding the fingertips with his own. He turns the hand over, says: 'Though the hands are damaged they are good hands. Have you worked as a painter, Mr Dyer, or as a musician perhaps?'

James shakes his head. He is alarmed by the man's questions, his perspicacity. As yet he has remained unrecognised, though he knows he has seen the Physician before, in London, in another life. At least two visitors to the hospital were men he knew. Neither smoked him. Now he is close to being uncovered by a stranger. He stares at the floor, says: 'I can neither paint nor play. I do not remember how I lived. I remember nothing before I came to this place.'

272

Rose leaves go of his hand. 'Sometimes it is necessary to forget.' He turns to the Physician. 'I believe Mr Dyer should be of the company. With your permission.'

'By all means, have him. What part shall he have? One of the conspirators? A ghost? What of that comical fellow in yellow stockings?'

Says Rose: 'Malvolio would be excellent. But our play is *A Midsummer Night's Dream*. I have a part in mind for him, but I must see them together before I decide. I should like to have them tomorrow in some large convenient room. One can never overestimate how long these matters will take.'

The Physician says: 'We have more rooms here than we know how to fill. I shall have one made ready for you.'

He calls into the gallery for Wagner. Wagner comes, stands in the doorway. The Physician says: 'Clean this fellow up. Fetch him fresh linen. Tell Callow to charge him accordingly.'

Wagner nods, stands out of the way for the gentlemen to leave. Rose turns at the door; the light catches the diamond at his ear. He grins at James, his face pure monkey.

'*A bientot*, Mr Dyer.'

O'Connor, swinging keys, leads them down the stairs. Adam is there. James walks beside him. He says: 'Are we put out?'

'Out?'

'Sent away from here?'

'We are to be players, James. This Rose is to make a play with us. We are to grow sane by playing sane men. By imitation.'

On the ground floor at the front of the hospital a room has been prepared. Furniture is piled together at one side and a small fire has been lit, though the heat does not touch the cold of the place. The women are already there with their keepers. Dot Flyer is among them. Her bruise has faded. Her face looks very young, very pale. There is no swagger about her today. There are marks on her wrists from where she has been chained. The keepers lounge against the walls, pick at their nails, look about as if uncertain how they shall wield their authority here.

Mr Rose comes into the room. He is a short man. He is beautifully dressed; a satin waistcoat, coloured like his name, a gold-and-silver coat. He climbs on to a chair, holds out his arms, brings the room to silence.

'I am Augustus Rose. Some of you know of me already, and have attended at my concerts here at the hospital. Some – I see Mr Lyle there – good day to you, sir – have taken part in my little theatrical parties. Well, dear friends, today I am inviting you to join with me in a most ambitious venture.'

He holds up a sheaf of coloured papers. 'These are tickets to a play. A tale of enchantment, to be performed by your good selves in

front of certain privileged and discerning members of the public.'
He flourishes the tickets. One floats free, flies to James's feet. He
picks it up.

AUGUSTUS ROSE Esq, CELEBRATED IMPRESARIO,
presents a THEATRICAL PRODUCTION of
Mr Wlm Shakespeare's 'Midsummer Night's
Dream' PERFORMED ENTIRELY BY THE LUNATICS
OF THE BETHLEHEM HOSPITAL in the gardens
thereof the 5 & 6 & 7 days of June 1769
2 Guineas Each

Rose leans down for the ticket; James passes it to him. Rose says:
'It is Mr Dyer, is it not? Shortly, sir, I intend to make you a duke.
How do you say to that?'

He hops from his chair and begins dividing the company:
Athenians on one side, Spirits on the other. When he has them
in two crooked lines, he steps back on to his chair.

'Now, to the naming of the parts. Mr Nathaniel Collins and Mr
John Collins, I have you for the lovers Demetrius and Lysander.
Mrs Donovan, you madame for the fair and warlike Hippolyta.
Mrs Forbellow as Hermia, who loves Lysander. Miss Poole as
Helena, who loves Demetrius. Miss Flyer as Titania, the fairy
queen. Mr Adam Meridith as Robin Goodfellow, Mr Asquini
as Oberon, Mr Dyer as Theseus, Duke of Athens. Mr Lyle for
Peter Quince, Mr George Dee as the weaver Bottom, Mr Hobbes,
Egeus, father of . . .'

'I shall play no weaver's ARSE.'

George Dee, a butcher from Houndsditch, fat-eyed, face flushed
with blood, elbows his way to Rose's chair. The keepers stir. Rose,
in gentle voice, says: 'Mr Dee, you are mistaken. Bottom is a sweet
part, a true comic part. He is an honest weaver, loved by his friends.
Why he even . . .'

'An ARSE! I will not! Did you not promise me I should play some duke or great lord? Did you not promise me?'

Rose holds up his hand to O'Connor. 'Dear Mr Dee. I am sure I never made any such promise. However, if Bottom is not to your liking, I may offer you Flute, which is a gentle part, though smaller, or Snug . . .'

The butcher shakes his head. It is as if a wasp has flown into his ear. 'No Flute, no Snug, no ARSE! You said I should be Theseus, indeed you did!'

Rose says: 'Faith, sir, I am sure I did not. And Theseus has many lines. To con them would be a mountain of work.'

Dee says: 'I cannot bear to be thwarted! I cannot bear it!'

Rose smiles. 'Why, this is most authentic! Quite like Drury Lane. Mr Lyle, will you save us, sir? Will you change places with Mr Dee? You have, I believe, the necessary genius to play the weaver.'

Lyle shakes his head. Dee bites his own hand; teeth in the old scars. 'I shall be Theseus or I shall set fire to my head! Why do you torment me? Why am I persecuted? It is because I have been a great murderer of animals. Ay, I know it.' His eyes crease, tears squeeze down his cheeks. 'You are right to persecute me.'

Mr Hobbes embraces him.

James says: 'Let him be Theseus. I do not know one part from another.'

Rose says: 'You are kind, sir. But I do not know if the weaver is right for you.'

Says James: 'It is one to me.'

Mr Rose consults his watch. 'We can settle this another time. I am certain when Mr Dee has seen the parts . . .'

George Dee unclasps from Mr Hobbes, wipes a wing of snot from his nose, stares delightedly at James. 'YOU shall be the arse! I shall be Theseus! I am Duke of Athens!'

He starts to hop, to dance. It is infectious. The lines dissolve.

Dot tugs at James's arm. He staggers after her. Those who cannot dance stand and shake like prophets. Miss Forbellow, skipping near to the fire, ignites her skirts. She is extinguished. A footstool sails through the air, shatters one of the windows. Over the stamping, the whoops, the barking, Rose calls. 'Until tomorrow, my friends! We shall all be perfectly famous!'

The keepers move in, swing their ropes, swing their canes. The lunatics flee before them.

7   On dry days they rehearse in the gardens, filing out, blinking like the denizens of an underground city, in their hands the tatty chap-book copies of the play. Rose mimes the parts, sings all the songs, shows the fairies how to dance, his legs like the legs of an elegant frog.

There are incidents. Helena head-butts Demetrius. Lysander unexpectedly shits himself. Dot, for chewing a keeper's nose, is confined for a week to the Coffin. Through it all Rose operates his craft. He is unshakeable. From the chaos of the early meetings a play emerges, not unlike the one intended. James, reluctant to begin with, miserable, mumbling his lines, at length takes refuge in the character of the weaver and, concealed in the weaver, he starts to move and speak with a freedom that amazes him. His mind grows lighter, his pains ease. On his hands the wounds of Gummer's needle, Canning's pincers, begin to dry. He hears himself laugh; it startles him. He has no recollection of the last time he laughed.

Dot shines; she has the knack. Her presence, though always fierce, even when she is tender or playing tender, no longer intimidates James. He makes eyes at her, walks close beside her so that sometimes the skin of their hands touch. There is still no love-talk between them. He cannot explain his heart to her; a lack of language more than a want of resolve. But when they make their scenes together, waking in imaginary woods under the imaginary moon, Rose and the lunatics hushed in a circle around them, then they are intimate and speak their lines as though they have invented them.

> 'Come sit thee down upon this flow'ry bed
> While I thy amiable cheeks do coy,
> And stick musk roses in thy sleek smooth head,
> And kiss thy fair long ears, my gentle joy.'
>
> [They sit; she embraces him]

The week after Easter the properties arrive. Pillars, schematic trees; a moon with the face of a man sleeping off his dinner. There is a basket full of clothes, wooden swords and crowns. Cloaks, doublets stiff with powder and the sweat of other players. Gowns in brilliant colours, harsh on the skin, none with its full complement of buttons or ties. And an asse's head. Rose presents it to James. James sits it on his shoulders. It is heavy and stinks of decaying hide. He looks out through the not-quite-even eyes. His breath sounds in his ears like the tide in a shell. The company is bunched about him. Rose cries: 'Oh, Bottom, thou art changed!'

James turns. Through the thing's left eye he sees Dot, naked, pouring over her head the gaudiest of the costumes; golds and scarlet. The dress is too big for her. She gathers it in her fists, turns, curtseys and comes towards him. He closes his eyes. Tears gum in the stubble of his chin. His hands shake. He staggers; he is afraid that he will fall. Someone takes the ass's head, lifts it off; someone else supports him. He blinks away the tears. The air wraps his face like a scarf. Dot is smiling at him. She is beautiful.

An evening in May. In the garden. The quality of Athens, the lords and ladies of the fairy world, make their exits and entrances under the creeping shadow of the hospital. Miss Poole, a tall, pocked, lunatic seamstress from the Isle of Dogs, is speaking as Helena. Adam – Puck now – dressed in a petticoat, hovers about her to work his magic. James squats outside the D of their arena. His cue is: 'The man shall have his mare again, and all shall be well.' He is wearing the head. He is quite accustomed to it now. He does not see Dot until she is sat beside him.

Adam says: 'On the ground, sleep sound; I'll apply, to your eye . . .'

Dot takes James's hand. Presses her lips against the scars, then guides it into the top of her dress, holds it against the swell of her breast, the nipple stiffening under his palm. He can feel the pulse of her heart.

Puck is singing. 'Jack shall have Jill; Nought shall go ill . . .'

What gifts are these? It is raining joys.

A voice summons them. They struggle to their feet, walk tipsily across the grass. James hears the whirling of a beetle, then Dot saying: '*Come, sit thee down upon this flow'ry bed . . .*'

Each time they meet they are bolder. They grope behind the wooden trees, in the shadow of the wooden moon or pressed against the stone face of the building. Around them the play lurches towards it final shape. Mr Hobbes suffers an anal prolapse and is replaced at short notice by John Johnson, a deranged schoolmaster. God speaks to the Collins twins, dictates to them new lines concerning the inheritance of a glue factory in Brentford. Theseus is slightly madder than he was. Mr Rose, stripped of his coats, his wig, understanding everything, admitting everything, herds them towards their first night.

The keepers grow lax. They sprawl, smoke, play dice; sleep off their binges. Dot and James, loitering during the last week ever nearer to the door of the hospital, now slip unregarded into the building and lose themselves amid its passageways. They peer in at rooms until they find one suitable to their purpose. A broad room, empty but for a hundred, two hundred, five hundred strait jackets piled up together; a single high barred-window for light; the noise of the world muffled like a dream. They lie on the jackets; the jackets sigh and give off their breath of sweat, dog blanket, midden. All the spices vented by the soul in mortal combat. This, thinks James, is how purgatory will smell.

Dot raises her skirts. James kneels, lightly touches her. She shivers then leans forward, tugs his breeches to his knees, finds his cock, plays her tongue around its head. It is a pleasure as vast, as shocking, as any pain that has come to him since St Petersburg. He reels away from her, gets awkwardly to his feet. He is afraid. Dot goes to him, holds him from behind, her head resting at the nape of his neck. He turns inside the ring of her arms, kisses her, hard on her mouth. They shuffle towards the bed of jackets, tumble backward, knocking teeth together, faces. His entrance is savage. Like the force used to stab a man or to kill an animal. He dreamt it would be gentle. Dot gasps, punches his ribs. The buckle from one of the jackets cuts into his knee as he moves. The pain is a black rope; he clings to it. He is laughing now, like a true madman. He sees that she is laughing too, and frowning and crying, fighting him and licking his face. He pulls out of her and spends over her belly. She wipes it with her hand, then wipes her hand on one of the jackets. James lies on his back beside her. There is a fly in the room, having followed them perhaps from the garden. A fly the only witness. Dot says: 'We must go back now.'

He calls her 'My love. My dearest'. She does not seem to be listening. He would like to tell her about Mary, and how he used to be one thing, one kind of man, a half-man. And how he is changed, like a man who has walked through an enchanted mirror, a man who has woken dishevelled from the grave. He thinks: Indeed, I am like Lazarus. Did Lazarus have a wife?

'We must go now,' she says.

Through the little window, blunt distorted sunlight falls between them. It strikes her hair, his patched shoes.

'Dot?'

She puts a finger to her lips.

'Dot, my life.'

'Peace, Jem.'

She is by the door. She holds out her hand to him. He takes it soberly in his. They go back to the garden. They are not running now. They have been away some fifteen minutes. Oberon is sending Robin Goodfellow to search for the magical flower. They have not been missed.

8 Augustus Rose, four o'clock on a Saturday evening, walks with the Physician in front of the Bethlehem hospital, showing him the tiers of seating the carpenters have been erecting for the last three days. There is still the noise of saws, a sudden crescendo of hammering, the tuneless whistle of a workman, but the work is largely done. Seating for two hundred, the first of whom may be expected in less than three hours' time.

The hospital wears its grandest face. Its windows show the sky over Moorfields, the streaks of feathery cloud. The gardens have been clipped. The smell of the honeysuckle comes near to hiding the stink of the Necessary. Only the bars on the windows of the upper floors and the cries like those of seagulls suggest that this is not the tranquil suburban seat of a grandee.

The Physician has changed his clothes and wears now a suit of resplendent plum in which to receive his guests. Rose dawdles with him on the lawn, indicates the court, the woods, the nooks and bowers where the action will take place. They have not talked of the money. They shall talk of it later. There is a mutual, workable distrust between them. Neither shall cheat the other by much.

The Physician says: 'There is nothing in the play to excite them too greatly? I would not want them doing any violence to the audience. That would not do at all.'

Rose says: 'It is a calm play. A very mellow play. It quite drugs them.'

'The woman called Dorothy Flyer. You have had no trouble with her?'

'Dot Flyer, sir, is our brightest light.'

The Physician says: 'I have given orders she is to be handled most firmly should she give us cause. They must fear us, Mr Rose.'

'I am sure that they do.'

The Physician jingles the silver in his pocket, mutters: 'For their own good.'

They stand watching the workmen. The last of them is stowing his tools in a canvas sack, wiping the warmth from his face with a cloth. A dog cocks its leg against one of the benches. The carpenter kicks at it, misses. At length Rose says: 'Should you care to meet your players?'

'My players, sir?'

'They think of you as their patron. You have no idea, sir, how large you are in their minds.'

The Physician nods, allows himself a smile. He says: 'By all means, then. Let us see them.'

Rose slips his arm through the Physician's. They saunter towards the great door of the hospital, towards the moat of shadow that surrounds it. From a high window a madman screams. Pigeons scatter. The carpenter looks up, spits for luck, shoulders his bag. The dog watches him go, then climbs on to a bench, turns, and settles into wary sleep.

9 The company are in the room they first rehearsed in. They have had wine at Mr Rose's expense, though no one is yet drunk except for two of the keepers. The costume basket has been drained of its contents. There have been fights over the choicer items – a paste tiara, a pair of extravagantly pointed boots, a plumed helmet from a forgotten production of *Tamburlaine*. But now they are peaceful, some conversing with themselves, some hand in hand, staring at the floor, some rocking in a corner.

James sits on top of the empty basket. Dot is beside him, dressed as the fairy queen, her face disturbingly painted. He has the asse's head on his lap. He strokes its bristles and wonders how it is he can remember none of his lines. Rose and the Physician come by, inspecting them like generals taking a turn in the camp on the eve of battle. After they have gone the flambeaux are lit around the stage and the first guests arrive, then the musicians, setting up at the side of the stage, trying their strings, their reeds. Concentrated, unobtrusive men.

When the benches are full – the women fanning themselves, the men loud, the servants at a distance, hot in their liveries – Mr Rose emerges from the hospital. There is light applause, some heckling. Rose raises a hand, welcomes them all to the Mad House. He says: 'Expect the unexpected. Tonight we shall dream together, but the manner of the dream, that I must leave to our players. Ladies, be not afraid . . .'

On first is Mr Dee with Mrs Donnelly. They reach the green in front of the benches and stand like lost children, huddled together, staring fearfully at the faces of the strangers. From the audience there is a fascinated silence, then a muffled remark, a gust of laughter.

Mrs Donnelly begins to speak, first her own part, then Mr Dee's, both at enormous speed. The audience cheer, someone flings an orange. The butcher sits on the grass, takes off his shoes and rubs his feet. A young man in a gorgeous coat darts out and steals the shoes; a voice mimics the bray of the huntsman's horn and Mr Dee chases the young man around the back of the benches. The Collins brothers come on. Mrs Donnelly, eyes tightly shut, speaks their lines, until Nathaniel Collins pushes her to the ground. Mr Dee reappears with one of his shoes. He has a bloody lip. He waves the shoe over his head. There are cries of 'Bravo!' Mr Rose comes on. He looks happy, as though the evening were progressing far better than he had hoped. He settles the audience, winks, and points to Dot Flyer, padding downstage with her attendant fairies. The flames of the torches show in her hair. She delivers her lines – part Shakespeare, part babble of her own – with a sweetness, a lewdness, an endearing distractedness, that seduces the audience to silence. Hecklers are heckled. Coins are tossed into the grass at her feet.

James acts his part as though he were sitting in the air above his own right shoulder, watching himself. For an instant, in the middle of the play, he slips violently through time, and becomes again the creature of his past, cool and proud. It is a shock, nauseating him like a blow to the solar plexus. Then it passes, and the words he feared he had forgotten spill out of his mouth and his hands resume the gestures Mr Rose has so patiently taught. He is a broody, melancholy Bottom, but this makes his gambols the more ridiculous and Titania's love of him more absurd. There is laughter from the benches; they are authentically amused, and when Dot embraces him they clap, sentimentally.

10 On the second night, the players are calmer. It is the audience who threaten. Sunday-drunk, restive, spoiling for a fight. They are quick to cheer, quick to turn. A quarter-hour before the end of the play part of the tiered benching collapses, men and women spilling backward, howling on to the grass or into their neighbours' laps. One woman's arm is snapped above the elbow. No one is killed. A bottle is thrown at Rose's head at the end of the play. He dodges it neatly enough. The Physician is furious. There is no celebration that night; no wine, no dancing. Adam sits with James in his cell. Distantly they can hear them, Rose and the Physician, shouting at the top of their lungs in the offices below.

James says: 'Have you loved? Loved a woman?'

'I had a wife, James. It was long ago. She was young. She died.'

'I am sorry for it.'

'It was long ago. I have seen how you are with Dot, James.'

'Ay, but I cannot tell if it is love, for I do not think I have ever loved before.'

'I have seen the light in you, in your eyes when you look at her. That light is love.'

'Adam, I cannot say what I fear most. That she will love me or that she will not love me.'

'It is always dangerous, brother, loving.'

The third night of the play. The final performance. The benches are shored up, the Physician is in temper again. The players recite their parts lovingly, taking their leave of the borrowed words. After the performance Lord C sends a guinea to Dot who gives it to Dolly Kingdom, an elderly, honest keeper, sending her out for wine and oysters. The players dance again, still in their costumes. When the wine and oysters come, Dolly Kingdom and a boy from the wine shop carrying them between them, the music pauses, the bottles are emptied, the oyster shells crunch underfoot. The air is rich with sweat and sea smells.

James looks for Dot. He cannot see her; nor can he see Asquini, who was whispering in her ear, the two of them together, Oberon and Titania, while waiting for their cues. Asquini is a handsome man; his madness is not offensive. He often speaks well; he has seen the world, and what he has not seen he fluently invents. Nor does he stink like most of the Bedlamites, and James has seen how he looks at Dot, his come-hither eyes.

When Wagner moves away from the door, searching among the bottles for one still with a mouthful of wine, James slips out. His leg is throbbing. He leans against a wall and takes off his shoes, then runs like an ape towards the room with the jackets. There is a light at the foot of the door. He knows what he will see when he opens it: Asquini's arse bobbing in Dot's lap. He puts his ear to the door, hears nothing. Have they heard him coming in the passage? Are they listening to his listening? He presses the handle. The door moves almost silently on its hinges. His sight is drawn to the candle, the flame burning very straight until the draught from the passageway rolls it over. Dot says: 'Close the door, Jem.'

She is alone, sitting on a stool beside the candle. Across from her is a second stool, and on top of it a chipped porcelain bowl. The bowl is full of cherries, their skins luxuriously dark, the green stalks catching the light.

Dot says: 'They are from Mr Rose.'

'He gives you presents?' James looks around the room as if its shadows might be hiding Asquini or Rose or both.

Dot laughs. She moves the bowl and sets it on her lap. James sits on the other stool. She takes a cherry in her mouth, then draws James to her by the edges of his coat and passes the fruit from her mouth to his. In this manner they work through half the bowl. There is nothing brazen. Nothing louder than a smile. They bury the stones under the jackets. Tinker, tailor, soldier, sailor.

When they have eaten they lie on the jackets. He tumbles her. She marks his back with her nails, stickies his face with her cherry tongue and cherry lips. It is quick, tender; almost unimportant.

Dot says: 'God keep Augustus Rose.'

'Amen to that. Dot?'

'What, Jem?'

'Marry me.'

'Mad people do not marry, Jem.'

'Then we shall not be mad, for we shall be married.'

'You do not know me, Jem. I cannot always help myself. Inside a month I should be here again or at Tyburn with a rope at my neck.'

'I would help you.'

'You who can barely help yourself.'

'Dot!'

'Hush, Jem! Set your lips to this.' She pulls the cork from a bottle. Rough green glass. He takes it, swallows angrily. It is not wine. He sputters, spills some of the liquid out of his mouth. Warmth spreads through his chest. 'Brandy?'

Dot takes the bottle. James watches the slide of her throat as she swallows. He did not understand it before, this manner of drinking. It was part of the ugliness and mystery of other people. Not something he would ever do, ever need to do. Now when she passes him the bottle he is greedy for his share. When it is empty they lie in each other's arms on the jackets, their breath a fiery cloud around their heads, the candle burning lower and lower, consuming itself, the flame bobbing and snapping in currents of air, the room trembling with shadows. They doze, wake, doze. James hears the jostling of carriages, the noise of a distant dog-fight; hears footsteps in the passage. He frees himself clumsily from Dot's arms. His movements are urgent but slow, like a man undressing under water. He means to snuff the candle so its light will not betray them. It is a long way to the candle. He touches the flame. It burns him, then goes out, a speck of red at the wick's end.

Dot says: 'What is it, Jem?'

As she speaks the door opens. At first they cannot see who is there; it is a man with a lantern, two men with lanterns, perhaps more. Then O'Connor enters the room. There is the gleam, the ring, of chains.

The brandy takes off the worst of the pain, and in truth, O'Connor was too drunk himself, too idle to do much harm. Some kicks, a dozen strokes from the cane; vile, but bearable. James is learning to survive, to bear pain; uncovering the springs of courage. Love is his teacher.

He licks his fingers, reaches down, rubs gently between the fetters and the chafed skin of his legs. Chains, irons; Iron Garters they called them in the Navy.

Thanks to God they did not make him wear a strait jacket, nor did they chain his hands. Dot they carried off quietly enough. A keeper on either side of her and she looking back sleepily, drunkenly, smiling. She did not speak. He heard her laughing as they carried her into the women's wing.

He pictures her, sitting in her cell, in chains as he is, sitting in the hot air, thinking of him as he is thinking of her. It is too hot to sleep; his mind is busy with plans.

He looks at the shadow of his hands. Might he not, one day, regain his touch, his gift? It cannot all have gone. Why not be a sawbones in some county town? Somewhere in the north or the far west. Away from here, from ambition. Patch up farmers; bleed the squire. He would only need a horse, and the patience to ride over the county. He might roll his own pills as Mr Viney once taught him to, and Dot would sell eggs and what not and they would ride to church in a little cart and be like Adam, no man's enemy.

The phantasy warms him like the brandy. He squirrels down into the unclean straw, arranges his feet to be as easy as they may and lies there through the body of the night, picking over the details of his future joy. Towards dawn he rises and shuffles to the window. To the right, over Bishopsgate Street, over Half Moon Alley and the London Workhouse, the sky is streaked with pearl. He waits, hearing the flat tolling of the bell from the Dutch church, and the calling of birds, just a few at first, distant to each other, tentative, as though afraid that the dawn might be false, or else awed by the great hush over the London fields. Then hundreds are calling together, a great complexity of sound, the air quivering with the noise of them. It is as if he has never heard birds before, never seen the dawn. He has never wept like this. The world is good. It is astonishing.

11 The truth seeps out. In whispers, in rumours. In the underbelly of lies. How they took her to her cell; how she fought with them; how they overwhelmed her and chained her, hands and feet; then put a collar on her, a steel collar, and fixed it by a length of chain to the ring on the cell wall. How they left her, spitting at their backs; damning them and calling hell to be her witness.

In the morning they find her sat up against the wall, legs straight out in front of her, head twisted in the collar, eyes half open, her tongue showing past her teeth. They free her from the chains, knowing at the first cool touch of her that she is dead. One of the women in the gallery sees them lifting the body on to the pallet bed, and before they can reach her, silence her, she has screamed the news. The cry is taken up by others, travelling through bolted doors, past iron bars. The keepers, fearful for their safety, quit the wing, returning a half-hour later, a dozen of them with ropes and blackjacks. The Physician is with them, unshaven, striding at their head. He examines the body, pronounces her dead: a seizure. Common enough among the insane; to be expected with a violent creature like Dorothy Flyer. He issues orders: the cells are to be kept locked. They will bury her, as early as possible the following day. As he is leaving, word comes that O'Connor is being murdered by a lunatic in the men's wing.

O'Connor is sitting on the stairs. He cannot speak to them because his jaw is broken. There is blood on his neck and shoulder. The lobe of his left ear is bitten off. He shows it to them, a scrap of flesh in the palm of his hand; then he points to James Dyer's cell.

James is lying, apparently calm, on the floor of his cell. He asks the Physician if it is true. At first the Physician will not answer, keeps asking questions of his own, viz: What did he mean by attacking O'Connor? What was Dorothy Flyer to him? At length, thinking perhaps to end the interview and go in search of his morning comforts, he admits that it is true. She has suffered a fit in her brain. She is dead. Then, testily, he repeats the word, shouts it: 'Dead!'

At this second 'dead', the Physician observes a curious trans-formation in his patient, as if a delicate stem of glass inside him has shattered. There is a small though profound exhalation, then an utter stillness, then a spasm in the muscles of the face such as accompanies certain kinds of poisoning. Wagner asks if he should chain the patient's hands. The Physician shakes his head and leaves, saying: 'I have subtler chains than yours, Mr Wagner.'

Next morning, Adam stands by James at the window of James's cell. They watch the funeral party: the chaplain, Dolly Kingdom, Passmore, and some men unknown, hired for the occasion, there to handle the coffin. A slovenly cortège, trailing from the hospital gates and turning towards the hospital burying ground beside New Broad Street, the coffin on a cart pulled by a single horse. It is not possible to see the interment. After half an hour they come back, the chaplain and the keepers. The hired men ride in the empty cart, smoking.

12 They reduce him with physic. Vomits and blisters, worse than when he first arrived. He cannot stomach his food. The keepers pour broth down his throat; he brings it up, back into the vessel. They feed it to him a second time.

She has left him nothing. No locket, no keepsake, no letter. No parting words. Nothing that might console him or sustain him. What is he to do with his love? Where is it to go? It is rotting inside of him. He is rotting.

He steals a razor from the hospital barber. The edge is rusty, but it will cut well enough. He treasures it. Hides it in his shoe.

If she were to be hid for twenty, thirty years, he could bear it. It is the never that is destroying him.

Flies settle on his face. He lets them crawl. Then the flies are gone. It is colder. The wind snags in the bars of his window. The visitors who stroll, squeamish and delighted past the cell doors, wear furs and warm cloaks. One morning there is snow on the grey straw of his bed. He looks out. The Moorfields are buried in a fall inches deep. A dozen children are snowballing beside a pond. Two men with packs on their backs trudge towards the town. They are black and stubborn as insects and leave behind them a tiny trail of footsteps. One stumbles; the other pauses, goes back, and lets the stumbler lean upon his arm. How slowly they go! What is in those packs which warrants such effort?

Then the memory, wholly unexpected, of watching another figure move slowly across the snow. The parson on his way to the forest by the monastery. The fat, good-natured parson, stopping and turning and waving.

13   On Christmas Day there is a concert organised by Mr Rose. The keepers take James down to the room where he once rehearsed for the play. The razor in his shoe makes his limp extravagant. The keepers parade him in front of Rose, showing off their handiwork. Rose comes forward, bows, looks sombre and says: 'I am sorry to see you are not well, sir. If these gentlemen will permit it, I should like you to sit here at the front.'

When the Bedlamites are assembled, when they have been

hushed by prods and stares, Rose introduces Faustina Bordoni, a slight, spangled figure dressed in the high fashion of 1730. When she moves she sounds like a ship at sea; it is the creaking of her whalebones, the hissing of yards of silk and taffeta. Her face is sleepy and magnificent; the papery skin rouged and dotted, her eyes brown, burnished under the heavy lids. A fat young man accompanies her at the piano. She sings, faintly but very sweetly. The lunatics are moved. A man named Clapp leaps from the benches and embraces her. The keepers drag him away. Signora Bordoni smiles, jokes in Italian with the fat young man and sings again while the rain that has followed the snow drips and patters musically on the window.

After the concert Rose speaks again with James, speaks of Dot Flyer, his esteem for her. Later, James sees him speaking closely with the Physician. On Boxing Day the chains on James's feet are removed; a parcel of blankets arrives. On Twelfth Night Wagner delivers to him a suit of dark blue wool. James is afraid to wear it. It is like a ruse to draw him back into the world again. For days the parcel sits half opened on the floor. Then he peels off his rags, stands naked, shivering, sharp-boned in his cell, and draws on the suit.

The keepers avoid him. Even the Physician is content merely to look into the cell as he passes, nod his head, and move on to try his arts upon less visible, less protected men. James takes the razor from his shoe and gouges upon the palimpsestic surface of old wainscotting a crude heart, Dot's name, his own, and the date: February 1770.

'Adam?'
  'Speak, James.'
  'I shall never love again.'
  'We cannot always choose.'
  'I shall never love again.'

'Nothing stays, brother. And never is a poor word.'
'When she died, your wife. What did you do? Adam?'
'I ran mad.'
'And have you loved since then?'
'It is like the rain, brother. You cannot always be out of it.'

He waits, faintly appalled to find he is recovering, that he does not have the character to die of grief, that the life in him is too stubborn.

And he waits for her, whom dreams have assured him will come. The architect. The subtle witch. He looks for her from his window, day after day, until an evening in March when he is certain of her presence. A group of men, foreigners, are standing near the steps leading up to the hospital gardens. They are admiring the hospital, pointing out its features with their gloved hands. Fragments of their voices drift up on the blustery air. Then they move and he sees her, stood behind them in a dark dress with a red scarf at her neck. He does not wave to her. She will know that he has seen her. She waits ten minutes, still as a tree, then walks off towards Finsbury.

She is there again the next day. How she tests him! Does she not understand that it is too soon? That he has not the strength? That he is not yet well? Yet he trusts her, more than he trusts himself. She has come for him. He must go. The certainty of it is a relief. He goes to Wagner and begs an interview with the Physician. The interview is granted. Three days later, early, Wagner comes to collect him from the cell, and James limps behind him through doors noisily unlocked by Wagner's keys. Stone gives way to carpet, darkness to light. The air loses its stink of incontinence, smelling instead of wax and cooked meats and sea coal. On a table by an open window is a vase of daffodils. James can barely pass them: exemplars of all beauty, all perfection. Wagner calls to him, not unkindly. Calls as if he has often seen men in James's state, stunned by flowers.

A door, broad and brilliantly polished. Wagner knocks. They are summoned. The Physician, his pendulous face topped with a velvet cap, vermillion, gazes at them from behind his desk. A secretary sits at a smaller desk deeper in the room, his arms in cotton covers to protect his sleeves from the ink. In front of the Physician is an open newspaper and next to it a half-empty glass of claret, a plate of queen cakes, and a cup from which drifts a rich perfume of coffee. He says to Wagner: 'What does he want?'

'Begging your pardon, sir,' says the keeper, 'but he wishes to leave the hospital.'

'Leave?'

'Ay, sir. That is what he has told me.'

The Physician stares at James. For a moment James meets his eyes, then he looks down. He is afraid that his legs will begin to shake.

'Does he consider himself recovered?' asks the Physician, looking from James to Wagner. Now Wagner looks at James. Standing here among these men who mean him no good, James does not feel recovered at all. He is afraid that somehow he will betray himself, that he will say some mad thing; that he will start to sing or to slobber or he will fall on to his knees shrieking. He knows he must find his voice. The silence in the room is already dangerously extended.

'Yes,' he says. The sound of his own voice, almost aggressively loud, breaks the spell. He looks up.

'What does he mean?' says the Physician. 'What does he mean by "yes"? You wish to be gone, Dyer?'

'Yes,' says James.

'Well, sir,' says the Physician, taking another cake, 'and what will you do with yourself should I see fit to discharge you? Speak up.'

James says: 'I shall live quietly. I shall be no man's enemy.'

'And how will you live? How shall you eat?'

James glances at the secretary. He says: 'I can read and write. I might use a pen . . .'

The Physician laughs, slaps the table, twists in his seat. 'Y'hear that, Price? He wants to be a secretary. A clerk! Tell me, is that suitable employment for a former lunatic?' To James he says: 'Where will you go?'

'I have a sister,' says James, surprising himself with his answer. 'In Somerset.'

'You think she will be glad to see you, eh? Her mad brother? You intend to walk there?'

'Yes, sir.'

There is a long pause while the Physician eats his cake. James looks down again at the carpet. There is a particular pattern on the carpet, a blue and red arabesque, which he can barely take his eyes from. He knows that his destiny is being decided.

'Mr Price,' says the Physician, 'have the patient sign for his discharge. If he is to be a secretary he should be able to sign his own name.'

Price beckons James to his desk, opens a ledger, turns it around and offers a pen. He taps the page at the place where James must sign.

The Physician has taken up his newspaper again. He says: 'You are released. Take no strong liquor. Avoid all excitement. Women in particular. Other than a sister, of course. A sister is acceptable.'

James tries to speak but cannot. He feels exhausted, as if during the entire interview he had been holding over his head something as large and heavy as the Physician's desk. His fingertips are sweating. He knows that if he does not leave the room immediately it may still elude him, this questionable gift of freedom.

Wagner plucks his elbow, leads him out, then takes him by a private staircase to a door at the side of the hospital. There are no goodbyes to Adam, to the Collins brothers, to Asquini. Wagner grins at him, as if it has all been a sly joke in which they were both required to play their parts. James looks round at the light, steps outside. Is this what he wants? Are not the familiar horrors of the hospital preferable to the unknown ones of the world outside? The urge to hide is very strong; to creep into the shadows, to bolt up a tree.

The door closes behind him. He flinches as he hears the turning of the key. He closes his eyes for a moment, concentrates, then walks very slowly across the formal gardens – once the woods outside of Athens. He half expects, half hopes, to hear a voice recalling him, but no one calls. He steps through a smaller gate at the side of the main gate, closes it carefully behind him and goes, faster now, almost running, towards the woman who is waiting in the white dust of the road to rescue him a second time.

SEVENTH

1770

 'Kyrie, eleison.'
'Christe, eleison.'
'Kyrie, eleison.'

The words scatter like bats into the shadows of the arches. Simon Tupper breaks into a fit of coughing. George Pace in the pew behind slaps the round of the old man's back. The fit subsides.

'The Lord be with you.'
'And with thy spirit.'
'Let us pray.'

It is the usual Easter Sunday congregation, swaying gently now upon the keels of their knees. Lady Hallam is there, of course, lovely in a gown of yellows and golds. His Lordship is in London; politics or whoring or both. Behind Lady Hallam is Dido, hair – not all of it her own – piled on to her head with pins and grease and Spanish combs. The Reverend thinks: At night she must sleep with it in a wire cage, as if it were a beast. A pretty fan she carries today; gold stars on a sky of ultramarine. Fashionable; practical too in this weather. Warm in the church today. The old ones will be asleep before long.

'Almighty God who through thine only begotten son Jesus Christ hast overcome death and opened the gates of everlasting life . . .'

In the balance sheet of the Reverend's fortunes there is for the moment a slight surplus upon the credit side. True, he remains obstinately constipated, and true, he rowed unpleasantly with Dido last evening over some detail of household expenses. Not their usual sparring. Things best unsaid had been spoken on both sides and the Reverend went to his bed with a heavy conscience, tossing and turning until at last he climbed into the cold of his room, found a pen, and scratched an apology, slipping it under his sister's door, noting as he did so that she had a light in her room. And true, he finds himself this Easter without his faith again, one of those occasional fallings-away that used so to trouble him but which now worry him less than the constipation. God plays hide-and-seek with him. Experience has taught him that he will find a way back, that it is better to lie still upon the surface of the waters than thrash about in a panic.

To set against these he has the following: his good-tempered cow, Ruby, has calved. Pace came in with news of it at breakfast-time, his hands still slick with the birthing of it. They had all gone out then – the Reverend, Dido, Mrs Cole and Tabitha – to the stable where the animal had been brought the day before. A glorious sight! The cow's expanse of tongue licking the calf, and the calf itself, trembling, delicately stunned by its passage into the air . . .

Then there is his garden, ignited by the season, the red earth seeping flowers, blossom crowding on to his fruit trees, petals cupping showers of rain. The previous Sunday he caught Sam dipping the point of his tongue into the blossom cups. It had looked so odd at first, a boy on tiptoe with his tongue in a flower. Later, when Sam had gone, he was tempted to do it himself. He was afraid, however, afraid of being seen.

'Almighty God, Father of Our Lord Jesus Christ, Maker of all things, Judge of all men: we acknowledge and bewail our manifold *sins and wickedness which we, from time to time, must grievously have committed . . .'*

In the midst of the words he has a clear mental image of the excellent Mrs Cole in her jacket of fragrant steam, working her knives, her spit, her fire. Today, he thinks – the thought like a triumphant blast on the trumpet – we have a pig's face! A pig's face, a knuckle of veal, and asparagus from Mr Askew's asparagus bed . . .

'Grant us therefore gracious Lord, so to eat the flesh of thy dear son, and to drink his blood, that our sinful bodies may be made clean by his body . . .'

What old bread this is. Trust there shall be no surprises. Blessed are the weevils.

'The Lord be with you.'

'And with thy spirit.'

'Lift up your hearts.'

'We lift them unto the Lord.'

The light, dusty streams ending in coloured spangles on the stone floor, fails suddenly with the passing of a cloud. The Reverend loses sight of the rear of the nave but is dimly aware of the door opening and swiftly closing, of the presence of a figure in the aisle. He recites the Lord's Prayer. Then: *'The peace of God be always with you.'*

'And with thy Spirit.'

Lady Hallam plucks at her gown, rises, approaches the rail. Dido is a little behind her, then Astick with Sophie, his peevish daughter. Behind Sophie, Dr Thorne, adjusting the crotch of his breeches.

The cloud departs. Light unfurls the length of the aisle, and as the Reverend breaks the bread for Lady Hallam, he sees who it is who has entered the church, knows her immediately, yet distrusts himself, sure that it cannot be her, not here, not here in his church. She who belongs irrevocably elsewhere.

A gentle clearing of the throat. He looks down. Lady Hallam

raises her eyebrows, not unkindly. For the space of three beats of his heart, he is lost, cannot at all remember where he is, what he is about. Then he lays the bread in her cupped hands.

'*The body of our Lord, Jesus Christ . . .*'

With her eyes Dido asks: Who is she? He leans down by her ear, whispers: 'Her name is Mary. A foreigner. Sit with her.'

Others also question him with their eyes. Thorne grins as if there were something intrinsically lewd in the advent of a strange woman. The service acquires a new vigour. Conjecture and counter-conjecture are threaded from pew to pew through the forms of prayer, behind the din of bad singing. Necks, not very discreetly, swivel to view this unlikely intruder. The Reverend hears, quite distinctly, the word 'gypsy'.

'*The peace of God that passeth all understanding, keep your hearts and minds in the knowledge and love of God . . .*'

At last the door is thrown open. Richer air reaches the Reverend as he drinks off the remaining wine. Were it possible he should like to pour himself another, though it is poor stuff as wine. He wipes the lip of the goblet with a cloth and walks, swiftly, down the aisle, vestments billowing behind him. To Mary he gives a long look, a quick nod. To Dido he says: 'I shall be back as soon as I may. Will you stay here?'

Dido asks: 'Can she understand us?'

Both look at Mary, who is gazing without much interest at St George slaying the dragon in the east window. It is as if she comprehends there must be some to-do, some wonder, that only afterwards will they do what she wants of them.

'Mayhap,' says the Reverend. 'You might try some questions.'

A movement of yellow by the door catches his eye. He turns, goes. Dido looks at the side of Mary's face, the high cheekbones, the eyes the colour of soaked wood. She does not feel alarmed by her. Oddly, she finds her presence reassuring.

In the churchyard, a dozen parishioners tarry by the path, reading familiar names off crooked gravestones. Now and then they look towards the door of the church. Lady Hallam smiles a welcome at the Reverend, remarks on the size of the congregation.

'One more than I had expected,' says the Reverend.

'Why, yes, indeed,' says Lady Hallam, as if she has all but forgotten the incident. Thorne comes up. He and the Reverend shake hands.

'Fine service, Reverend.'

The Reverend nods, mutters his thanks. That grin again. Thorne, receiving a cool glance from Lady Hallam, goes off, swinging his cane like a cat twitching its tail.

'I wonder', says the Reverend softly, 'if you can possibly guess who she is?'

'Oh, I think that I may. We spied each other as I came out. What eyes she has! Quite as you described her in your letter from – where was it now – Riga?'

'Riga it may have been. I confess, Lady Hallam, I have never been more surprised by anything in my life, though I believe she has a talent for surprises.'

'She will require a great deal of explaining.' A broad smile; amused and sympathetic. 'Your best course may be to explain nothing at all. You know that you and your sister may count on me for every assistance.'

'I know it. You are very kind to me. To us.'

'I am your friend. Now I shall go, and seek to draw the curious after me. Call on me soon.' She offers her hand, he takes it; one, two . . . That elusive third second.

'Well, Mary,' says the Reverend. 'You have given us quite a shock.'

Mary reaches into the pocket of her apron, takes out some manner of rolled leaf and pops it into her mouth, chews it like a quid of tobacco.

'Mary, do you know anything of Dr Dyer? Do you know his whereabouts?'

She stands and walks slowly out of the church. The Reverend moves as if to call her back. Dido touches his arm, says: 'She means us to follow her . . .'

They walk behind her along the path between clumps of daffodils, through the wicket-gate, along the lane by the churchyard wall and round the jammed and broken skeleton of a gate – a trellis now for weeds – into the orchard. The land here belongs to Makins, a widower, his sons gone to stretch their legs in the world, one halfwit daughter at home. Here the apples either rot or are taken by children. On summer evenings the place is visited by courting couples. Sometimes the Reverend hears their sighs on his way home from Vespers.

The grasses drag at Dido's skirts. A court of flies starts up angrily from a human turd. There is a sound of bees, a smell of wild garlic. For a moment they lose sight of Mary as she weaves between the crooked aisles, through the blue shadows, through cloudbursts of blossom. It would, thinks the Reverend, be quite her manner to disappear like a rabbit into a hole. But they find her, standing under a tree somewhat larger than the others, one hand, one finger pointing upward into the head of the tree, like a figure in an allegorical painting. Dido and the Reverend look up. A man's shoes, a man's legs, a grey shirt. A face, very thin, very white, garnished with the shapeless, peppery grizzle of a beard.

'Dr Dyer!' calls the Reverend. 'This is as happy as it is unexpected. I was afraid . . . that is, I had no news of you. Are you well, sir? Will you come down? The branches there are rather slender.'

The face looks down. The transformation is remarkable, ghastly. What manner of sickness does this to a man?

Says Dido: 'This is Dr Dyer?'

'Ay,' says the Reverend softly. 'What remains of him. Dr Dyer!

It is I, the Reverend Lestrade. Sure you have not forgotten me? Do you require some assistance?'

A voice, but barely the right side of sound, drops from the roof of the tree.

'. . . the finch . . . the sparrow and the lark . . . the plain song cuckoo grey . . . whose note . . . a man doth mark . . . and dare not answer . . . nay . . .'

Says Dido: 'Is it a song?'

'. . . the ousel cock, so black of hue . . . with orange tawny bill . . . the throstle with his note so true . . .'

The Reverend catches sight of two young faces peeping round a trunk. One he knows for the sexton's boy, Sam Clarke.

'Sam! Here, child. Come, I am not angry with you.'

The boy comes, looking from the Reverend to the tree, from the tree to Mary.

'Are you a fast runner, Sam?'

'Middlin'.'

'Well, middling must do. Get to Caxton's place. You shall find George Pace there. Tell him to bring the ladder that is in the vestry here to the orchard. Tell him I wish for it now and not when he has finished his porter. Wait! Do not make a great kerfuffle, and do not say what you have seen. We do not require an audience. Go now.' They watch him race away, his feet clearing the points of grass. Mary squats by the roots of the tree. Says Dido: 'I am afraid he will fall. He shall kill himself for certain if he does. Could you not climb up to him, Julius?'

The Reverend says: 'Pray have the sense you were born with, Diddy. Even supposing I were able to reach him, what would it serve to have the pair of us trapped there. Are you not afraid for my neck?'

'You were a very neat climber of trees once.'

'Ay, once. Thirty years since. I remember you, sis, climbing that great elm at the back of Father's place.'

'I did too,' says Dido. 'But when girls become women they lose the freedom of their bodies. Custom requires it.'

'Not all of 'em.'

'You are being vulgar, Julius. It is your least attractive suit.'

They wait, watch shadows, hear the peace of Sunday. Now and then, from overhead fall snatches of croaked song, whispered verses.

Sam comes back, marching like a drummer boy, George Pace scowling behind him, the ladder on his shoulder.

'Well done, Sam! My thanks to you, George. I shall see you right for it. This one here. You see him. Steady now. His name is James Dyer.' The Reverend holds the ladder. 'Can you reach him? Have you got him?'

George Pace comes down, alone. He says: ''E's crawlin'. I can see 'em in 'is beard. That an' he stinks worse than a laystall.'

The Reverend says: 'Should you like it better if we had him doused in bergamot? Heavens, George, I only wish you to carry him down. You do not need to wed him.'

'Wi' respect, sir, I'd rather not. 'E looks plaguey to me.'

'Plague? Have you perhaps made a study of the subject – between laying traps for Lord Hallam's birds?'

'Do not rant so, Julius,' says Dido. 'If he will not fetch him down, he will not.'

'Are you volunteering, sister?'

'George may be right,' she says. 'He may have a disease. Nothing more likely.'

'In which case we are to leave him in the tree? I see I must do it myself. It is ever thus.'

Still garbed in the robes of his office, the ladder bellying out beneath his weight, the Reverend ascends, hand over hand, his mouth dry as a stone. A branch rakes off his wig and drops it like a shot bird at Dido's feet.

'Dr Dyer?'

An ankle presents itself before his nose. He grasps it. 'Dr Dyer? We must get you down, sir. You cannot stay up here. Place your foot on my shoulder. No, like this . . . ooof . . . come come, sir . . . and the other now, gently does it . . . steady, steady – keep the ladder still, George! Now then . . . good, sir, that's the way . . . so . . . and . . . so . . . ah . . . a little more . . . now . . . there . . . Help me, George, damn your eyes. So . . . another step . . . and . . . we have him . . . thank God.'

'Bravo, brother!'

The Reverend claims his wig, slaps it on, silently congratulating himself. James Dyer crouches, panting in the grass by Mary's knees. Out of the tree the full extent of his alteration becomes apparent. To the Reverend he looks like the survivor of a shipwreck, one who has escaped with his life, but barely, barely. The Reverend gets on his knees beside him. Pace was right about the lice.

'Can you walk, sir? We have a conveyance by the church. A very short step from here.'

At the house there is a small party to meet them. Mr Astick and his daughter, over for dinner; Sam, who has cut through the fields ahead of the cart and broadcast the news; and Mrs Cole with Tabitha, the pair looking anxiously out from the kitchen door.

Astick comes up and takes the horse's head, then goes to the back of the cart to help down the ladies.

'This is Dr Dyer,' says the Reverend. Astick looks up. The man he sees in the cart reminds him of the prisoners he saw after the Battle of Plessy in '57. Men whose beards seemed to sprout straight from their skulls. Eyes too big for their heads, seeing things invisible to fatter men.

'He's verminous,' whispers the Reverend as Astick reaches up to lift James down from the high seat of the cart.

'Never mind that,' says Astick. He is a powerful man, swings James down easily.

'Mrs Cole,' says the Reverend, 'is the room next to mine fit for use?'

'Lor', there's no bed made up, and as for airing . . .'

'Airing is not of the first, Mrs Cole. Tabitha, get some sheets upon the bed, quick as you like. Mrs Cole, can you make a little of your beef tea, or' – seeing the objection forming on her lips – 'any of your most nourishing beverages that may be quickly prepared. Where is Mary?' They see her sat with her back against the wall of the barn, head lowered, sniffed at by a cat.

Says Dido: 'Poor woman. She is quite done up. Miss Astick and I shall attend to her.'

'Oh my,' says Miss Astick, seventeen, 'I never looked after a stranger before.'

The Reverend and Mr Astick move the sick man up the stairs between them, gain the room where Tabitha is setting up a breeze with the sheets, and sit the doctor down on a dusty seat beside the fireplace.

'That beard must come off,' says Astick, 'and all the hair elsewhere. If you bring me a razor, Reverend, I shall see to it myself. And hot water. Look! On your sleeve . . . Allow me . . .' Astick destroys the insect between finger and thumb. Fine, thinks the Reverend, fetching the razor from his room, how the unexpected shows the character of a man. What a good soldier Astick must have been, a good Christian soldier. Glad to call him friend.

They strip their patient, bundle his clothes to be burnt, shave him like a corpse. He is as white as one, as white and as yellow. James gazes up at the ceiling as they work above him. His breathing is rapid, feeble. Sam is sent running again, this time to Dr Thorne's. There are lice in James's eyebrows. They shave the eyebrows, crack the lice.

Mrs Cole comes in with the tea. The Reverend takes it from her at the door. He blows on its surface and seeks to spoon some

310

between the frayed skin of James's lips, but it spills over the sick man's chin. He says: 'I believe I never fed a man before.'

'Nonsense,' says Astick. 'You fed the whole church this morning, Reverend. Bread and wine.'

'True, sir. But this is devilish hard to do. The stuff goes everywhere but his mouth.'

'Raise his head a little. There now. We must not drown him in broth.'

'Aha! He took some that time. And swallowed it down. This will be as new blood to you, Doctor.'

James drinks, spoonful by spoonful, half a cup. A heat spreads inside of him. For the first time in days he becomes aware that he has a body. He is not entirely pleased to remember it. When did he last eat? Mary fed him some manner of roots in the New Forest. Then in Salisbury, an orange from the market, crushed upon one side, and some bread. Nothing since then, nothing but greenstuff from the hedgerows. With enormous effort, as though rolling a stone off his chest, he turns in the bed. Who is that man there? He shouts: 'Mary!'

Says Astick: 'I believe he said something. Say again, sir.'

'Mary.'

'Mary?'

'Ay,' says the Reverend, 'the woman he came with.'

'She is his wife?'

'His companion. Or so I believe. Easy there, Doctor. She shall come directly. My sister and Miss Astick are setting her up. You have come a long way, I think.'

James says: 'A long way, a long way . . .' He is uncertain now if he is speaking aloud or only to himself. He thinks: It would not be so bad to die here. This is journey's end perhaps. Lolling his head to one side, he sees the Reverend Lestrade and Mr Astick stripped to the waist and facing each other as if about to wrestle. Up flies Astick's arm. 'Got one!' he cries. 'Well done, sir,' says the Reverend. 'I have not been so verminous since I was last in France.'

James, moon-bald, floats in the subterranean rivers of fever and exhaustion. Thorne comes twice, makes his observations, standing a yard from the bed, and leaves a box of Dover's Powders, a box that disappears without much mystery after one of Mary's visits.

Mary has her own regime: no one feels inclined to interfere. She forages in the Reverend's garden. At first light and dusk she sails up to the woods, returning with her apron full of angelica and cowslip and woundwort, and other plants less readily named.

She wears one of Mrs Cole's old dresses, the housekeeper being the nearest in size, though it was necessary to take up the hems in Dido's chamber, Mary standing before them, quite at ease, like a princess in the company of her maidservants. It was then, as they dressed her, they saw the tattoos, a shower of blue stars over the soft of her thigh and rump, extending downward to the crease of her knee.

She gives rise to talk, of course. Talk of spells, of the evil eye, of necromancy. And yet there is such a mildness in the stranger that come St Michael's Day, Mrs Cole, somewhat to her own amazement, consults Mary about her swollen knees, and Mary treats her, pressing with her hands against the joints until there is a puddle of fluid around the housekeeper's feet. ('Lor',' says Mrs Cole to her gossip the following Sunday, holding up her skirts to show the evidence, the newly restored, muscular ruby globes of her knees. 'What hands she has. What hands!')

By Whit Sunday, James is out of his sick-bed for the first time; a clownish figure in an old suit of the Reverend's, shuffling about the yards and garden, often found asleep, lying in the grass, or even curled on the carpet in the parlour.

To the Reverend's relief, James shows no more desire to climb trees, no evidence of a continuing distraction. Whatever he has been, whatever strange latitudes he has travelled in, he now appears quite sane, answers sensibly all enquiries, though these do not as yet extend beyond the simple catechism of: 'How do you do today, sir?' 'Better, I thank you'; 'Will you walk today?', 'I shall'; 'Will you take some refreshment?', 'A dish of tea if I may, sir'.

Little or nothing is learnt of his history between the last time the Reverend clapped eyes on him in his rooms in Russia, and his reappearance in the apple tree at Cow. Lady Hallam, following the case from the airy prospect of her park, counsels patience.

With summer flying into the trees and woods, the fields high with corn and the village braced for the great work of the harvest, there is an air of transformation about the Reverend's house. Tabitha – the talk is not hard to come by – is enamoured of a soldier, a northerner, down for the harvest, spilling stories of war and cities at the far ends of the earth. George Pace wears knots of wild flowers in his hat as though he were a guest at a perpetual wedding. Astick visits regularly to view James's progress, and his daughter, such an awkward, spiky creature six months before, has acquired a fragile and unnerving beauty. What, ponders the Reverend, is not possible in such a season?

The nights of the first week in August belong to some more southern country, have flown up from Italy or Moorish Africa. Squadrons of slowly sailing stars inch across the heavens. The narrow casement windows of the cottages and the great sash windows of the Hall stand wide to stray breezes. Lady Hallam sits up till dawn, dabbing at her temples with a scented handkerchief, looking out over the paling darkness of her parkland, listening to the shriek of the peacocks and allowing herself, in the privacy of isolation, the luxury of a profound melancholy.

The Reverend also keeps late hours, walking softly about the heat-ticking house, hearing occasionally from the rooms above the creak of a floorboard as someone goes to the window for a draught of this musky, mysterious air. It cannot last, but if it could! The

Reverend imagines the village of Cow translated into La Vaca, the fields full of vines, the villagers tanned and swaggering, the church a mysterious pool of shade.

Near the last of this halcyon season, the Reverend steals out of his house in the small hours, wigless and coatless, a good stick in his hand, the taste of wine in his mouth. He sets off towards the woods across fields of grazing. He has no conscious destination in mind and only after twenty minutes' steady progress under a moon that throws on to the grass behind him a clearly defined shadow does he realise where he is headed. The 'ring', he calls it – it has no more proper name he knows of, is marked on no maps. Indeed, there is little or nothing to mark, merely a circle of oak trees, though he has found there, while picking mushrooms, certain stones, suggestively marked, that make him think there was once something there, a pagan temple perhaps, and it pleases him to imagine some white-robed predecessor of his, officiating at ceremonies before the woolly-haired ancestors of the present villagers.

He walks for ten minutes under the canopy of trees and breaks into the ring, certain now, seeing it lit by such a moon, that he is walking into sacred ground.

A man is sitting on a tussock in the centre of the ring. The Reverend freezes, grips his blackthorn more tightly, readies himself to melt back into the treeline, but the figure turns towards him and the Reverend stops. 'Is that you, Dr Dyer?'

'It is.'

The Reverend approaches, still cautious, as if this figure, not quite substantial on the tump, might yet prove false, a figment of his own mind, or worse, some familiar of the place. These woodland spirits, whom the Reverend cannot quite bring himself to disbelieve in, are said to be very ingenious. And who better to play tricks on than a portly, middle-aged, moon-drunk cleric?

When they are close, James says: 'Pity the poor lunatics on a night such as this. I have heard three or four since I have been here, howling at this great moon.'

'Bless me, it *is* you, Dr Dyer. How did you find this place?'

'I merely wandered into it. In these days I do very little intentionally. Here, sir, drink a little of this comfortable cider. I took the liberty of bringing out some from the kitchen. There is plenty left.'

The Reverend drinks from the stone lip of the jar. James is right. The cider is good. One can taste the whole tree in it.

'I perceive you have been sketching, sir.'

'I like to try my hand. Do you wish to see them?' He lays on the silver grass five sheets of paper, each of which has only a single inky circle, crudely done, yet with an undeniable energy.

'These two I did with my finger.' He shows the dark tip of his index finger as evidence.' I have more paper – will you not have a turn? The trick is to think of nothing. Not how beautiful it is, nor how difficult to catch, nor of catching it at all. The doing of it should surprise you.'

'You mean I am to do it and not to do it at one and the same time?'

James says: 'Precisely so.' Then, seeing the look of confusion on the Reverend's face, he says: 'Perhaps we have not drunk enough of the cider.'

Each man takes three long swallows. The jug gives back a strange, hollow music. The Reverend belches, then plunges his finger into the open ink bottle and draws a ragged loop that is yet, somehow, very moonlike.

'Bravely done!'

They sit, untalking, long enough for certain stars to slip beyond the fretted horizon of the oak-tops.

'Dr Dyer, sir, I should wish you joy of your recovery, for I see now that you are indeed recovered. I confess we all greatly feared for you at Easter.'

315

'If I am recovering – I would not say recovered, not yet a while – then it is your kindness, and the kindness of your sister, your household . . .'

'And Mary . . .'

'And Mary, of course. Her ways must appear very odd. But then, you know something of what she is. You were the first to see her. In some measure she owes you her life.'

The Reverend nods and remembers: torches, dogs, the woman's silent running.

'She is,' says James, 'so I believe, an infallible judge of a man's character. It was no accident she brought me here.'

'That is an endorsement, Doctor, that I will cherish. You know you must stay, of course – you and Mary – quite as long as you wish to. The room you occupy at present can be made more homely with a few alterations, and Mary' – he treads lightly – 'is, I think, tolerably comfortable in the little room next to Tabitha.'

'We are both very comfortable. But I feel as if I should explain to you . . . I mean, you must wonder . . .'

'I confess it, but I require no explanation. First we must confirm your recovery. Is that leg still sore?'

'It gives me some trouble. It is a very old hurt. It is the same with my hands. The pain is not violent now. It is almost companionable.'

'Forgive me, Doctor, but you were once, so it seemed, impervious to its fangs. Pain, I mean.'

'Not "seemed", Reverend. I did not feign it. It was precisely as I said. I never had a moment's physical suffering until . . . well, until Petersburg. I begin to find it hard to believe in it myself. Suffice to say, I have been making up for what I missed.'

'He is quite gone, then?'

'Who sir?'

'The old James Dyer.'

'Quite gone.'

'And you do not regret his passing?'

'There are times when I think of the great certainty my immunity provided me with. I have become something of a coward. Always filled with some morbid dread or other. And whereas once I was as free from hesitation and doubts as any man may possibly be, I am now constantly prey to them. Ha! I am half an hour deciding what coat to wear in the morning, and as you know, I have but two of 'em.'

'This will pass. It is but an effect of your being . . . so unwell.'

'I wonder. I have been born into a new state, a new self, one as distinguished by weakness as the other was marked by strength.'

Says the Reverend: 'Is not this new self marked also by a certain softening, a gentleness?'

'It may be. I hardly know yet what I am, what I may expect. Sure my days with a knife are done with. Perhaps I might turn a shilling with my painting.'

'Lady Hallam remembers you from your Bath days. She says you had the most remarkable reputation.'

'I had several, and it is kind of Lady Hallam to remember me, though God's honour, I could wish myself, my old self, as unremembered as if it were a handful of dust.'

'We shall not chase you with your shadow, Doctor. After all, a man must be free to change. Many are trapped in old skins they would do better to shed.'

'Like the adder? I hope, sir, you shall not shed your old skin.'

'I would not have your courage, though you call it weakness.'

'It was not a thing I chose.'

The Reverend, feeling the intimacy of their meeting in such a spot, emboldened by it, says: 'In Russia, at the apartment on Millionaya, I witnessed something that . . .'

James raises a hand, leans suddenly forward, staring, as if, in the summer night air, he had glimpsed some large and elusive matter, some form that signed to him a message which he must immediately grasp. The Reverend, following the other man's gaze, sees only a family of rabbits, their coats silvery in the moonlight, romping in the grass ten yards from their feet. He looks at James's face, whispers: 'What is it, sir?'

James settles back, shakes his head slowly, sniffs, reaches for the jug.

'Ghosts. Merely ghosts. You were saying?'

'Nothing at all, sir. Nothing at all.'

EIGHTH

1772

1 'Mrs Cole,' says the Reverend Lestrade, wiping his mouth, 'not only are you good enough to laugh at my stories but these are the juiciest pigeons in the world. I cannot think what we should do without you. Dr Dyer, will you not second me?'

James raises his glass. 'Mrs Cole is the finest cook in Devon. She is an artist.'

'An artist indeed!' The Reverend fills his glass. 'You have said the necessary thing, Doctor. Tabitha dear, will you pass the prawns. I thank you. Now tell me, is this sergeant of yours coming to see us before he embarks for the Americas?'

Dido says: 'Leave the poor girl to eat her dinner, Julius.'

The Reverend says: 'She may eat her dinner and talk, may she not? It was a simple question. I take an interest in the fellow's fortunes. He is a very able botanist. Did you know that? Nothing he cannot tell you about roses.'

'You are making her blush, Julius. Do give it it over.'

A tear falls from Tabitha's downturned face, plops in the buttery gravy on her plate. Mrs Cole pulls a cloth from her sleeve and forces it roughly on to the end of Tabitha's nose. Tabitha blows. Dido scowls at her brother, who shrugs guiltily and sips his wine. James winks at Sam, who is sat opposite him.

It is Sam's birthday. In his honour the entire household – with the exception of George Pace, who would be uncomfortable in such company – is dining together. It is May. A light rain is falling. Mary is sitting next to Sam.

James says: 'Miss Lestrade tells me, Reverend, that you are going up to Bath.'

'I think we may. Astick wants to go with his daughter. My sister likes the place.'

Dido says: 'I should like to go to the theatre again. They are performing *The Merchant of Venice* with Mr Barrett and Mr Death. Perhaps, Doctor, you should join us.'

The Reverend says: 'The doctor does not care for theatre.'

James says: 'I used to go sometimes, to the theatre in Orchard Street.'

'What did you see?' Dido asks.

James smiles. 'I am afraid I did not notice.'

'In the winter,' says Dido, 'I always have a dream of going to Bath. It is always a fine day, all the world dressed in their best clothes, and I am going to a ball.' She laughs, blushes. 'It is a very foolish dream, to be sure. Do you care for Bath, Dr Dyer?'

James reorders the pigeon bones on his plate. 'I find it somewhat . . .'

The Reverend claps his hands. 'Here come the puddings! I hope you have kept some room for these, Sam.'

Tabitha and Mrs Cole lay cakes and syllabubs on the table. There is a warm smell of almonds and cinnamon. When the cakes are cut, Mrs Cole gives a large slice of the seed cake to Mary. The cook says: 'I know this is to her fancy. She likes the sweetness.'

Mary eats the cake, breaking pieces off with her fingers, rolling the crumbs into a pellet. James grins at her. She looks up at him, briefly.

Tabitha, recovered from her tears, says: 'There's a show over at Cow this afternoon.'

'What is it?' asks the Reverend.

'It is a Negro,' says Mrs Cole, 'from Exeter.'

Sam says: 'He's going to wrestle. An' lift up a cart an' a horse an' two men on each of his arms.'

Tabitha says: 'His wife is there an' all. She's no bigger than your thumb.'

'And does the wife also wrestle?' enquires the Reverend.

Dido says: 'Tabitha could go with Sam to see it. It is not indecent, is it, Mrs Cole?'

'I do not believe it is,' says Mrs Cole, 'but I shall go with them in case. The boy is too young to know, and Tabitha has not the wit.'

The Reverend says: 'You are a female Solomon, Mrs Cole. Now then, Sam, if you wish for that last piece of cake we must have a song from you. I know the doctor likes your singing.'

James says: 'As it is his birthday, should we not sing to him?'

The Reverend nods. 'Then we shall all sing together. Sister, will you start us off on something?'

The rain stops. By the time they have drunk their tea, the afternoon is glittering with watery light. They go out into the garden. The Reverend inspects his yellow roses, his lilac and his wisteria. He says: 'There is some tying-in to be done on the creepers.'

Dido wraps a scarf around Sam's eyes. She turns him twice, says: 'Off you go!'

The others scatter, whistling and calling, all except Mary who, to James's great satisfaction, looks genuinely puzzled. He says: 'It is a game, Mary! You must not let him catch you.'

Sam, standing half a yard in front of her, senses a presence, reaches out both hands, then pauses, cocks his head, turns, and runs directly to where the Reverend is bent over his tulips.

Dido calls: 'He can see! Shame on you, Sam!'

'It was not that,' says James.

Sam takes off the blindfold and gives it to the Reverend. The boy looks at Mary. He laughs. The Reverend puts on the blindfold. After several minutes he catches Mrs Cole. Mrs Cole catches Tabitha. Tabitha, surprisingly fast on her feet, catches James. James catches Dido. They are all flushed, slightly breathless. Tabitha, Mrs Cole and Sam set out for Cow. Dido goes into the house and comes out with a book in her hand. She holds it up. James recognises it: *The Life and Opinions of Tristram Shandy*. The last volume. They have been reading the book aloud two or three evenings a week, sometimes Dido reading, but mostly James. He says: 'You wish to read some now, Miss Lestrade? In the garden?'

'I thought we might walk a little first and read by the river. Julius, will you walk off the effect of Mrs Cole's cakes with us? I will find your strong shoes.'

The Reverend says: 'The effect of Mrs Cole's cakes is entirely benign, my dear, which is more than I may say for Laurence Sterne.'

'Twaddle, brother. You were laughing like a horse last time James read.'

The Reverend says: 'Sterne was a doubtful man. No, you two go ahead. I am happy here. Make her go, Doctor. It is her who needs the exercise. Why don't you go and see the wrestling Negro and his wife while you are about it, eh?' He chuckles, takes a ball of twine from his pocket. From the stable courtyard comes the sound of a saw. George Pace working something up. Dido goes into the house. James follows her. A cloud twists for a moment in front of the sun, then passes. The light seems stronger than ever.

2 The track to the road is muddy but the air under the young leaves is pleasantly green and cool. They walk on the bank, in single file, to save their shoes. Dido asks James how his leg is today. He replies over his shoulder that the weather agrees with it, that it is not near so achey as it was.

When they come to the bridge, they cross the road and go down the bank on the other side. There are flat stones here, shaded by trees and out of sight of the road. They have stopped here before, to read or talk or gaze at the river, though the river is little more than a stream here, the water flowing in shallow tresses over the stony bed.

Dido gives James the book. There is a ribbon marking the page. He rubs his eyes. He does not wear his gloves now. He clears his throat, looks up, meets Dido's smile. He wonders briefly, and for the hundredth time, if he is misleading her, if she expects him to talk love to her. Has she never heard or seen Mary coming from his room? Has she chosen to ignore it? But then, he himself could hardly begin to explain his relationship with Mary. It has so many aspects, and is in many ways quite innocent. It would be no betrayal of Mary to court Dido. It may even be what Mary intends.

Dido says: 'Can you not find the place?'

James says: 'I have found it now.' He begins to read.

'*Upon looking back from the end of the last chapter, and surveying the texture of what has been wrote, it is necessary, that upon this page and the five following, a good deal of heterogeneous matter be inserted to keep up that balance of wisdom*

325

and folly, without which a book would not hold together a single year . . .'

James reads to the end, closes the book and lays it on the stone. Dido says: 'It is not a very proper book, yet I cannot help liking it. I am sorry that we have finished it.'

James nods. 'Mr Askew was of the opinion that it was only the author's death that finished it. That he would have written more had he been able.'

'Well,' says Dido, 'if I were to write a novel I think it is the ending that should give me most trouble. Perhaps it was the same for Laurence Sterne.'

'You mean,' says James, 'it was easier for him to die than to finish the book?'

She laughs. 'I am sure I cannot mean that. That would be extreme.'

'No. But death is certainly an ending.'

Dido raises her eyebrows. 'You must not let my brother hear such heresy.'

James grins at her. 'You misunderstand me, Miss Lestrade.'

From the village comes the single note of a horn. Dido says: 'That must be the show. They must be beginning.'

After a moment of silence, James says: 'Should you care to have a look? I have seen them once before, last wintertime, but I have not seen their performance.'

Dido stands, pats her gown. She has a sweet, sad, patient smile. She says: 'We might just peep. I should not care to be much noticed.'

'We shall only look from the door. There is no harm in that.'

The horn sounds again, just as they reach the empty road.

The afternoon is growing hotter. The sun has almost dried the puddles in the road. The booth is on a scrap of land near Caxton's place; the canvas, once red and white, is faded now to cream and rust. As they walk towards it there comes a burst of applause and cheering. They stand by the side entrance where the flaps of the booth have been tied back. The smells that come to James's nose are vividly familiar: crushed grass, sweat, canvas, beer. He would like to tell Dido how he once performed in a place like this, Marley Gummer sticking him with pins.

There are some forty people in the booth watching John Amazement bend a poker. He is stripped to the waist; his shoulders tremble, he narrows his eyes, then holds up the U-shaped poker. He passes it to his wife, who is smaller even than James has remembered her, and she takes it among the villagers, letting them handle it and nod their heads and mutter to their friends. In a shrill voice she calls on some strong lad to challenge 'the Moor'. The young men bay. Jack Hawkins is pushed forward. He tries to get back into the crowd but they push him out again. He shuffles into the ring and raises his arms awkwardly. The woman takes his waistcoat and his shirt. He is almost as tall as the Negro, and twenty years younger. A solid build, working on his father's land since he could walk. The crowd settle. A fat man just inside the door shouts: 'Kill 'im, Jacko!' John Amazement looks round. For an instant he sees James, and briefly gestures as if he has recognised him. Then he turns to face his opponent.

They grip up, their feet scuffing in the dirt, the muscles in their backs and arms gleaming and distended. Hawkins charges; the Negro staggers, goes down on one knee, though his face is still calm, as though he were thinking of something else, something serious and peaceful. The crowd huzzah. Some shift about as though tussling with ghostly opponents of their own. James feels the faint pressure of Dido's shoulder. Jack Hawkins is driving the Negro back towards the wall of the booth, his head hard in the

327

Negro's belly. Then John Amazement pivots, adds his own force to Hawkins's drive, and flips him over, lightly and neatly as if the farmer were a boy of Sam's age. Hawkins lies a moment on his back, winded, then gets to his feet, the dirt stuck on to the sweat of his back. He shakes his head, grins and takes his shirt and waistcoat from the woman.

The woman issues a second challenge. 'Who can beat the Moor?' John Amazement is standing quietly behind her, massaging his left shoulder. Suddenly he staggers backward, bawls, snatches at nothing and collapses, the ground shivering under his weight. The quickness of it stuns them. They stare at the great outstretched body, its weird stillness; the woman walks towards him slowly. She calls his name. There is no response. Dido whispers: 'What is it? What has happened?'

James's strongest instinct is to leave; to walk quickly away, with or without Dido. He knows that if he does not go now, this very instant, it will be too late, but the now passes and he has not moved. The woman is kneeling by the Negro's head. She is calling for someone to help him. She is begging.

James steps into the shade of the booth; heads turn to stare at him. He hears his name. He does not look anywhere other than at the Negro and the woman. When she sees him coming she stops crying out. His presence seems to calm her. She holds up her arms to him, blabs something he cannot understand, is not listening to. He is looking down at John Amazement. It is no more than half a minute since the attack but already he seems long dead. James kneels. He wants to say to her: 'He's dead,' but he cannot; he cannot stand the thought of her grief. He puts his hand lightly on the Negro's chest. The skin is clammy but he feels a warmth at the heart. He has felt this before; it lasts some minutes after the patient has ceased to breathe, after the heart has stopped. He remembers an evening in Bath, a young woman at a dance dropping down as suddenly as this. They had been dancing the hornpipe. He was there with Agnes Munro, and he had stooped over the girl, guessing it was her heart. For a moment then, he had considered something wild: attempting to resuscitate her by opening her chest. It had come to him quite spontaneously, and the thought had excited him, yet he did not have his bag to hand, and the sight of him cutting open a young woman in a ballroom was unlikely to have enhanced his reputation. Now he has no reputation. He looks at his hands. They are steady, steady enough. He reaches into his coat pocket and takes out his clasp-knife. George Pace sharpened it on the whestone the other day while he was doing one of the scythes. It has a good edge on it now. Pace said: 'You could bone a fish wi' that, Doctor.'

James looks at the woman, manages a smile, a grimace. She sees the knife in his hand. 'Trust me,' he says, speaking to himself as much as to her. 'Trust me.' She nods. Perhaps she understands. She looks away. He has Grimaldi's watch in his pocket but no one shall time him today. He presses the point of the knife against John Amazement's breastbone, then eases his grip on the wooden handle. He knows how hard it is to cut into human beings, how stubborn the flesh can be with its knots and grains; but the knife must not be held as a child holds a pen. It must float in his hand, like the brush of an artist.

He cuts, unaware of the sighs of horror, of disbelief, from the watchers all around him; unaware of the heat of the booth, the pain in his leg as he kneels. He opens the chest, cuts the costal cartilage of the ribs, sites the heart inside the fibrous glove of the pericardium, half hidden behind the sac of the left lung; feels for it, grasps it, squeezes. For a single minute he has regained his former purity of attention. This is the target to which the arrow of his life has been flighted. In this act, all his experience unites. It is the true and unlooked-for harvest.

His hand mimes the rhythms of the heart. Life bobs to the surface of the Negro's eyes. The dead man lives, gasping, sputtering, as though he has been under water and has come suddenly, fiercely into the air again. He speaks, a voice retrieved from silence, from death. He gasps, then speaks, soft and clear, a half-dozen words that sound to James like words inverted, mirror words, the language of the dead, a sentence smuggled back in the mouth. The woman looks at James. There is dust on her face which has adhered to the path of her tears. She says: 'That's 'is own lingo. That's Africa.'

3 In time he grows a great grey scar across his chest and changes his name. He does not wrestle any more. He lives. It is the surgeon, whose name the Negro forgets, but whose face floats in his sleep all the years of his life like the moon on water, who was a friend of the parson and his sister, and who had been, some said, truly or otherwise, as far as Russia and met the Empress and had adventures; a neat, sad, limping, clever sort of man; it is he who does not live out the summer, dying on an August morning in a field of summer barley near the village, his sketchbook on his lap; pole-axed by death, keeling backward from his stool, a single short yell of surprise, and only a boy beside him, a boy and a dog. No one to reach inside and bring him back.

For almost an hour, while the boy runs for help, James lies there alone, a dark and cruciform figure, his face brushed by the shadow of the clouds, the crop swaying all around him like a crowd, an incurious golden crowd. In the kitchen of the

Reverend's house, Mary, peeling apples for a pie, pauses in her work, lays down the knife and the apple on the chopping-board. Mrs Cole, looking up from her pastry, is amazed to see that her friend is smiling.

EPILOGUE

The coffin is brought to the bridge by cart, then carried on the men's shoulders. George Pace, Mr Astick – at his own particular request – Ween Tull, Killick, and Urbane Davis, all of them tricked out in their best, with black silk hatbands and black shammy gloves, two and six a pair, courtesy of the Reverend. The Reverend walks ahead of the coffin with his sister and Lady Hallam. Behind come Mary and Sam, Mrs Cole and Tabitha, Dr Thorne, Mrs Clarke, and a dozen of the small farmers and tradesmen who knew the deceased, enough at least to greet him on his road.

It is a day for a funeral: cool air, low cloud, a light drizzle. Clarke, the sexton, meets them at the gate. They carry the coffin into the church, up the path under the tolling of the bell.

'*The Lord is my shepherd; I shall not want. He maketh me to lie down in green pastures; he leadeth me in the paths of righteousness for his name's sake . . .*'

Dido mops at her eyes, as do Mrs Cole and Tabitha, and Sam, learning grief for the first time, the tears unstoppable despite his best efforts. The Reverend thinks: Shame the boy had to be there when he died. A terrible shock. And James had seemed to be getting better, stronger. Happier too. You could almost have called him a happy man, the last months.

'*And I saw a new heaven and a new earth: for the first heaven and the first earth were passed away . . .*'

The coffin is shouldered into the yard. Mr Clarke and his assistant, Mr Potter, are waiting respectfully by the grave's edge. The grave beside it is fresh still: Sally Caxton and her child. Dead flowers on the turf, brown-edged petals turning to mulch in this drizzle.

The mourners gather. The Reverend, the book in his hand, but not looking at it, says:

'*As for man, his days are as grass; as a flower of the field, so he flourisheth. For the wind passeth over it and it is gone; and the place thereof shall know it no more . . .*'

Mr Astick strips off his gloves and takes a clod of earth, breaks it in his fist and scatters it over the coffin lid. Lady Hallam also; then she gives some earth into Sam's hand and he leans forward and lets it drop, tentatively, as if the coffin lid were a surface that could bruise. Mary, at the head of the grave, eyes slits of brown light, is conducting a service of her own, summoning her own spirits to mix with those who inhabit the air above Cow.

When it is over they walk to the gate. The Reverend invites them to drink a glass of wine at the parsonage. Lady Hallam takes Dido and Mrs Cole in her coach. The others set off on foot for the bridge. The cart will take some of them and the others have their horses there, tethered to the trees and watched by a boy. The sky is discernibly brighter. They do not talk much. From the fields comes the sound of the harvesters. A woman, carrying an infant in one arm and a stone jar in the other, stops and bows her head as the party passes. The Reverend nods to her, mutters her name.

Something in the ditch beside him catches his eye. He stops. Mr Astick looks over the Reverend's shoulder. 'Poor devil,' says Astick. The men move on; the others look down briefly but do not pause. Only Sam, trailing at the rear of the group, stops and crouches. On the slope of the ditch is a kitten with its throat cut. It does not seem to have been there long. The fur on its chest is crisp with blood and there are cherry spots on the grass around it. Its eyes are tightly shut, as if against its own suffering, and in the part-open mouth he can see the creature's tongue, and its teeth, still pearly white. Sam picks up a stick and prods the kitten, almost as if, in this age of miracles, he expects it to wake and run off. Then he slides the stick beneath its body and rolls it down the bank, through larkspur and harebell and buttercup, to the bottom of the ditch.

AUTHOR'S NOTE

James Dyer, the Reverened Lestrade, Dido, Mary, Lady Hallam
– all these are fictional characters, citizens of the imagination
living imaginary adventures in an eighteenth century of the mind.
Some of the characters however are based upon real historical lives.
Foremost among these is Thomas Dimsdale who in 1767 was
invited to the Russian court to inoculate the Empress Catherine
against the smallpox. His journey was without incident, the
inoculation – always a risky procedure – a complete success.
There is, unfortunately, no record of a race across the snow, nor
of Dimsdale meeting so formidable a rival as James Dyer.